THAT WHICH DIVIDES

THAT WHICH DIVIDES

A Novel By

Andrew R. Davidson

Kindle Edition published via KDB

Written & Edited & Designed by Andrew R. Davidson

Cover design by Andrew R. Davidson

Visit my website:
andrewdavidson1981.wixsite.com/iwritethings

Disclaimer: All names, characters and events contained within are products of the author's imagination. Any resemblance to actual persons, living or dead, or actual events is purely coincidental.

ISBN-13: 978-1-71-281008-8

For Sharon;
for keeping my feet on the ground and my head in the
stars

And for Philip & Jack;
for constantly reminding me that it's not about me

ABOUT THIS BOOK

Colonising the solar system was our greatest achievement. It should have seen in a new age of mankind – enlightened and inclusive.

Instead the colonies have fallen into the same traps which have ensnared us all for generations – political corruption, personal greed, anger and selfishness.

We reached for the stars, but brought all of our baggage along with us.

Bernard Kiebler offers the chance to make a change – to follow his leadership into a new era, but how many people must be hurt along the way?

To what extent must our humanity be sacrificed... by Kiebler and those who look to oppose him?

Table of Contents

CHAPTER ONE

T he question offended him. He'd worked hard to suppress his instinct to react with anger, and he made a forceful effort to present a smile on his face.

"You're asking me if these people shouldn't hold the same rights in Jupitoan society as I myself enjoy? Is that the question?" The host nodded agreement, while his opponent on the far side of the stage flashed her own smug smile at the gathered audience. Four and a half thousand people crammed into this tin shack of an arena. The smell was as disgusting as most of the people.

Bernard Kiebler looked around. A sweating mass of inferiority, poverty and braying voices. His own supporters. The very ones he was here to please. Deep down he hated that he shared a world view with these types of people. He found comfort in the fact that once he gained power over them he would never have to set his eyes on them again – unless it was in the newspapers when his policies forced them out of their rat trap homes to make way for some serious development.

This planet needed a vision, and needed someone with the foresight to make that vision become a reality. Kiebler knew he was the man to do just that.

"These 'tourists'," he spat with venom, "are here under our grace, living by our laws and working our jobs. Those are the rights we have afforded them," he looked his opponent up and down, "and have been allowed to do so by the spineless government Mrs Calhoun represents."

Whooping from the crowds, and a pathetic attempt by the host to calm them, gave Bernard a breather. He flashed a look at his own family, stood by the stage exit on his right. His son, six years old, was taking it all in, while his two teenage girls couldn't have looked less happy to be at work with daddy. His wife was dressed head to toe in designer clothes, all generously donated to the campaign. He had to laugh that the same fashionistas who had been waiting with column inches to spare for him to slip up in his previous career were falling over themselves to get into his good books now. When he was president their whole business would be hung out to dry – he'd see to that.

"No, for too long we've allowed the tourists to come here and feed off Jupiter's bountiful resources. No longer will they eat at the table we have laid for them."

He was getting better at pausing for the big moments. Those kinds of lines killed in the industrial belts such as this one. He let them have a moment to voice their approval, then calmed them with the palm of his hand.

"I am turning off the supply. I am giving this land back to its own people – deportation, defamation, I don't care how we get it done, but we will get the job done."

"This is a good time to bring up the Belt issue. Mr Kiebler, you have made some strong remarks on this in the past – would you care to begin?"

The host was out of his depth. Painfully reading from his script, trying to pretend that he cared for balance and equality in these debates. Kiebler knew the truth; Sam Heighway, producer and host of all sorts of lefty garbage television, was born on Mars and truly believed that Jupiter was the galaxy's own little capital – where people could just pop over and take a living with both hands.

He was also weak, as his fall from eminent personality to Z-list front man of trash TV and hand-picked host of this debate evidenced. The opposition obviously held him in some regard – or else felt they could walk all over him. Neither trait enamoured the man to Kiebler very much.

"Thanks Sam, I believe I can sum this up fairly succinctly as it ties in with my previous point," he spoke calmly. "A few decades ago, we left the inferior planets behind us. We moved on and became the frontier of science and business and human growth. Jupiter is a beacon to those we left behind. A shining example of becoming whatever you want to become, through sheer force of will."

"We left ninety-five percent of them behind for good reason. Now they come through the asteroid belt in their ramshackle shuttles, dreaming of the 'Promised Land'? Fuck that. I'm promising this land to YOU!" He emphasised his point with a dramatic finger waved at a blur of faces in the crowd. "And YOU", another finger pointed at anybody or somebody.

"And you, and you, and you!"

The crowd ate it up. The noise became unbearable, as Sam Heighway tried to usher them to silence for the opposition's retort. Good luck, Bernard thought, while stalking the stage, riling up his people. They had bought it, as they always did. The little people, with nothing to show for their lives, and only themselves to blame, always *always* lapped it up when you gave them someone else to lay their blame on.

He took his seat and allowed the noise to subside, just enough to let his opponent step up to the mic. At 65 years old, she was pushing her luck, he thought. She thinks she can run a planet? She'd have trouble running to catch a bus.

Heather Calhoun was the leader of the opposition – just as she had been twice before. Twice she'd stepped up to this stage and pleaded with the people to vote for her. Twice she had been trounced when it came to the vote. How they had dragged her back out into the open for this Kiebler did not know, but he expected to send her back into her box with a third defeat. He didn't really mind what kind of box it was she ended up in.

"I have long held the belief," she started and was immediately drowned out by the volatile crowd. A rising torrent of noise rose as she began to speak until, mid-sentence, she found that even she couldn't hear her own voice.

The people were speaking and the people were angry. They chanted one thing, and they chanted it long into the night.

"Block the Belt! Block the Belt! Block the Belt!"

***

The press are all over him, anyone think he went too far?" The General spoke in hushed tones, knowing his words wouldn't leave this room.

However, looking around at the faces of his peers, he wasn't sure he had any support here. The gathered group were the proposed leaders of the next government on Jupiter. The brightest and best.

General Wilson Hasting stood amongst the gloom of the candidates' private study in full uniform. He recognised the prominent scientist Daxler Scion immediately, and was introduced to Valerie Marlborough of The Mars Banking Corporation. The other three people present were recognisable only if you followed television and the digital media – neither of which interested Hasting in the slightest.

"Mr Kiebler speaks his mind. The people like that, after so many years of hearing the ramblings of politicians," Scion responded to his question. "I think it is great that the media are paying his words the attention he deserves."

"The majority of the stories this morning were attacking his 'block the Belt' idea, I'm not sure it's doing his campaign much good." Marlborough replied.

"Nonsense. They are run by companies with interests in Mars Tech and various other businesses which would be affected by the block. You won't hear a word of truth out of their mouths until it's over."

Marlborough leaned forward. "That's all well and good, but who's going to pay for the block once it's all over? My bank can't fund it, this government can't fund it, and we're pissing off the very people who might have the money."

Scion eyed her up, calmly sipping from a fine china cup. "Ms Marlborough, you worry about money too much. Change will always cost. It's about what you are willing to pay."

"But-" Marlborough began to respond, only to be interrupted by the door swinging wildly open.

"Daddy's home!" Kiebler entered the room, beaming. A bottle of champagne in one hand, and a stack of papers in the other. "What are you kids talking about?"

Silence.

"Alrighty, we need some loosening up in here, I can tell," he shone his smile across the room, as if its artificial moonbeam radiance could affect a smile in anyone. He noticed Marlborough almost giggle when his eyes passed hers. Scion stood and greeted him respectfully. He was a loyal little excuse for a man, thought Kiebler. He will be a great asset to the future government.

"I have gathered you all here, as you know, because you have been selected to lead. I need strong, forceful, loyal people working to keep my government on the front foot– when I win – and I believe you are just the people to do that."

He offered the bottle to Hasting, thrusting it into his chest before he could say no. "Have a sip, fella. We're celebrating a great day!" Hasting stared at the bottle but declined to take a sip, instead gracefully hiding it back on the desk behind him once all eyes were looking elsewhere.

"What is it that we are celebrating, your honour?" Scion crawled.

"Lay off the 'your honour' stuff for now, Dax. Bernie will do," he told him, as he flicked through the stack of papers in his hand. "This, ladies and gents, is my first key to the kingdom. I have been given access to the treaties, deals, contracts and just about every other piece of paperwork that exists in this fair land."

"Now does anyone want to guess which precious piece I hold right here?"

The group looked around at each other, not sure where to even start guessing.

"I'll just tell you, spoilsports. It's the trade agreement made more than two decades ago with the Martians. Any Martians in the room? Good – and my sweet lord it makes for good reading!

"This document grants Mars free reign to name their price on anything we want to buy from them. The services they provide in the tech industry, and the support they claim to be the best at, is costing us billions every year."

"Isn't that vital infrastructure? We can't afford to play games with that stuff," Hasting said.

"It is vital, yes. But at this price? It's robbery. I'll tear this deal up on day one. Mark my words."

"Shouldn't the people be involved in that kind of decision?"

"Were the people asked when the deal was signed? Have the billions of Jupitoans born since had a chance to have their say? The world is changing, the Martians need to catch up or get left behind with the rest."

"I feel that Jupitoans deserve the right to guide those changes," Hasting spoke again, stepping forward to stand in front of the candidate. "All the more so if, like you say, they have been short changed without their knowledge in the past."

"You weren't born here, were you Hasting?" Kiebler asked.

"My father and mother were Jupitoan born. I was born on Saturn, during the Uzstaz rebellion when my father was stationed there."

"So, you identify as Jupitoan?"

"I have no memory of ever living elsewhere, sir," he spoke proudly.

"I was born here, myself. I remember distinctly being barely a tot, watching my mother and father struggle to raise us kids in this society. The poverty on the streets, the inertia in government. Nothing has changed."

"With respect, sir, I spent my first waking days in a muddy field on the back end of Saturn, before it was developed, with bombs dropping not 200 yards away. Your mother and father owned a penthouse, if I'm not mistaken?"

Kiebler looked Hasting up and down, unsure of what to make of the man. He had balls, that's for certain. He could be moulded into a resolute force for change – but his mouth would get him into trouble.

"You're correct, but don't mistake money for an easy life. I said we struggled, I didn't say we were poor," he responded, before quickly wheeling around to the silent majority in the room. "You folks are awfully quiet! Have some champagne; tell me what you can do for your new government-in-waiting."

"Sir, we represent the Board of Trustees for the Jupitoan State Television Department."

"Represent? Don't put yourself down, I've seen your show, you're stars in your own right."

Kiebler spoke, not knowing the names of the people who sat at his couch right in front of him, the very people he had been told he should get on his side no matter what.

"You're too kind, sir" the youngest of the group spoke. "We do all right, but not as well as you have been doing in our latest polls. Up by seven points in the last three months."

"But it's not enough is it? She's still winning."

"Yes, sir. However, the performance at the debate last night should change things for the better. In our latest polls this morning you are tracking higher with businessmen, celebrities, the elite. The one-percenters love you."

"The one-percenters have always loved me. They always love their own. What else?"

The only female in the group stood and unfolded a touch screen flip chart to show to Kiebler. "That's the interesting thing. See here," she said pointing at the graphs which she was rapidly flicking through on her screen "Up four percent in working class, up seventeen percent with the unemployed and thirty-five whole percentage points with Jupitoan-born nationals."

"The workers of Jupiter are a proud people, they want to see Jupiter mean something to them again," Scion spoke, still sipping from his cup. "You give them hope, sir."

"Sir is better. But 'hope'? I'm just giving my people the chance to outshine those who would get in their way."

Hasting cleared his throat. "There are still many immigrants who shine just as brightly, sir," he spoke forcefully.

"That may be so – but just you wait until our society is run by Jupitoans for Jupitoans, with pride and passion for their homeland."

"With all due respect, Mr Kiebler, this is nobody's homeland. Our true homeland lies 600 million miles away."

"That's exactly the thinking that got us into this mess we are in, Hasting." He turned his attention back to the general. "You speak your mind; we have that in common," he spoke calmly. "You'll need to be persuaded to bend your views slightly if you are to serve this planet of ours."

"My views are meant for me alone, sir."

"Your views are made to be shifted, General." They stood almost eye to eye. In another time and place it could be called toe to toe. "Have dinner with my family and I tonight, Hasting. We will discuss every view you can think up."

"I'm afraid I am on duty this evening, sir. I must return to my bed before midday if I am to be ready to lead my command. If you'll all excuse me?"

The room was full of collective nods in agreement, as Kiebler watched the General prepare to leave.

"General Hasting," he spoke before Hasting could open the door.

"Yes, sir?"

"My first order when I'm in charge will be for you to call me Bernie."

"Yes, sir," Hasting responded without pause.

Kiebler waited for the door to close behind the General, and then turned back to his people. "That man is going to make an excellent face for this government, and I'm going to see to it that he does."

Scion shuffled in his seat. "Sir, there are some who believe the General's views on such matters are a little antiquated. It is time to move with the times."

"Indeed, and I agree," Kiebler responded coolly. "Don't get me wrong, the man's strength lies in his command and his lack of fear – his views will be beaten out of him one way or another. As they all will." He looked to the TV delegates once more.

"Seven points, eh? Show me what I need to do to blow that bitch out of the water."

Kiebler knew these were the great minds when it came to this kind of thing – popularity and image. In his former career as your average pin-up, Ken-doll, action movie star, he had made every public appearance imaginable, sat through every media day they could fit into his schedule and kissed every baby that crossed his path. The differences between being an actor and a politician really were minimal. He considered the stroke of luck that had landed him in both roles, while the two experts rattled off reams of detail about how he was going to win the public over.

"Sounds like a lot of effort just to win a shabby little office, don't you think?"

His eyes sparkled as he caught the look of the young girl. He couldn't tell her age, or much about her, but that had never been too important. He knew that if he wanted her, all he had to do was ask. In fact, he rarely even had to put himself out so much as to ask. He smiled, making light of his comment. The girl laughed, the others less so. They were nervous, he could tell.

"Look, don't worry about the details. Have my team confirm the dates and appearances. I'll handle the rest. We're going to rule this planet, people. Let's enjoy it!"

***

Late that night, with the television playing in the background, Kiebler stirred. He hadn't slept well for a few weeks now. It wasn't the pressure, like his wife told him, or the stress, like the doctors advised. He was just agitated. He was excitable. He knew that the press were talking about him. He knew that some 24-hour news channel was discussing him as he slept, and that some little guy on minimum wage, all the way across the globe where it was dawn, was writing some poorly written and poorly read copy for a sub-editor who just wanted the Kiebler name above the by-line. It thrilled him, and sleep didn't come easy with that running through his mind.

The girl turned at his side, pulling the covers off him. She squinted at the TV then up at Kiebler's face. "It's early..." she said, barely awake.

"It is, honey. I like to think while the world around me sleeps. Keeps me ahead of the game."

He smiled at her and she forced a smile back. "What exactly are you thinking?" she asked, pulling herself up to rest upright against the headboard. Kiebler couldn't help his eyes drifting, taking her in. He loved his life at times, and this was one of them.

"What do you think can give me that edge? I don't want to just claw back into this thing and scrape through an election. I sure as hell don't just want to make a show of it and walk away proud that we gave her a run. Do you follow me?"

The girl looked a little confused, unsure of the thought process. She had never slept with such a great man, she thought.

"I want to crush her. Calhoun. All of them. That snivelling party, sucking up to every side. The minorities, the immigrants, the unions and the councils and the... Ugh. Makes me sick. I want a landslide. I want to crush them so huge there is no coming back."

The girl smiled, seeing his absolute power and the possibilities of it all. She would do anything to help him achieve it in that moment.

"What about your wife?" she asked.

"My wife? Little girl, don't bring up my wife when you're in bed with me.... I thought you had more class than that?"

"No. Not like that. Silly, Mr Future President... I mean to boost that popularity. We have to play the family angle. Get your wife up on the podiums with you, have the kids surrounding you. Play to the heartlands. Play to the grandmas. Show them the perfect life they can have with you in charge – by presenting it to them in full view."

"You, girl, are a piece of work," he chuckled. "The family life. Vote for me and live the perfect family life..."

He paused, and watched as the girl's smile turned from sweet to deviant, and she slid down, down, down, under the covers.

"… just like mine."

CHAPTER TWO

The arching domed entrance to the Martian Embassy Senate building was a monument to a civilisation left behind. Its architecture representing the spirit and freedom of the people; the first colony in the galaxy. It had taken decades to plan and longer still to build the machinery and infrastructure which allowed for Mars' inhospitable atmosphere to be converted. It was a time of incredible social and economic success, as humanity lifted itself from the confines of Earth and out into the stars.

The people of Mars were proud to be the first colonists. They set up home in the northern-most regions to begin with, where thousands of miles worth of technology was housed in vast hangers and used to pump a finely balanced chemical mixture into the atmosphere. Solar winds and other natural elements were harnessed to power the creation of a magnetic field, which in turn allowed the planet to develop its own ozone layer and comfortably support life on the once dusty, red planet.

The process was a long and arduous one, and many of the volunteers, scientists and explorers who first set out to the new colony did not get to see the final plan to fruition. After years of toil, the first residential buildings went up, and people began to move to Mars on a regular basis; setting up house and home, finding work in the hangers and in the increasing need for construction. The first settlers were revered and admired back home on Earth. The Senate was created soon after to allow the newly formed Martian people some sovereignty and a sense of control over the matters which governed them.

Sebastian Raylor looked up at the Senate building and felt its weight in his heart. The old building, falling into disrepair, was still a sight to behold but weather damage and lack of care were taking their toll. He knew the money wasn't there to protect it anymore. The last estimates to have it fixed up and returned to its once pristine condition were astronomical. The opposition had joked that it had cost less to colonise Saturn than it would to give the Senate house a lick of paint.

His reverie was shaken by the man approaching him. Well into his fifties, the Senate representative for the Northern District was in almost as poor a condition as the building itself.

"Senator Sutherland. So glad you could find the time," Raylor greeted the bustling man. He was stocky yet small, a good foot shorter than Raylor himself. This came as a surprise to Seb Raylor – he wasn't often the tallest in man in any room.

"I don't have long, Raylor. I'm late as it is," he replied.

"I understand Senator, I was hoping I could just relay to you the thoughts of my constituents before we head in there today," he spoke, trying to keep up with the bustling walk of the Senator who did not look interested in holding the conversation.

"May we stop walking for a moment, sir?"

The Senator slowed and turned to face Seb. His jowly face showed the stress he was under as he tried to catch his breath.

"The people in the North East District are riled up, sir. Bernard Kiebler is causing some real debate."

"Isn't that the way everywhere, Mr Raylor? Your people are no different to mine."

"With respect, Senator, your people are all of us. We just want to ensure that you make our thoughts clear in the Senate today. The Galactic Union reps must be made aware of our concerns."

Sutherland sighed, giving the impression of a man who did not need the hassle of a Senate debate and Galactic Union intrusions.

"The GU is monitoring all of the candidates in the Jupiter elections, Raylor. They know all of the concerns and many more on top. No jumped up little celebrity is going to challenge their abiding jurisdiction over the colonies."

"That may be so but the way Kiebler talks; he doesn't have much time for the GU or the other colonies."

"Do you think it matters what he thinks?"

"You don't?" Raylor stared at his compatriot. He was unsure if the man was unwilling to see a problem or just unwilling to deal with it. "If Mr Kiebler is elected as President of Jupiter, what is to stop him pulling out of the Union? He has stated many times in his campaign that he wishes for Jupitoans to be ruled by a Jupitoan. That is worrying talk, Mr Senator."

"It is just that. Talk. He knows no planetary colony can stand without the GU governing above all. It's as simple as that. He is not a politician; he doesn't have the power or the nerve to do such a thing. He cannot and will not leave the GU"

"Are you sure about that?" Raylor asked finally. The Senator did not respond, simply giving a weary look and trundling through the open doors of the Senate building.

***

Inside, the Senate chamber was a wall of noise. The four sitting Senators, Sutherland included, were seated at the front of a large observational room, holding court over the visiting foreign and domestic dignitaries. The Elected Officials of Mars' eight geographic regions sat in the floor seats, with Raylor amongst them. Behind the EO's sat the visiting attendees – today's main invitees being representatives of the Workers' Council of Mars.

The Workers' Council had grown from a small union of workers back in the formative days of Mars' colonists. They had developed a strong presence on the political scene, giving voice to a population of workers and servicemen who ensured that the planet continued to run perfectly.

The foreman of the Senate introduced Senator Sutherland, of the Northern District, and invited him to speak. Sutherland stood and adjusted his already tousled tie. He shuffled through his pile of uneven papers, finding the correct piece. Delaying the inevitable.

"Ladies and gentleman of the Senate, and honoured guests," he began shakily. He was never one for public speaking and it was his least favourite part of the role. "I am speaking on behalf of my people, the Northernmost of Mars, and directly address the gathered dignitaries of the Galactic Union."

A hushed chorus of whispering grew, echoing around the room, then died off just as quickly.

"As we are all aware, Bernard Kiebler is gaining ground in the Jupitoan elections and we – that is my people – feel it only right to make public our concerns at the policies he has publically proclaimed."

A Galactic Union emissary interrupted, standing from his comfy seat in the back of the hall. "Mister Senator, as you are aware, matters of planetary politics are beyond the reach of the GU and as such are not a concern of this meeting."

"Of course, I understand. I am merely raising the concerns of my people. We feel some of the ideas that have been brought forth are in direct opposition to our views on... Well, they are against several views we all hold and some seemingly in extremely non-constitutional ways." He could fool himself stumbling over the words, but ploughed ahead. The Galactic Union was not to be messed with, he knew, and this was pushing their boundaries just a little too far.

"Mr Sutherland, I assure you the GU will uphold our constitution for the good of all of the colonies it represents, and will challenge the legality and process of any new policy it feels is in opposition to our own." The GU members surrounding this man looked as bored as he sounded.

A member of the Workers' Council took to the floor before Sutherland could conjure up an apology to his galactic higher-ups.

"With respect, does that mean the GU opposes Mr Kiebler's policies?" James Bellson spoke clearly. A hanger engineer himself, he was elected to the Workers' Council by his colleagues, and wanted answers from this visit of the GU

"The GU will work with whoever is elected by the people of Jupiter. Whatever policies or persons they see fit to warrant office on their planet will be regarded in the same manner as all other elected officials."

"And what about his policy to tear up the trade agreements with planets like Mars? Ones that are already heavily biased against the industrial workers who provide the backbone to this great galaxy you all revel in? Or his desire to kick all immigrants to the curb, and the knock-on effect that will have to the economies of every other planet?"

"We cannot condemn the policies of one man simply because we disagree with them, economically or morally."

"That is where we disagree, sir. That is exactly why we should condemn his policies, and the man himself."

The Workers' Council representatives cheered, and one or two regional elected officials joined in. Sebastian Raylor remained quiet, but couldn't help to admire the conviction and composure of the young delegate. He had not spoken to James Bellson before, but had seen him at events like this in the past. He had never been quite so outspoken, however, and for a man no older than thirty years he spoke like a veteran.

"Order, order," the speaker shouted across the room.

"I would say a word if I may?" Raylor spoke as the cheering subsided. "The Workers' Council merely puts into words what many of us have thought over the past weeks, as we watch this man grow ever popular. He will say what he likes, and do as he pleases, and yet he remains unchecked." He could sense the tension in the room, and knew his words were a catalyst.

"Mark my words – his policies and ethics with regards to workers, citizens and genuine, honest human beings are both ruinous and unforgivable. Choose your footing carefully in the coming days, or you may find yourself on the wrong side of history."

Again, cheers erupted from the Workers' Council and polite applause from the sitting Elected Officials of Mars. James Bellson caught Raylor's eye and nodded his appreciation.

***

The confines of the Workers' Council offices were cramped, even by Martian standards. Raylor was reminded of his old college dorm room, from the lack of space and abundance of clutter, right down to the clammy, pervasive air. He shuffled in his seat as Bellson fussed over preparing drinks for the pair of them. He wasn't sure if he would grow to regret his decision to come here but was fairly certain that his constituents would be very interested to hear that he was in liaison with the Council.

The Workers' Council had been a thorn in the side of every government Mars had appointed since its inception. As a rule, Elected Officials were expected to pay them no heed and only give in to their demands as and when the public began to ask similar questions. That said, the Council stood for the rights and moral code of all of the hard-working men and women of Mars, and that was no small thing. Mars was built on the blood and sweat of brave and hardy souls. Those who had taken the risk to be pioneers and visit this strange new world – not just to say they had seen it, but to build it into something they could call home.

He admired that spirit, and counted himself as a Martian through and through. However, the aggressive anti-politics of the Council had grated on him throughout his career as they protested and argued and flat out sabotaged amendment after amendment in the civil courts. The Senate duly paid them no heed, but he had to admit they knew how to make their case heard despite having no official political pull.

"That was quite a showing you made this morning. Strong words from an elected official. Aren't you supposed to hold your tongue until they put you in those cushy Senate seats?" Bellson teased.

"I've never been one to hold my tongue, I'm sure you've heard", Raylor responded. His reputation preceded him wherever he went. "Tell me honestly though; do you think he can win?"

Bellson took a moment to consider the question. "There's a long way to go yet. But there's also a long line of instances in humanities past which show that people sometimes make very stupid decisions." He smiled and Raylor gave a begrudging smile in return.

"We have to make all the noise we can before the election. Let the opposition be known."

"We reached out to the opposition – Calhoun's people want nothing to do with us. Martian workers are beneath them you know?"

Raylor let out a snort, the kind of laugh that takes you by surprise. Calhoun had run two hugely unsuccessful campaigns in the past, trying to ride the coattails of popularity left over by her late husband.

In the first, she had leaned too heavily on her husband's legacy, alienating many voters in the process. The second time around she swung the opposite way; relying too heavily on polls and bad advisement from short-sighted political hacks. She had sold herself as the Jupitoan embodiment of the Workers' Council, and that just wouldn't wash with voters who knew her past life, private school upbringing, membership of every exclusive club you could name and the upper-class accent she tried and failed to disguise for all of her years in public service.

Now she found herself somewhere in the middle – unwilling to look too upper-class while not fully committing to the working class cause.

"Calhoun is a changed woman these days," Raylor said.

"She's a walking campaign – I don't know what she truly actually believes in."

"I suspect the current Heather Calhoun is more the real her than anything we've seen before. We just can't rely on her support."

"No surprises there," Bellson replied.

"Did her party give an official reason for not wanting your help?"

"Just that they had things in hand. They either have something huge on this guy, or they are not taking him seriously enough."

Raylor found himself considering both options as he lay sleepless in bed for the next few nights. He couldn't conclusively settle either argument in his head but knew, either way, the people of Jupiter were in for a major shock.

CHAPTER THREE

"That sun is blazing down; get us a canopy or an umbrella or something," Kiebler barked as aides rushed around the garden of his private home. This was his favourite of the many mansions he owned – despite being located so close to the capital it was a peaceful and beautiful area. Thirty-something rooms, acres of gardens to roam in, a bar, pool, tennis courts. He didn't need much more in his life. He came here alone, mostly. It was his home when he was working, and he didn't like having family around him when he was working.

Xanthe hassled him to stay sometimes, but the kids hated the capital anyway. Seo-Sing City wasn't a place made for children's minds - it was built by businessmen, for businessmen and Kiebler revelled in that atmosphere. He allowed Xanthe the odd visit, usually for a state dinner or some function where he needed his wife in tow. She made an excellent accompaniment by his side at any event, and he admired that about her. He gave her run of the house when she was around, choosing to retire to his office with his scotch and whatever reading his aides would give him each night.

Truth be told, the reading didn't interest him all that much either. Many aides had been let go after providing a morning question and answer session based on last night's reading. Most knew to give him the highlights, briefly, in the morning and politely assume he knew it all anyway when he dismissed them with a hand wave. If they had asked him how his popularity ratings were looking, or how well reviewed his production company's latest television efforts were then he could have given them a speech off the top of his head every morning. Nobody ever dared to strike up that conversation.

These charity events called for the full brunt of the family man image, however. So he had the bullet train chartered to bring his wife and kids along for the occasion early in the morning, to ensure they were raring to go on arrival. He hated being up and ready for the day and having to watch as the kids bundled around the house until the very last minute.

They arrived fully ready for the day, and they had breakfast together. The aides gave him a quick briefing while they all ate. His eldest daughter, Ali, earned a rebuke for bringing up her 18th birthday celebrations yet again – he made it clear this was not the time or place for that kind of talk. He had drilled it into his children from a young age that business came before pleasure, and he expected them to hold to his ideals.

Melanie, his 15-year-old, understood better than them all. She engaged with the briefing and offered advice to the aides on what information he would need before he could make any decisions. Xanthe was off somewhere in the house, messing with floral arrangements or otherwise getting in the staff's way.

The final piece of the familial set was young Bernard – or Bernie Junior as they liked to call him. Kiebler hadn't intended on having another child, not really. Although he had always wished for a son, and hadn't hid his disappointment with Xanthe at the birth of two daughters, he was happy with the girls they had raised. When they found out that she had fallen pregnant again, nine years after Melanie was born, it came as a shock. However, Kiebler knew – and told anyone who would listen – *he just knew* that this was the one.

His only son and heir.

The day of Junior's birth had seen the biggest party the capital had ever witnessed. He recounted its events and passed on the well-wishes of every political name or entertainment industry luminary to his wife the next evening in her hospital bed.

Bernie Junior was growing into the very image of his father. Kiebler hoped that a couple of terms as President would show his son just what his father was made of – and give him plenty to live up to. It would also do no harm at all in getting him into the enhanced study scholarships at Jupiter's most prestigious schools. It had cost a lot of money to secure his place in the junior academy he currently attended – the next step would be a lot cheaper, he was sure.

An aide arrived and erected an imposingly large umbrella over the family table. A microphone sat in front of Bernard only; the family would be present but not active in any of the questioning from the public. Bernard had suggested as much and his team agreed. In reality, the public made up less than forty percent public of the gathered crowd. The rest was made up of a small number of political allies and more press than he was really comfortable with. A necessary evil.

He fielded questions with a smile on his face and a bottle of water in hand. The charity folks rolled out the standard old questions about his charitable legacy and where he saw the government's role in supporting and guiding the many people, who did great work for the citizens of Jupiter. He thought he could answer most of them with just a smile and they'd still coo and aw over him.

The reporters' questions weren't much tougher, and he fielded the odd issue on policy and upcoming appointments to his staff. He felt these types of things were out of place at an event like this, and told them so, but he answered them anyway. He knew that if he didn't do it now he would just be bothered by them on the golf course later where he really preferred to be left in peace. He hated press intruding on the golf course. The day someone publishes his handicap in the morning news will be the day he buys up every newspaper on the planet, only to shut them down and humiliate all involved.

"All right everyone, I really must be getting home and hosed, I'm sure you will all agree it's been a long and fruitful morning," he waited for applause and received plenty of it.

"One more question from you rabble before I ask my security to chase you off my property." He played out his practiced pause, deployed his public laugh and turned on the 'let me shake your hand and kiss your baby' grin. It was all too easy.

A ragged looking presser in a brown suit waved frantically from the edge of the seating area. Kiebler had spotted his hand raised several times throughout the afternoon but hadn't seen his face before. He didn't trust new press men. Or at least, trusted them even less than the ones he knew well.

"Yes, Martin," he said and pointed at an older man standing front and centre.

"Thank you, sir. Can you tell us more about your plans for the weekend?"

"Oh, horseshit!" came the shout from the brown suited man. All eyes turned to him as he began to walk between the tables and press men, edging toward the centre for full effect.

"Tell us about last weekend instead, sir. Stop ignoring me, and tell us about Sonya Medina."

The crowd came to life with whispers and chatter, but Kiebler kept his focus on the intruder, eyeing him up. He never had to think too hard on how to react in any given situation. He was blessed with a coolness of blood and a way with words that he had counted on many times in his life.

"Sir, I have called my final question. Don't you go ruining a lovely day for these incredible people by being so selfish."

"Selfish? Wouldn't you say it was selfish for a man wishing to be the President of our great people to withhold the truth? To deceive his own people?"

"There has been no deceit, my friend. Now kindly step down before I have the security team take action."

The man looked around and could see the security detail in full force – two suited men either side of the family table, a further three or four lurking on the outskirts of the crowd. They were dressed as civilians but the conspicuous shades and bulging jackets were a dead giveaway.

"I'll gladly leave, sir. Just answer me one thing – you say there has been no deceit. Then I wonder how you wife and children are enjoying this lovely day, as you put it, while knowing that you spent the weekend in your private suite, at your own hotel in Seo-Sing City, with Miss Sonya Medina. Now there was nothing Presidential going on there, was there... Sir?"

The crowd let out an audible gasp at the insinuation, one of those perfect moments when the collective reacts in the same way, in the same instant.

"Get this guy off my lawn," Kiebler screamed as chaos erupted. The security team burst into action, and tables with half eaten cake and empty bottles of expensive champagne were thrown aside.

Kiebler turned to his family and shook his head. Xanthe could only stare ahead, watching as the man in the brown suit was wrestled to the floor, screaming about his democratic rights to question and inform as a member of the press corps.

"Come on, let's get inside. There's only one crackpot you have to listen to in there," Kiebler smiled, offering his hand to Melanie and motioning Junior to stand too.

"Xanthe. Get out of your seat and get inside," he intoned to his wife. The spell broken, she looked away from the madness and into his face. She seemed for the briefest of moments like she might be shocked, or about to ask him something important, but the moment was gone in an instant.

"Of course. Come on, kids," she said, "do as your father says."

"Why did that man say those things, Daddy? Why is he being arrested?" Junior chimed in as a security detail joined them for the walk to the residence.

"We've discussed this before, Junior," his father replied while placing his hand on the young boy's head. "Daddy is famous, and has money and soon to be power. Some people don't like that. Some of them are jealous or just plain mean. They can't stand to see one of their own doing better than they are, so they try to do whatever they can to sabotage our happiness."

Xanthe shot him a look and he returned it. There was something stern in that look. Something that told her to remain silent, and that whatever she might be thinking should be buried away so deep it should never see the light of day.

***

Bernard Kiebler stormed into his private study and hurled his phone across the room, watching the man in its path duck out of its way. It shattered with a satisfying crack against the wall.

"You didn't think to vet these pricks before letting them into my own home?" he screamed.

Donald Orsay, his Chief Advisor on the Presidential campaign, stood upright and took the abuse. He knew what was coming and he knew no way of avoiding it.

"Sir, the man had full press credentials and a legitimate reason to be here." He replied, remaining calm in the face of an uphill battle.

"Then how come I've never seen his fucking face before?"

"He was on the staff at the North Shore Herald for seven years, sir. Until last month he was their star boy. Then he jumped ship for the Ganymede Media Corporation."

"One month ago? Just like that? And suddenly he's insulting me in front of my family?" Rage and fury spilled from Kiebler's mouth with every word. He wanted someone strung up for this, and he had a few people in mind already.

"We have reason to believe he was offered the job due to his, uh, ambitious style of investigative journalism. He has been pursuing you aggressively, making claims and publishing theories which appeal to a certain fan base." Orsay took several deep breaths as his boss took in that information. He knew what was coming, and the anger that would ensue. He also knew that he hadn't given half the story yet, and the worst was yet to come.

"We can show him to be a crackpot. Put his previous claims together to show his vendetta against me. Discredit him before anyone looks too closely."

"I'm afraid it's beyond that point, sir." Orsay replied.

"I swear to God, Don, if you're holding on to something I need to know I will not hold back. I have never wanted to bludgeon the life out of you more than I do right now."

"Sir, the Ganymede networks are already running the story. This event – his attendance at it at least – was a set-up. They wanted your reaction on camera."

Kiebler let it sink in a moment. He stared at the man in front of him – a man who had advised him through two difficult elections, local then state. A man telling him the world was collapsing around him.

"Don't just stand there, put the fucking TV on!" he screamed at an aide. "And shut the door! You want to invite the press in here too? My wife and kids?"

The aide quickly shut the door, and ran to the TV to find the news stations controlled by Ganymede. A picture of Sonya Medina filled the screen, as a reporter talked about her background and how she had come to meet the "wannabe President."

"Motherfuckers," Kiebler almost whispered. He picked up a desk lamp and ripped it from the socket, severing the cord. Turning viciously and without warning he slammed it against the head of the young aide. Blood immediately began to seep from the wound, as the aide sunk to the floor with a scream of fear and pain.

"How much do they know, Don?" he spoke, breathing hard.

"As far as I can tell? Everything."

"Tell me you have put out a denial?"

"I have asked for an immediate retraction and for the footage from today to go unaired. I'm not sure it will help us."

"Don't you fucking tell me its worse. Don't you fucking dare!"

A knock sounded at the door, and Daxler Scion slunk into the room. He stood on the periphery, consumed in shadow and entirely unfazed by the bleeding aide who had pulled himself to a chair in the corner.

"Its worse, sir" Donald continued. "I demanded a retraction in the strongest possible terms, and the response was to ask us why they should. They claim to have pictures. Video too."

He allowed a moment for that to truly sink in. Bernard Kiebler was not used to losing, but this seemed a step too far even for him.

"I'm afraid the cork is already out of the bottle, sir. There's no putting it back in now." Orsay stated, as solemnly as he could manage.

"I'll smash the fucking bottle over your misshapen head, you spineless-"

"Sir, if I may interrupt?" Scion spoke, sensing the appearance of more blood in the room soon enough.

"No, no! I've come so far! Too far. To be ruined by some whore? Do you realise the pressure? Do you *even know* the pressure I am under?" Kiebler raged on, his fury directed at his friend now.

"The people do not want to hear of the pressure, sir. They want to see you take action. To shake off the pressure. Rise above it," Scion spoke, with all the perspicacity of a serpent.

"Oh, they want a superhero! They want me to be impervious while I save their fucking planet? They want me to stop them being shafted by every liberal, every off-worlder, and every snivelling, wishy-washy, harebrained disgrace that steps foot into a presidential race?"

"Yes, sir," Scion offered back.

"And how do they suppose I relieve that pressure, Scion? Who do I get to fuck while I prevent them all from being fucked by these vultures?" he said, pacing the room. "The frigid, leathery sack of bones I call a wife? I'd rather put my dick in one of you useless pricks." He picked up a waiting bottle of whisky from the drinks cabinet by his desk. He took a long, hard glug directly from the bottle, keeping his eyes locked on Daxler Scion, and wondering if he would dare to answer.

When no response came he launched the bottle at the wall, where it shattered into a thousand pieces and took down a portrait of his own father along with it. He let out a sigh, and slumped into his seat behind his antique desk. Silence filled the room like a poisonous gas.

"Where is she from... this... girl?" Scion asked after a moment.

"What does it matter?" Kiebler replied, flat and lifeless.

"It may matter. Where is she from?" Scion repeated the question, looking to both men now.

"She's from one of the islands, I believe. Just off North Shore." Orsay offered.

"A capital girl," Scion whispered, looking into Kiebler's eyes. "An honest to goodness Jupitoan girl?"

On the same wavelength, Scion and Kiebler shared a moment which went beyond Orsay's understanding. For whatever reason, it did not comfort him one bit.

**

Senator Calhoun had finally allowed a smile to work its way across her face as she hung up the old-style telephone in her study. She immediately moved through into the main house, across the polished wood floors of the hallways and into the warmth of the kitchen where her eldest daughter, Caroline, sat at the dining table, clutching a large glass of wine.

The kitchen had been boisterous and chaotic in the past – especially during election season. Her husband, Marty, and his entire staff tended to decamp to the kitchen at the end of particularly long days and turn them into particularly long – but substantially more fun – evenings. Their two daughters would lend a hand with cooking and provide laughs, while the wood-burning fireplace in the corner of the room warmed them against the chilled Jupitoan nights.

Now it was just Caroline and her, and all this space. She wondered what they might do with it if she won the election. She couldn't see any way of letting go of the house and all of those memories but the thought of anyone else staying here and keeping the house right for four years bothered her – and the fact that she would be approaching seventy-four by the time she returned to from a second term weighed heavily on her mind.

But that was all 'if' she won.

She couldn't let the reality of the situation sink in, but surely tonight's news granted her the right to indulge in thoughts of victory. She smiled and Caroline smiled right back.

"So? How does it look?" she asked while simultaneously pouring a large glass for her mother.

"They have refused to comment on the allegations. No denial, no threat of a lawsuit. They are rocked, Caroline."

"You think there's truth in it then?"

"Who knows? It looks that way," she replied, taking a seat. "Why wouldn't he deny it? He is on TV at the slightest mention of his name. Publicity is the only thing he knows how to do right. Why aren't they denying it?"

"Because it's all true. His lifestyle has caught up with him. He was never going to win this thing. Skeletons don't stay hidden for long, especially not in politics," Caroline replied, raising her glass and offering it up to her mother. They clinked together and each took a sip.

"His momentum is done for. He's been catching up for weeks now but they tell me it's over. A two-point slide already and the story only broke a few hours ago."

"His approval rating will be shattered like the ships he wanted to obliterate in the Belt. They call that 'karma' back on Earth." Calhoun said as she relaxed back into her chair. It wasn't her chair, she thought to herself. This was Marty's.

Her husband had served every office imaginable and had popularity ratings through the roof. He was a man of the people who had dragged himself up by his own sheer will. She had admired that about him from the day that they met until the day that he died. She wished for just an ounce of his nobility or his drive. She wished for those who loved him to love her too.

She wished that he was here, in his chair, holding court on another campaign so she could merely watch it unfold.

"Do you think they will release the things they say they have?" her daughter asked.

"The video? Yeah, I imagine it'll be out there soon enough. Maybe they will wait a few days for maximum impact."

"I don't know how I feel about that. His poor kids," she said, looking to her mother for comfort. Scandal and media games came with the territory, she knew, but she had also lived through the trials of Presidential scandals as the child of the Head of State. She wouldn't have wished that on anyone.

"You can't worry about that. That's his family. They should have been his first thought when he was off dallying with other women. We can't assume the blame for the things he has done, and neither can those who expose him for it."

"No. I know who is to blame for all that. I just can't help feeling like I'm on the wrong side of things when I find myself agreeing with what the press is doing."

Heather reached out to squeeze her daughters hand over the table and gave her a reassuring smile.

"We have to look at the positives and let Kiebler worry about his life. This is a major boost for me – for us. Who knows if I could have halted his rise without all of this?" she asked, wondering if it really mattered how she won, or just that she was winning.

"I know, I know. I just wish it didn't have to get so messy. Better now than a year down the road with him already in office, I suppose."

"Exactly, you take a moment to think about that. The most important thing is that the right person is going to win. The bad guy got his. How often does that ever happen? In the entire galaxy, never mind politics?"

They both laughed, relaxing more. She always knew the right words to cheer her kids up and this time she actually believed it herself. She knew that she was in the race for the right reasons. Not for the popularity, or the money. Not to further some racist agenda or to boost some failing businesses.

She had failed in the past by trying to latch onto her husband's legacy and ride his popularity, and she'd failed again when she was advised to flip her stance on practically every matter.

Now she was succeeding – or at least leading the race– by being bold and saying what she truly believed in, using her experiences on both sides of the fence to try to find a balance between the two.

She saw that people were struggling and her planet had space and ideas and passion to burn. She wanted to see that expanded, to see it blossom and win over those who were filled with fear or hate. She wanted to make things better.

"It doesn't matter how we get there. As long as the right person gets there," she stated quietly.

"That's the spirit," Caroline replied. "I'm so proud of what you've done, and I can't wait to see what else you can achieve."

"Cheers," she offered her glass up once again, and her eldest daughter reciprocated.

"Á la vôtre" she whispered, as their glasses chinked again.

"A toast to the future President of Jupiter!"

CHAPTER FOUR

T he Ganymede Media Corporation had been based on the actual Jupitoan moon itself for a number of years, until atmospheric pressure variances led to its sudden and complete evacuation. In the early days of Jupiter's own colonisation, the scientists and atmospheric experts thought of a way to recycle the old machinery and potentially revolutionise the way they terraformed these galactic terrains.

Having no atmosphere of their own, the moons were blank canvasses for experimentation. Work on Saturn's atmospheric conversion had already begun at that time and was monopolising the time of the solar systems system's leading scientists and experts, therefore a small group of die-hard visionaries and entrepreneurs was formed and tasked with making Callisto and Io habitable.

After some early success, the government of Jupiter decided that the ideas were good enough but the scale wasn't – the moons weren't of sufficient size to justify the cost of the expansion that the program required. Plans were put in place to convert Ganymede instead, being the largest moon known to man – larger even than the planet Mercury.

It took a number of years to perfect the science but relatively quickly the moon had a basic hydrogen atmosphere and a small community of scientists, builders and ecologists who called it home. Land was cheap and plentiful and big corporations flocked to it, looking to break into the Jupitoan markets.

The Ganymede Media Corporation operated there for six years before the bubble burst. It started with little things, like extreme drops in temperature overnight, or snow storms in the midst of a heat wave. Everyone knew something wasn't right and the best and brightest minds were lured back from the outer edges of the galaxy to consult on the technical details.

After months of investigations and site surveys on areas that had been particularly affected, they eventually found serious flaws in the conversion methods that had been used to make the atmosphere breathable. The artificial O-Zone was wasting away, day by day and while it was assisted by the heavy-duty machinery, installed on day one as in every other terraformed colony, it wasn't enough to counter the rate of decay. They ordered an immediate mass evacuation – an exodus of hundreds of thousands of people.

Jupiter opened its doors to the beleaguered colonists, gifting them large plots of land to re-populate, along with tax breaks to help them adjust to the resettlement. The moon's atmosphere generators were switched off remotely after the last ship departed. Within a couple of days the moon had returned to its previous barren state.

Ganymede Media made a killing from the disarray caused by the whole situation. As the primary media outlet on the moon, they had every live satellite link and every interview with the top experts as an exclusive. They made millions in deals with media companies from across the galaxy as everyone wanted to see how things panned out for the great failed moon experiment.

The owners exploited the resettlement deal offered by the Jupitoan government and took full advantage. They bought up cheap land which was meant for honest, hard-working settlers, and they used every tax break afforded to them. Two weeks before the final evacuation, Ganymede Media's executives had their monumental head office building taken apart like a kid's toy and relocated to Jupiter – just outside of the newly thriving capital of Seo-Sing.

They had played the situation perfectly and now stood as an experienced, extremely well-placed and very well financed organisation. They bought out several smaller media firms and built an empire on Jupiter – unrivalled and unprecedented in the entire outer solar system.

Sam Heighway approached their imposing skyscraper office in awe every day. He had worked in Ganymede Towers for three years, consulting or producing projects in the television department and hosting a handful of shows of his own. Still, the building represented a foundation stone in television and print here on Jupiter, and the ingenuity of the original board made them heroes to Sam. They saw an opportunity and took full advantage until they dominated all of their adversaries – he could see some real merit in there somewhere.

The awe he felt usually turned to trembling fear or a very tangible feeling of self-doubt when he stepped inside. Since his early career had slid into decline, places like this were intimidating to him. That's why Sam liked to produce things under his own banner – after an initial pitch he was basically his own boss, with little in the way of consequences if he got things wrong along the way.

Not this day, though. This day felt different. Sam felt his stride widen, his step more bouncy than fearful. He gave a nod to the receptionist girl whose name he hadn't yet learned. He gave a cheery 'good morning' to the elevator full of people he stepped right into. This day was different for many reasons.

The truth struck him in that moment, contemplating his sudden rise in confidence. He was terrified of this place. He held his head low, keeping himself under the radar at all times with good reason - he was washed up. He was a washed up, fading, hopeless TV star with one hand grasping at the last vestiges of any fame he could ever have claimed to have had.

In this building of up-and-comers and already-made-its he was nobody. He was less than nobody – he was so inconsequential as to not even warrant the time it took to say hello or to offer your name. His mind flashed back to that receptionist. He had wanted to ask her out on so many occasions, and had barely managed a conversation with her even once. This day was different.

He recognised that he had always known the truth of his lowly level. Only now that he was free from the mental shackles he had constructed for himself, did he see just how much he had been affected by it all. He would walk in here every time feeling inferior and acting inferior.

Today was different. Today he breezed through reception and was that annoyingly cheerful guy in the elevator. Today he waltzed through the news room – the place where the big boys played – and walked right up to the News Editor's office. He considered knocking for a brief second then decided to go with the flow of his mood. Today everyone would feel the tables turning.

"Heighway? What the fuck are you doing here, and who the fuck said you could come into my office?" the editor spoke, more annoyed than angry.

Wally Molinaro was an institution. In his mid-40s and at the peak of his powers, he was News Editor for all television, digital and print media put out by the Ganymede company. They said his distribution was so good even the priests back on Earth and the savages of Venus read his stuff. Galaxy wide and utterly dominant, the man had style, power and success to spare. Sam had weaselled and wormed his way into his good books, all the while remaining utterly in fear of the man.

"Mr Molinaro-"

"Heighway. I don't have time for your bullshit today. I got no debates coming up, no radio hosts down with a cold, and no desire at all to hear another shitty reality show pitch. So, would you kindly get the fuck out of my office?"

Sam hesitated for just a moment, as muscle memory or some hidden gene in his DNA almost made him turn and walk away. He steeled himself against his own ingrained instinct, beating himself up for even feeling that way. 'Not this time' repeated over and over in his head.

"Pull the Kiebler thing." He blurted out, not half as coolly as he had planned.

Molinaro laughed, briefly, then finally looked up from his tablet screen to which he had been transfixed since two seconds after Sam walked in the door.

"Have you finally lost it, Heighway? Because I think there was a pool with the office girls."

"Pull the story. End it. Bury the video footage," he spoke, calmer this time, settling into it.

"Sam this is the biggest story we've ever reported on – potentially the biggest in Jupitoan history. Why the hell would I pull it on the word of some washed up kook? No offence."

"Offence has absolutely been taken, and will not be forgotten – but pull the story immediately. Cancel whatever you have airing at 8pm and get me a crew and a fine-ass looking suit like that one you are wearing now." He flashed a smile Molinaro's way, causing the man to pick his glasses up from the desk and place them on very carefully. He looked back at Sam as if he had never seen him before in his life.

"The story-" he tried to reason, but Sam wasn't looking to lose momentum now.

"You don't have a story. You have half a story, and some seedy footage of some whore and a faded movie star who you will turn into a nobody overnight, if you air it."

Sam smiled again and read from the look on Molinaro's face that he had him exactly where he wanted him.

"What you don't have, Mr Editor, is an exclusive, confessional, one on one interview with the future President of this planet."

"Confessional?" Wally asked, reeling. He didn't recognise the man in front of him, and refused to accept he had any relevance in the world he knew.

"He's going to spill the beans on the biggest story you will ever have broken and couldn't even possibly contemplate, my friend. And you'll hear it all from his mouth, as will every person on the planet, on your very own network."

Wally sat back. He hadn't any reason to trust Sam Heighway on any matter whatsoever – never mind something so huge. However, the man in front of him bore no resemblance to Sam Heighway. Not today.

"I'll embargo the footage until 10pm tonight. You deliver the goods and it will disappear." Molinaro looked Sam dead in the eyes.

"You screw me over and it airs 10pm sharp, along with a footnote at the bottom of the hour regarding your dismissal from this corporation. You got that?"

Sam heard it loud and clear. He was about to become the second most famous face on the planet and Molinaro didn't even know what he had yet.

***

Bernard Kiebler adjusted his shirt collar and stared up at the studio lights. It was hotter than he remembered under the glare, and he regretted the choice of shirt and tie. Thinking about it more, he realised in this particular case that the sweaty, pressurised look might not be such a bad thing. He should look nervous; he should look like the weight of the world was on his shoulders.

"I'm sorry I missed the question, Sam. It's really quite hot in here," he spoke to Heighway and smiled. The cameras were on him and he knew that a record audience would be tuning in. It was remarkable, he decided, that he didn't feel any of the pressure that the people expected of him.

"I'll repeat, Governor. You have asked for this time here, in front of the voting public, to offer your response in person to these scandalous rumours and tabloid stories. Are you ready to be honest and open with your people?"

Sam was relaxed and in his element. He knew the boost this would provide for his career and the elevation in social and political standing which would come along with it. He knew that he just needed to bring this one home.

"Sam, I need to be honest. And I need to agree with you – it is scandalous. The media have hounded me from day one. You know what this is like – the way they build you up to be the poster boy for whatever agenda they have in mind this month, then knock you down the next. It is exhausting and immoral and an insult to our people and our planet as a whole"

Kiebler was glad there was no live audience for this one. Just a crew who knew to keep quiet. He had his words mapped out carefully and the baying crowd at this point would have been enough to send things off the rails fast.

"So, you are here tonight to admonish the press and strike a blow against the false media?" Sam said, reigning in all of his natural, genuine emotions on the matter.

"No, Sam. I must admit I am not. For while I have been a victim of their abuse, and a pawn in the popularity schemes of these vultures, I must confess to my wrong doing. The reports of my indiscretions are all true, I am ashamed to admit. I have indulged in an extra-marital affair."

Pause for effect. Kiebler waited. He eyed Sam up, hoping he would allow the moment. He imagined viewers at home - gasps of shock, screams of anger, the full range of emotions. He paused and waited for their clamour to calm down. He wanted them to hear every word.

"I know that is a shock to many. I know I have done wrong, and I know the upset and torment I may cause by my actions. To my family, to my friends and colleagues and to this beautiful campaign we hoped to run to take back the planet I love. I know I have done wrong," he spoke passionately, and haltingly, hoping to convey emotion but not to appear weak. It was a fine line.

"Mr Kiebler, please – take a moment," Sam offered.

"No, no, Sam. It's OK. I have only myself to blame. I know these things – these hurts I have caused – but I fear I must act now and be truthful. I am a God-fearing man and I know the power of confession. Despite what the advisors from the party have told me – they wanted this all kept hush-hush, like the dirty secret it was. Well, that's not me. This isn't me. I had to let the truth be known."

"That is very admirable of you, Mr Kiebler."

"You know, these things will always get out, Sam. It isn't an accident, and it isn't misfortune. The truth will out."

"That's correct, Mr Presi... Mr Kiebler, I'm sorry."

Kiebler smiled. Sam had sold him on the idea of that fumble. He hadn't liked it, and wasn't convinced the bumbling mess that was once Sam Heighway could pull it off. But this guy – *this* Sam

Heighway was as slick and professional as any interviewer he had ever encountered. It seemed this game was right up Sam's street.

"Sam, honestly, I feel that now the truth is out there a weight has been lifted, but it is not the full weight. The people have a right to know the thoughts and motivations of the man they had put so much faith in up to now. They deserve the full story."

"The world is watching, sir. We are all eager to hear your words," Sam spoke softly now, playing the calming, soothing, confessional interviewer.

"I've been carrying this around for so long, and it is one that has not leaked or been used against me until now. I'm sure they'll twist this and turn it against me, and maybe I deserve it but the truth is," he paused, choosing his moment, adjusting the collar, the tie. "I have fallen out of love with the woman I thought of as my everything. Xanthe and I have been through many many trials and tribulations. We have endured through a long, hard road together but we have both agreed that we have reached the end of that road now."

The audible gasps from the assembled crew told Kiebler his words had hit home. He took a gulp of water from his waiting glass.

"The pressures of a long and arduous campaign have taken their toll. The realities of bringing my vision, my will, and the will of those who support me, to light have been too much to accept for my wife. She is not from Jupiter – she is not one of us –

and I believe she finds it hard to understand my passion and my pride in my people. My planet."

Kiebler knew now, could see in the eyes of everyone in the room, that the tide was turning. Daxler Scion's words and ideas spilled from his mouth, and his soul was lifted with every revelation.

"I dare say she doesn't agree with some of my policies – my policies to make this planet a great place to live once again. To give it back to *our* people. I suppose I can see why, and maybe I can forgive her for that if I am to ask forgiveness for my sins too."

Sam sat forward in his seat, concentrated and fully focused on the end goal now. They had dropped the bombshell, and now it was a case of running for cover and waiting to see where the dust might settle.

"The girl in the stories, Mr Kiebler," Sam spoke "Did your wife know about her – was she aware of your sordid moment of weakness?"

Kiebler took a long hard drink from his glass. He wished he had taken up the offer of masking vodka as water in there.

"I'm afraid she did, yes. And I must confess more – there was nothing sordid about the affair. It was much worse than that. I have fallen in love... In love with a younger woman, a woman who is not my wife. Yes, she is the mistress I never intended to have, but she is so much more. A woman who understands the pressures I am under and who believes in the right way for Jupiter and its people. She sees nothing but glory in the Kiebler promise. A genuine Jupitoan born girl with fire in her belly and love in her heart, and the freedom and future of you people as her desire."

He thought it was too much, and he could have heard a pin drop in that little studio for a moment or two. Just enough time for people to catch their breath. Then, faintly, and growing louder by the second, Kiebler heard the applause of the crew. They were clapping and now cheering and the mood had shifted in an instant.

Sam Heighway looked at the Governor sat before him and saw the President to be looking right back at him.

***

Kiebler greeted the aide backstage with all the contempt he could muster. Sycophantic fawning did not impress him in the slightest and this boy was practically hanging around his neck shouting 'look at me, look at me!'.

"Give me the numbers, and none of your bullshit" he stated, drowning out the boy's words.

"Yes, sir," he responded, disappointment oozing from his every pore. "Ratings look to be monumental! Initial figures in the high-hundreds – the whole planet saw you out there, sir."

"And the polls? Where are those?"

Daxler Scion stepped forward, having patiently watched the entire act from backstage. He smiled when he greeted Kiebler; a sickening grin.

"Mr Governor, it is safe to say that your confessional hour was the turning of the tide.

Approval ratings steadily increased throughout the hour. You're now more popular than you were before the scandal broke. A complete and perfect turnaround."

"Maybe my wife was the albatross you always suspected, Dax."

"I am sure it is not my place to comment, sir," Daxler replied and somehow made the grin grow more ominous.

"Your wife awaits in your hotel room. She is quite... agitated."

Kiebler sighed. He knew this would come next, but the exhilaration of the show itself was enough to keep his mind off it until now. He hadn't had the time or the patience to pre-warn his wife about the interview, and he couldn't imagine her reaction would be calm and understanding.

"Dax. I need you to go there now. Speak with her. Calm her, if you can. She must be made to understand, but for now I have things I must do. You understand."

Daxler Scion was not excited by this new task, Kiebler could tell. The look on his face was worth the effort, and he knew Dax would do his best. His wife was a whirlwind of emotion at the best of times and he did not wish to face the initial brunt of it himself. Dax could take the worst of it, the man had no soul. He would lay the groundwork and then the pieces would be swept under the carpet.

Kiebler had more important things in mind. His team had found the girl already and all he needed to do was convince her to be his new bride. He could hardly see any downside from her point of view – new life, new home, future wife of the most powerful man in the solar system? Still, she had to be locked down before he finally confronted his wife with the state of affairs.

Sam Heighway finally joined the backstage throng and moved to congratulate Kiebler. His beaming smile was like a beacon, and he couldn't wait to make the trip upstairs and visit Molinaro's office. The thought of that arrogant prick kissing the ring and throwing offers at him was enough to make Sam's dreams come true. Soon it would be a reality.

"Sammy boy. Come here," Kiebler shouted over and extended an arm. He took the younger man under his wing, and guided him off to a quiet corner.

"You know you did me good out there, Sammy boy. You seen the numbers?" he asked in conspiratorial tones.

"They're record-shattering, Sam. The highest ratings in history, anywhere, ever. Thanks to you." Kiebler let the words flow, as he always did. Truth and fiction were one and the same when he had someone in his sights.

"That's incredible news, Governor. We really did it," Sam responded, eyes wide now.

"Listen up, Sam. I just made you relevant again, you hear me? Never forget that. Never forget what you owe to your future President, OK?" Kiebler spoke up now, looking Sam in the eye and sharpening his tone. He didn't want the kid to misunderstand anything.

"Bernie I..." Sam started.

"Mr Kiebler. To you my name is Mr Kiebler and it will remain so until it is Mr President. Get that straight, OK?"

"Yes, Mr Kiebler."

"You never forget, you hear? I resurrected your life tonight. You forget about that and I send you back to that reality TV garbage." Kiebler knew where to hit him hardest.

Sam, for his part, stood motionless, the arm of his Governor and puppeteer draped over his shoulder. He had come so far in less than a day; he didn't want to ruin anything at this stage.

"You ever get record breaking ratings with that garbage, Sammy boy?" Kiebler asked, not waiting for a response.

"You just remember what your President did for you."

Kiebler released Sam from his hold and began to walk away. He looked back at Sam, who stood rooted to the spot, staring aimlessly. A man at odds with himself.

"Cheer up, Sammy. I got one more piece of the puzzle for you to play with. Gonna make you a star, my boy. I'll be in touch tomorrow - you make sure they give you air time. It'll be huge."

CHAPTER FIVE

General Hasting waited outside the Presidential office like a naughty school boy. He hated this part. As a leader of Seo-Sing City's major armed forces unit, he was often called to babysit various dignitaries on visits to meet the President. It almost always resulted in him sitting outside the Presidential suite, wasting half of the day away.

Normally this was followed by escorting the dignitary back to wherever they needed to be and gave rise to some unquestionably dull conversation along the way.

Senator Calhoun had only been in the office for an hour, give or take, when the door was flung open and allowed to bang against the desk inside. Hasting jumped to attention to see the Senator storm out of the current sitting President's office and march towards the exit. Nobody followed her out of the room, so he took it upon himself to follow.

"Mrs Calhoun – please," he shouted after the Presidential candidate. Her fury was plain to see in her walk.

"I have no need of an escort, General," she hollered back.

He quickened his step to catch up with her, and fell into stride by her side. He decided to walk in silence as they passed out of the grand arch of the Presidential building, and down the steps outside. She stopped at the bottom of the stairs, looking lost.

"May I be of assistance, Mrs Calhoun?" he asked.

"You may tell me where my car is, and I'll be on my way" she responded, her anger turned to annoyance now.

"I have been asked to escort you while you are in the capital, Mrs Calhoun. Your car was sent away but I will happily take you wherever you wish to be."

She eyed him, not knowing whether to explode with fury now or just give in and let him win. She settled somewhere in between and asked if he knew anywhere that she could get a cold, hard drink without too many prying eyes being on her.

Hasting smiled and signalled for his car to be brought around. It was a military issue vehicle – slick but unremarkable all at once, with reinforced steel and bullet-proof windows wrapped in a shell that was acceptable for a lady of Senator Calhoun's standing to be seen climbing into.

As they drove he felt her mood lighten, and slowly began to lay some small talk groundwork.

She didn't seem to be interested in the stuff that usually worked – and he wasn't much of a conversationalist even on his best day. Usually the delegates he picked up on this assignment didn't need much encouragement to tell him everything he didn't want to know about their meetings with the President.

"I met with Mr Kiebler for a position in his cabinet," he blurted out. He noticed she immediately sat up, looking at him for the first time since they got into the car.

"Why are you telling me that?" she asked, hostile.

"I figure we have some things in common. Or at least plenty to talk about," he said with a smile.

"You're considering taking the job?" she asked him, feigning disinterest again. He was always good at reading people, and he knew he had chosen the right subject.

"I've considered it. I don't particularly like the thought of working for the man, but equally I have my concerns if someone else was in my place."

"Concerns for your own career?"

"No ma'am. I'm concerned for the planet and for Seo-Sing itself. It is a very dangerous time at the moment, and a leader like Kiebler could set things on fire."

She looked at him intently, unsure how to take this talkative General.

"You think if he picked the wrong guy to lead his armed forces we could see things go very wrong, very fast?" she asked, knowing the answer.

Hasting nodded. He was usually a man of few words, but he had wanted to have this discussion with Senator Calhoun for some time.

"There are a lot of wrong guys out there at the moment," he told her.

She thought it over for a moment. "You know I shortlisted you from day one, don't you?" she asked.

"No ma'am."

"Well I did. I know your reputation; you're a fine General by all accounts. I didn't ask you in to speak with my team because we'd heard about your meeting with old 'Honest Bernie.'"

She let out a laugh and Hasting joined her. He had hoped she had a good reason for not choosing him on her staff. He had it now.

"I met him out of reluctance, and out of hope that he wouldn't then be able to choose another. I think he sees me as someone he can mould into... whatever it is he needs. I know plenty of men who would fall for it. If he is going to lead our government, he needs a General behind him who sees right through all of his bullshit."

He said all of this without hesitation, and with no aim to impress the famous Senator by his side. He spoke his mind and sometimes had to hope for the best. He felt in this situation that he would have no trouble.

"It's an admirable thing you are doing. Looks like you're going to have a job, General Hasting."

"Is it that bad?" he asked.

"It's bad. The President just chewed me out for not 'finishing him when he was down'. The party thinks we let the ball get away from us with the affair rumours – we didn't touch it, waited to see the aftermath. Who could have known the level he would stoop to?"

"You think he was stooping? I heard he filed the divorce papers this morning."

"It's a sham, General. If the people only knew. Or rather, if I could only prove it."

"There's no proof of any wrong doing?"

"Only his poor wife, ditched on television to right a sinking ship. He's concocted the whole story – the only marital problems he ever had were that his wife didn't like him sleeping with younger women. I suppose she got everything she asked for when she let him get away with it."

Hasting let it all sink in, confirming many of his own suspicions but opening up a whole canyon full of new questions.

"His wife knew about the affair then?" he asked.

"Yes, she knew about several of them. She stayed with him for the perks, and no doubt the kids played their part. She knew what he was from the beginning, and now with the finishing line in sight he has kicked her to the curb and moved the younger model into his home."

"How very Presidential," Hasting observed as he turned up a side street and parked in an alley out of sight.

"Well get used to it – I'm clinging on for my life right now."

Hasting nodded in agreement, then motioned to the non-descript building by their side.

"We're here," he smiled.

***

Inside the shabby-looking apartment building was a hidden gem – a bar in the style of an old speakeasy. Hasting knew it was popular with politicians and any other secretive types who didn't want their every move to be watched. The doormen were conspicuous but also very good at recognising a reporter – a handy trick to have in such a place.

Hasting carried drinks over to the table for Calhoun and himself – making sure his was the non-alcoholic glass. They relaxed into general chit-chat, about life in the city and how it compared to the green spaces outside. Calhoun waxed lyrical about growing up on her parents' farm, and raising her own kids on the very same land.

"I can't imagine life being so open. As a kid, I knew only concrete and steel. We played sports indoors," he told her, as a waiter placed a bowl of nibbles on the table between them.

"I thought you grew up off-world?" Calhoun replied, surprised by this.

"No ma'am. People tend to assume a lot about me."

"I'm sorry, I didn't mean..." she was flustered a little, not sure enough in his company to know how serious he could take things.

He waved a hand to brush off the comment, and smiled.

"It's OK; I didn't mean you in particular. People just see a black man in a uniform. They hear about my being born on Saturn and assume some crazy lineage. Truth is my parents grew up about a mile from where we sit right now."

"So, this is your local, I suppose?" she laughed and raised her glass to him before taking a sip.

"I frequented this place a few times in my youth, yeah," Hasting replied, allowing himself a laugh too. "Back when it wasn't quite so fancy or secure."

"How long were you on Saturn?" she asked.

"I'm not sure really. Weeks or months at most. I don't remember a thing about it. The Uzstaz rebellion was on its last legs then. My father was still on the front lines, and wouldn't let my mother leave without him. She was well looked after in the military hospital."

"They both survived the fighting?"

"Yes ma'am. Once they knew I was healthy and my mother was feeling up to it they let her come home. Dad joined her a few weeks later after finishing his service."

"You must be proud. They fought for Jupiter, and they fought for you, and now you get to repay that honour."

"I just do what I feel is right. I don't like to see folks put down, and I don't like to see anyone shut out. We all deserve the opportunity to thrive in this world, or on any other." He spoke with passion and pride, and she got a sense for who he was now. A man who knew right from wrong, who would put his life on the line to stand up for his beliefs.

"You must have some issues with your potential boss' plans then?" she asked him, incredulously.

"Mr Kiebler seems to believe that being born on one planet or another manifests a change in a person's ability to work hard or feel patriotism or endeavour to achieve. I have never felt any lack of love or honour for this planet. My place of birth is irrelevant – this is what I call home."

"He looks at you and sees a foreigner – on a giant piece of rock that was once an unreachable ball of gas to all of mankind. He forgets where we all come from and that we all share in this incredible enterprise together." Calhoun replied, sensing the politician in her coming to the fore and shying away from it. She didn't need to sell the idea to Hasting, she could tell.

"His ability to look behind the facts for something more convenient is astonishing," Hasting added. That was the point which frustrated him most of all out of all of Kiebler's many flaws.

"What's astonishing is that people are following him," Calhoun replied.

"I can understand that, in a way. People want to be led. It's a natural instinct – to be told what is right and what is wrong, and to be led towards the good path. It's why my title exists. It's why religion exists. It's why we vote for our leaders in the first place. They have simply lost sight of the difference between what is good for the planet, and what is good for themselves."

Calhoun agreed, and leaned in close.

"I've heard there have been increased security details in the streets around the capital. Is it true that they've been covering up something major?"

"I wouldn't go so far as to say major. Or covering up for that matter. There have been small uprisings – groups of young men with nothing better to do with their time."

"Organised groups?"

"Not especially. Just boys mostly. They cause a little scene, some incidental damage to the city. They sing racist songs and paint signs on doors. It hasn't taken a lot of force to put a stop to it."

"But that's not the point is it, Hasting?" she exclaimed. "Where are these kids learning these lessons? From where do they draw their spite and hatred for hard-working, fellow citizens?"

"They look to their leaders. As we all do."

"That is the greatest worry of our times, General."

Hasting stared into his glass for a long while. He knew things would need to get worse before they got better. He sincerely hoped the woman sitting opposite him could find the miracle she needed – or else he wasn't sure how long those extremes of society could be held at bay.

CHAPTER SIX

"**M**r Kiebler you are in direct contempt of this assembly," the Galactic Union speaker shouted above the rabble in his chambers. "Can we have some quiet in the room, please!" he screamed, making himself heard at last.

Bernard Kiebler had gone to the Galactic Union General Assembly as a show of good faith. He was the leader of the opposition in Jupiter's most hotly contested election to date, and the run-away leader in the race to the polls. Senator Calhoun had visited much earlier in the campaign and had been received well, although she had made little impression on the assembled members.

Kiebler noticed that the speaker did all of the talking inside the chambers, as well as in the general assembly which he saw broadcast every week to anyone dull enough to bother watching it. The Chair of the GU did not speak much at all – he simply sat, stony-faced, in the middle of it all, allowing the chaos to pass over him.

"What you suggest is not only akin to carving up a piece of the galaxy for yourself, it is also in direct breech of one of our core principles," the speaker said, as Kiebler watched the Chair alone.

"I am doing what needs to be done for the good of my planet, and its people. People like me who are threatened, day in and day out, by those who wish to corrupt and distort the very values we stand for," Kiebler responded, venom in his voice.

"Your planet?" the GU emissary from Earth spoke up. "I wasn't aware you had been elected yet, Mr Kiebler. Have you been appointed to our council already?" He spoke with disdain, his face contorted in its disgust. Kiebler knew he was unpopular here, but suspected a lot of this aggression towards him was just for show. Too many men with nonsense powers, acting like lords of the Universe.

"Forgive my presumptive attitude – however, I believe I have been asked here to discuss my policies in the likelihood that I do win the vote, so let's take that logical leap for a moment, shall we?" He enjoyed speaking down to them. He knew they felt it in their bones and reviled him even more for it.

"You are right of course," the speaker butted in again. "Mr Kiebler you must understand, the GU will not, in fact cannot, support any act to block or thereby restrict access to the asteroid belt which separates Mars from Jupiter. We are as one in our union, and in our exploration of the far reaches of our own solar system. This has always been the way."

"And I say that way is at its end. Not a negotiated cooling off period, not a time for re-examining our treaties together, not a fucking time out."

"Mr Kieb-"

"I don't want to hear it, friend. I'm here to give you fair warning. The day is drawing nigh. Make your plans, rewrite your laws, do whatever you must do. Jupiter is waking up."

Kiebler felt proud of himself and wished the cameras were on him – the people back home would have eaten that up. He tried his best to commit it to memory but the ruckus his words had caused was distractingly ferocious. Then a loud hammer rang out – a deafening banging sound, echoing harshly around the small chamber.

The Chair had finally seen enough, and banged his gavel furiously, demanding quiet. The gathered representatives of the eight planetary systems all hushed instantly, looking to the Chair for guidance.

"Mr Bernard Kiebler, you have heretofore been warned that any attempt to carry out your stated policies on immigration control is the first of many policies which will be in direct opposition to this union. We will have no choice but to come together as a joint operating force and punish any actions taken in this regard – should you be the winner of the democratic vote of the Jupitoan people."

Silence filled the room. The Chair had spoken and Kiebler looked around at the dumb-founded faces which surrounded him. They looked as if God himself had just entered the room and laid down their fate. He could not stand it.

"Mr Chair. Forgive me for not heeding your powerful words, but I must tell you a tale of my own. Jupiter is the strongest power in the solar system, of that there is no doubt. In terms of population, monetary wealth and military strength, we hold the key to peace in this system – not the GU In fact, as a vital piece in the fabric of this union, I feel it only fair to warn you," he looked from the Chair to every face gathered in the room, "all of you – that Jupiter will remove itself from this union if you stand in my way."

"Then as powerful as you may be, you will face the might of all of the system combined. The Galactic Union will not be held to ransom" the Chair responded.

"There's no ransom, don't be so overly dramatic," he replied with a crooked smile. "If we were going to be dramatic about this I could let you know that rent will be due on this cathedral to politics and ego as soon as I am in charge. Your obstructions and immigrant mongering will not be allowed to manifest themselves within my city boundaries. You'll be forced to relocate beyond the belt – to some backwoods slum where nobody will hear from you ever again." He paused a moment, letting the idea sink in. He loved the smell of fear in the room. He lived for those moments.

"Your loss of face and positioning at Jupiter's high table will be ruinous. You all need to think long and hard about that."

The representatives all stood silent; dumbfounded by the sheer abrupt and shrewd manipulation that Kiebler had spun. They could see no way out, other than the hope that he might still lose the election.

"I pray to God almighty above that you fail in your task, Mr Kiebler," the Earth delegate stated, raising his head to the sky as he did so.

"Pray to all the Gods you want. I will be President of Jupiter, that is a fact. Be ready to offer your unending support to me when it happens – or start clearing out those offices."

"You are too assured of yourself. Pride goes before a fall," the speaker responded.

"You want assurance? You want to see a fall? Watch Ganymede News Hour tonight. You have 24 hours after it ends to pledge your commitment to my cause." He smiled as he stood from his seat.

"I'll be expecting your call. Gentlemen, it's been a pleasure."

With that he walked out of the Galactic Union chambers, and left the most powerful men in the galaxy impotent.

***

"Two nights ago we revealed the biggest story of any of our lifetimes, here in a Ganymede News Hour exclusive. Tonight that story gets bigger. Stayed tuned for the shocking revelations which will rock the Presidential elections to the core."

Sam Heighway spoke with a confidence that had belied him for the best part of a decade. He watched as the producer signalled the incoming commercial break, and flicked through his notes for the coming show. He was on the brink of something massive and he was eager to get it out.

The last 48 hours were a blur now – the Kiebler interview had been watched by millions of people, though not quite the record audience Kiebler had promised. Tonight they had time to plan and to advertise correctly – the second bombshell would be the biggest thing television had ever witnessed.

Sam planned it out meticulously. As soon as Kiebler had called to confirm the story, he had stormed into Molinaro's office and made his demands. He walked out of the GMC head office building as the new full-time host of Ganymede News Hour, with a six-figure guaranteed contract, creative control and most importantly this very slot tonight – primetime, superseding all regular programming.

It would just be Sam. No interviewee to take the spotlight, and no one to rely on to sell the tale to the public. He did the rounds in the early morning to record precisely-worded pieces from the relevant parties. He left nothing to chance.

The producer counted him down and the 'On Air' light flashed green.

"Good evening, Jupiter. Tonight we bring you a shocking and disturbing tale – one that will shake confidence in our political process and cause great concern to you, the voting public, and the sitting President with the stunning allegations against his party."

He plastered on his most earnest look, and waited a moment. The space between words was ever so important in allowing people to anticipate and inflate their notions of what the story would be.

"I spoke today with Sonya Medina – the campaign worker accused this week of indulging in an unlawful affair with Mr Bernard Kiebler. As we all know, Mr Kiebler has very publically declared his affections for Ms Medina but revelations uncovered by myself here at Ganymede News have given the tale a shocking twist.

Sonya Medina is an honest, hard-working girl. She believes in doing what is right, and is a girl of honour and principles. Unfortunately, the Calhoun campaign failed to see this. I have a statement from Sonya now, please be advised the things being discussed are not for the faint hearted."

The net cast, he watched as the pre-recorded clip was played into the live feed. Time to reel it in. Sonya Medina appeared in the video monitors and on every TV screen on Jupiter.

"I was working late, helping on a campaign drive to support homeless shelters on the outskirts of the city. There had been rumours all day of strange cars and men passing through the area who wouldn't normally be seen there. I was approached by two men in suits – it was intimidating and I was scared for my life so I just went along with everything they were saying.

"What were they asking of you, Ms Medina?" Sam hated his own voice coming from the monitor. Even worse when it was echoed through his earpiece.

"They asked me into a car and I refused that – but they told me they were professionals, from the government, and they could help me. I didn't need any help but the fear was hitting me hard, I had heard plenty of stories from the girls who lived on those streets. I knew what to say to survive."

"So, these men propositioned you, is that right?"

"At first I thought that was all this was. They saw a young girl walking the street and these city types assumed I was a hooker. But it was more than that. They asked me something that still makes me sick at the thought." She broke off at that, tears coming to her eyes. She looked off-camera, struggling to maintain herself.

"As you can see, Ms Medina had great trouble recounting her story to us," Sam spoke, back on the live feed. He had wanted to tell this part, there was no way he was allowing Sonya Medina all of his spotlight

"What those men offered Ms Medina is abhorrent. She was given details of a time and place where Bernard Kiebler would be present. She was given access to secure areas which are off-limits to members of the public. And finally, she was given specific orders to seduce and blackmail Governor Kiebler.

As an honest woman, Ms Medina protested and was threatened rather harshly for her actions. They offered a reward and specific details which we cannot repeat at this time. What is undeniable is that she was asked to ruin a man's life, to destroy his marriage and his public reputation and provide photographic evidence to do so."

Sam looked directly into the camera, putting down his notes. Sincere time.

"Ladies and gentleman, we at Ganymede News have received the footage which eventually resulted from the meeting of Mr Kiebler with Ms Medina. Needless to say, it does not contain what the conspiracy theorists and sabotage artists claim. We will not air that footage, and it will be kept safe until such a time that a criminal prosecutor may use it to build a case against the blackmailers.

"Furthermore, the shocking testimony of Ms Medina – which, as mentioned earlier, is partly unsuitable to air at this time – will be made available online within the next few days - after our lawyers, and those on behalf of Mr Kiebler, have had access to the files."

"We can play you some of the truly sensational confession from Ms Medina now – and I urge you to remember Mr Kiebler's similar confession two nights ago."

He leaned back, part one of the night's work complete. The major revelation was out there now, and Sonya's words would only soften the blow and support Bernard's story. Part two of the story would finish this race for good. He wished he could smoke a cigar on set. He had never even held a cigar before, but the monumental feeling of triumph he felt in that moment was a revelation.

"I knew I couldn't do it, of course, and it was just a matter of how to tell him. As it happened he was a gentleman from the start – far from the monster the media portrays him to be. For a few hours we talked and he was charming and kind and I felt something for him I have not felt before.

We connected on a level I cannot explain and when talk turned to home life -marriage and kids – he confessed to me that he had lived apart from his family for months. I don't think anyone knew that, and it came as a shock to me. He was heartbroken, of course, but he had chosen to move on as he saw that his vision for us all was the most important thing right now."

"You felt for him on an emotional level, but also respected his ability to focus on what was required of him as a Governor and a leader, rather than as a man in his own self?" Sam added in the video. Studio Sam smiled at his own tying together of all those stray pieces.

"Yes, I felt for him. And I felt the powerful, transformative bond that was forming between us. I told him I was behind him all the way, his policies were the policies of the people and he should not stop, ever. He was bringing revolution to his people."

"We saw the Governor tell the world that he fell in love with you that night."

"Yes. And I love him too. He has already begun the proceedings for an amicable divorce and Xanthe understands the situation. Sometimes things just aren't meant to be. I hope my marriage to our future President can be one of those dreams which does come true."

"That is a lovely thought, Ms Medina. Finally, do you have any thoughts or words for those who involved you in this scheme?"

"Yes. I want them to see what good came of their awful acts. You tried to destroy an incredible man's life, and all you have done is strengthen his soul and his resolve. Evil deeds are harsh and scary – but love will win every time."

In the studio, Sam sat back up into his seat. He thought that she had overblown the ending, slightly. He wondered if the soap opera types who would buy that line would ever vote at all – never mind for Kiebler. He knew those people well – they were his demographic in the reality TV business too. He had considered cutting it from the footage, but it was too perfect as segues go.

It really was showtime now, and his heart was pounding in his chest. He had one last blow to deliver, and he took a deep breath before delivering it.

"Lovely sentiments there, from Ms Medina. Unfortunately, I must shift our focus⸱ to more unpleasant acts now, as my investigation has uncovered some disturbing facts about the would-be blackmailers.

After trawling hours of security camera footage and gaining eyewitness reports -including from Ms Medina herself - we have identified the two men responsible."

A picture flashed up on the screen – one smartly dressed man, mid-20s, holding a portfolio, and another late-30s wearing a similarly high-priced suit.

"If you are thinking they don't look like your average blackmail hoods, then you are correct. These men are senior staffers on the Calhoun election campaign team. You heard me right - these men are directly in the employ of Heather Calhoun."

He revelled in the moment.

"The Calhoun campaign did not respond to requests for comment today."

He hadn't asked.

"State police have been informed and have asked the two alleged 'gentlemen' to hand themselves in to authorities for questioning."

They were already locked away in a cell somewhere, with no idea of the crime they had allegedly committed.

"It is clear the Calhoun campaign has some very serious questions to answer, and I suspect these two men will have a very severe sentence to face should they be found guilty."

He suspected those two men would never even make it to trial. Rigging a trial is hard work. Making two reviled men disappear was not.

***

Bernard Kiebler enjoyed the quiet of his office. He wondered what the rules were for conducting presidential business from your own office. He could imagine the furore the opposition would kick up – how dare he reject the traditional offices of the President of this fair land, how can he be sure of the security in his private office compared to that of the government's own?

It was all just noise, he knew. They'd kick up a fuss but there would be little they could do about it. His office was plush and refined – the dwelling of a statesman, and a gentleman. The presidential office was cold and unwelcoming – like standing in a waxwork museum exhibit, except you were the main attraction.

Daxler Scion slunk into the room silently. Kiebler always thought the man moved like a shadow. He made him feel on edge when he lurked on the edges of the room, then he would suddenly burst forward with some piercing observation and devious little plot to solve any problem. That ability far outweighed his creepy demeanour, and Kiebler was glad to have him on his side.

"What say you, Dark Lord," he joked as Scion positioned himself in front of the Governor's large desk.

"Mr Governor, I have news."

"Sit down, man, you make me nervous when you act all formal," Kiebler admonished.

"Yes. Sir," he began, taking a seat facing Kiebler, "I have come to you directly from my meetings with Mrs Kiebler. She ugh... she has agreed in principle to the divorce settlement."

"Great news. Now what am I giving her?"

"Well she has asked for a reasonable deal. Surprisingly acceptable, on all accounts. The only sticking point, of course, being the children." Scion lowered his tone at this, anticipating the difficult conversation ahead.

"She wants me to have them?" Kiebler responded.

"No, no sir. She demands full custody and claims they don't wish to speak with you after the... unpleasantness." Scion spoke carefully, choosing his words. After a moment, he started to speak again, hoping to sooth his superior's mood, but Kiebler moved first.

"So, what is the issue, Dax?"

He appeared entirely unmoved by the news. Scion wasn't sure how to react, fumbling with his words as he tried to think of the appropriate response.

"Dax, you crazy bastard, when are you going to join me for a cigar?"

Kiebler reached for the drawer of his desk and pulled out a hand-carved cigar box. "Some of the finest ever produced. You know how hard it was to get these through customs?" He smiled and Scion relaxed, if only a little.

"I'd hate to waste it in that case, sir. I've never cared for them myself."

"Suit yourself," Kiebler replied and lit up his own cigar, leaning back into his chair. He savoured it for a moment, allowing the smoke to gather about him.

"The thing about kids, Dax, is that they are so needy. They start off needing you for everything – wiping their ass, feeding 'em, clothing 'em. Then they just want everything – begging for this, must have that, all their friends have got this. Selfish little pricks.

"Then suddenly – poof! You're as useful to them as shit on your shoe. My kids haven't wanted to spend time with me for a long while now. The boy is good – daddy's little boy that one. But I see the tide turning. And you know why?"

He looked at Daxler and Daxler looked right back at him, unsure where this particular rant was heading.

"I couldn't offer them any more. They milked me dry, Dax. So, I hear they don't wanna talk to me – fine. We'll see if they want to speak to daddy when he's the President of this fucking planet."

Scion could sense the fury hidden beneath the words – he spoke the truth, or what he believed to be true at least. However, underneath it all he was hurt. Daxler wondered if he regretted the scandal breaking when it did, and if Kiebler really felt any remorse for the way he unceremoniously kicked his wife to the curb. He knew that he would never find out.

A knock sounded at the door, drawing Kiebler's eye. Daxler took that as a sign that he should answer it. He moved quickly across the room and pulled the door open by an inch. He spoke for a moment in hushed tones, then silently closed the door and returned to his seat.

"They have a call for you. I thought you would like to take it personally," Daxler advised him, smiling.

Kiebler looked confused, but put out his cigar and sat up straight. He picked up the phone from his desk and pressed the flashing line.

"Bernie Kiebler, Sausage King of the North Shore," he spoke with bluster and mocking.

"Kiebler you're a disgrace," came the voice from the receiver. "You have spun a story so vindictive and manipulative that I can't believe it - even from you."

Senator Calhoun's anger was tangible in her voice.

"Ah, Calhoun. I trust you watched my bride-to-be's performance on television his evening?" he laughed, and Scion joined him with a snivelling, sinister chuckle of his own.

"Performance is the only word for it. You know damn well I didn't pay anyone to do a thing! You were derailing your own campaign just fine without our help."

"Mrs Calhoun. Are you calling my dear beloved a liar?"

"You disgust me, Bernard. You have grown into a despicable shell of a man. Have no doubt that we will fight back on this. The people will see what a conniving little toad you are."

"Oh, calm down Heather. Have you seen your approval ratings tonight? I could ski down them. The election is in four days – the only way you could come back from this if I accidentally slept with some other young, easy to manipulate whore."

"You bastard. The people won't continue to fall for your lies, Kiebler. We'll take you down."

"Aw that's nice, sweetheart. Such a lovely thing to say. Now you get some sleep, you'll need your rest to make up such a *huge* deficit in the morning. Bye bye."

He hung up the phone in fits of laughter, with Scion almost mimicking his laugh like a man who has no discernible joy of his own.

"It appears our opposition did not take our gambit tonight too well, Mr Scion."

"Indeed, Governor. Maybe we should send her some flowers," he replied, eliciting a genuine guffaw from his boss.

"That's an outstanding idea. Can you ask Orsay to arrange that, please? And on your way out, send in those gentlemen waiting outside my office."

"Yes, of course. May I ask...?" Scion enquired.

"GU delegates. They arrived about twenty minutes after the show tonight. I've had them waiting outside since then." Kiebler told him.

"That was three or four hours ago now, sir." Scion told him, looking at the clock mounted high on the wall above Kiebler's desk.

"Oh, I'm well aware, Mr Scion," he responded with a smile. "Send them in."

***

While the city fizzled out into darkness in the dead of night, Hasting stood in full riot gear on the outskirts. Looking at the lights of the skyscrapers beyond him, and the brief blinking flashes from the spacecraft passing just out of atmosphere, he wished the streets were as calm as the sky above.

Calhoun supporters had begun the evening with a peaceful march through the city's financial quarter – timed to coincide with Senator Calhoun's visit earlier. It was a standard operation for the city police, ensuring the crowd stayed on track and traffic was diverted appropriately.

The trouble began around 8.30pm when the first half of Sam Heighway's interview had aired. Kiebler supporters, infuriated at the revelations from Sonya Medina, took to the streets. Police tried their best to separate the two groups, and only minor skirmishes were reported for the first hour or so.

Hasting had received his call at around 9.45pm and immediately assembled his own task force. As the highest ranking General in the city forces, he had an emergency response unit assigned to his command.

The streets were absolute pandemonium when he arrived. He spotted known gang members and hate group leaders within the ranks of Kiebler supporters – he wasn't sure if they were genuinely out to support the man, or if they had their own agenda, but it added up to the same thing.

The peaceful march of the Calhoun group was torn apart by the raging throng – Hasting ordered riot police and tear gas, and when that didn't work he ordered the first deployment of armoured tanks to Seo-Sing City in over twenty years. These modern tanks were quick and agile little machines, capable of negotiating all types of terrain and unleashing a vast array of different weaponry.

It didn't take long to break the large Kiebler group up into small pieces with the tanks engaged. The worry had been that the group would continue to grow, and Hasting had seen mob mentality in action before. It wouldn't be long before they were storming the GU building, or attacking a foreign embassy. His biggest fear was any leak of Calhoun's whereabouts. He knew she was staying in the city and the risk to her would be great should the crowd find out.

He was glad the heavy-duty tactics worked, and had his force split up with various ranks of the local police squads to chase down the remaining factions. In the relative calm that followed he heard through his control comms that Calhoun's people had ordered a private transport and she was safely out of the capital now.

The noise of the last vestiges of the mob became louder, and he knew that they approaching quickly. He gave orders to the men around him and they took to their positions. He had chosen a spot not far from the docks, on the river's edge. The South Shore had a great view of the city by night but he turned away from it and faced the pitch black of the industrial buildings and the side streets which hid in their shadow.

The host of rioters charged suddenly out of the dark streets, screaming and shouting at the sight of the armed force awaiting them. They wielded signs and banners, but hidden amongst them Hasting spotted bats and knives. Glass bottles were launched towards the riot police and shattered against their shields.

A tank rolled into the path of the mob and a warning was issued from the loud-speaker system. The crowd cheered at the threat of arrest, and just as a flaming bottle smashed against the sides of the vehicle, Hasting barked his order to advance. He didn't like resorting to attacking – he knew it was overkill in some ways.

However, he saw no way around it in this situation. The crowd had taken on a mind of its own and had ignored all warnings. It was growing more violent and had nowhere to turn now that it had reached the South Shore. The next logical step for this group would be to cross the bridge into the suburbs – and they could not allow the violence to spread where families and children slept.

Hasting trusted his men to move with precision. He himself aimed for the left of centre section of the group, disarming several men along his way. After a few moments he was in the thick of the action but his riot gear hindered him in close quarters. He shook off the heavy-duty gloves, and dropped his shield. He brandished a standard-issue truncheon and electronic shackles, which could be deployed quickly in a fight.

He began taking down and locking up anyone who attacked. Several men took one look at him in action and turned the other way. He was trained in hand to hand combat, various martial arts, boxing. There was very little they could throw at him for which he didn't have an answer.

A woman screamed as she launched herself at him, clawing at his eyes. A bottle bounced off her head and smashed against his shoulder. He looked up and spotted the perpetrator attempting to flee, running along the tops of several dumpsters nearby.

He grabbed the woozy woman's head and flipped her over his shoulder. She hit the ground hard and he left her, confident she wouldn't get up any time soon. Thinking quickly, he picked up his riot shield and tore away the top half – a handy thing to have in very tight spaces when full length protection wasn't required.

He had a different use in mind now, though. He pulled the shield back above his shoulder and spun it like a frisbee, watching it sail over a few heads and crash directly into the legs of the bottle thrower as he attempted to jump from one dumpster to another.

Hasting marched towards him, grabbing the shackles that hung from his waist. He ducked a punch from another protester, and delivered a blow to his body that saw him sink to his knees. He came to his quarry as the man dragged himself along the floor into a blind alley.

"Stay where you are, your night's over" he spoke with conviction.

The guy on the floor looked back and tried to stand up and run when he saw Hasting had pursued him. His leg buckled under him and he faltered, hitting the ground hard.

"Stay down. There's nowhere left to run." Hasting said, unlocking the shackle and looking for a convenient place to tie the man down while he rejoined the fray. In that moment he felt a strange sensation – like a wave of static flowing through him.

His knees gave way and he found himself suddenly kneeling in the street. He dropped the shackle as his left arm fell entirely limp. He couldn't turn his head but the thought dawned on him that he knew what had happened.

At the mouth of the alley, behind Hasting, stood three men. One brandished a truncheon from some fallen officer. Another held a glass bottle in his hand. The third was holding an illegal Uzstazi electro-mech rifle.

The rifles – along with other Uzstazi inventions – had been outlawed under GU law centuries ago. The Uzstazi had taken many lives in their rebellion on Saturn, and the advances they had made in weaponry to further their cause were exceptional, not to mention brutal and unsettling.

Hasting didn't see the weapons until the three men approached him. He was paralysed from the neck down, stranded on his knees in the dark. The man he had knocked to the floor scrambled away, himself fearing the three intruders.

"You look like you could use a lie down, outlander," the man with the bottle spat at him, before crashing the glass against Hasting's forehead. He tumbled to the floor in agony, unable to resist.

The men laughed and crowded round. Hasting could only barely hear the sounds of the fight in the distance, and realised that his men were winning – driving the fight away from his position. He was alone.

"You're going to die in the fucking gutter where you belong, tourist," another spoke to him. His head was already spinning, eyes losing focus.

He felt the truncheon slam against his arms and legs, and boots crunch into his ribs. Their words died out soon enough, and the world seemed far off. He saw his own blood mix with the mud in the cracks of the road, and finally passed out as a solid kick landed square against his jaw.

CHAPTER SEVEN

T he velocity had always made Bellson ill. Ever since he was a young boy he had despised outer-atmosphere travel, but it was the quickest way to get around if you could afford it. Air traffic below the atmospheric rim was too congested with cheap, anti-pollutant airbuses taking up all of the space, making flying a slow and frustrating process if you were going further than a handful of miles.

Outer-atmosphere crafts were bigger and faster animals. Bellson had never got used to the speed, and his body liked to remind him of that fact whenever he attempted it.

"You never been off planet before?" Jeffrey Sutherland asked him, after Bellson's third trip to the toilet in the thirty minutes since they took off.

"I've travelled out of atmos. A few times. Never been off-world." Bellson replied, feeling his stomach shake at the thought of it.

"I guess you get used to it after a while. I think it bothered me when I was a boy, but I've been through the Belt and back again so many times now-" Sutherland saw the look on Bellson's face at just the mention of the asteroid belt, and stopped in his tracks. Too much, too soon.

Seb Raylor sat in the row in front of Sutherland, quietly seething. They had been about to take off for a Workers' Council meeting in the south when the Galactic Union had issued a statement. He had no choice but to read it and hustle aboard the craft immediately after.

"Did they say 'in the best interests of all free peoples' – did they say that?" he asked Sutherland.

"I can't remember the exact wording. We'll have comms back in two minutes, the crew say. We can look at it again," he replied.

"I'd love to know which people they meant. It sure as hell wasn't in the interests of the people of Mars – and Jupiter is beyond help right now," Raylor said.

Bellson's phone lit up, signalling that communications were back online. He eagerly grabbed at it and flicked through his incoming messages.

"Fuck," he uttered, eyes fixed to his screen.

Raylor and Sutherland both turned to see the younger man; sat as he was nearest to the small cubicle they called a bathroom in these crafts.

"My source says the GU stood up to Kiebler a few days ago. Told him there was no way they could support him. Everything you asked of them, Jeff," he nodded at Sutherland in appreciation. "Kiebler threatened a complete withdrawal from the Union and the reps shit themselves."

Raylor glared at Sutherland, who in turn looked like a man about to burst. He had begged the Senate of Mars to send a strong presence to the GU meeting with Kiebler – and had even volunteered to go alone if they allowed him to. The Senate voted him down, and in the end sent only a spokesman – believing that the other planetary representatives would take their opposition to him in the right terms.

"Spineless, arrogant, selfish arseholes. Every one of them," Sutherland blurted out. "They walked in with a smoking gun! A red-hot mandate to say no to his insanity. They've walked out with their dicks in their hands."

"It may not be that bad – maybe it's all talk? They said the same things to Calhoun when she met with them," Bellson spoke, trying to be the voice of reason.

"The time to stand up to him was now. He's streaked ahead in the polls, he's got the people brainwashed. The time to act *was now*. They've failed," Raylor ranted. He felt like ranting was all he had really done lately, and he couldn't stand the sound of his own voice. He also couldn't handle the thought of a man like Kiebler winning the most powerful office in the solar system. It would be disastrous for Jupiter and worse for anyone beyond that. His policies reeked of nationalism, and xenophobia. His tactics were out of the Stone Age but the man could talk anyone into anything – and the biggest fear was that he would talk himself into being a despotic overlord that the GU was entirely unprepared for.

"There has to be something we can do," Raylor said, looking to the others for help and advice. The faces staring back at him were blank. Sutherland was breathing hard, his big frame not meant for the small chairs and light air up in the outer atmosphere.

"It's time we let the people of Mars speak on this. Give them the full truth and let them act," Raylor offered.

"You mean let them decide on how we work with the GU if he wins?" Sutherland questioned, looking confused.

"If he wins? We're days away, Jeff. He's untouchable. We have to wake up!" Raylor was shouting now, unsure to who or what his rage was directed.

"Seb, stay calm my friend. Lay it out for us because we're not seeing this path you're on," Bellson spoke again, slipping into the seat beside Sutherland. Raylor stood and took a moment to gather himself, remembering how much he hated his ranting self.

"If the Galactic Union acquiesces to Kiebler's policies, then Jupiter effectively *becomes* the Galactic Union. They do his bidding, they sanction his policy. How long before he interferes more? How long before he pushes the hold he has over them? Kiebler becomes the President of the entire solar system in all but name."

The three looked at each other, the full weight of the matter dawning on them simultaneously. Raylor could see the panic and desperation which took hold of each of them as it sunk in. He hoped they had come to the same conclusion that he had. He waited in the hope of one of them vocalising it first. Silence hung heavily in the air.

"He has bullied the GU by threatening Jupiter's exit from the Union," he finally spoke. "There's only one course of action we can take now," he said, feeling his voice shake as the words spilled out.

"A referendum?" Bellson asked.

"We give the people of Mars the chance to act now, before it's too late. Vote out of the Union. Give them exactly what they feared," Raylor answered. He knew from their eyes that they were in agreement, although their collective demeanour screamed doubt and fear. Raylor felt sure of the course he had suggested, and had confidence in those he had trusted to help make it happen.

"Sutherland – you're going to have to be the match that lights this on fire. You can stand in the Senate and call for a vote. We'll make sure the public is on side," Bellson grinned, growing ever more excited at the prospect. He glanced at Sutherland only to find the larger man struggling.

The air pressure, combined with the actual pressure of the task at hand, was getting to him. As soon as the word 'referendum' was mentioned Sutherland knew what was coming next. As a ranking Senate member he was the only one of the three who could genuinely make that call.

The intense psychological pressure became a very real, and very present, pressure on his chest and lungs. He felt the edges of his sight grow blurry. The last thing he could remember before passing out was the worried looks of his colleagues. He wondered if he might ever see them again.

CHAPTER EIGHT

T he polls closed at midnight on Jupiter. Daxler Scion awoke his boss at sunrise to inform him of the result.

"Mr President," was all he had to say.

Kiebler leaped around the room like an excited child, screaming and shouting at the top of his lungs. He lashed out at Heather Calhoun, and spat venom at the leadership of every other planet in the solar system.

He had done it. He had achieved the impossible. He could go to work now.

He showered then dressed in his most pristine suit and gave himself a look in the mirror. He stared into his own eyes and considered everything he had been through, everywhere he had been and everything he had sacrificed to reach his goal. Pride rushed through his veins, carried by adrenaline as he rushed down the stairs and prepared for his speech.

His notes were a dripping mush on the hard-oak podium by the time he made it outside. Rain lashed down harder and harder. Kiebler had never seen a victory speech held under such conditions. He applauded himself for his determinedness to continue with the plan. He stood in front of hundreds of thousands and spoke directly to the people.

His people.

"My friends. Tonight, Jupiter has decided. *You* – each and every one of you – have decided that the future is *ours*. It is truly an honour to stand here and make this promise to you – that no more will Jupiter be the ark that keeps humanity afloat. No more will Jupitoans fight and strive for a better way, only to be forced to give it all away to our neighbours. No more."

He paused for effect. He had always loved the pauses in every speech he made – sometimes he gave his staff odds on how long he could leave it, or how many he could get. The applause always came. The cheers always came.

"I know this night feels like a culmination. The end of a long, hard road. We will put our feet up tonight. We will toast our future tonight. But let us not take our eyes off tomorrow. I promise you all a better tomorrow – I have promised you as much for many months now. Today you have accepted that promise, taken me into your hearts and voted me into your office."

Another pause. He revelled in it, drawing power from it, knowing the biggest was about to come.

"We'll sleep tonight, and tomorrow I will give you your planet back!"

Kiebler stepped back from the podium. The movement caused the rain to splash out of his hair and down his forehead. It was relentless – crashing against the wooden stage, forming puddles all around. He took a moment to indulge himself – feeling the rapturous response from his people. His people, almost hidden behind raincoats and umbrellas, or cheap waterproof ponchos which his staff had handed out on the street.

With a final wave and a beaming smile, he retreated to the cover of the tent behind, and the makeshift tunnel they had erected to get him to his office comfortably. Dripping wet, he assessed his bone-dry team waiting in the wings with mixed feelings.

An aide passed him a towel as various 'well done' and 'congratulations' poured in from the bystanders and hangers-on. Daxler Scion and Valerie Marlborough were huddled around a TV monitor, watching the news coverage of his victory speech.

"How did I do?" he asked them, while furiously rubbing at his soaking hair with the towel.

"Mr President," Daxler replied, "you were a phenomenon. A true force of nature and freedom, speaking for your people. The news people, the TV people, the actual *people* loved it."

"It was a momentous occasion, sir," Marlborough added, "and you met it greatly. It is an honour to call you my President."

She reached for his hand and kissed it awkwardly. Kiebler caught Scion's look and quickly walked past the two, heading for the house.

"Come with me, you two," he shouted back as he opened his front door, still under cover of the temporary tent.

He was glad he had made his base here for the night. His own home was a comfort to him. He had imagined every scenario, and truly believed a few weeks ago that he would be stepping through that door tonight as the Vice President of Jupiter – and flying into a rage in his study where it would be hidden from prying eyes.

He wondered at his own monumental shift since then, and at the steps taken to push his campaign across the line, and to denigrate Calhoun. The woman infuriated him. He felt such a genuine gladness at her defeat that he wondered for a moment if that pleased him even more than the fact that he was now President.

"Any word from Calhoun's office?" he asked a passing aide, handing her the now dripping wet towel.

"No, sir. Want me to call them?"

"No, let them stew on it. I want her to come to me," he replied.

"Heather Calhoun will come crawling to you soon enough," Daxler spoke as the three entered the plush study. Kiebler motioned for his guests to sit at a leather sofa and took his own place in a high-backed, leather wing chair.

"I'm going to enjoy listening to her crawl and beg. Utter defeat will look good on her," Kiebler sneered.

"It's almost a disgrace that she gets to be your Vice President now, after all she has done," Marlborough offered.

"I have suggested we look at ways we can legally remove her from the picture, sir," Scion butted in. "I have my staff reading constitutional law through the night."

"I appreciate the effort, Dax, but there's no need. I know the constitution better than anyone. She has the right to take up the VP role, and knowing her she will take it. We'll just have to ensure she hates the damn job," he laughed, and Daxler Scion offered his unnatural laugh back.

"Have you put more thought into your cabinet, Mr President?" Marlborough asked, hoping not to seem too obvious.

Kiebler eyed her up, then pulled an old-style tobacco pouch from his pocket and began to roll himself a cigarette.

"I have done as much thinking as any man could take on the matter, Ms Marlborough," he told her. "Have you heard any updates from the hospital tonight?"

"About General Hasting? No, sir. Just that he is stable and there should be no lasting damage," she replied.

"That's good. The man will make an excellent leader one day. Hopefully those thugs have beaten some sense into him," Kiebler spoke, taking a draw from the freshly rolled cigarette.

"The truth is often revealed to a man in times of great strife," Dax offered. "Perhaps the General will now realise the brutality of the world we live in, and embrace his role in bringing the future to our people."

"Don't underestimate the man, Daxler. He's seen plenty of strife in his time. The man has served the military for twenty-odd years now," Kiebler said. "He just needs a little moulding to our way of thinking. He's an asset."

"A great asset", Scion agreed.

Marlborough listened intently, and agreed for the most part. She had seen General Hasting in action and had read his service file. He was a man who commanded respect in his peers – and that in turn was enough for her to fear and respect him.

"So, he will make an excellent chief in your military, I'm sure," she said with a leading smile.

"Indeed. And Dax here, he's going to be my right-hand man. My lead advisor and Chief of Staff," he nodded to Scion, who grinned a sinister response, turning to Marlborough as he did so.

"Our President, of course, needs no advice from someone like me," Scion spoke. "He has already crushed the Calhoun campaign, and brought the Galactic Union to its knees in front of him."

"Nonsense, Dax, you were instrumental in all of the above," Kiebler responded, a haze of smoke surrounding every word he uttered.

"I will need someone strong to get a hold on that lot," he mused out loud. "The GU has been led by straw men for too long. It needs someone powerful at the forefront to lead their agenda," he spoke, looking into Marlborough's eyes across the small table in the centre of the room.

Her eyes strayed from his face to the table – catching on the magazine which was proudly laid out; a political publication with Kiebler's glowing face looking right back at her, 'Kiebler's Promise' printed in bold yellow across it glossy front page.

"What do you think, Daxler?" Kiebler asked.

"Oh, I think Ms Marlborough here has shown she is a strong leader, wrangling that appalling bank back into shape after the previous government's many *many* missteps. She's loyal, and intelligent, and quite the negotiator, if the tales I hear are to be believed," Daxler responded.

Marlborough sat up in her seat, looking between both men, and feeling her anxiousness rise. She knew a position was on the table, and she hoped to further her case without slipping up.

"Sir... Mr Daxler... Mr President... I assure you any tales that have been..." she started.

"Ms Marlborough, relax!" Kiebler interrupted. "The tales have been thin on the ground - nobody you have worked with seems very keen to speak out about any dealings you have had. It has taken us quite some time to vet you, actually."

She smiled, pleased that her staff and those she had made deals with in the past had kept to their word to not disclose too much. She had a fierce negotiating style and she accepted nothing short of silence from anyone she had dealings with.

"I want you to be the new General Secretary to the Galactic Union, Ms Marlborough," Kiebler said with a smile. "It's not quite a position within my government but I have taken the liberty of drawing up an employment contract with my team, and offering your services to the GU at no cost to the Union."

"And the GU leadership have accepted those terms?" she asked.

"Accepted? They damn near bit my hand off. You'll be leading them into this union with my government here – it'll be the strongest alliance the solar system has ever witnessed," Kiebler replied.

He stood and stubbed out his cigarette in a small whiskey glass on the table in front. "So, what do you say?" he grinned at Marlborough, offering her his hand.

CHAPTER NINE

Sutherland didn't enjoy attention. He wasn't a man to court publicity, or to solicit a crowd. He had stumbled into politics, and he supposed his natural inclination to remain focussed on issues that would help his constituents was what had led to them putting his name forward for a role within the Senate. He hadn't asked for it, nor had he campaigned for it until he realised the force of popular opinion flowing his way was something that could not be ignored. His comfort level with the idea of being a Senator already stretched him to his absolute limit, and so the added pressure of a mounting inter-planetary conflict was all too much for him to take.

He had awoken in his hospital bed to find his own face plastered on the front papers of every broadsheet and tabloid, and taking up a fairly large portion of the fifteen-minute news cycle on any local station he could find. He had given up any hope of a distraction from his woes when the national stations had picked up the story. He was out there. Big news. The speculation was inevitable, he knew. A Senator taking ill during outer-atmos travel, and a hastily called private Senate meeting in a hospital room were rare occurrences. Unheard of until now, he supposed. He didn't much like the idea of being seen as a pioneer in the matter, either.

The other Senate members arrived before lunchtime and Sutherland asked a nurse to keep the room as quiet as was possible; he didn't want an insistent orderly barging in on a potentially fiery meeting.

He adjusted the bed so he could at least sit up and speak to his colleagues eye to eye. His three Senate colleagues looked sympathetic, but he had a feeling a lot of it was bluster. There was a certain vulture-like character to any personality who willing put himself up on the highest table Mars had to offer. He knew they were all wondering how to spin his condition into some gain for their own interests.

Marien Lyndell, Senator for the East, was a close ally to Sutherland and the North. She greeted him warmly and he knew that he'd get her onside without too much trouble. Marien held much the same values as the hard-working and little-rewarded north and north-eastern Martians, and they saw her as one of their own.

He was less sure of Ramsey Pierce, representing the West, and Edward Royce from the South. The former was never eager to wade into any fight, carefully choosing his words and deeds, while the latter was opinionated and often divisive. Royce had won the Southern vote on an aggressive platform, appealing to the wealthy and settled Martian citizens who, for the most part, resented being thought of as second-class citizens when compared to the industrious North.

"Well, we may as well get started," Sutherland spoke as they all settled into the random assortment of chairs that had been sourced from around the department.

"First things first, Jeffrey, how the hell are you feeling?" asked Pierce.

"I'm at my peak, Ramsey. Can't wait to get back to work," Sutherland offered.

"Seriously?" Pierce asked back, after a longer-than-expected pause.

"As a heart attack," Sutherland answered, with a chuckle, as his audience looked at him with all the humour of a man waiting on death row. He mused for a moment that he wasn't far from being just that.

"I had a major myocardial infarction, Senators. A heart attack. I'm about as far from all right as you can be – but I'm a hell of a lot better than I was a day ago," he smiled, hoping to lighten the mood once again.

"Sutherland, you have our sympathies, of course – all of us. The office is doing a collection," offered Royce.

"Very kind, but there's no need," Sutherland said, pausing for a breath. "I won't be returning to my office."

All sound in the room seemed to be sucked out into the vacuum of space. Sutherland wondered how much of their shock was genuine, and how many of them had secretly guessed, or even wished for, this to be the purpose of this hasty gathering.

"I'll be giving up my seat. The doctors say I have a good chance of a recovery from this, but a huge lifestyle change is in order if I want to see 65 and it's time I took heed," he continued.

"You want to give it up right away?" Royce asked, incredulous. He would remain in office until his death, if given the chance, Sutherland thought to himself.

"Nobody has ever done that, Sutherland," Marien Lyndell chimed in.

"There is legislation in place. There's a contingency for the death of a Senator and my office have checked it out in full – it applies to anyone unable or unwilling to carry out the office too," he told them.

"That legislation requires you to call a new election, if I'm not mistaken?" Royce asked.

"Within six months," Sutherland spoke. "I can name a temporary replacement in the meantime, but they can only hold the office un-elected for six months."

The room quickly degenerated into chatter of who was a good candidate for the role – Ramsey wondering if they could hold their own vote of candidates they all agreed on, while Royce offered up an old friend, "a great Southerner - a worker. His people love him."

"Please, please," Sutherland said, calming the rabble. "I know how we like to protect our ranks – and the idea of being able to pick our own man in the seat is something we've all dreamed of at one time or another."

"But you get to make that call, right?" Lyndell spoke. "I studied the legislation in law school. Only the outgoing Senator gets a say in the matter."

"That's right," Sutherland responded. "It has to be someone I choose, to ensure no region is unfairly over-represented in the house."

"So, who have you got in mind? No offence, but there aren't many northerners in your party making a strong case for themselves, Jeff," Royce responded.

Sutherland had thought long and hard about his choice. His heart, in its weakened state, knew exactly who he needed to call on, and his head told him exactly how his fellow Senators were going to react.

"My man isn't a member of my own party," he said and waited for the expected outrage. It came with questions and furrowed brows and anger to spare.

"I'm naming Sebastian Raylor as my replacement as Senator for the North," Sutherland spoke confidently.

"Raylor!? Isn't he a Council guy?" came the protest from Royce immediately.

"No, he's an elected official," Lyndell interjected.

"But he's been cosying up to Bellson from the Workers' Council for weeks now," Royce spat.

"As I'm sure you can appreciate I am in no condition for a shouting match on this, nor do I care for one." Sutherland spoke, remaining calm and surprising himself in the process.

"Well hell, Sutherland what do you...." Royce spoke but Sutherland cut him off with a raised hand.

"I don't expect anything from any of you. I know you will respect the law of our lands and will uphold the decision of a man who may be making the final call of his long and hard career," he told them, looking Royce in the eye as he did so. "I believe Raylor is a man of the same moral and a-political valour I hope to live up to myself. Make no mistake, folks - we are approaching a storm we have never encountered before and we've been preparing for it as if it were my nine-year old's birthday party."

The Senators looked around, not daring to make eye contact with each other and barely able to look at Sutherland himself.

"Kiebler is the focus. Raylor is the man to turn to. Listen to him – I beg you to listen to the man."

Sutherland's voice cracked as he spoke his plea – he knew it was his last act as a servant of the people of Mars.

***

All of the swearing in and formalities of becoming a Senator to your people were a huge honour. They were also a monumental chore, and Raylor found himself day dreaming throughout the process. However, any chances of a happy reverie were always intruded upon by the thought of the coming storm.

An emergency session of the Senate had been called, and Raylor's swearing in was immediately followed by a frog-march to the Senate Chambers where the crowds had already gathered. Outside, the people lined up in good numbers – he spotted Workers' Council banners and the odd independent group making their presence known. Inside, the chambers were packed with every man and woman with the credentials to get inside.

Everyone present knew how big a day this was in Martian history. Raylor considered that for a moment; considered that he was at the centre of it, thrust into the middle of history with little warning and no preparation.

"Are you OK?" the chairperson spoke to him, as he entered the chambers.

"I'll be fine," he replied, flustered. "Just having a bit of a day," he added. He nodded to James Bellson, sat in his nominated space with the other Workers' Council reps then made his way to his own seat at the high table.

"Can we get some order in the Chamber please?" Edward Royce shouted, glaring at the Speaker, prompting a more official announcement for the Senate to come to order.

"Let me begin by welcoming our newest member – Senator Raylor, it's a pleasure to welcome you to this honoured seat," Royce spoke stiffly. Raylor gave a nod of recognition and a smile to his fellow Senators.

"If we are all OK to start, I will ask the Speaker to call the first order of business?" Royce asked.

Marien Lyndell stood from her seat and addressed the chambers.

"Good morning all. I believe we have all gathered for this extraordinary meeting of the Senate to mark the occasion of Senator Raylor's appointment. While I would like to express my sympathies for former Senator Sutherland and offer my prayers for his good health, I believe we should yield the floor to his replacement for our first order of business," she spoke confidently and gestured towards the Speaker to make it official.

"Indeed, Ms Lyndell you are correct," the Speaker took her lead, "Mr Raylor, an opening statement?"

Raylor recognised the slowing down of time around him as he moved to stand. He would swear it took him the best part of thirty minutes to get to his feet, as the jumble of words and thoughts sloshed around his head. He had considered what he might say at this moment constantly over the preceding few hours, but still had not convinced himself that he knew what he was doing.

"Thank you, Mr Speaker," he opened, "and thank you Ms Lyndell for your graciousness. I too offer my best to our former colleague, Mr Sutherland. He has been a great servant to our people – and I owe him a lot for elevating me to the position I find myself in today."

There was applause from the galleries; the gathered people showing appreciation for the fallen Senator. Raylor was sure the man would make a strong recovery, and didn't think for one minute that he would be able to keep his nose out of politics when he felt himself again.

"Today I must begin to repay the debt I owe the man. Jeffrey Sutherland saw what was coming for Mars and he didn't approve. He has placed his belief in me as an individual and as a citizen who shares his concerns, knowing me to be a man who will fight for the rights and freedoms of the people of Mars – not just the Northerners within our constituency," Raylor spoke, not sticking even remotely to the script he had gone over in his head a hundred times.

"Bernard Kiebler, whichever way you spin it, is an enemy of Mars. His movements to tie his government to the leadership of the Galactic Union are a threat to freedom and autonomy for the entire solar system. Now, more than ever, we are under the thumb of a super-powered union which was intended to protect our interests, but instead has declared its own interests in the policies of a dangerous man."

Raylor paused, letting the words sink in. He knew what he was saying would be inflammatory and divisive, yet a unifying call to the majority of Martians who he believed would feel the same way.

"We must make a stand against those who threaten us. If we lie back and accept meekly the jurisdictions of a failing institution then what message are we giving to the universe at large? That Mars will continue to work its fingers to the bone to support a union from which it benefits little? That Martians will give their hardest working years, and bravest fighting sons, for a cause that gives nothing back? That Mars is happy to be left behind while mankind uses it as a foundation for its advancement, never looking back to appreciate those who made it possible?"

The reaction surprised him. Whooping and cheering from half of the room, polite applause from some smaller sections and even support from Royce's Union-loving cronies. The silence from the Galactic Union delegates to the left was not so much of a revelation.

"I call for a referendum of the people of Mars. A vote to leave the Galactic Union versus a vote for climbing into bed with Bernie Kiebler and his Belt-blocking, immigration-hating, Union-bullying, totalitarian institution."

The cheers grew louder, the applause more wide-spread. Raylor allowed himself a smile.

"The Workers' Council supports this call for a referendum," Bellson shouted, above the clamour in the chamber. "We believe there has been collusion and blackmail at work from the Kiebler administration. The Union is broken, its mandate in tatters. Mars should have its say!"

It took a few minutes for the noise to die down. Raylor took his seat and breathed a huge sigh of relief.

"Not a bad first day, Mr Senator," Lyndell leaned over to speak into his ear. He couldn't form the words to respond right away.

The Speaker finally wrested control from the raucous crowd and put the vote to the Senators. Royce had a lot to say but Raylor heard none of it. He was numb. He listened intently as Lyndell fully supported his motion and was relieved to hear Pierce reluctantly follow suite – the man tended to fall under Royce's thumb but he was too smart to say no to this. His people would riot if they weren't at least given the chance to vote.

Royce voted against, a mere protest vote. He stared at Raylor across the Senate bench and reached over to shake his hand as the vote was certified by the Speaker.

"Looks like Sutherland got what he wanted," he spoke with an unpleasant tone.

Raylor simply shook his hand back in response, gripping it tighter as he looked into the man's eyes. He knew that the South would be no opposition to this. Martians would get their say on the matter and they weren't scared of Edward Royce and his right-wing politics, nor of Bernard Kiebler and his hand-picked Galactic Union.

CHAPTER TEN

"General Hasting!" Kiebler announced as he bounded down the steps of the grand old Presidential building. The General had climbed out of a military transport, and approached the house to greet the President.

"Mr President, thank you for the welcome," he said, extending a hand which Kiebler took all too enthusiastically.

"It's great to see you back on your feet," Kiebler spoke, "but are you sure you're ready for this?"

Hasting had expected the question as soon as he arrived. His bruises hadn't healed as quickly as he had hoped and as a result he presented an appearance of a beaten man. Inside he felt fine and had been out of the hospital for over a week. He was pacing the floor at home, a man too full of energy and ideas to sit back and let the world pass him by.

"I'm as ready as I ever have been, Mr President," he said firmly.

"Good, good, we need a firm presence in this building, General, and you know you're my man," Kiebler began as he led Hasting into the building. "The work has already begun without you; I made sure they kept an office clear for you."

Inside, the building was a hive of activity as painters and cleaners poured from every corridor, touching up here or cleaning up there. Hasting had visited the building under the previous administration and had revelled in its history. It was teeming with art work and offices named after the greats of Jupiter's past. The place had been built by the planet's ruling body way back before the formation of the first government, in preparation for the long planned first general election.

President Oliver Greenville had taken up office and residence there on day one of his presidency and every sitting ruler had lived and governed from it ever since. The office part of the building was a maze of rooms and detail which Hasting had admired on his way to countless meetings with government staff. He had never visited the second floor, where the President held office; nor had he witnessed the elegant, designer-built Presidential residence which was only accessible through the private gardens or the Presidential office itself.

"Finally getting this place up to a suitable standard for living in, Hasting," Kiebler spoke buoyantly. "Couldn't have the family moving into the dusty old relic the previous administration left behind."

Hasting smiled and played along, but he knew the truth – Kiebler had wanted his own offices to be his Presidential base but was overruled within his own party. The people wouldn't like it, for starters, they argued. Then there was the slight matter of it being potentially unconstitutional to carry out Presidential operations from a private office. In the end he had settled for gutting the heart out of the old place.

They made their way through the busy lobby, flanked by two of the Presidents security detail. Hasting noted the large presence of armed officers around the building – both uniformed and undercover in civilian clothing.

"There has been a lot of unrest in the capital of late," he spoke to the President.

"You've been watching too much television, General," came Kiebler's flippant response.

"It's about all I have done since getting out of the hospital, sir," he responded.

"And how are you feeling? They tell me the doctors were happy to let you go, but you don't look your usual perky best," Kiebler offered him a smile, hoping to lighten the mood.

"As I said, I've never felt better, sir," Hasting replied. "In fact, I have a few ideas to get me back on the streets. The unrest won't just go away, we need to act."

"On the street?" Kiebler responded, incredulous. "General, you are being appointed as Lead General of the Jupiter Armed Forces. We have no war on the streets."

"No, but you have unruly gangs of revolutionaries, fascists, democrats even. They only grow larger, and more diverse groups appear each day,"

"And how do you suppose we crack down on them, exactly?"

"With a special task force. Led by me. We'll track down the ring leaders, the high-profile ones to make a show of it. Maybe find the men who attacked me."

Kiebler stopped in his tracks as they approached the staircase to the second floor. He turned to face Hasting.

"Listen to me, General. Those men who attacked you will be made to pay for their actions. But that's the job of the police."

"With respect, sir, I want to get out there. Show my face. Show them that they didn't win."

"They'll see your face on the news tonight after you take up your office. You'll be out there without having to actually get out there, General," Kiebler said as he began to walk up the stairs, pausing to look back at Hasting.

"I could really use you on this Mars thing."

"Martians are voting for their own rights, sir, I don't see my place there," Hasting responded carefully.

"I see. I have Senator Calhoun waiting in my office and I suspect she feels the same as you on that matter."

"If I know the Senator like I think I do, I'm sure you're right, Mr President," Hasting replied.

"Go and speak with Daxler Scion about your ideas. He'll talk some sense into you. I promise this is for your own good, General."

With that Kiebler made his way up the stairs, guards in tow. Hasting glanced around at the hive of activity surrounding him and wondered where Scion's office might be.

***

"I accept!" Kiebler announced loudly as he forcefully pushed open the large oak door to his office. He grinned unbearably as Heather Calhoun turned her head, remaining in her seat by his desk. Kiebler's smile dropped when he received no response.

"Senator Calhoun, I said I accept; you are free of your duties as my Vice President. I release you." He spoke with a flourish, teasing and poking at the Senator.

"I'm sorry to disappoint, Mr President," Calhoun responded, "but I have no intention of handing you my resignation today. Nor have I come here, tail between my legs, grovelling at your feet."

Kiebler almost enjoyed the aggressive way she spoke, with the smile firmly fixed to her lips. He wished he could be as cool as she was under pressure. In reality he was always one wrong word away from meltdown.

"Well there will be no need to grovel, Senator. The laws of the land grant you the office of VP and nobody wishes to stand in your way. I simply offer you the opportunity to avoid serving as the right-hand of a – now what was it – a 'despicable shell of a man'? A 'conniving little toad'? Your words, Senator." He was enjoying this too much, he told himself, and poured a large whisky before taking his seat, hoping it would settle the giddy child inside him.

Calhoun eyed him warily, barely reacting to his taunts. She stood by her every word and didn't regret standing up to a duplicitous and galling man. She waited for him to sit so that he was able to lock eyes with her and truly hear her speak.

"Mr President. Bernie. I won't make any apologies for my actions, and I won't stand idly by while you run this planet into the ground. Your own people are making you look bad – riots in the street, racist graffiti on our walls."

"The people are free to do as they wish," he replied smugly.

"We've regressed a hundred years in a matter of weeks and meanwhile Mars is kicking you where it hurts."

"I'm afraid you can't be so self-satisfied, Senator. The people have been oppressed for too long under your party's rule. It's about time they let off some steam."

"You have duped the people you purport to stand for. You've poisoned the minds of the weak and the vulnerable. What kind of morals does a man like that hold?"

"Duped is such a strong word. Actually, it's a pathetic word. A liberal, half-measure of a word," he replied with a snort of laughter.

"You're nauseating. The only thing that brings me pleasure at the moment is how it must gall you to have me working by your side. You can't replace your VP and you know I won't quit. Trust me; this won't be the last time the constitution gets in the way of hurricane Bernie."

Kiebler took a deep swig from his glass. He stood and made his way to the drinks cabinet in the corner – a relic from a bygone administration which he had found rather useful in his initial weeks in office.

"The funny thing about hurricanes, Mrs Calhoun," he spoke quietly, not turning to look at the woman burning a hole in the back of his head, "is they don't seem to give a damn about rules and history." He turned to face her again, raising his glass.

"They just blow right on through."

Calhoun had heard enough and she felt she had made her point loud and clear. He was clearly riled, lashing out with his words. That gave her some satisfaction but she knew Bernard Kiebler could be dangerous when cornered. She wanted to play him just right.

"I'll be in my office if you need anything, Mr President. I have work to do for the good people of Jupiter," she said, heading for the door.

"Senator Calhoun. Don't get too settled, will you? The shuttle leaves at midnight, I believe."

"Shuttle?" she asked, puzzled.

"To Mars. You will be my representative in talks with the Senate. And meet with the Workers' Council too – it seems their top man is developing a big head and it's just full of *wacky* ideas."

Calhoun forced a smile.

"Anything I can do to help," she said graciously.

"Oh, don't be under the impression you are there to help. You're there to represent us. To represent me. When you are on official business you are Bernie Kiebler's number one cheerleader. You got that?"

Calhoun stumbled with her words slightly, just enough to tip him off that he had knocked her confidence.

"To do anything other would, of course, be treason."

Kiebler downed the last of his whisky and again raised the glass to Calhoun.

"Safe journey!"

***

Daxler Scion sighed heavily, hunched over his small desk in his office. He was beginning to learn that working so closely with the newly elected President, and having the most senior-ranking office on the ground floor of the Presidential building, was a never-ending job. He had people at his door at every minute of the day, and phone calls to return whenever he had a chance to come up for air. He blamed the previous administration for this open-door policy and was resolved to shutting as many of those doors as possible over the next few months.

Scion was of the belief that those who had been elected to power should be left to rule. He didn't need meetings with lobbyists and lunch with senators or governors, or anybody for that matter. He preferred to lock himself away and plan all alone. He knew Kiebler hadn't hired him for his communication skills, or his personality. He had a job to do.

He wasn't surprised to hear that General Wilson Hasting was asking to see him. He knew the man was out of hospital and making his inaugural visit to the office today - he also knew that Kiebler hadn't the time or the nous to fend him off all on his own. He pressed the buzzer under his desk to let his assistant know he was ready.

"General Hasting, what a pleasure to see you on your feet again," he spoke with all the slime and guile of the political creature he truly was. He lived for the politicising and pandering.

"Thank you, Mr Scion," Hasting replied as he stepped into the office.

"Please take a seat," Scion indicated.

Hasting sat wearily in the faded chair opposite Daxler's desk. His host hadn't stood from his own seat to greet him, remaining with elbows resting on the edge of his desk, hands clasped together.

"You'll be delighted to take up your office, I'm sure?" he asked.

"I'm eager to get to work, that's why I am here."

"I'm sure they explained to you that the refurbishments are taking longer than expected. I believe your office is due to be complete by the end of the week. Meanwhile you must excuse the dusty old state of mine," Scion smiled.

"Its fine, I don't foresee me spending much time within the building when I take up my post," Hasting replied.

"No indeed, you will want to be out in the field. Observing and commanding."

"The President asked me to speak with you regarding my plans. I intend to set up a special task force from the ranks of the army and police units."

"With what aim, General?"

"To make it clear that race and hate crimes will not be tolerated within the new regime," Hasting responded. "To show them that we won't stand for it."

"Is this about your attack? General I assure you-"

"This isn't just about me," Hasting interrupted. "This is about the freedom and rights of every citizen. We have minorities, groups of settlers and generations of immigrants with Jupitoan children cowering in fear from these groups of delinquents."

"We have our intelligence sources out in the field looking for those leading these groups. They are small groups of young men, mostly. Barely even organised. They will be found, General," Scion assured him.

"A presence on the streets will serve a warning. We need to make our position clear."

"Our position will be clear when they are caught, believe me. In the meantime, we can't have police searching the city high and low. We will create more fear and lend the rumours credence."

"There was no rumour in my attack, Mr Scion," Hasting scolded, "and I do not think the people believe that to be true either."

"Wilson, please. The people have just voted for their freedom. We cannot make them think they are living in a police state."

"That may be so, but we aren't doing enough to get the message out there. If I wasn't about to take up a post in this government I might be questioning the stance of this administration myself."

"The stance of the administration, of President Kiebler himself, will be all too obvious when we catch the men who did this to you, General. But until then we must play this the right way," Scion spoke matter-of-factly. Kiebler's decrees falling from his lips.

"So, what am I to do in the meantime? Sit on my hands in some half-finished office? I am a military general, an advisor to the President."

"We'll find you some bigger fish to fry soon, General, make no mistake. Our true enemies have yet to come to the fore. Return to your command – lead your men and wait this out. Your time is yet to come."

Scion's smile sickened Hasting. It had done so from their very first meeting, and he liked it less each time.

***

The Press Secretary had been hired by Daxler Scion. Kiebler knew it from the way she spoke in matter-of-fact tones and gave nothing away to the assembled mass of accredited media. She was also a dull, middle-aged, uninspiring woman. Kiebler would never have hired her, and he knew that was exactly why she had been chosen.

"Ladies and gentleman, I pass you now to President Kiebler," she spoke and stepped aside from her podium. Kiebler hustled onto the stage, wanting to show that he had passion and purpose for the cause he was about to speak on.

"Citizens of Jupiter. I am sure you have all seen by now the inflammatory and libellous speeches made by the Martian Senate this morning and will join me in showing our abhorrence to the dangerous theorising being spouted. For a Martian Senator to declare a sitting President of another GU planet as "an enemy of Mars" you might expect some major breakdown in talks and relationships."

Kiebler smiled. His love for addressing the people was only growing as he settled into the power that he now yielded. He served it, and they ate it up.

"The thing is – I have had no dealings with the Martian Senate as yet in my short reign here. I have not met, nor even heard of, Mr Raylor and the Workers' Council have made no efforts to contact me to the best of my knowledge." The press corps were silent, with only the irregular mechanical click of their cameras snapping pictures to punctuate his words.

"Let me make things clear. There is no collusion or blackmail at work. The Galactic Union has not declared its interests in anything other than a peaceful and co-operative future for Jupiter; and by extension the entire solar system. Maybe the Martians would have received the same level of hospitality from my administration had they bothered to speak to me before lashing out at some perceived injustice."

He spoke with confidence, knowing that no member of the Galactic Union would be brave enough to step forward in public to speak out about the talks he had held with them. They were indeed under his thumb, he thought, and he took pleasure in the fact that they all should knew there was no way out. Someone had clearly been speaking off the record to the Martians and that sickened him – he couldn't run a tough government which cracked down on unruly superpowers like the GU and have some young hack leak information and undermine his grip.

He resolved to pressure the GU into giving him a name for this informant. He would keep it quiet, but make sure they knew precisely what the consequences of going behind Bernie's back were.

"Our ties to the Union are being strengthened to allow us to bring freedom and equality to Jupiter and to spread our success to the far reaches of the galaxy. If every planet could be as successful and flourish as we will then there will be no more rush to flood our land with immigrants. Everyone will have their fair share. The Martians must be made to see that," he spoke more determinedly now, trying not to sound too earnest.

He believed the policies would work, but he detested politicians who spoke in clichés and made abstract statements for 'the good of all mankind'. Jupiter first, that was all that really mattered.

"As has been reported earlier from this office, I have dispatched the Vice President to Mars to speak with the Senate and come to a resolution. I firmly believe the talk of shady links between my staff and the Galactic Union are being touted purely because these are things that Mrs Calhoun would love to hear," he couldn't help but get some digs in for his new understudy. "Now she has pledged to support my leadership in her constitutionally appointed role, and won't waver from her task in talking down this nonsense about a referendum on GU membership."

"With that said, of course, I wish Mrs Calhoun to have the full support of my government and the Galactic Union has expressed the same sentiments. That is why we have also asked the new GU General Secretary – Valerie Marlborough – to attend the meetings as well. I hope very much that the Martians will listen to reason from two political powerhouses and that I can bring you more news in the coming days."

Kiebler turned and left the podium immediately as the barrage of questions filled the air. He had no intention of facing the press and had instructed the press officer to follow him out of the room as soon as he was finished speaking too. Another holdover from the previous administration – their abnormal proximity to the press. He intended to speak only when something needed to be said and feed the press corps only the absolute minimum amount of information.

He'd make sure that the people of Jupiter were kept well informed of the government's success stories and that they barely got a sniff of anything that didn't quite go his way.

CHAPTER ELEVEN

Heather Calhoun entered the Workers' Council offices under cover of darkness. Her shuttle had arrived late and the press had watched her go straight to her hotel. She pleaded with her own team to smuggle her out of the back door when nobody was looking, then put in a call to Sebastian Raylor.

She had seen Kiebler's statement and heard of Valerie Marlborough's pending arrival to assist in the talks with the Senate. Calhoun saw exactly what this was and she didn't like it. Marlborough had been in Kiebler's pocket from day one of the campaign. Her placement as the GU General Secretary was a smart move on all accounts.

She was now the most powerful person in the Union and had the closest ties to Kiebler - ideally placed to run the government's agenda from inside the Union and make it look like the common course of politics.

"Senator Raylor," she greeted Seb as he welcomed her into his cramped old office, "it's great to finally meet you."

"We've met before, Mrs Calhoun. Must have been ten years ago. I wrote speeches for your husband once upon a time," Raylor replied.

"That's right, I remember you. Your speeches were always-"

"A little too on the nose, for your husband's campaigns, I think?" Raylor said with a smile. "Have you met James Bellson, he's the representative for the Workers' Council in our Senate chambers."

Calhoun had not met Bellson but had heard plenty of his antics in the past. She had admired his pluck and spirit, if not his actions, in fighting for workers' rights. She greeted him warmly and took a seat with the two men. Raylor asked the aides to leave the room and she appreciated the smaller crowd.

"Gentlemen, I'm sorry to pull this cloak and dagger sort of thing on you in the middle of the night," she started, "but Valerie Marlborough will be here by morning and I wanted to get some time with you alone before then."

"We understand, don't worry. I've heard rumours of Marlborough's style of negotiation over the years. I can't imagine her methods working too well alongside yours," Raylor offered.

"No indeed. The main issue I have is that Kiebler insists I toe the line. He enjoys having me at his command and he wants to ensure that I'm not speaking out of school."

"He's a precious man," Bellson spoke, "I can't imagine he'd be happy to have his VP speak out against any of his actions."

"He point-blank ordered me not to do so. I'm here to speak for the Kiebler administration only. The worry is that Marlborough may have been given the same order."

"So you believe there is collusion between Kiebler and the GU leadership?" Raylor asked.

"I can only tell you what I have seen. Marlborough was part of his campaign, behind the scenes. I have it from a very reliable source that she sat in on several meetings of his potential cabinet before the election," Calhoun said, hoping they would not opt to ask questions of her source. General Hasting had told her of those meetings as a friend and she would not betray that confidence.

"Her appointment to the GU came days after his meetings with their leadership; it has to have been decreed by him, right?" Bellson asked.

"It doesn't look good. But it's not really evidence of anything," Raylor stated.

"You made those big speeches in your Senate about all of this – did you have any proof? Any links to prove the Union is in Kiebler's pocket?" Calhoun asked hopefully.

"We had steady intel from a well-placed source in the Union until yesterday," Bellson informed her. "Since Kiebler's statement we've had no word from the source. He's disappeared off the grid."

"Proof enough, for us in the room at least," Calhoun spoke, rubbing her forehead, "but not enough for the voting public."

The shuttle had been a rough ride and she hadn't been able to sleep. The thought of the impending Galactic Union crisis only made her weariness more potent.

"I wish I could have won and we were working together to strengthen the Union," she said quietly.

"You can speak out now. Make it clear you're in direct opposition to him. It sends a very clear statement to the GU if his own administration isn't in full support," Bellson offered.

"It would fall on deaf ears," Raylor replied. "No offence, Heather, but your reputation is full of holes after the campaign scandals. Throwing your weight behind the cause just gives him reason to remove you from office. It would do none of us any good."

"Treason. He threatened me with that charge already," Calhoun informed them. "Coming from a man who maliciously twisted a scandal of his own into defamation of his rival – at the expense of his own family? All just to win that office."

"The Sonya Medina thing?" Bellson asked.

"Manufactured. She was just a whore, one of many. My people knew about it all but I forced them to stay quiet. I wanted to win a real campaign, by fighting over issues, not throwing dirt. I knew he'd fall into his own mess eventually."

"And once one of the stories leaked he was cornered. He had no choice but to shift the blame," Raylor said.

"On to me," Calhoun responded. "He ditched his wife, made up some tale of love and patriotism. You have to hand it to him – he worked for it." She smiled, and the two men offered faint ones back.

"The scale of his corruption doesn't surprise me; it's the things we don't know about that truly scare me." Raylor said after a pause. "Who knows what he is getting up to behind closed doors? There aren't many who can get into those rooms with him now."

"You understand that's why I can't make my support of your cause public?" Calhoun asked.

"You can – you'll have the full backing of Mars, we'll see to that," Bellson said, almost pleading.

"She can't, James," Raylor replied. "Mrs Calhoun holds the second highest office on Jupiter. Like it or not, Kiebler can't stop it and can't restrict her access to certain things."

"I'm in the Presidential office building every day, just waiting for someone to slip up. If I gave that up he would fill the place with even more of his own people. The government, and by default the GU, would become a closed book."

Raylor looked at Calhoun and knew he had found an important ally. He didn't know how she could be effective, but he sensed the deep will and strength of conviction that she held and admired her for it.

"We'll call a Senate meeting first thing in the morning," Raylor said. "Let's find out what Valerie Marlborough has to say for herself."

***

Valerie Marlborough and Heather Calhoun left the Senate chambers around midnight, after a full day of debate. The back and forth had been long and arduous, as the Workers' Council, Galactic Union reps and Senate members of Mars all had their say.

"An entire day wasted to the ideological murmurings of people who don't know how good they have it," Marlborough commented, as the pair headed for their car.

"I enjoyed the chance to discuss the issues. It's worth seeing things from the other side sometimes," Calhoun responded.

"Please. If they could choose a side it would be more tolerable. They can't seem to agree on anything other than 'Jupiter Bad'. It's childish," Marlborough said, climbing into the nondescript vehicle. She found that her patience was always stretched rather thin and in the presence of people who couldn't agree on their own discourse she struggled to bottle up her feelings.

"So you think the Martian cause is voided by the fact that they can't agree on what comes next?" Calhoun asked as she settled into the car beside the GU General Secretary.

"They have asked their own people to vote on independence from the very power which makes them a force on the bigger stage, and yet offer no clear plan for how Mars survives without it."

"They believe the Union has lost its relevance, with corruption and conspiracy never far from its actions. It doesn't provide stability anymore," Calhoun chided.

"We provide trade agreements. Jobs. Money. Subsidies and benefits. The GU gives every Martian the same rights of every citizen of the entire solar system – with freedom to live, work and pursue the life they choose." Marlborough spat in response.

"Aren't those the same rights our President is looking to take from them?" Calhoun asked. Marlborough gave her a stony look and the Vice President decided not to labour the point. She didn't want to get into an anti-Kiebler argument with one of his biggest cheerleaders.

"The Union must remain an independent organisation, overseeing the welfare of us all. It mustn't be seen to be taking advantage of the 'little people' to benefit those with more wealth and power," Calhoun spoke, diplomatically. "No matter what the agenda is, nor who the GU decides to work closely with, those values must remain."

"I admire the simplicity of your ideas, Heather, I truly do," Marlborough said, pausing to gather her thoughts for a moment. "I have decades of experience in the banking industry and do you know what the most important lesson I have learned is?"

Calhoun looked at her with a questioning expression, wondering how she was going to spin the deceit the GU and Bernie Kiebler were concocting. Marlborough waited a moment, as if swilling the words around in her head, savouring them.

"The little people rarely know what is best for them. They have their heads in the ground and only pop up to complain at some perceived slight on their way of living when it is too late."

Calhoun couldn't quite work out if this was prepared dialogue, or an off-the-fly thought. She imagined Marlborough wringing her hands at night, writing her own speeches in her head for moments just like this.

"The universe needs people who lift their heads above the ground. Forward thinkers who can see the future clearly and balance the good and the bad to ensure change comes for us all."

"So, would you admit that you plan to advance Bernard Kiebler's agenda from your position as General Secretary?" Calhoun asked, affronted by the notion.

"We'll certainly work very closely with him to ensure things are as they should be," Marlborough answered, her eye line never veering from Calhoun's.

"And how should they be, madam Secretary?"

"They should be balanced fairly, Mrs Calhoun. Jupiter stands alone as the centre of power, of wealth, of trade on all levels. Big business and big government. It is time the Galactic Union recognised that strength and weighed its decisions accordingly."

"A fairer deal for Jupiter, at the expense of humanity?" Calhoun asked. "The same humanity which will be locked out of this economic haven by his ridiculous 'Block the Belt' idea?"

Marlborough opened her mouth to respond but immediately felt the sudden change of gravity.

Searing pain quickly followed.

Only then did she notice the screech of metal on metal. The smashing of glass.

Something had hit them hard.

She flew across the back seat of the car and crushed Calhoun against the opposite side door. Calhoun herself had been strapped in and felt herself rebound against the door, then was pinned flat by the weight of Marlborough's already limp body.

The sound of gunfire, close but distant all at once, reverberated outside. She felt for the back of her head and found her fingertips sticky with blood. She couldn't tell if the car was spinning from the impact of the crash or if it was her own dizziness making the world around her loop and whirl about wildly.

She passed out as the door was thrown open and the gun shots grew louder.

CHAPTER TWELVE

M arlborough opened her eyes reluctantly, feeling both the stinging pain in her temple and the nagging fear in the pit of her stomach. She had faded in and out of consciousness since the crash, but had pieced together the snippets of conversations and the sounds of engines enough to know that she had been taken somewhere.

She took in the dank, dark space around her and decided it must have been some long unused factory. Tin walls rattled with a strong wind and no source of light or heat penetrated the building. Looking around she saw Heather Calhoun tied to a post in the middle of the room, slouched on the floor, blood stains on her clothes. Marlborough immediately pulled her own arms forward and realised she too was trussed to a post, arms tied behind her back.

Four shadowy figures emerged amid a torrent of shouts from an unseen room. She heard an engine running somewhere outside and then the door slammed shut and blocked the sound out entirely.

The figures approached – all four hooded and wearing black combat fatigues. Marlborough tried to take them in as they roused Calhoun. She did not think they carried themselves like military officers. As she focused her ears to the words they were speaking amongst themselves she realised that three were men, one a woman and they were speaking plainly in an accent she recognised all too well.

"You're from Earth? Why? Why have you done this?" she asked out loud.

The figures seemed startled at first, expecting her to still be unconscious. One approached her with a forceful step and she determined not to blanch if she was to be struck.

The blow did not come and she found the man reaching over her and cutting the ties at her back. He motioned for her to move along the floor to join Calhoun and she quickly forced down any notion of getting physical. She slid carefully along the dusty floor and sat alongside her waking colleague.

"We represent a group of fighters for justice and for the return of humankind to its promised home," one of the hooded men spoke. "For too long the greed and corruption of mankind has infiltrated the solar system around us – our reach exceeds our grasp. We, as a people, have allowed the rape of this galaxy and we must end it."

Marlborough sat for a moment in silence and took in their words. She was unsure why they were being directed at her. Calhoun was awake now and equally perplexed with the abruptness of the speech.

"We bring to you – as messengers of the powerful – our promise. Mankind has-"

"Mankind has expanded itself beyond the thoughts of brainless idiots like you," Marlborough interrupted.

"Man has overreached and now some believe themselves to be above God himself," the woman replied angrily.

"We wish the powers that be to know that God does not forgive what they have done. Punishment and judgment is coming for us all."

Calhoun sat up, touched her bloodied head tenderly, and tried to shake the cobwebs loose.

"You are wrong. Mankind would have died without the invention of the colonies. Earth was dying and humanity needed to find a way. There is nothing bad or sinful in survival." Calhoun tried to rise to her feet as she spoke, but wobbled and settled for a knee. She looked up at her captors and could see only eyes under thick black hoods.

"Mrs Calhoun, please do not tell us who is wrong. We have watched as the simple experiment has grown beyond our needs, to take from every inch of the stars. We were put on Earth for a reason and the planet's cycle is tied to our own."

The voice came from the smallest of the four – Calhoun could not get a good read on him through his outfit, although she guessed he was not a young man. He spoke confidentially and calmly. She was reminded of the speakers at her church back home.

"When the resources dry up, so too should mankind. We have perverted His natural order."

"And you think killing us will advance your cause, how...?" Marlborough asked, indignant.

"We do not intend to kill you. We wish to warn you only."

"You crash into us and take us prisoner - tell us we should all be dead and our judgement is coming - and you only wish to warn? These are terrorist acts," Marlborough was angry now, her blood boiling as her circulation returned.

"We came to you, against our own principles, as a show of intent. To make a statement."

"A statement? You'll be laughed at on every news broadcast in the system! The Earth extremists who believe space travel is the devil, and God is just, have come to us in their spaceships to make threats on our lives. You haven't helped your cause. You've made it a punchline."

Marlborough felt the words as she spoke them and delivered them like a boxer delivering a knockout flurry. She allowed herself a crooked smile and knew she must look like a crazy old fool to these people. She did not care for a second.

"We will do what it takes to be heard," the lead speaker said defiantly, but somewhat resigned to the truth of Marlborough's words.

"I sympathise with your stance," Calhoun spoke, hoping to ease the tensions. "I understand the view you take on the life we all lead – but you must understand that there is no going back? You hope to gain two spokespeople in us but even if we agreed, all you would gain is two more voices shouting into the abyss. There is nothing to be done to make things right in your eyes."

"Miss Calhoun, you do not understand the full weight of our actions. We have stood back, in the knowledge of what you say – there can be no action which returns us to our glory days. Only God can judge you now."

"Then what is it you want from us?" Calhoun asked.

"We have watched Bernard Kiebler rise to power and betray the basic human dignity we hold at heart. We have seen the things he does and have intelligence from informants throughout Jupiter. We know what he did to you. How he betrayed his own family, and the sanctity of marriage to steal power."

Both women were amazed at the knowledge the extremists had gathered. Marlborough considered arguing the point for a brief moment, defending her President. A look in Calhoun's eyes told her not to bother – Heather Calhoun knew the truth and any denial would be a waste of everyone's time.

"How have you come about this information?" Calhoun asked the pseudo-leader of the group.

"As I say, we have sources. Many informants and persons agreeable to our cause. They are in your government. In your campaign teaMs They work in your TV and media. Hidden in plain sight and exceptional at their jobs."

"For what purpose?" Marlborough asked.

"We intend to gather enough evidence and place enough people in places of power to topple the Galactic Union. It cannot stand on its own right and must never be allowed to continue with a man like Kiebler pulling the strings."

"You have a GU rep from Earth – they can make your case, veto any action Kiebler influences," Calhoun offered.

"We cannot trust any GU member. It is a compromised organisation. The few will take our beliefs to the system, planet by planet, government by government. Any way we can."

"And to achieve this you will travel in space craft, live on foreign planets? Participate in the future mankind has built. It's hypocrisy."

"It is sacrifice, Ms Marlborough."

The four figures stood looking down on their hostages, as Marlborough glared with absolute fury into each of their faces. She wished to be able to see behind the hoods, to have any clue to the identities of these people. She would see them brought to swift and brutal justice when she did.

Calhoun, meanwhile, thought things over in her still hazy mind. She didn't believe in the extremist view for one moment, but she understood it. She didn't agree with their methods either but she could emphasise with the desperation and hopelessness of seeing your enemies progress through lies and deceit, while all you can do is watch.

"I cannot do you any good here. You must let me return to Jupiter. You have misjudged the situation and your actions betray your cause. Kidnapping, or whatever you'd like to call this, is not the way. This can only harm your cause."

She spoke kindly, hoping to gain some trust. She knew having Marlborough snarling next to her would work in her favour. Good cop, rabid cop.

"In my role as Vice President I can influence people and policies – attempt to broker peace, and bring our sides closer together. We must find a way to live in peace."

"The people must know that judgment is coming," a so far silent extremist spoke up in a gravelly voice.

"I will make sure your message is heard. And people will have the freedom to repent their ways and join your cause, should they wish."

"Ridiculous!" Marlborough scoffed. "You'll be laughed out of office or locked up. These lunatics are the dying embers of a past humanity has thankfully left behind."

The figure closest to Marlborough reached out, incensed at her words, and grabbed her by the hair. He pulled a gun from his belt and raised it stubbornly to her head.

"We are being good little Earthlings and asking you to spread our message today. Do not forget what we are capable of."

The memories of past extremist flare ups flashed through Marlborough's head – they had always been a joke to her, a group who break their own rules whenever it is convenient for them, and never offer any real terms to end the terror they spread. Various groups had claimed the lives of hundreds, potentially thousands, over the years. She had witnessed the bombing of a government reserve building on Jupiter with her own eyes and knew many who had died in the aftermath.

"Put down your gun. It is not human to murder and people spreading your brand of hate have not advanced your message any further than Earth's atmosphere in the past. It is not right to do as you please to gain what you wish. That is the way Kiebler thinks – and you will be no better than him if you do this."

Calhoun's words blew a cooling wind through the room and the presumed-leader of the group stepped forward to put a hand on the gun and lower it from Marlborough's forehead. Calhoun found herself admiring her for the first time – the way she never took her eyes off the aggressor as he towered over her.

"We did not come here to kill. We have made our point and thank the Vice President for hearing it, as she has heard the views of the Workers' Council and other fringe groups here on Mars." Marlborough shot a look at Calhoun, taking in that nugget of information. Heather Calhoun and her secret meetings; Marlborough was almost proud of how well she had played that.

The leader nodded his acknowledgement to Calhoun. "Do not be mistaken in this – we will not stand idly by and watch Kiebler and his Galactic Union take control of the system. Violence is not our chosen route, but is one we will not spare when it is required."

He motioned for his people to gather their things and they hastily followed his order. Within a moment they were gone, the waiting engine outside growing louder then fading into the distance as they sped off into the night.

***

The security escorts arrived within minutes and Calhoun was safely in the back of a transport receiving medical attention before she had time to think over the events of the evening. Marlborough sat opposite, gaining the attention of another doctor. Calhoun was glad of the time to gather her thoughts before the inevitable shouting match.

They arrived at the aerospace terminal and eyed each other warily as they were left alone in the vehicle. They would fly home separately, each of their newly acquired roles coming with their own personal inter-planetary spacecraft.

"Let me guess - you want me to go easy on this whole thing when the press come asking in the morning?" Marlborough asked, her cracked, dry lips pursed with every word.

Calhoun had thought it over carefully on the journey and nodded in the affirmative.

"What exactly do you hope to achieve with this nonsense?"

Calhoun struggled to find the words. Weariness had crept into her bones, and the shock or the adrenalin or just sheer fear had finally made her seize up inside. It annoyed her that Marlborough seemed little fazed. She took her time to find the right words.

"Earth extremists will never achieve anything. They are fighting for a goal that was lost generations ago. But we can't let them bully the entire solar system without acknowledging them. To ignore them is only to encourage them further."

"Oh, I don't intend to ignore them. Believe me, once I'm finished here they will be known throughout the cosmos as the arrogant fools who tried to take on a giant, and were brought crashing to their knees."

Calhoun blanched at the words, partly unable to comprehend how an educated and successful woman like Valerie Marlborough could believe such aggressive rhetoric, and partly wondering if she even believed the words she was spewing forth.

"You won't beat them down with guns or bombs. Violence won't end their cause, nor will it appease anyone. War will simply breed more extreme views, more intolerant people. You will feed what already divides us."

"You propose we cosy up to the bad guys?"

"I'm saying I don't know who the bad guys are any more."

Marlborough sat forward in her seat, hoping somehow it would help her words to get through to Heather Calhoun – she suspected she was fighting a losing battle.

"Your idealism astounds me; do you know that Heather? You play nice with the Martian Senate, flirt with the Workers' Council. Now you want to hug a terrorist. They know nothing but violence. Their attempts at a peaceful warning tonight nearly involved our deaths in a high-speed crash, for God's sake."

"They are ill-advised and out of their depth. Now is the time to talk them off the ledge, bring them into the political fold. Give them a voice and let them know that they are being heard."

"Let them be tolerated. Let them know that their views and their bullying tactics were a success, and send that message to every other fringe group in the goddamn galaxy!" Marlborough's voice raised, and she could sense her already wafer-thin patience disintegrating.

"I won't speak to the press. Say what you like to them but The President will personally hear my account of tonight."

With that she excused herself, leaving Calhoun to sweat on the President's reaction.

**

The diplomatic transports gave the faux-luxury of a small pod-like office for higher-ranking officials. Marlborough was enjoying her first experience of having one to herself. Locked away in her sound-proofed room, she sat and contemplated the evening's events long and hard.

She didn't trust Heather Calhoun to represent her government. Between secret meetings with the workers on Mars and standing up for the rights of known terrorist organisations – her own kidnappers, no less – Marlborough decided that she couldn't trust this woman in the slightest and that Bernard Kiebler would be glad to be informed of her deceit.

She felt a twinge of delight in the knowledge that she had information to hold over Calhoun. The woman who had married a President and looked down on all around her for so long. The woman who just couldn't stay out of the limelight, even after her husband's retirement from politics. Time and again she tried to make herself relevant; and now here she was, Vice President of Jupiter.

Marlborough smiled as she thought about how this was the most power Heather Calhoun would ever hold. The smile only widened when she considered that the Vice President's role really had no worth in her hands – she was not trusted or well liked by any stretch and now Marlborough had the information which would break her.

She picked up the secure receiver and asked for a direct line to the Presidential office. Daxler Scion was delighted to take her call and he listened eagerly to her tale. The President called back before they had cleared the Belt, happy to hear from his Galactic Union trustee.

She told of Calhoun's lies and her overriding mistrust. She told her President of the VP's poisonous talks with the rebellious Workers' Council and how she believed that Calhoun may have defected already and that at this very moment she may be attempting a dangerous game of subterfuge within their very own government.

She told of the Earth extremists and their growing influence – and how Heather Calhoun had made peace with them, making promises she could not keep.

She made her case well and warned of the dangers of Calhoun talking with the press on such matters. Even worse, talking to the Martian Senate and the extremists – making shady deals to plot against her own government.

President Kiebler thanked her for her efforts on this trip. He wished her goodnight. He sounded proud.

Marlborough went to sleep with a smile on her face, having given herself more power than the Vice President – all through one simple phone call.

CHAPTER THIRTEEN

The shuttle veered wildly as the pilot changed its course. The Belt was never easy to navigate but it felt particularly vicious this time. The asteroids themselves appeared bigger – giant balls of rock, tumbling through space, locked into an orbit together but free and wild and entirely unpredictable.

The pilot watched as a lump as big as his ship collided with a gigantic asteroid and spewed out plumes of rock and dust, leaving only a small crater on the surface of the larger entity. The dust clouds were hampering visibility and he was growing more anxious. The hardest part was to find an opening that was easy to navigate into and then to pick a path through its centre.

He spent fifteen minutes circling, waiting for an opportunity, then seized the briefest of opportunities

– darting into the belt amid a cloud of dust and seeing the particles bounce off his front viewing screen. He knew the smaller rocks wouldn't do any damage but couldn't help glancing at the gigantic boulders which periodically ducked past, all too close for comfort.

It soon became apparent something was wrong. The dust grew worse and the activity rebounding off the ship's outer body increased, sending the various motion-sensor displays wild. He took evasive action three or four times, dodging between asteroids he had never seen at such close quarters before.

He had flown the Belt hundreds of times and never witnessed a night like this. His nerves were frayed as he jerked the controls up time and time again; performing miracles just to stay in the air.

His radio link fizzled out soon after entering the storm of rock and debris. He knew there was no sanctuary and no respite to be had – he had to make it through to the other side. His training in the Jupiter Aerospace program stood him in good stead and he reassured himself that average pilots don't get to fly the private craft of senior government officials.

He was elite.

He breathed easier, finding a moment of calm, and swung the ship hard left, hoping to find a way around the dust clouds up ahead.

His radio crackled into life and he heard some chatter – it seemed to be government code but faded quickly. He hailed the mystery crew but gleaned only silence in response. He checked his view ports and through the cloud of debris he thought he saw a glint of silver.

His hopes rose and he considered updating the crew so that his highly valuable asset on board could be relieved – he was sure news of imminent rescue would be greeted warmly.

The first blast tore through the hull of the craft with ease. The pilot didn't fully understand what was happening until the second blast hit – his thoughts of Vice Presidential praise shattered into fragments as his front view screens did likewise.

In the split second before all oxygen was sucked from the cockpit he wondered why. Who would attack a government vessel so close to home? He lost consciousness as he was pulled violently into the blackness of space and did not live to witness the brief flash of fire as the craft was fired upon twice more.

The smoking hulk of the government-issue spacecraft careened serenely into the next approaching asteroid and disappeared in a ball of smoke and dust, lost to the Belt.

***

Kiebler felt the energy in the room as he took his place on the dais. He scanned the faces of the crowd that had gathered on the lawns of the presidential office building. They had heard the rumours. Every news channel was now reporting some form of tragedy that had struck his new government in the night.

He had tipped off Sam Heighway an hour ago and knew that as soon as he had finished making his statement here, Sam would be live on the air giving people the Kiebler spin on the tragic developments.

Deeply tragic, he thought to himself and it took all of his skill as an actor to ensure the melancholy look on his face was not replaced by a smile.

"It is with deep regret that I must announce the tragic death of our Vice President – Heather Calhoun."

He savoured the words. He had hoped for Calhoun's end as a political opponent for so long, and had wished for a thousand different ways for it to come about. He could have planned nothing better than the situation which had unfolded through the night.

"As you are aware, Mrs Calhoun had completed a very tense and stressful trip to Mars to negotiate peaceful and productive talks with the leaders there. Her craft met with severe turbulence while passing through the Belt during the night. There are no survivors."

His advisors had assured him that nobody could survive the crash. The pilots who were stationed in the Belt were due to search for any wreckage throughout the day and report back. They had provided a short clip of the doomed pilot of Calhoun's craft and his plea for help moments before he died. Kiebler had sent it directly to Sam Heighway to be broadcast to the people.

The pilot would be a hero. Kiebler would have to host some sort of ceremony for his family. It was a small price to pay. Calhoun, however, would not be afforded the public image boost her death could provide for her.

"We would like to express our deepest sympathy with Heather's family at this time and ask that you respect their privacy. I would personally like to express something else," he said, removing his reading glasses to ensure nobody thought he was reading from a prompter. He wanted them to take particular notice of the impassioned, unscripted and emotional words of their president.

"Heather ventured across the solar system to speak for my government and to deliver my message. We know she held positive talks with the Senate on Mars. We also know, from very reliable sources, that she met with other undesirable elements while on the planet. Now, who knows the intentions of these people? Now is not the time to point fingers - but I'm told she may have met with an Earth extremist group, as well as the Workers' Council of Mars. Some might think it suspicious that she never made it home to report on everything she saw and heard there.

"Needless to say, I will assign a special task force to investigate the circumstances of her death over the coming days."

He listened for the murmur of the rumour mill churning into gear. The reporters within the gathered crowd were already prepping questions, he could see their eager lips pursed, respectfully waiting for him to finish his announcement before they pounced.

"It is just tragic what happened here, make no mistake," he continued. "You have my word that I will exhaust the full breadth of my powers as President to find out what really happened out there. May you find rest, Heather."

He slid his glasses back into his breast pocket and nodded a 'thank you' to the audience as the reporters filled the air with questions. He turned and left, only allowing the smile to break out onto his face when he was firmly ensconced within his office.

***

The referendum hadn't come quick enough for Raylor. He wished they had convinced Sutherland to ask for it months ago and he regretted that his friend was not in a position to help them, now that the day had actually arrived.

He wondered, as the Senate introductions were made, how Heather Calhoun's death would be seen by the solar system at large and if Kiebler's comments on the circumstances surrounding her death would be taken at face value.

The speaker made the necessary introductions and Marien Lyndell began the first order of business.

"My thoughts and prayers go out to Heather Calhoun's family. May she rest in peace," she spoke, with head bowed. A murmur or respectful agreement swept through the room.

"It is sad that we must discuss these matters today, however in light of President Kiebler's comments this morning it feels only right that we do."

"The South feels it would be an egregious error to hold a referendum on this day. We must stay the vote and think what is best for the people of Mars in the current climate," Edward Royce joined in. His subtle objections to the referendum had grown more aggressive in recent days and now that the day had arrived he was growing desperate. Raylor saw it coming and had already coached his fellow senators on what to expect from him today. He hoped they would see through his words to the truth behind them.

"Mr Royce, staying the vote will not change any matters of life or death in the universe. It is about the rights and liberty of the Martian people, I don't think you get to stand in the way of that," Raylor responded.

"Equally I don't believe anyone appointed you as the spokesperson for the people, Mr Raylor," Royce spat back.

"The people don't require a spokesperson on this matter – they will get to vote with their own hearts and minds."

Raylor eyed his fellow Senator, waiting for his snide response but it did not come. Ramsey Pierce, usually precise and tactical in his words within the Senate walls, spoke up instead.

"I feel that President Kiebler's words have thrown our good intentions into shadow. What he said this morning was tantamount to an accusation against the Senate and the Workers' Council. That must be dealt with, regardless of this vote."

"He was using his political enemies as a very unconvincing scapegoat for a tragic death. Turning what should have been a respectful announcement of a great woman's loss of life into a witch-hunt," Raylor spoke angrily, hoping to rouse his own supporters in the room. He knew if even the more liberal Pierce were leaning away from the vote he would have a hard job convincing the rest of the Senate.

"I propose we cancel the referendum and hold peaceful talks with Kiebler and the GU We must ensure Mars is not seen as an aggressor here," Royce spoke.

"Banding our name in with terrorists like the Earth mob was a stroke of genius by Kiebler," Raylor said. "Has he even convinced all of you – who were present for the talks with Calhoun - that you are part of some devious plot to overthrow the Galactic Union?"

"It is propaganda. It's as simple as that. Kiebler has twisted a terrible situation to his own means. That should tell us everything we need to know about the man you propose peaceful talks with. He will do anything it takes to achieve power and he'll continue to take more and more. Where will it end?"

Raylor looked around at the wider room. Bellson was sat in the front of the Workers' Council section and he knew he could rely on their support. Other lobbyist groups and local officials seemed less sure and Raylor wondered how the people became so disenfranchised with their own nation.

He remembered being a boy on Mars and growing up fiercely proud of his heritage. His father would tell stories of the great builders and scientists of Mars' past. Pioneers who shaped the future of the planet and all of mankind along with it. They had argued for their own administration, to be allowed to govern themselves and to shape their own future outside of the rule of Earth's leaders at the time.

He wondered where that fight had gone. He thought the people - the real people outside of this building - would agree. He wanted to give them the chance to have their say more than anything.

"Bernard Kiebler is a proven liar. He manipulates the truth and we have all seen it in action many times before today. After the awful events of last night we have even more reason to leave now, before it's too late."

"What will removing ourselves from the only body capable of standing up to Kiebler prove exactly?" Royce added, hoping to stem the tide of popular opinion which he could feel edging Raylor's way.

"The Galactic Union is already broken. Raped and pillaged by Kiebler's people. It's a shell of what it once was," Lyndell admonished him.

"And without planets like Mars it is devalued even more so. We would strike a blow to the coalition, weaken it possibly beyond repair. At the very least we might give other governments, on every other planet, a reason to question their role in the GU too. That might just be enough."

James Bellson led the applause in the chambers and soon a vast majority were on their feet. The Speaker called for order, before asking for the Senate members to make their final vote on the opening of the polls.

Raylor smiled as Lyndell and Pierce both voted in the positive. Royce scowled and left his seat before the speaker made the result official. Raylor guessed that the south would vote against a full withdrawal from the GU and he hoped that the numbers in the north and east would come out strong.

The polling stations would open within the hour and the future of Mars and the Galactic Union would be revealed once and for all.

***

James Bellson stepped out of the voting booth and shouted at the top of his voice - "Freedom!"

The handful of people assembled in the city hall barely reacted, but his friend Sebastian Raylor applauded.

"I'm glad we could rely on your vote," he told him as the pair walked side by side out of the building.

"I'm glad we could rely on you to give us the opportunity," Bellson replied.

"It's in the people's hands now, where decisions like this belong."

Bellson admired the way Raylor could come out with bold and moral statements with such ease. He knew that hidden not-all-that deep down Raylor wanted the people to vote 'no' and to do so emphatically. The fact that he respected the process and that he would respect the result, whichever way it fell, was testament to the man's character.

"I hope this place isn't a reflection of the turnout. I've seen maybe 30 people since we walked in here."

Bellson had seen far less popular votes in his time. The Senate called many procedural votes of little importance or interest to the common man every day and Bellson would take the short walk from the Senate chambers to the city hall and make his voice heard for each and every one of them.

"City workers don't tend to leave the office through the day. Industrial types up in your neck of the woods work all hours of the day. There's no such thing as a reliable poll on Mars. We just wait."

Raylor didn't seem to be put at ease by his reasoning but Bellson knew it to be true. The pollsters had given up on Martian voting practices years ago. Of course Raylor knew this too. He was an emphatically anxious man. Bellson thought it was one of his most admirable traits.

"So, we had our Council meeting after the Senate this morning. Your name was mentioned."

Raylor's eyebrows raised but he only ventured an almost inaudible "uh-huh" in response.

"The guys were really impressed with what you said. As much as we love Sutherland, we all knew he wasn't the backbone we needed in a Senate seat. Add to that the fact that he liked to play inter-planetary favourites rather than really get his teeth into the issues of his people."

Bellson shrugged. Sutherland had been a long-serving and loyal member of the Senate, and his people continued to vote him into office, but he had shaken off the causes of many of the organised groups in recent years. The Workers' Council felt marginalised and its membership had dropped steadily.

"We wondered if you might do us all a great honour, Seb?"

Raylor stopped in the street to look at his friend. He hadn't thought about the implications of their friendship until he felt the angling in Bellson's words today. He suspected this was coming.

"The honour of...?" he asked.

"We'd like you to be our representative in the Senate. The Leader of the Workers' Council."

"I can't lead an organisation while sitting on the Senate – it would be seen as a conflict."

"Seb. You know as well as I do that there is no rule against any such thing. And who is going to be misled by any conflict of interest? You think anyone has any doubts about where your priorities lie after the arguments you made this morning?"

Raylor thought it over. His views were well known to the public and the Senate. They knew he was close to the Workers' Council already, so image wise he couldn't see any problems.

"Why not you?" he asked Bellson.

"Everyone knows me. They're used to me. I've left it too late to start piling the pressure on these issues – it'd be seen as a purely political move and ignored. You – you're a phenom in there. You speak with passion and control. You aren't afraid to tell them how it is to convince them to agree. The power of your words, and the Workers' Council history behind you when you stand up there, is an obstacle nobody will want to face down."

"Royce will hate it," Raylor replied after a beat.

"So that's a yes then?" Bellson said with a smile.

***

The polls closed at two o'clock in the morning, Martian time. The counting of the votes took a further six hours to complete and confirm. Once complete, the House Speaker would present the results for immediate ratification from the four serving Senators.

This presented several problems for the Senators, as they would perform any last minute lobbying nearby up until midnight, then be required to wait around until morning when the first signs of victory or defeat would be clear.

Raylor found time to meet with the Workers' Council during the evening and officially accepted their leadership. He thanked as many members as he could individually and urged every last one to make sure they had voted before the day was out.

Bellson paraded Raylor around town as much as possible – he wanted a grass-roots feel to the announcement. He felt that Raylor was the natural, organic choice for head of the organisation and wanted the public to see that. For that reason he resisted calling a press conference or even calling in favours from journalists friendly to the cause. Instead, they met the public, talked to voters and visited the local zones where Martian workers were the main populace.

By the end of the day, Raylor thought he may have shaken every hand of every Martian who had ever picked up a tool or got their hands dirty this side of Jupiter. He felt more like he was running for office than a man who had stumbled his way into two new jobs in no time at all.

Valerie Marlborough appeared on every TV broadcast she could manage throughout the day. She drilled home the Kiebler administration line of how disrespectful it was of the Martina Senate to press ahead with a referendum on a day like today. She alluded to Martian involvement in Calhoun's death all too skilfully, using her past as a lawyer and a banker to know when to say just enough without making an outright accusation.

She launched scathing attacks on Earth extremist groups, and Earth leaders who refused to do anything to combat them. Watching the coverage, Raylor and Bellson agreed that she was only making their cause stronger – as leader of the Galactic Union, of which Earth was a founding member, she should be able to exert influence and convey a message of peace and safety. Such a show of strength was not forthcoming; instead she only succeeded in giving Raylor another talking point to lay at the GU doorstep when he met with Martian tech workers over lunch.

Senators Royce and Pierce appeared on a political debate show in the early evening and, predictably, Royce battered the Senator from the West into submission. The two had long been allies in the Senate chambers and the South-West links were long and storied.

Pierce's decision to side with the "No" vote had galled Royce and he did not hold back on attacking his colleague's record of flip-flopping on decisions and voting against his own party in the past. He painted a picture of a man more interested in his own political ascent than the wants and needs of his constituents.

Royce's own voters in the South would lap that up, Raylor knew. Some might judge it to have been a step too far, but Raylor had a good handle of the Southern mindset. They enjoyed seeing themselves as the elite – or at least a vast majority did – and watching their own representative lambast a fellow Senator in such a way would be high entertainment for them.

Bernard Kiebler remained uncharacteristically quiet throughout the day. He listened to his advisors when they told him to put on a show of respect for Calhoun's passing. He sent Marlborough out to face the media and coached her on everything that needed to be said.

In private he seethed over the referendum. The fact that it even existed burned him up and he caught himself pacing in his office on more than one occasion. He hoped the Martian people would hold their nerve and recognise the Union as the strongest entity in the solar system – and the only hope many of them had of maintaining the high quality of life they currently enjoyed.

He resolved to ensure that their quality of life was significantly reduced if they voted out of the Union.

When eight o'clock in the morning rolled around, the Senate reconvened in the chambers and the Speaker was handed an envelope. It took him fifteen minutes to get through each region's individual results.

The South overwhelmingly voted to remain in the Union. Senator Royce accepted handshakes and congratulations from those around him and flashed his artificially-whitened smile at Pierce on the opposite end of the bench.

Lyndell delivered the East to the leave campaign and Raylor nodded his gratitude for her support.

The North was a landslide. The press told Raylor afterwards that it was the biggest turnout in the region's history, with upwards of eighty percent of registered voters having had their say. They wanted out of the Galactic Union and they had made their point loud and clear.

Senator Ramsey Pierce was a mess of nerves and fury as he awaited the results from his region and felt the glowing stare of Royce on him all the while. He would either be vindicated or laughed out of the Senate when all was said and done.

In his worry he almost missed the call. The Speaker said his name and went through the formalities and yet his ears wouldn't quite take in the information until people were cheering and hugs were being thrown his way.

In a tightly won 53-47 split vote, the Western region of Mars voted to leave the Galactic Union.

Raylor and Bellson jumped from their seats, while the northmen and Workers' Council reps alike all cheered loudly and rushed the bench. The speaker protested but his words were drowned out quickly by the host of well wishers eager to congratulate their Senators.

Mars had voted for freedom from the Union. Freedom to rule over itself and to see to it that its own people's interests were at the heart of every decision.

Freedom from Bernard Kiebler's increasingly toxic grasp.

***

Kiebler watched the result in his study, with his closest advisors surrounding him. They each shied away from comment when the final votes were announced. Kiebler remained silent, a stony expression on his face as he swirled his whisky around a vintage glass.

Marlborough was the first to move, quickly switching off the monitor which was showing nothing but glorious celebrations on the streets of the Martian capital.

"Is it possible we have handled everything wrong? Is there some scope to backtrack?" She glanced at Daxler Scion, then back to Kiebler.

"And do what, Valerie?" Kiebler slammed his glass down on the table then relaxed back into the leather sofa's cushion. "We backtrack and put them in charge of the Union? There is no backtrack, even if we wanted to."

"The only acceptable position the Martians would accept is if we pulled out of the Union and left it to governor itself," Scion offered.

"Exactly. A Galactic Union which would seek control over Jupitoan law, without our involvement at the top. Or we pull out entirely and the whole thing falls to the ground. We are the backbone of the GU – more so today than ever before."

Marlborough mulled it over and could not see any better options. Her GU was weakened now either way. She had no power to stop that.

"Who would be left in our stead, to curb the Martians whims?" Scion asked. "The Earth extremists who hunted you down and tied you up like a prisoner? Are we to trust them with the running of our solar system?"

"Indeed not," she replied contemplatively. "Maybe I should return to Mars. Without Calhoun's pandering influence I may be able to talk some sense into them."

Kiebler liked her front. She had just returned from an eventful trip, having been kidnapped and held at gunpoint. Her travelling partner had been killed in transit on the return leg and yet here she was offering her services again for the good of the Union.

"You're a strong woman, Valerie. If you were Jupitoan-born I would have you sworn in as my Vice President on the spot."

"It's an honour to serve you, sir. No titles required."

"If I may, President Kiebler," Scion interrupted. "We are still searching for a Secretary of Communications who fits our very exacting needs. There is no limitation on nationality for a staff role of that ilk."

Kiebler smiled and looked at Marlborough for any sign of a reaction. She was hiding it well but not well enough. He could see the gleam in her eye and the tiniest curling of her lip.

"How about it, Val – wanna be my right-hand woman?"

Marlborough stood and approached him carefully. She knelt on the floor at his feet and he sat up, unsure of how to react. She reached for his hand and kissed it gently.

"Mr President. It will be an honour to serve you," she said while looking into his eyes.

He knew he had her - and he knew just exactly what to use her for.

CHAPTER FOURTEEN

R aylor stood to acknowledge the visitors as they entered the plush meeting room in the Martian Senate chamber building. He had seldom set foot in the hidden depths of the building and felt very much the outsider among the other Senate members as they all stepped forward to shake Valerie Marlborough's hand.

He worked his way down the line of her advisors and hangers-on and briskly shook her hand too. Ed Royce was already talking by that point, launching into his welcoming speech which his fellow Senators had heard time and time again. Marlborough smiled and nodded but didn't offer much back.

Marien Lyndell and Ramsey Pierce took their seats at either end of the table, leaving Raylor facing Marlborough. Royce sat by his side and ushered their own advisors out of the room. The Senate did not allow any citizens to bear witness to their meetings, a policy which offered some degree of secrecy in decision making but no end of trouble in recording and monitoring such meetings.

The Senators had gathered an hour early for the arrival of Marlborough and worked through strategy for the day. They hoped to lay some good groundwork for future discussions at the very least. Royce and Lyndell cautioned against coming on too strong but Raylor made his case for starting strong and then giving the impression of loosening the strings to work towards a compromise.

None of them believed an easy exit from the Union would be possible. They were sure Kiebler had briefed his new favourite advisor on what she could and could not say, and that only made them nervous. His unpredictability was perhaps his worst trait.

Raylor finally gained agreement that he should lead the talks. He could push further than the other Senators were willing to push, as he could hide behind his role with the Workers' Council. If he overstepped the mark, he could claim that it was his own fault for speaking out of line on behalf of his people and that he did not speak for the Senate.

Royce loved the idea. He pointed out that if Raylor made a mess of this he would take it public and make sure he was ousted from office as soon as physically possible. "For the good of the negotiations," he insisted. Raylor agreed. He would need to step down if he made any such error – removing himself from office could reset the clock on negotiations and allowed him some freedom to be as aggressive as he wished.

"Ms Marlborough, I believe it would be only proper for you to get us started," Royce spoke, the smarm dripping from him with every syllable.

Raylor noted that Marlborough's expression had not changed since she entered the room. The plastered-on smile and the deep, untrusting look in her eyes were plain to see. He wondered if the trauma of her previous visit had truly affected her or if she now had an even deeper mistrust of the Martians in general. Did she believe Kiebler's hype machine and buy into his every crackpot theory?

"Senators, I will gladly begin and I hope to keep this brief. As General Secretary to the Galactic Union let me be perfectly clear – Mars cannot, and will not, be allowed to secede from the Union. I have not come here to negotiate on any terms and will not discuss the matter on any level. Leaving the GU is off the table."

She spoke with a conviction Raylor was unsure he had seen in her before. He had done his research on her past and knew her from her public life over the last decade or two. She was a strong leader, with strong opinions, but he had seen her flip-flop on many a decision when the situation suited her. In normal circumstances he might have thought her an excellent choice to lead the GU In any circumstance which did not involve Bernard Kiebler, that is.

"Ms Marlborough, you have to understand the people made a choice. We have voted out of the GU" Lyndell spoke, smiling.

"The people should never have been given that choice. It was reckless and irresponsible to do so and you, as their leaders, should be ashamed."

"What the GU is doing is irresponsible – getting into bed with Bernie Kiebler, and selling out the entire solar system in doing so," Raylor retorted.

"He has installed me as General Secretary to ensure-"

"Oh please," Raylor interrupted, surprising even himself by how quickly his patience had worn thin. "He connived and faked his way into power. Everyone knows it. He's corrupt and you should know better than to piggy back on his fraud."

"Let me remind you that the people of Jupiter voted for President Kiebler in great numbers. Record breaking turnouts, across the planet. Why do you think that is, Mr Raylor?"

She eyed him like a sparring partner who had crossed the line with one punch too many.

"Think what you want of the scandals and the accusations laid at our President's door; you forget that ordinary, everyday Jupitoans wanted him. They are the biggest population of any single race in existence and they needed a voice. Bernard Kiebler has provided that voice and he speaks for us all."

"You're not even Jupitoan!" Raylor fumed. "Under all the grime and cheap, populist, baying-mob baiting ideas which won him all of those votes, there are people like you. Using him as an opportunity to rise up. Lending him your political credit as you ride his populism to the top."

She stared into his eyes, and he held it, knowing she was seeing them as a serious political threat for the first time. He knew in that moment that Mars could not back down and that Marlborough would do anything to beat them into submission.

"That's an outrageous accusation, coming from someone who has not even been elected to his post."

He could handle the dig at his path to the Senate seat. He knew deep down she probably held some jealousy – someone so power-hungry must hate to see others do well, especially when fate lands them in such a fortuitous position as his.

"What happened to you, Valerie?" Pierce spoke up. "You were a woman of great repute – we loved you when you were in charge of our banking sector. Such a strong leader and a force in the community. I remember you supporting my church. You were a good woman."

"No, she wasn't," Raylor said.

Marlborough seethed silently at Pierce's words. She had hired him once, for a lowly position on some task group or other. The financial sector had been the making of them both but now she looked down on him and resented him bringing up a life long since passed.

"How dare either of you question my record, past or present. It is not for you to judge me as a good, or right, or reasonable woman. I keep my own faith." She was proud of herself for keeping her head.

"Were you keeping your own faith when you abstained from voting to allow greater freedoms to Jupiter's smaller religions?" Raylor asked. "On whose faith did you base your decision to sell out your local community, where you yourself grew up? It doesn't even exist anymore, Valerie."

"I defy anyone to build the career I have had and not have to make the tough calls when necessary," she defended herself.

"They weren't tough calls, Ms Marlborough. They were opportunities. Chances for you to gain from other people's suffering. You step back from history and you wait for the dust to settle, then you pick at the bones."

Marlborough had heard enough. She gathered her paperwork and swung out of her seat, looking to Ed Royce and Marien Lyndell.

"There will be no deal – ever – with this man in the room."

The senators remained silent, allowing Raylor to take the lead.

"That's unfortunate as I will be in every room, both Senate led and Workers' Council meetings to represent my people. Mars has spoken, Valerie, just as the Jupitoans did."

"The Martian people will be disappointed then," she seethed as she turned from the table. "You should not have made them a promise you cannot keep."

"It isn't in our hands to keep it. We strike a deal with the GU or the people will come and do it for us. Revolution is in the air. Martians will willingly fight for the rights they are owed, and the freedom that they seek, whether Bernie likes it or not."

Marlborough flashed him one last vicious glance as she spun to exit the door behind her. Raylor could feel the venom in it but relaxed into a smile as the door closed.

His smile gave way to the giggles. He lost control and for a moment he could have been anywhere, laughing harder than he had for years. The tension and relief had done for him. He slowly gathered himself and looked back to his fellow Senators and found only Ramsey Pierce was smiling along.

"No turning back now," he told them.

"Did we push too hard?" Lyndell asked.

"I'm wary of pushing any harder, that's for sure," Royce joined in. "We can't be seen to be making any dramatic moves against the GU or Jupiter – if we look too aggressive and they have reason to strike back, we would be crushed."

"The only way forward is to enforce the vote. Officially declare it and give them a date. Start the process."

"I'm not sure – if we do it before securing trade deals, and god knows what else we haven't thought of yet, then we could just be throwing ourselves into the dark," Lyndell spoke, looking nervous.

"We need to take our time. Work on the negotiations," Royce agreed. "It's in your hands, Mr Raylor."

Raylor's smile shrunk only a little. He understood their concerns – a broken relationship between the Senate, the leadership of the GU and Jupiter would be hugely problematic. He wasn't sure there was any way around that while still delivering an exit from the Union to the people of Mars.

***

By the end of the day Raylor knew everything there was to know about the Galactic Union and the various treaties which had brought it into being. He researched every aspect of the trade deals and the rocky political paths and hoops that had to be jumped through, to allow a planet to walk away from the table.

He was more confident than ever that something could be done – and if Marlborough, or Kiebler, decided to stand in the way he had the firepower to strike back politically. He made a call to Bellson as he walked down the stairs and made his way into the crisp night air.

No answer. He hung up on the voicemail, knowing the man never checked them anyway and would most likely call him back whenever it pleased him, even if the phone was in his hand. He was a strange sort, James Bellson.

A shadow caught Raylor's eye as he moved across the deserted main square outside the Workers' Council offices. A man in a long, dark grey coat walked in parallel with him on the opposite side of the square.

They both arrived at the gated exit onto the main street at the same time and Raylor took the opportunity to look at the man's face, seeing if he could place him. He worked later than anyone he knew, with the exception of the security team, so it was rare to see anyone else around at this hour.

He gave a courteous nod and held open the gate and had just decided that he didn't know the man when he spoke. A gruff, unexpected voice.

"Sebastian."

"Good evening," Raylor managed to reply through hidden surprise.

"You don't know me, I'm sure," the man spoke. "I am Alexander. I have been waiting for you for a few hours now."

Raylor took a step out into the street, warily eyeing the man again. He gave away no real clues to his identity and his dull but neat clothing didn't divulge anything further. Raylor felt safer carrying on this conversation on the street, with passing traffic and handy witnesses, rather than the shadowy confines of the Workers' Plaza.

"If it's about anything to do with a legislative issue, or the GU vote, or anything along those lines you need to come back in business hours and make an appointment," he said, hoping to sound casual.

"It's not about that. Not entirely. I don't think I'd get in the door for a meeting."

"And why is that?"

"Because I work for the Peoples' of the Earth organisation."

"Earth extremists?" Raylor asked, incredulous.

"Well, we don't particularly like that label, Mr Raylor," Alex responded. "However, I understand your mistake – we don't receive a lot of time on any political platform and we certainly don't get invited to meetings with Senators on any planet, even our own."

Raylor tried to take it all in but thoughts of the kidnapping of Calhoun and Marlborough flashed through his head and hindered his own thought process. He knew of the PoE by name and reputation only – their leaders were largely anonymous and their actions highly disputed. The majority of the solar system classed them as terrorists and events such as the Calhoun kidnapping and subsequent assassination were routinely pinned on or claimed by the PoE.

"What do you want from me? I can't grant you anything, not here and now, and not without agreement from my fellow Senators. There's nothing I can do for you."

"I actually want to ask what I might do for you, Mr Raylor," Alex replied. "We waited with anticipation for your briefing after the talks with Marlborough this morning. I notice you didn't deliver that briefing."

Raylor had decided, with Senate agreement, that the content of their first negotiation with Marlborough should remain on a need to know basis for the time being. They had to piece together a clear strategy before mouthing off in public about what the GU could and should do.

"The details aren't important at this time. We'll give a full update in due course."

"I'm sure. As I'm sure you also don't want the public to ever know that Marlborough refused to even discuss the leave process. What were her words again – reckless and irresponsible?"

"How do you know that?" Raylor asked, stepping closer to the man. Any fear he had of the situation was easily clouded over by hints of a leak in his office. "Only a handful of people are aware of the details of that meeting. Who have you been speaking to?"

Alexander laughed lightly and smiled at Raylor. He held his hands out in a sign of openness which Raylor saw as a rehearsed move.

"Calm down, Sebastian. We are not the enemy. I promise you. But my sources are very good."

"Not the enemy? Is that why your people kidnapped the Vice President of the most powerful entity in the system?"

"We have not made any claim to that act. It was most likely a silly group of young men, trying to fight battles they know little about."

"Yeah. And the rumour of Calhoun's death? You want to claim that one?"

"You know as well as we do what happened to Mrs Calhoun, Senator."

"Is that right? Do you have any evidence to that end, Alexander?"

"As I say, my sources are very good."

"I bet," Raylor responded, coming almost nose to nose with the man. He hated letting himself get fired up like this and had worked hard to combat his own combustible nature over the years. You can't fully change your nature, he supposed.

"Sebastian. Please. I did not come here for a fight. Rather to tell you that Earth is ready for war too."

"Excuse me?"

"You told the General Secretary of the Galactic Union today that your people are willing to go to war for their cause, did you not?"

Raylor waited, fuming. He nodded his confirmation.

"Then I am telling you, the PoE and our affiliates are willing to stand by your side. We have a common enemy and we believe their defeat is more important than anything at this time."

"You expect me to welcome the help of murderers? You have orchestrated countless attacks on innocent people over the years. You and others of your faith. Nobody will ever give you the trust you wish for."

Alexander reached into his coat and produced a cigarette. He offered Raylor one too, even though he knew he would say no. Raylor hadn't touched the things for a decade.

"The attacks you speak of are in the past. Very much ancient history for the PoE. We have made an effort to clean up our image and remove any remnants of the inglorious past from our ranks. The other groups – I cannot speak for them any more than you can speak for the southerners of Mars."

"What's the aim of this sudden change of tact? You expect anyone to take you seriously?"

"They already have, Mr Raylor. How do you think we know about the meetings today? How do you think we hear tales of Mr Kiebler's deeds? Our message is out there. Many are beginning to see things our way."

"Is that right? And all it took was you having to stop killing people."

Raylor looked at the man with contempt but also with some degree of respect for his defence of the organisation he worked for. He wondered how far up the ranks 'Alexander' had climbed and what his real name might be. He couldn't imagine he held much power and having been sent here on a dark night to wait and deliver a message, he couldn't imagine the man had much say in how that message was shaped.

"If your superiors in the 'organisation' are serious," Raylor said "you will promise me that you stick to your word. No violence. No threats. We stick to the right and proper means."

"You will have the word of us all."

"What's your end goal? You want out of the Union?"

"Ultimately, we want to stand free from all union and see humanity return to its birthplace."

"You realise that's a crazy goal, right? Even if it was possible to return humanity to Earth – the planet would be wiped out in no time."

"It would be the end of our times, yes."

Raylor took a breath, letting the man's words swill around in his head for a moment.

"And that's fine by you?"

"It is an 'end goal', as you say."

Raylor couldn't wrap his head around the Earth extremist mentality and he was almost thankful for that fact. A devout religion based on the theory that mankind should have died with the planet Earth and dedicated to bringing about that exact objective. He considered for a moment the idea of dying for a cause and wondered if he could be bold enough to make that choice.

He wasn't sure that he could ever be so committed but he knew for certain that he could not support a cause that expressly desired the destruction of its own people.

"Negotiations. Threats of political ideas. Proper ways and means."

He looked the Earthling in the eye. The Earthling looked right back at him.

"No violence. No extremism."

"You have my word, Mr Raylor."

***

"Come in, Ms Marlborough," Kiebler shouted from the comfort of his leather sofa. He had been slouched in front of his television for two hours since dinner and had lost track of the time. As Marlborough entered the room he raised his nearly-empty beer glass to her by way of a greeting.

"Good evening, Madam Secretary," he spoke with a smile.

"Evening, Mr President. I hope it's not too late?"

"Don't be silly, Valerie, I'm just getting warmed up!" he replied. "Can I get you a drink? We have wine, if beer isn't your thing?"

He couldn't imagine beer would be quite to her taste but equally couldn't conceive of her saying no to it if it was all he had offered. She shook her head to the wine, however, and ploughed right into work talk. Kiebler admired her eagerness. He wished he could find that kind of motivation on an evening but having every television station in the known universe available to you, and knowing your face might be on a good percentage of them, was a distracting business.

"I feel that we dealt with them firmly. They can be under no illusions that Mars will not be allowed to dictate any terms to the GU" she spoke confidently.

"You met with them all? Just the Senate leaders?"

"Yes, Mr President. Sebastian Raylor seems to have taken on the role of the gang leader. He's got teeth, but in terms of playing these types of games he is just a pup."

"I like how you think, Valerie. Keep us one step ahead of them at all times."

"With regards to that, sir. I had my people do some digging while we were on the ground. I've got some very reliable intel that high-ranking members of the Senate House on Mars are meeting with PoE members."

"The extremists? Are you sure...?"

"I took my best people with me. I don't doubt what they saw and heard. It seems the PoE are cosying up to the Martians."

"Or vice versa. Who have you told?"

"Only you, so far."

"Keep it that way. But have those House members followed for now. We could try to exert some influence there – just keep it close to the chest for now."

Kiebler knew the PoE were reaching out into the solar system, trying to get their hooks into as many people they could. The higher the rank, the more pressure they would put on. He wasn't sure if a terrorist group such as the PoE aligned with some real political weight could really do much harm in the scheme of things but the thought of it reminded him of playing chess with older and smarter kids in school. The feeling that every innocuous move may be the first step in some grand stratagem.

"I wish we could deal with them more decisively but the Senate is the bigger fish right now," he smiled. "I've got a lot on my plate, Valerie."

"I'm all too aware, sir. How are the arrangements for the wedding coming along?"

"All systems go, Val. The bride is safely off with her family, the venue is prepared and I'm one-hundred percent divorced – just in the nick of time." He gave a wink with the last statement, drawing a shy smile from Marlborough.

"You know, I'm very impressed with your work on this," Kiebler pushed. "You have proven again that some experience and guile are far more useful than a successful political history – or a successful political husband for that matter."

"Thank you, it's honestly an honour."

"I mean it. I'm impressed with you as whole – who wouldn't be?"

Kiebler's smile was a sight to behold when he wanted to truly make an impact. He knew exactly the effect it would have on Valerie Marlborough in that moment.

"I could never have trusted Calhoun with this. She was flirting with the other team and she got burned."

"It's lucky she is no longer in the picture then you might say," Marlborough spoke tentatively.

"Yes indeed. A shame she ran into such awful trouble. It's almost a blessing."

"Have you had any luck in finding the perpetrators, as yet?"

"Valerie. Let's just say we can call off the search. I have a feeling they won't ever be caught for such a tragic, tragic crime."

He knew in the moment that he had gone too far. He often caught himself a fraction too late and watched his ego run off with words he shouldn't have uttered out loud. He smiled and played it off casually but could see the look on Marlborough's face – not quite shock, not quite understanding.

"Now Valerie. Don't read too much into those comments. I've had more beers tonight than I care to tell you."

Marlborough stood from the edge of the sofa where she had rested herself awkwardly. She looked Kiebler in the eye.

"I don't believe you are a man who brags haphazardly, Mr President," she spoke. "Rest assured I won't speak a word of this to another living soul."

She straightened up and Kiebler could see how tense and prickly she had become. He reached for her hand.

"Valerie, listen to me. We have had some serious obstacles to climb on our path to where we are now – and the road ahead is all uphill. You know the belligerence of Calhoun's ways when it came to this administration. We could not have her climbing into bed with the extremists and the Martians and looking to build walls around our ability to make change."

He looked into her eyes and watched as his words filtered into her brain, waiting to see her soften.

"The people want change, Valerie. The people voted for change. Bernie Kiebler is that change. Heather Calhoun was just another obstacle to climb."

"She was resistant to change..." Marlborough uttered, barely even audibly.

"She was that. We would have been foolish to let her go on that way," Kiebler spoke softly, putting an arm around Marlborough's shoulder.

"Valerie, you have to understand that it isn't going to come easily. Some blood will have to be spilled. Casualties are an inevitability of war."

She nodded softly and Kiebler knew he had her. He was convinced that he could persuade her into believing anything in that moment.

"Make no mistake about it, Madam Secretary; we are at war."

CHAPTER FIFTEEN

The people of Seo-Sing City flooded the streets on the morning of their President's wedding day. The sun blazed as the crowds grew, until there was barely a foot of free standing space within three miles of the ceremony itself. Kiebler's car – a traditional gas-guzzling Oldsmobile – ground its way through throngs of citizens slowly, as he waved and smiled at his people. He loved it for all of fifteen minutes, taking in the adoration and feeling the genuine love of those who had voted for him.

He began to grow tired of it as they swarmed around the vehicle, causing noise and chaos as the driver incessantly beeped his horn to clear the path and they ignored his every beep. They had left an hour early in anticipation of the crowds but Kiebler dispatched two security men from the car in his impatience, forcing them to muscle the baying crowd away from the vehicle to allow it to move ahead at a steadier speed.

He was glad to arrive at the church – a grand, old-style cathedral, built of twisted metal and glass. The crowds were kept well at bay from the actual building, allowing him to climb from the car, give a final wave and head inside to the sound of cheers and screams from his supporters.

In the gloomy reception area he asked the guards and various hangers on to stand down as he approached his family. He had seen very little of his children since the news of 'the other woman' had broke and Xanthe had taken some persuading to get them here today. Kiebler had to hand it to Dax – he had put in all of the work and there they were; Ali, Melanie and Bernie Junior alongside their statuesque mother.

"Junior!" he yelled as he stretched out to shake his young boy's hand. Bernie Junior took it meekly, looking up at his mother as he did so. The girls were greeted next – Ali, the eldest, barely able to hide her contempt for the man she called her father, and Melanie, always more of a daddy's girl clearly struggling to hold back. She wanted to hug her father, give him forgiveness for all of the family and welcome him back into the fold, but at the same time she was all too aware of the purpose of their gathering.

"I'm so glad you all could come – life keeps on changing but family is family," Bernie smiled.

"We do as we are forced to do," Ali replied, under her breath. Kiebler looked at her then to her mother; his anger just barely disguised behind his disappointment.

"She's got a smart mouth on her, your daughter," he spoke directly to Xanthe. "It'll serve you well in college I'm sure but you'd best start thinking about the real world and how people might treat you," he continued, now looking his daughter directly in the eye.

"You want to start a lecture on how to treat people?" Ali snapped back.

Bernie looked again to Xanthe, hoping for some support. His now ex-wife offered only a stoic look in return.

"You get control of her. I'm sure Mr Scion has expressed how important today is going to be. No cock-ups." He spoke with aggression, not liking when things don't go exactly as planned. He gave one last look to his kids and ruffled Junior's hair before wandering off.

"I'm your daughter too," Ali shouted after him.

He turned to look back at her and his former life. He knew it all too well – she was growing up to be her father's daughter and he didn't enjoy it one bit.

***

The ceremony went off without a hitch, and at around twenty minutes past midday, Bernard and Sonya Kiebler walked down the aisle to rapturous applause from their friends, family and critics.

Five rows back, alone on the end of the aisle, sat Xanthe. The children had been placed in the front row to show their public support for their father and his new bride. As the happy couple passed by, Xanthe stepped out into the aisle for all to see. The applause died for a moment, and silence filled the vast cathedral. Finally, after what felt like a lifetime to Bernie, his ex-wife gave a graceful bow of her head to him and then took Sonya's hand in hers and gently kissed it.

The response in the cavernous old space was loud enough to give him chills every time he thought back to that moment. Pre-planned or not, it went down perfectly as intended. President Bernard Kiebler's image as the loving leader of the solar system was cemented in stone.

***

The reception was held at one of his own hotels – a grand jewel in his property portfolio. Guests paid upwards of three thousand Jupitoan dollars per night for the privilege of staying here – and he had raised it to five thousand for this weekend only. People flocked to the hotel – the upper crust of Jupitoan society would have paid twice the price to be able to say that they spent the night celebrating with the President himself.

He made his speech to the assembled guests with little preparation, standing on ceremony alone. Flanked by the Presidential guard alongside the high table, his highest ranking staff by his side and

General Wilson Hasting in full military regalia, he felt the words didn't so much matter. The visual would remain with people for all of their lives.

He spoke to his wife personally and invented a well of love and inspiration for her on the spot. She smiled and cried. Kiebler was impressed for a moment. He wasn't sure if it was genuinely overwhelming or if she really was that good of an actress. Not bad for a common whore, he thought to himself.

He spoke to his children and promised them a life of happiness and of two families merged together in one beautiful future; one in which Jupiter would prosper just as they all would. He thanked Xanthe and wished her happiness too. She remained stony faced throughout. He warily eyed the photographers who had their lenses trained on his ex-wife and made a mental note to ensure Daxler had coached them well. A picture of her bitter face in the press tomorrow would undo so much of their good work.

It was the biggest day of his life, so they told him, but he worked through it like just another day at the office. A process and a procession and a damn fine acting job. He almost wished he could confess to the entire plot, just to receive the credit he thought he deserved for actually pulling it off. He smiled to himself at the notion and thanked the people for attending.

"Now if you'll excuse me, I must retire to my room for some urgent Presidential business," he spoke with a laugh and looked at his new wife.

Ten minutes later, Sonya Kiebler was left to her own devices in a plush high-level suite, while her new husband retired to his top floor penthouse alone.

***

General Hasting escorted the President from the dining hall and waited until Kiebler was safely in the custody of his own presidential guard before taking his leave. He had stood by his president's side throughout the speeches and the dinner and remained the loyal servant, all the while looking forward to getting away from the stuffy hotel and discussing the events of the day with someone less fake than those surrounding him.

Climbing into the elevator to leave, Hasting stopped in his tracks. A group of men entered the building via a fire exit door, which led directly to the car park. He eyed the men intently, not recognising them as guests from the wedding nor as security staff. The majority of the personnel on duty were either military or law enforcement and Hasting knew them to a man.

He stepped away from the elevator and calmly followed the path of the group. There were six in total, all dressed in fine, ill-fitting, suits. They barged through the hotel hallway and crossed the lobby quickly.

Hasting remained at a distance behind, seeing that they were heading towards the dining room. Small groups of guests were now lingering in the area, waiting for the evening festivities to begin.

At the dining room entrance, two of the men split off from the group and tried their best to inconspicuously take strategic positions at either side of the double glass doors. Hasting took a breath and proceeded past the two men, not making eye contact. He felt their gaze upon him as he passed into the room.

He watched for the remaining four, and saw them making their way to the far corner of the room. They turned down the waitresses offering nibbles and champagne along the way. Halfway across the room Hasting paused and took up the offer of champagne. He made a show of sipping at it, without ingesting a drop.

His eyes were locked on the corner of the room. A larger group was positioned at the table there. Some faces he had seen throughout the day, others he guessed had joined the party for the evening only. As the group parted to welcome the four newbies, he saw them. Without their truncheons, bottles and electro-mech rifles, the three men were unremarkable. Hasting would never forget their faces though and he felt his blood boil as soon as recognition dawned on him.

The three men who had attacked him and left him for dead were sat at the table, laughing and joking together with the rest of the group. From their movements he could tell they were armed.

Mustering all of the subtleness he could reach for, he coolly turned his back on the thugs and caught the eye of one of the deputies standing guard at the high table. Within minutes his orders were set and he knew that these men wouldn't be leaving the building as free men.

He waited.

He checked on assignments and congratulated the family of the bride. He mingled with guests from politicians to reporters to high financiers who wanted to touch the insignia and ask about the wars he had seen.

All the while he kept an eye on the corner of the room, and on his three assailants. Finally, an hour or so later, one of them made a move for the restroom. The tallest of the group – the thin man who had brandished a truncheon on that fateful night - strode confidently through the room. Hasting followed.

In the toilets, the thin man ducked into a cubicle and left the door open. Hasting stood patiently by, listening to the sound of his piss mostly missing the toilet. As the flow slowed he chose his moment and kicked the door hard. It slammed against the back of the thin man and knocked him off balance, sending him stumbling forward against the toilet.

"What the fuck!" he yelled, desperately reaching to avoid smashing his head against the wall, putting his leg in his own piss and trying to zip up his fly all at once.

Hasting was on him before he could adjust. He spun the man around, and held him by his suit jacket – then slammed him hard against the wall. The man groaned and, after a few seconds, took in the sight of his attacker. He almost laughed a resigned and doleful laugh, then spat in Hasting's face.

"How sweet of you to remember me," Hasting growled.

He struggled but had little chance of escaping. General Hasting was two or three inches shorter but was built solidly and was entirely unmovable when he wanted to be. The struggling gained the man nothing but a wet, piss-soaked trouser leg.

"What are you here for? How did you get in?"

The man shouted for help, screaming loudly. Hasting had taken care of the door on his way in. There was no help to be had.

"Nobody listens to the pleas of racist thugs. It's the society we live in," Hasting started. "Now tell me – how did you get here?"

"I won't tell you shit. We should have made sure you were dead," he came back.

"I'd have to agree. You're already a racist, neo-fascist scumbag – you didn't need 'failed murderer' on that CV did you? You think you could get much lower?"

"Fuck you!" the thin man instinctively replied, as he again struggled for freedom.

"I can think of lower, actually," Hasting answered for him and pulled hard on the lapels of his suit jacket, bringing the man's head down hard and fast. He adjusted quickly, tucking his head to avoid it banging against the toilet bowl – and plunged it directly into his own urine.

Hasting held him for a moment. Just long enough.

"Tell me why you are here?" he asked again as he pulled the head from the toilet.

"S-sec-security! We're working security!" the thin man gasped and spluttered, rancid liquid running from his eyes as he was pulled upright like a ragdoll.

"I'm in charge of security here. Try again," Hasting told him and motioned to pull his head below once more.

"Scion! Scion! He hired us... private stuff... needed muscle to protect the Pres-" he wasn't able to finish his sentence.

Hasting pulled him close with one arm and slammed his other elbow hard into the man's head, knocking him out cold. He let go and allowed the man's limp body to fall awkwardly over the toilet.

He washed his hands and face carefully then left the restrooms and ordered an officer in to make the arrest.

Back in the lobby, Hasting looked around. He needed to find Daxler Scion.

***

Valerie Marlborough stalked through the dining room with one man on her mind - Daxler Scion.

She found him cosying up to a group of banking associates she herself had hired many years ago. They seemed pleased to see her but she didn't give them a second thought – former colleagues were just as useless as former lovers, in her book.

She asked their forgiveness and dragged Scion away from the crowd. He was reluctant, feeling the time was ripe to make some acquaintances – Daxler was of the opinion that you could never have too many friends in high places.

"What is so urgent that it should take me away from our guests?" he asked her when they had strayed far enough from prying ears.

"The police just arrested a man in the toilets. The press are all over it,"

"Arrested? For what?"

"I don't know that. And neither do the press. So you can imagine..." she said.

"Yes. The rumour mills will be grinding into gear. Do we know who this man was?" he asked.

"He looked like one of your men," she whispered in reply. "One of your, ah, 'private' security team."

Scion felt a pang of nervousness at that – not due to the apparent arrest, but at the fact that Marlborough knew about his private security. Only Kiebler could have shared that information with her, which tipped him off on just how valued Valerie Marlborough was becoming in the eyes of the President.

"I will take care of the press. I'm sure the story is nothing anyway, but I'll deal with my people too," he assured her.

"Daxler, I hope you know what you are doing?" Marlborough asked.

"I'm not sure I understand what you are implying, Ms Marlborough?"

She took a moment to compose her thoughts. He was being facetious and they both knew it, so she would have to be careful in pushing the matter any further.

"I have simply noticed a large segment of some very well known undesirables around the hotel this evening. I'm sure they didn't get in here alone," she said bluntly.

"Mr Kiebler is a man of the people, Valerie. Anyone is welcome here."

"Anyone who could pass the pre-checks and pay the hotel bill, surely?"

She eyed him carefully, wondering if he would defend his position at all. Scion stood and eyed her back, silently.

"If you have hired a personal security force out of the dregs of society then so be it – but make sure they are behaving themselves. How many arrests can you cover up?"

Scion took that on board and nodded his acknowledgement. The pair stood in an awkward holding pattern for a moment, neither having much to say to the other in any other context.

"I'm going to find our President and ensure he hears about this in the right manner. No doubt he's in his room studying the news coverage of the day, rather than playing his part in it."

She took her leave and Daxler watched her go quietly. As she strutted away across the room he spotted someone else marching towards him with clear intent.

"General Hasting, I thought you had retired for the evening," he spoke as the General caught up with him.

"I'm sure you have heard by now that there has been some trouble. I couldn't step away just yet," Hasting replied.

"Yes, unfortunate business. I am just on my way to get to the bottom of it," Scion hissed.

Hasting used all of his inner strength to resist laying hands on the man and shaking the truth out of him.

"You hired men to work here tonight?" Hasting asked.

"That's Presidential business and I'm not at liberty to discuss it, General,"

"You hired men. Do you know who you hired? Were you aware?"

The General could feel his anger growing and forced it back down. He had to remain calm and hear the full explanation or the excuses.

"General, we have to ensure the privacy and security of the President at all times. We know what we are doing,"

"Did you know that you have hired the men who attacked me?"

Scion didn't speak. A brief hesitation.

"Did you know them before, Scion? Did you know these men before they left me for dead in the gutter?"

Hasting was almost chest to chest with Daxler now – towering over the diminutive man.

"How do you know it was these men, specifically? General, you suffered serious brain injuries that night – your mind could tell you I was responsible for the attack and you might believe it."

"There are many layers to that term, Daxler," Hasting responded, pushing closer still so that Scion had to take a step back. "Responsible?" he questioned, letting the word hang in the air. He pressed forward again, backing Scion fully against the wall. Hasting lowered his head to look down into the face of the Presidential advisor.

"Quite," Daxler replied, breathlessly. "Perhaps, Wilson, these men who attacked you weren't quite the men you made them out to be. Not racists or rioters at all. Perhaps they simply did not like this aggressive side you are displaying now. Perhaps the whole thing was your own fault after all," he spoke.

Hasting stared a moment more into the threatened eyes before him. He stepped away from the man and allowed him space to breath.

"I will speak with the GU tonight. I have one of your men in custody and the others will find my forces waiting for them when they attempt to leave this building."

He smiled as he backed slowly away from Daxler Scion.

"The truth will out, Daxler," he warned.

***

Marlborough pressed the button for the penthouse suite and stepped back. She was surprised to see no guards in the elevator but knew, even before she heard of Scion's personal security team, that the hotel would be the safest place in the known universe on this night.

As the doors opened slowly to the penthouse floor, Marlborough heard the sound of muffled voices. She stepped cautiously into the hallway and approached the inner doors, which were left ajar. The noise became clearer as she moved and she recognised the sound of Bernie Kiebler's silky voice. A female voice followed his but was abruptly cut off as his own tone rose up a notch.

She crept towards the open doors and peered warily inside – darkness filled the elaborate living area, with only a warm glow of light from a far off bedroom spilling into the room. She could tell the voices were in there and a sick but thrilling feeling filled Valerie Marlborough – she was listening in on Bernie and his new wife's first time alone after their wedding.

She hovered at the door, not daring to disturb the happy couple, but straining to hear every word and noise emanating from the bedroom. She felt a gnawing in her gut that she was doing wrong and a wan smile stretched across her thin, withered lips.

"Shit doesn't always go the way you want it to, sweetheart," Kiebler's voice was almost booming now. "But I'm the President of this fucking place, and this is my hotel no less."

Marlborough couldn't hear the response but could sense the frustration in Kiebler's voice in his reply.

"You like what you see? You always were one for watching and not doing. Don't like to get those manicured hands dirty?"

The voice responded louder this time and Valerie's ears pricked up as she tried again to pick out the words. She didn't glean anything from her efforts but thought she heard a soft groan mixed in with it all.

"I won't ask you again," Kiebler shouted this time, making Marlborough jump as the sound something being thrown echoed through the empty living room, followed by the sound of glass shattering.

She stepped gently into the room, hoping to hear more, and the sound of a belt and the rustling of clothes again hit her in the pit of her stomach.

The moaning came louder and more aggressive than she expected. She could have sworn she could pick out a sob in between the expected noises.

A moment passed. Marlborough felt her own exposure greatly now and stepped back into the hallway, reluctant to move further and reveal her presence. The cries grew louder now and she didn't know what to make of those.

"Turn over you fucking whore," came Kiebler's voice and, a moment later, a slap of skin and a definitive shriek of pain.

Marlborough froze on the spot, incapacitated.

The grunts and moans and the sickening cries grew louder and more frequent until Kiebler's guttural call echoed again through the room and the noise abruptly ended. A fumbling, rustling followed.

Silence.

"Now get the fuck out of here. And say one goddamn word... Pay very careful attention to what I'm saying here, Xanthe. Not a fucking word."

Marlborough staggered back a step in shock as Xanthe stumbled and fell out of the bedroom and into the darkness. Her hair was messier than she had ever seen it; her dress looked torn in places. Her underwear was in her hand as she struggled to her feet and made her way towards the door.

Marlborough stepped forward, feigning as if she had just arrived. She reached to knock on the door, hoping she would not be found out. Xanthe barely glanced at her as she passed by and barged into the waiting elevator.

Marlborough saw the red raw patches on her body, the filthy stains on her dress, as she struggled to pull her underwear up. Their eyes locked on to each other as the doors slowly closed, leaving Marlborough in near total darkness.

Marlborough gathered her senses. She felt the shock flowing through to her limbs, felt weakness in her legs. Her head spiralled out of control. She heard the movement of Kiebler in the room next door and knew she couldn't make a clean escape quickly enough.

She knocked on the door and entered. Kiebler appeared from the bedroom, looking as dapper as earlier, while redoing the knot in his tie.

"Valerie. This is a surprise. Come to check up on your fearless leader?" he spoke cheerily.

"Yes... No, sir. I came to..." she fumbled her words and hoped she could recover before it was too obvious.

"Spit it out, Valerie, I'm missing my big day for this," he said, beaming.

"I just hoped you weren't spending the big day alone watching news coverage. I know your ways, Mr President," she finally spoke.

"You know my ways, Valerie?" The smarm dripped from his voice.

"I mean to say," she started but again faltered.

"Did you see my ex-wife leaving the penthouse, Valerie?"

She didn't utter a word. He looked at her calmly and pulled his tie firmly up into place, folding his shirt collar neatly over the top.

"Valerie, I know you are the type of person I can trust. I know you understand the ways, as you say, of a man in my position. I work hard – harder than anyone – and I suffer for it every day. No rest for the wicked, didn't they used to say?"

He asked it with a twinkle in his eye, walking ever closer to his Secretary of Communications.

"And I admit I have a little wicked in me, Valerie. You've seen it. You know it. It's what keeps me driven, what makes me so vibrant. Should I have to give that up to be 'The Man', Valerie?"

He reached Marlborough, standing not two foot inside the door of the suite. He reached one hand out and gently touched the side of her face as she looked down, unable to make eye contact with this man she admired but could not rationalize.

"What do you want to do here, Valerie? Do you dare to judge me? Do you understand the pressures of being Bernie Kiebler, day in and day out? A man of many tastes and desires – a man who naturally holds such sway over certain people."

He smiled and raised her chin gently with his hand. He looked directly into her eyes, more intently than ever before.

"You know this, Valerie. You know all about my sway over the fairer sex."

He reached slowly forward, leaning in to kiss her cheek. She blanched, pulling away but he grasped at her wrist and pulled her firmly towards him.

"Valerie," he whispered.

She squirmed for a moment, then relaxed into it. She considered his words and wondered if maybe he wasn't wrong. Maybe he wasn't as mad as he had seemed. There's an explanation for everything, in a just and logical world, she thought to herself.

She looked back into his eyes and allowed him to lean closer still. She pursed her lips and closed her eyes slowly, waiting to feel his kiss when the room shook.

Suddenly and violently.

A millisecond after the shaking, the booming sound vibrated through the walls. A shuddering, dull, deafening sound followed by glass breaking, alarms sounding. The lights went out and the whirring of the back-up generator was heard amongst the chaos, before that too cut off.

A second boom blasted out and the resulting tremble throughout the penthouse suite was enough to send picture frames tumbling from the walls and knock both Kiebler and Marlborough off balance.

Screams could be heard from the streets below. Sirens wailed.

CHAPTER SIXTEEN

C hoking dust filled the air in one dense cloud. Hasting lay motionless on the floor of the dining room, holding his breath deeply. He waited a moment or two to gather his thoughts and make the right decision. He looked around and saw that the dust to his right was flowing away. He began to crawl in the same direction, hoping to find an open window or door. He was acutely aware of the rising temperature in the room and knew that soon he would be following smoke, not dust, to the way out.

It didn't take him long to reach some clearer air. His senses recovered, he managed to get to his feet and help several others up too. Chaos reigned around him – screams and calls for help mingled with the hotel's fire alarm and the sound of sirens coming from outside. From a standing position, he found that he could see clearly through the settling dust.

To his right he could see the high table was completely destroyed. Ash and fire stood in place of the bride and groom's spaces, while the table itself was mangled and tossed across the floor. Fire raged in the far corner, where Hasting's attackers had sat with their gang of hired goons earlier. To the left, the smoke spiralled outwards through a huge chasm in the wall and ceiling; the early evening sky could be seen perfectly clearly beyond.

Hasting had his bearings now and could hear the emergency vehicles approaching outside. He resolved to stay and guide people to safety, knowing that the further back that people were sitting, the less likely they were to have any visibility of the way out. He made his way carefully forward, approaching the area where a band had been setting up to perform. The bass player's amp fizzed with electrical current, while fire crackled at its centre. The player himself lay face down nearby and Hasting could see the charred black texture of his face. The rest of the band were not to be found and the sounds of screams came louder still from the darker corners of the room.

Hasting ploughed ahead, grabbing a table covering and holding it to his mouth to protect himself from the smoke. The high table lay in his path and he pulled at it, then watched it crumble to nothing. He kicked out at the remaining section and walked through, unhindered. Flames licked at the edges of the room and he saw another hole blasted into the wall – this time opening out into a hotel hallway, itself now filling with thick black smoke.

He pulled a struggling guest from under a pile of rubble, and set her back on her feet. He passed the cloth to her to cover her mouth and pointed in the direction of the exit. He could hear the gush of hoses now and voices shouting and organising. He knew anyone making their way towards the demolished wall section would be rescued. He pressed forward, grateful that the smoke was flowing quickly, creating some small airflow under the thick cover above.

He reached the crackling flames of what was once the bride and groom's seats. As he shielded his face from the heat with one arm, he looked at the damage and surmised that whatever had been set off in the room it had to have been here. It had to have been aimed to take out the most honoured guests.

A speck of white caught his eye. He poked at the rubble around his feet to reveal more. The white became black and charred quickly. He followed it up and found a leg, bent and twisted. Panicked, he grabbed at the debris with his hands and dug out a hole furiously.

The new Mrs. Kiebler lay in front of him – burnt and broken. He picked her off the floor as gently as he could. Her head bobbed, her lips kissed by fire. He turned to leave with the bride in his arms as the fire licked at his heels.

As he stepped carefully back through the way he had came, he heard noises coming from the hallway, closely followed by three of Kiebler's security team bumbling through the gap in the wall. Behind them stood Bernard Kiebler, peering into the room he had left as his wedding venue and returned to as his own personal hell.

Hasting looked into his eyes as he stared across the room and saw him catch sight of his now dead wife. He saw fear cross Bernie Kiebler's face for the first time. Then he watched as it turned to anger within a second.

Hasting knew in that moment that war was coming; no matter who they found to be responsible.

CHAPTER SEVENTEEN

K aleb had worked hard for weeks in his so-called office, figuring out a way to take every TV network in Jupiter out of commission for one night only. He had broken every firewall and rewritten hidden policies for endless hours, creating himself a pathway into the frameworks which would, when the time was right, allow him to replace the standard scheduled programming with his own feed.

Isaiah didn't feel bad. He kept him working at it as a back-up but knew it was all in vain. The capacity to achieve such a thing was incredible and he loved Kaleb's mind for being able to crack things that he himself couldn't even begin comprehend.

However, he knew that once the big night came and the bombs exploded, the networks would be begging the Peoples of Earth for interview time.

Isaiah had the word put out on a strict deadline – the notion of the PoE being responsible for the attack was on the streets before the building had even been evacuated. The fires were still being put out when the first calls came.

Every network, on Jupiter and beyond, had made contact within the hour. Only a small cell of people knew the details of the attack and only a select few contacts had been given the correct information on who was truly behind it all. Isaiah began to field calls himself after a while, knowing that those who had managed to get through to him directly had really done the hard work in getting there.

He demanded thirty minutes of air time and that he be left alone to speak to the people. He didn't want an interviewer, or a hack like Sam Heighway, messing with his words and twisting the meanings. He wanted it to be live so that no producer or editor could bury the message or make the PoE out to be cold-blooded killers with no agenda.

He wanted to ensure that every person on the planet, along with anyone watching off-world, would have no doubt of the motives and intentions of the Peoples of Earth. That went for those on Earth who still did not believe and refused to turn back to the old ways. He needed everyone to understand.

At midnight all stations gave their air time over to the PoE and Isaiah Redman, the stubbled and tanned, thirty-eight year old leader of the Peoples of Earth organisation.

"Bernard Kiebler. Your loyalists, supporters and friends are dead. Your wedding day is over. Your honeymoon is over. Your beautiful new wife, now a victim of your greed and blasphemy. I'm sure you are very upset.

"Locals, immigrants, men, women and children alike have all been punished for your acts. For the acts of all mankind at this time.

"Tonight was retaliation. Retaliation for the way you rape the solar system. Retaliation for the way you dishonour your God. Retaliation for the pressure and demands you have made of the Galactic Union in recent days.

"It is not acceptable for one man, and one planet, to exert this influence over others. There will be no end to your corruption, just as there has been no slowing down of the abhorrent defiling of the worlds created around us. Earth is enough and we will now make our stand against your affront to our Lord and our People.

"The expansion of business into the further reaches of space beyond the known planets is absolutely forbidden under our holy laws. Earth is enough.

"The Martian Senate agrees with us on this point. The Workers' Council of Mars agrees with us on this point. The Galactic Union must agree too, or there will be further consequences.

"We suggest you leave your post with immediate effect, Mr Kiebler. Worse is to come."

He abruptly cut the live transmission there, depriving the universe of the thirty minutes of voyeur television they so badly wanted. Kaleb fed in a pre-made video of Earth as it was and as it is now. The PoE had devised the narration and Isaiah had agreed to air it although he didn't think it matched their new ethos.

The Peoples of Earth were openly and publicly a terrorist organisation now. They would fight the war they so badly wanted – Isaiah hoped it was a war they could win.

CHAPTER EIGHTEEN

The air in the office of the President was heavy with melancholy. There was anger and pain and frustration too but, as the advisors filed in, gloom was the pervasive feeling on all of their minds.

Kiebler arrived last, his jet black suit and tie looking perfect while his face told a different story. His staff had not seen him cry before. He had refused point blank any time they had asked him to show some emotion and weakness in public.

At the funeral of his new wife, he cried. Many people saw this strong and powerful man broken and cried too. Those who knew him well had a feeling this was not coming from the grief of a newly widowed husband – those tears were of humiliation, of defeat and of pent up anger at the situation life had dealt him.

"Let's make this crystal-fucking-clear, right off the bat," he spoke as he stepped behind his desk. "I will not ever be giving up this office. The people of Jupiter voted me into this place and if anyone wants me out they will have to take out the entire population first."

Daxler Scion bristled at this statement. General Hasting, Valerie Marlborough and Donald Orsay all stood from their seats to greet the President.

"Mr President, while I wholly agree with your sentiments, we may want to be more careful with our words when you speak out publically against these terrible events," Scion offered.

"You want me to mince my words, Dax? Want me to soften my image?" he snapped back.

"Not at all. I just think the words you have just said to us could be construed as war-like by anyone who would wish to take them obtusely."

"Dax, look me in the eye." Kiebler leaned forward, pressing his palms flatly against the desk and looking intently into his Chief of Staff's eyes.

"I am declaring war on the Earth extremists. I'm going to wipe them out, every last one. Their mothers, fathers, children, pets. All of them. Not only that, but anyone who is found to have collaborated with them - on this attack and any future attempt. Any link I find, no matter how small and trivial, will be punished severely. I'll blow the whole fucking planet Earth out of the solar system if I have to."

Scion sat back in his seat, recognising there was no arguing with his senior here. The silence hung heavy for a moment.

"Orsay, Marlborough. You know who met with these people on Mars. You know their links to the Senate?"

"Ms Marlborough provided us with detailed intel after her last visit, yes sir," Orsay replied.

"I want a warning sent out to the governments of Earth and Mars specifically, letting them know that we will leave no stone unturned and if they offer up any information now they will do themselves huge favours down the line."

"What about the Workers' Council of Mars?" Marlborough asked.

"Oh the Workers' Council! Raylor's gang. They got special praise from our friends the terrorists, didn't they?" Kiebler laughed. "I want them watched and followed; I want every detail of their lives documented. I want bank records, call logs. I want to nail them to whatever it is they're up to."

"What about links on the inside, sir?" Hasting spoke up.

"The inside?" Kiebler asked, incredulous.

"General Hasting has it in his head that your wedding party may have included several undesirables. I have assured him that if they were involved in the plot, surely they would have left the building before the explosion? As it happens they have been left dead or horribly disfigured."

Kiebler considered this for a moment. He understood that some of the so-called undesirables had been hired by Scion for good reason but had no proof that they weren't involved in any other dealings. He supposed it didn't matter for now, as they were all out of the picture.

"Hasting, we don't have time for personal vendettas or for grudges to be held," he spoke to his General. "I'll take care of things from the inside, don't worry about that. I need you on Mars duty – the Belt more specifically. I want you stationed there and within easy reach of Mars. Your presence will be well noted."

"I will carry out whatever duty you have for me, Mr President."

"I knew I'd make a loyal commander out of you one day, General," Kiebler said with a smile.

"It's my duty to my nation and my people, sir." Hasting said, hoping that the distinction was very clear.

***

The Martian Senate resumed two days after the Jupiter attacks. Much of the initial discussions were full of fury, as speaker after speaker denounced the terrorist actions and made clear that nobody in the Senate approved of such disgusting tactics.

The Peoples of Earth had a representative group on Mars and they chose this day to attend their first open Senate meeting. They were roundly heckled by the Workers' Council reps at their first attempt to contribute to the discussion, to the point where nobody heard a word of their point. James Bellson was happy with that turn of events and gave a smile towards Sebastian Raylor, up on the bench. He received a concerned frown in response.

Raylor knew that the PoE were here for the publicity and that most likely they hoped to be lambasted and shouted at to the point of rage or even actual aggression – what a great story that would be in the evening press, showing those on the morally right side of history losing their minds. He pleaded for calm when it came time for him to speak.

"People, from all walks of life, have come today to hear the words and truths of a democratic society. We will talk, we will debate and we will furrow a clear path through these dark times.

"Reason must prevail. So with a heavy heart, I ask that you all remain quiet and allow our Earth representatives to answer my questions."

The raucousness was only roused by this but died down in a moment as people settled into the idea of Raylor questioning the outsiders.

"So, gentlemen. Do you have any rationale to begin with, for the atrocities your people have taken credit for?" Raylor asked.

The representative for the PoE was a gaunt man, with hollow looking eyes. He looked like he hadn't slept for a month and his voice was barren of any real tone or inflection.

"We neither agree with nor denounce the actions of the small band of PoE cells who have taken such drastic actions. However we must stand behind the cause – it is one which will affect us all."

"You believe people must die for you to have your way?" Raylor forced.

"Some believe that a forceful approach is the only way to make our case now. We have been ignored for too long. We must be listened to, Mr Raylor."

Raylor laughed. Openly and viciously.

"Listened to? You will never be listened to again in any serious political forum. Your presence here today is a mockery. You – or these small cells - who you don't agree with but do? – have destroyed any chance you had of legitimacy. And don't get me wrong - that was an infinitesimally small chance to begin with."

Howls of laughter, whoops and cheers filled the Senate chamber for a moment. Raylor didn't smile, but kept his eyes locked on the PoE reps.

Edward Royce stood to speak and Raylor gave him a nod to go ahead. He had figured the man would have his say at some point today and was eager to find out where he stood – he knew he couldn't stand for terrorism but at the same time knew Royce could never bring himself to align with the left.

"Mr Raylor, your baiting and deriding is all well and good but wasn't it you yourself who first had contact with these shady... people?"

"I met with some representatives of the PoE organisation, yes. I have been open about those talks," Raylor replied.

"Is it not then true that you involved them in the political discourse?"

"They came to me in secret as they didn't have a voice and wanted to be heard by someone. They had the same thoughts and fears as we all share on Kiebler and the GU"

"And now look what has happened. You give these people a voice and they take a President's wife."

"I made it explicitly clear to them – and to all of you in this room – that there would be no violence of any sort. Not with the sanction of the Workers' Council, or the Senate of Mars."

"Well I'm afraid Mr Kiebler does not listen to your words of idealism, Mr Raylor," the PoE man spoke again. "He has committed acts of violence that the greater public does not even know of yet. He has begun something and our movement cannot now be stopped."

"This is not a movement. This is a rot. Your organisation, your terror cells, are a disease. It will destroy us all unless it is checked."

"The words of a bitter man. A man who promised the people their freedom and did not have the balls to deliver it. Why have you not abdicated from the Galactic Union yet, Mr Raylor?" the gaunt man asked, his tone still level and unwavering.

"He makes a sound point," Royce joined in. "These people see terror as the only way to gain freedom from the GU and Jupiter's rule. Our people were led to a vote and you stand and talk but don't deliver the rights and freedoms you have promised. The people grow impatient."

"Ever an opportunist, Mr Royce?" Raylor asked. He had worried about this – the first sign of any distraction, or any disruption in the process of things, Royce was there to pick holes. He wanted the idea of failure to begin festering in people's brains and for the public to grow restless with the seeming lack of movement. He was a clever politician; he had to hand that to him.

"I am merely suggesting you may not be focused on the real task at hand and should you wish to step aside and let someone else take the lead, then so be it."

"So, you would step into the breach? And do what differently? Have the Senate cosy up to the PoE and adopt their tactics? You're as much a part of this Senate as I am, Royce. You haven't set the wheels in motion because you don't believe the planet should leave the GU. You've made that quite clear."

"I have been clear that I represent our people, Mr Raylor. As do us all. You have been leading on this matter and I am simply saying there must be ways to handle our business which we have not discussed, I am sure-" Royce began, but Raylor could not let him finish.

"You make me sick, Royce. Scheming at a time like this? Representing our people? You'll represent whatever makes you look good on any given day," Raylor spat with ferocity.

"These people have killed – murdered innocent citizens, at a wedding no less. It's not the first and won't be the last time that they will go to such disturbing lengths. We will fight to get out of the GU any way we can - but not like that. If you, and anyone in this room, believes that the Senate of Mars should get further into bed with these fundamentalists then you should know the Workers' Council and all of our members will oppose you at every turn."

The Workers' Council representatives in the front row stood to applaud the words of their leader. The rest of the chamber was in harmonious uproar. Raylor could feel the tides of revolution coming and hoped in that moment that he could keep his head above water long enough.

***

The shuttle shuddered as it turned in mid-space, the internal gears working away with a satisfying wrenching noise. The crew in the pilot's cabin grabbed onto the side rails and adjusted their footing, while watching the breathtaking view of the solar system spin away to their right.

Kiebler knew he could be in a comfy chair in his office down the hallway. The stabilisers and soft lighting back there made you feel at home and never once alerted you to any kind of movement of the ship itself. However, it also had no windows to speak of and the views from the pilot's cabin were never to be missed.

He also didn't like to miss out on any action. Be it just a routine change of flight plan, or the simple sight of another ship ploughing its way through space nearby, he had to witness it. He talked with the pilots and other crew, imagining they were impressed by his presence up here where he didn't belong.

He tried to imagine past President's riding up here. He was willing to bet that very few of them ever had. He tried harder to imagine Heather Calhoun up here and almost let out a laugh. He couldn't imagine she would inspire much hope or confidence in the flight crew; the best she could have achieved was to see her own demise coming sooner.

"Sir, we are about to dock. If you will please take a seat, we'll bring it in," the co-pilot spoke with a smile.

Kiebler thanked the crew, and wandered back to his office. He lit up a cigar and sat back in his soft leather seat, feet firmly planted on the desk.

After a few minutes, the low hum of the engines died down and Kiebler knew they had docked securely. A gentle breeze could be felt as fresh atmosphere from outside of the ship swept inside. He wasn't entirely sure you could call it 'fresh' or 'atmosphere' when it was coming from another stale old source but he decided not to over think it as one of his staff poked his head into his office.

"Sir, we have successfully docked with the pod. Do you want the foreman to be escorted to your office when he is found?"

"No, no. I came all this way. I want to see this damn thing. Round me up some security and come get me in five minutes."

Ten minutes later he was greeting Robert Bright, foreman of the building squad posted to this station.

"It is truly an honour, Mr President," Robert spoke as he shook his hand.

"The honour is mine," Kiebler responded. "Let's see what you have been dreaming up for me, shall we?"

"Oh, the dream was all yours, sir. We are just making it come true, with a bit of luck."

Kiebler liked him. A good bit of sycophantic chatter was a great way to impress Bernard Kiebler. He led the way through some darkened hallways and out into an expansive space where slick, silver scaffolding clung to every wall.

"As you can see, we are making great progress with the structures. This is one of thirty we have in production at the moment," Robert explained, proudly.

"And how many more to go?"

"We'll need eighty or ninety when the project is complete, sir. But at the same time thirty is enough to begin rolling it out."

"And how do we go about rolling it out?" Kiebler asked, feeling a surge of excitement coursing through him.

"We can show you, if you like?" Robert replied, grinning from ear to ear.

Kiebler gave him the nod and Robert sprung into action, clearing all workers from the scaffolding and waiting until the chamber was empty. He released a small control panel, hidden under the metallic guardrail, and tapped away at the terminal.

The room began to shift. Heavy boulder-like walls rolled out of view, accompanied by a thunderous sound. The metal framework of the scaffolding was left bare, and revealed to be an immense structure in itself.

Kiebler looked at it in awe.

"The framework is designed to hold solid but will have millions of points of articulation once complete, which will allow it to adapt to any shape while remaining strong enough to absorb the heaviest blow. The engineers have tried this out on small asteroid fields and have had incredible successes."

"So the idea is that the asteroids will bounce off it and we can shift the thing to block any incoming ships?" Kiebler asked.

"Well yes, sir. That is one use. But the flexibility of the design allows for so much more. These structures will be able to navigate through the asteroid belt and can be used to trap asteroids wherever we see fit."

"Trap them?" Kiebler asked, his head spinning at the thought of so many different options.

"Indeed. Effectively we can trap very large rocks and link all of our structures together into one giant impenetrable field."

"A wall of rock?"

"An impossible wall, yes sir. Unbreakable and impassable."

***

Kiebler spent half of the day inspecting the work on the asteroid belt blocker and left a happy man. On the shuttle home he welcomed Daxler Scion into his office for a drink – despite the fact that his number two never actually touched a drop.

"That's one campaign promise we are going to deliver like nobody expected, Dax," he said proudly.

"It's just a shame we can't let the public know of your great deeds immediately," Daxler replied.

"One thing I've learned in my time, Dax, is to recognise when it's the right time to lay your cards on the table. This ain't it."

"The people would be rapturous in their approval. You have to think of that."

"Yeah but what do we gain from that? Higher popularity ratings? Yawn. I won the election, man. I'm in the office. I don't have to care what they think of me now."

"But sir, there's always another election ahead. And always those who would try to block your agenda if they felt the people weren't behind you."

"You're thinking too small scale, my friend. We need to aim higher. This block is going to stand in the way of some serious enemies if things keep going the way they are. Wouldn't you rather they didn't know about it until it was too late?"

"You think the Martians will really go to war for what they want?"

"I believe the voices of the people have to be listened to when they don't get what they want. Luckily, when the Martian voices rise up too high I'll be there with an asteroid-blocking wall to answer them with - all the while delivering my promise to the people of Jupiter."

Daxler Scion smiled his thin, sickly smile. The thought of conflict terrified him, but seeing the inner workings of a great man like Bernie Kiebler filled him with excitement.

CHAPTER NINETEEN

Edward Royce arrived, looking less than his usual suave self. He dumped his bag on the table and threw his suit jacket over the nearest chair. His fellow Senators watched him and allowed him a moment to compose himself.

"Thank you both for coming," he started, "we need to discuss some serious matters I'm afraid."

Marien Lyndell sat forward in her seat, looking at Royce intently as he stood at the head of the table in the small office he had hastily asked them to meet in.

"We are both very intrigued by why you would call us to a private Senate meeting and forget to invite one of our fellow Senators?" she asked.

"Mr Raylor does not need to be here for this meeting. I want to discuss these matters with you two alone," Royce responded.

"I think we can agree that this is uncomfortable. I don't wish to hold any official Senate business without Raylor's express knowledge or involvement," Ramsey Pierce spoke up.

"Call it whatever you like – I'm not asking for some official Senate meeting. I wanted the two of you in a room to discuss Raylor's actions yesterday. I was up all night and I don't think this can wait," Royce explained.

"You have a problem with Raylor's speech?" Pierce asked, knowing he himself had taken some worries away from the Senate questioning of the PoE members.

"He raised the notion of war, in our own Senate chamber. You can't tell me you two were happy with that?"

"I had my issues and I will discuss them with Senator Raylor in good time," Lyndell replied coldly.

"That's the issue, Marien," Royce continued, "I don't know if he's willing to listen. Look at his past. Look at his influences right now. He has the Workers' Council on his back now, thousands of voices to listen to and stand up for. He has their wishes at heart, not the people of Mars."

"Surely the workers *are* the people of Mars? The same people who voted for our removal from the GU and who would oppose terrorists in a heartbeat? Raylor may work for the Council but the people's will and what is right for Mars are one and the same," Lydell said.

"Agreed. But his stalling on the GU has sowed a seed of doubt. Surely you have seen it? I'm annoyed we didn't see it sooner."

"Explain," Pierce said, intrigued to a point by his colleague's excitable attitude – he had never seen Royce like this.

"My people, the southerners I represent, voted to stay in the GU by a vast majority. Now I know I ran a fair campaign, I lobbied hard for my point of view and my people saw things the same way. Can we say the same of Mr Raylor?"

"Are you suggesting he rigged the vote, somehow?" Lyndell asked.

"Not at all. I'm saying the vote was flawed, the campaign was corrupt. What were his motives for calling it? He seems to have an irrational hatred for Bernard Kiebler and used that to paint a picture of this maniacal despot – a man the Jupitoans, our friends – voted into power. Could they all have been so wrong?"

"So you think Raylor has a vendetta against Kiebler? I'm not sure..." Pierce offered, still running the idea through his head.

"I'm saying he twisted Kiebler's image and that of the GU into something which benefitted himself. Then he takes control of the Workers' Council while still remaining in a Senate seat? He is duping the public and I don't think his true intentions have been revealed yet."

"I still see no need to have this meeting without Raylor himself," Lyndell spoke. "Call the man, let's put these issues to him and have his word on the matter."

"I can't do that, Senator," Royce replied. "I have come to you directly from an early – and I mean early – meeting with the Peoples of Earth reps. They had info through the night that a separate cell was ready to make yet another statement."

"I'm guessing it wasn't a press release?" Pierce asked, sombrely.

"Indeed not. They were planning an attack here - on the Senate itself. On us," Royce told them.

The news took a moment to settle in before Lyndell began to question again. She had dealt with Edward Royce too many times in the past to take his word for anything too quickly, but the fear of terrorism at the door was always present in this day and age.

"You take their word for this?" she asked Royce.

"I fear we have no choice. They have been misled by Raylor too, just as the Martian people were. He pushed them to the brink by asking things of them, and promising to legitimise their efforts. His words yesterday caused serious internal issues within their ranks."

"He has been clear about the tentative peace he had made with them – and of course they will be upset that he denounced their terrorism. They broke the terms," Lyndell answered back, feeling her blood pressure rise.

"You don't understand, Marien. He promised them a voice in a future where he could provide that to them – Sebastian Raylor wants the GU out of the way so he can make a play for their role."

"This is ridiculous," Lyndell proclaimed.

"Is it?" Pierce asked. He had known Raylor as long as Lyndell had. They had seen his drive and determination first hand.

"Think how bloody-minded Seb can get. How he always knows the next step and knows exactly what he wants to get out of any situation. Do we know, for absolute certain, what his ambitions truly are?" Pierce asked the question. Lyndell sat back in her chair, considering it - and him.

"I have never had reason to doubt Seb's loyalty to any cause."

"Which cause is it, Marien?" Royce asked. "Is it the will of the people? Is it the way of the Workers' Council? Was it the promises he had made to these Earth extremists? He seems to be picking up causes at an alarming rate. You have to wonder just how loyal he is to any of them."

"If he's making deals based on what he can offer down the line then he must have an end game in mind," Pierce suggested.

"A man like Raylor? Of course he does."

"What exactly are you suggesting?" Lyndell asked.

"I'm suggesting that with the GU out of the way and the people behind him – what's to stop Raylor from taking anything he wants?"

"Nothing," Pierce spoke, under his breath.

"Not nothing, Mr Pierce. Us. The Senate is the rule of the land on Mars. Let us stand up for our people and let Sebastian Raylor know we aren't for the taking as his next cause."

"You heard what he said though – he is willing to go to war for this," Lyndell said.

"Don't worry about that, Marien," Royce replied. "I have already begun to make arrangements to ensure things don't get out of hand."

He smiled and both Lyndell and Pierce felt uneasy at the implication.

"We will have to be forceful to show our intentions – but war won't be necessary," he explained.

"And what about the PoE? If Raylor has made promises..."

"I have calmed them for now. They managed to stop the planned attack as they could see I was serious. We must be careful with how we play them now, but they are on my side at least. They have lost all faith in Raylor and that's probably for the best."

"I can't stomach the idea of the PoE being on our side of anything. But I agree they have to be kept at bay until something can be done about them. Things are too perilous right now."

"It all seems so underhanded. I hate that we are living through these times," Pierce spoke. "What do we actually do now?"

"All I need to know is – are you in?" Royce asked.

***

The tension could be felt on the streets, as Raylor and Bellson approached the Workers' Council offices. Protestors had taken up a position outside shortly after lunch and as they arrived at the gates they could see the Peoples of the Earth's banners everywhere. A smaller group of Council supporters had gathered on the grounds opposite and the police forces were out in numbers in order to keep some semblance of peace.

"See these numbers? Where are they all coming from?" Bellson asked.

Raylor took in the sight of the two sides, almost like battle lines had been drawn already. He questioned himself for his own part in escalating the issues – he should never have mentioned 'war' in the way that he did. He had used it appropriately enough, he thought, but maybe just the sound of that word sparked something in a lot of people.

"I don't know. Seems like the PoE have had more supporters around us than we knew. They're all out now," he replied to Bellson's rhetorical question.

"You would think they might have more shame. Their own followers murdered people, en masse, just days ago. It's sickening."

"People believe in what they believe. That rarely changes, no matter how many madmen twist and turn that belief into something nasty."

"You think there are sane, logical sorts on the PoE side of this?" Bellson asked, with a snort.

"I do. A few hundred years ago the majority of living humans believed in a God. A few hundred before that they believed in many. Millions have been killed in these conflicts. Now we treat those with belief like outsiders – it's inevitable some will turn to extremism to make people stand up and take notice."

"There's a difference between being noticed and outright murder. They should have made religion illegal in the way way back that you are talking about."

"You misunderstand faith, James," Raylor offered. "Repressing it only makes it stronger."

They entered the building only to be met immediately by an aide, who ushered both men into the nearby comms room. A hive of activity greeted them as they stepped into the doorway – aides and senior staff alike, rushing across the room, phones ringing off the hook.

"What the hell is going on here?" Bellson shouted through the chaos.

Eliza Bergman sighed.

"Where the hell have you two been?" she asked.

When Eliza was his personal assistant, Bellson would have checked her for her tone. As it was, he remembered he was no longer in charge here and looked to Raylor.

Raylor's eyes were fixed on the large-screen news feed at the back of the room. His face looked drained, mouth open. Bellson couldn't work out what the expression was but thought he had never seen it on his friend's face in the short time he had known him. It looked like he was hurt. It looked like fear.

Bellson turned slowly towards the screen himself, apprehensive. He saw the same look in Eliza's eyes as he glanced past her and focused on the live news feed.

Sam Heighway was speaking over shaky live images. Bellson recognised the area as downtown from the capital and saw the thick steel bridges of the industrial quarter in the distance.

Armoured tanks and military vehicles were rolling over those very bridges. A squadron of Southern Infantrymen had already crossed and were marching in formation.

Marching towards the capital.

"What the hell is this?" Bellson exclaimed, once or twice. He lost count. He looked to Eliza. She shook her head.

"They arrived maybe fifteen minutes ago. We've been calling you."

Bellson took out his phone to see several missed calls. He had been walking with Raylor through sirens and chants outside, he hadn't heard a thing.

Raylor stood in silence. He had worked through all of the options and possibilities in his head and knew exactly what had happened. He saw Royce's smug face and his manipulation of his fellow Senators. He knew. Royce wouldn't have had the balls to do this alone, but he had a silver tongue and Raylor was an outsider. Pierce would have been convinced fairly easily, Lyndell maybe not quite so.

"Seb," Bellson spoke. "Seb? We have to make a move. Now."

Raylor slowly awoke from his daydream. He looked around the room again, then back to Bellson.

"They're trying to squeeze us, James. To turn our minds back to peace with Kiebler. To negate the vote on the GU" He laughed a frustrated, resigned laugh.

"Who? What can they even achieve?" Bellson asked.

"Royce. He wants me out of the way. He wants to cosy up to Kiebler because it suits him and his business interests – and no doubt those of his supporters down in the south."

"The Senate can't-" Bellson started but was interrupted.

"The Senate cannot do anything officially, without meeting in the chambers. I have to go."

He gave a nod to Bellson and turned to leave.

"If those protestors have heard about this, the streets are only going to get more chaotic," Bellson shouted after him.

"If the army approaches the city and these Peoples of Earth supporters grow in confidence we will have riots on our hands," Raylor replied.

"What can you say, Seb? What can you say to make them see?"

"Democracy still reigns here. If Edward Royce wants to make up the rules and shape the future of our planet then he should do it the right way. Because his is no future I want to be a part of."

***

The journey to the Senate Chambers was an unforgettable one. Raylor never thought he would see the day when rioters roamed the capital's streets. Large groups, supporting a terrorist organisation, ran freely amok in the roads. He was glad of the armoured transport and the blackened out glass. He was scared for the future of everything they held dear.

He contemplated once more his own actions. Had he incited war by the mere mention of it? He hated the thought. He also resented the thought which accompanied it – that maybe all of this was exactly what Mars needed right now.

The tensions between North and South had brewed for too long. Senators and governors and representatives of every industry on the planet had been involved in ramping those tensions up over the years and eventually they had to reach a crescendo.

Civil war was surely never anyone's goal but maybe that tension had to be released. The presence of the PoE within it all worried him immensely though. They had been amenable to Raylor's ways up to a point but now they were coming out of the woodwork at an alarming rate. He had no doubt that Edward Royce had something to do with that.

He reached the Senate building and watched as gangs of people from the PoE and Workers' Council sides met in the street – some chanting, some throwing bottles or rocks. He watched the local police try to get in between the two sides and knew that was a losing battle – very soon this would all erupt into violence and bloodshed.

He stormed into the Senate Chambers and found several groups of people already waiting, arguing, shouting. Senators Royce, Lyndell and Pierce all sat at the bench, speaking to one another and ignoring the commotion in the chamber.

Everyone saw Raylor enter. Everyone watched him advance to the bench.

"It seems I am the only one not invited to this gathering, Senators?" he said loudly, as he took his seat. "Would anyone care to explain why we are here?"

Edward Royce smiled and Raylor felt the overwhelming urge to punch another human like never before.

"We have riots on the streets. We have Senators threatening war. It seemed a good time to discuss the current state of affairs, Mr Raylor. I'm glad you could join us at last."

"You two are in on this?" Raylor asked, eyeing both Lyndell and Pierce directly. "You've thrown your hats into the ring with this maniac?"

Royce laughed.

"Maniac? I have merely moved quickly to ensure your ego doesn't overtake us all. Surely you didn't think you would get away with it all, Seb?" Royce asked.

Raylor saw the writing on the wall and knew exactly how the conniving Southerner had convinced his fellow Senators.

"So I'm the bad guy now? I'm the maniac? I'm fairly certain that's your Southern Army marching on our own capital right now – isn't that correct, Ed?"

"That is a safety measure. The capital was in need of some stability at this time."

"What's the real reason? What's this all about, Royce? Is it religion – are you a believer? Is it just hate and jealousy of me? Of the north?"

Raylor again looked to the other Senators. Their expressions remained blank, happy to allow the two ring leaders to duke it out.

"Or is it just Bernie Kiebler? Your old pal. Mr Money Bags. Greed and glory."

Royce's smile had faded now, his anger was clear to see. Raylor couldn't be sure but felt the wedge between him and the others – like Royce's slickly worded spell might not be as permanent as he had hoped.

It was no matter now, he realised. The army was approaching the city. PoE agents were on the streets. Everything was coming to a head, whether it was what they had signed up to or not.

"If you come here only with accusations, you might as well leave, Mr Raylor," Royce spoke.

"I will do exactly that. How kind of you to offer. I'll be back to sit on my democratically decreed seat in this chamber – you three remember democracy, don't you? I'll bring you some reading material on the subject next time."

As he walked across the chamber floor, Royce stood again at the bench, leaning on his knuckles which he pressed hard into the thick wooden table in front of him.

"Raylor! You wanted a war. You came here today to drive a wedge further into this institution –

between yourself and your fellow Senators. You wanted a war... well you've got one."

The fury and bile in his voice reverberated around Raylor's head on the journey back to the Workers' Council offices. He couldn't quite comprehend just how quickly things had deteriorated. He worried about the coming storm.

He had never wanted a war, but he wanted to lose one even less.

CHAPTER TWENTY

The first week of the conflict was a nightmarish scenario for all Martians. The capital came under pressure immediately as the Southern Army reached the central areas. Local authorities mounted some resistance at first, and were quickly joined by a larger Martian military presence, however the influence of the Peoples of Earth within the city caused major disturbances.

Within three days, the PoE had organised themselves into a force comparable to the Southern Army which had already flooded the city. They did not follow military rule, cared little for the watchful eyes that were on them at all times, and acted out of hate and vengeance for their cause. The damage they caused in just a handful of days was incredible. The

Southern Army were soon forced to attempt to police their supposed allies, as well as hold back the growing dissent from the Workers' Council groups and bands of ordinary civilians.

The chaos escalated and fear took hold. The remaining Senate members voted three to one, to hand over control and protection of the city to the Southern Army and their allies via executive order. Royce was instrumental again in persuading his colleagues that they were taking the right course of action. He promised that his men could restore order.

Royce met in secret with his PoE contacts and begged that they pull back on their ruinous ways. Isaiah Redman himself sat with him for a face to face meeting. He gave nothing away. The cause was too great. He thanked Royce for allowing his people a window into the capital of Mars. He promised that their aims would be achieved, but he made it clear that Royce would have no say in the actions of the People's of Earth.

Raylor, for his part, bided his time. He urged caution amongst the Workers' Council members, despite the fact they had a small armed force of their own to call upon and many many ex-military members who had pledged their support. He talked down those who spoke too proudly and those who would incite an escalation of the violence.

For a civil war it was all so very tame, he thought, and he hoped to keep it that way.

The Workers' Council office building itself was surrounded for the most part, although protestors and council members made sure there was a tumultuous, but safe enough, way in every morning.

On day five, fighting broke out in the south of the city. PoE members clashed with locals. Reports varied but the story Raylor heard was of the Earthlings throwing their weight around and groups of locals regrouping with weapons before returning to the fight. Seven unarmed civilians were killed in the resultant shootout, with injuries reported on both sides.

Day six remained calm until the black of night, when the gut-wrenching sound of a bomb rocked the peaceful night air. Raylor was awoken from a restless slumber to be advised of the ensuing chaos. PoE members had taken out an office block downtown which was said to be housing a small band of Council-affiliated soldiers. Of the fourteen confirmed dead, only one was subsequently proven to be linked to Sebastian Raylor or the Workers' Council. Fourteen civilians, caught up in a game they had no idea they were playing.

Raylor wished it would stop, but knew it could only escalate now. The only reason they did not have all out war was him. He held back from unleashing those who would fight for his cause, knowing it would not be nearly enough.

Day seven came, much the same as all of the others, and news arrived through the night of more death and destruction. People were getting hurt because Raylor could not protect them with a genuine force.

That night he made a plan of action. He had to reach out, talk sense to people. He had to make sure that his side would be not be at a disadvantage if they were to go on the front foot, and it had to be now - before more skirmishes broke out. He couldn't live with the chance of more innocent, untrained, naive people losing their lives unnecessarily.

He reached out to the only man he could think of with the gravitas to help pull off the move he was aiming for. He had his doubts about putting him through the rigours of such a high pressure situation, but he knew that Jeffrey Sutherland was a man he could trust.

The former Senator had been recuperating at his holiday home for months now. He spoke with Raylor now and then, rarely about politics. He seemed at best content with his new life, and at worst bored of it all. He had led a long and industrious career and Raylor didn't know how he could slow to a crawling pace out in what passed for countryside on Mars.

It hadn't taken much effort to get him to visit the capital after he saw the news and understood the tensions that were running so high. Sutherland had arrived early in the morning on a private transport shuttle.

Raylor and Bellson met him at the Aeroport and whisked him away to an old rendezvous point on the outskirts of the industrial area of the city. There they were met by Sutherland's contact, and he proved his true worth as expected.

"Gentlemen, this is Harley Tyler, Chairman of the Armed Forces for Mars," Sutherland announced, to the surprise of both men.

Raylor immediately stepped forward to shake hands with the Chairman, while Bellson looked on in awe.

Harley Tyler was one of only a handful of four-star generals in the Martian armed forces. He was the highest-ranking military official on the planet, and importantly one of the only voices which had not been heard on TV and in public throughout the entire week.

"Mr Chairman, it's a great honour you agreeing to meet with us here," Raylor spoke. "We wouldn't ask you to come out of your way like this if it wasn't in great need."

It was highly unusual for a serving Chairman to meet the Senate in any setting. Mars' violent past had led to leglislation being written into the constitution which strictly spelled out the separation of military from the executive branch of government. They took orders from the Senate, as a whole, but otherwise should have no dealings with the standing Senators of their time.

"Raylor, I don't know if you've been watching the news, but everything is in great need at the moment. Shall we get down to business?" Tyler reached and shook Bellson's hand too, then motioned to a small table that had been set up with four chairs.

"Sutherland, you old bastard. Get us started here," Tyler said, smiling happily at his old friend.

Sutherland took his seat uncomfortably, and was followed by the other men. He adjusted his collar and wished he hadn't bothered with the shirt. He hadn't worn one for weeks now and he hadn't missed it.

"Harley, as I'm sure you know, we didn't ask you here for a good old gals catch up. These boys asked me to reach out to you, and I wouldn't have done it if I didn't think they had good cause to do so," he started.

"Seb here has been fighting a losing battle – trying to keep the peace as much as possible in the middle of a war he technically started."

"Keep the peace? I see plenty of fighting on the news every night, gentlemen?" Tyler questioned.

"We have no army to speak of, sir," Raylor answered. "The fighting on the news is either rebels or gangs, or just propaganda from the other side. They're winning by default."

"Didn't you threaten them with war? What were you thinking you might fight them with? The pair of you don't amount to much in front of an army."

"We were banking on you, Chairman," Bellson spoke. Tyler glared at him, accusingly.

"We hoped the Senate would back you," Raylor explained. "The Workers' Council and the people of Mars, united for the same cause. However, Edward Royce saw things differently and has manipulated the Senate into turning its back on what the people want."

"You made some rash and frankly stupid moves, Raylor. You put us all in a position of uncertainty.

But at the end of the day, you did it. You have to fix things."

Tyler was firm in his assessment, and Raylor wasn't sure how to argue with a four-star General. He didn't have the right.

"Tyler, listen to me," Sutherland spoke up. "You've known me for a hundred years now and we both know the score. You know the army side of life and I know politics. You've never been able to see the intricacies like I do."

"I see the military side very clearly though. I see orders from the Senate to remove my forces – all of them – from the capital and I have to follow," the General responded.

"And you don't question why the Southern Army is now holding our Senate Chambers – the very seat of our government? Why they flood our streets?"

"It is not my place to question," he replied.

"We have terrorists on our streets, unchecked. Our own Senate has validated, and rewarded, the leaders of an extremist group. They are here, in our capital, General."

The General had watched the news, catching snapshots of reality beneath the sanitised editing. He had pushed that reality out, his pride and professionalism not allowing him to see it for what it was. He considered both men, and their words, carefully.

"What can we do about that? Our government has made these calls," he finally said.

"More importantly, what happens if we don't do anything? Think about it, General," Raylor continued. "If the Peoples of Earth activists don't get their way with Royce and the Senate – they won't leave peacefully. If he tries to double-cross them he is asking for trouble too."

"There is no good end point to the way things are going, Harley," Sutherland joined in.

"Royce doesn't realise what he has signed up for. What is their agenda? They won't let him cosy up to Kiebler. That puts them at odds. And Kiebler won't tolerate their presence now. It's asking for a war so much bigger than the one we've already got," Bellson added.

"We would be crushed under Jupiter's military weight," Tyler spoke, despondently.

"Assume for a moment they find their way around those probleMs Royce appeases the PoE. What then? He's come this far, where will he stop? Who is in place to check him? He has his fellow Senators in his pocket. He will try to beat the opposition out of the Workers' Council - and all else who oppose him. Who is going to stand up for Mars?"

Raylor took a breath. He thought he had laid things on a little too much. He was passionate about his government and the democratic rights of every Martian. He eyed General Tyler carefully, seeing the cogs whirring behind his dark eyes.

"You're asking me to disobey a direct order from the Senate. To provide you with an army?"

"We're asking that the Martian Armed Forces stand up for Mars, to help us rid the planet of the biggest threat it has ever faced," Raylor replied.

It took a moment for the words to come. The General was a deeply patriotic man and had never so much as dreamed of disobeying an order before. Over the course of his career he had personally signed the order of execution for more traitors than he could even remember.

He had also faced down terrorism and extremism in its many guises. He knew the dangers they posed, and he could see the damage they had already done. He couldn't sit back and let them destroy Mars from the inside out.

"Gentlemen, I will provide you with an army on the proviso that this planet's government is returned to the people and that their will is done."

He looked into the faces around the table and saw determination in their eyes. They all nodded their agreement.

"The People's Army of Mars," Bellson said with a smile.

Raylor looked at his friend, then to all of those around him, and knew this was the turning point; no matter what happened next.

CHAPTER TWENTY-ONE

I saiah smiled to himself as he glanced back at the security gates. He had sailed through, as predicted. Kaleb followed behind, dragging his feet as he looked at the murals on the walls, and took in the sights of the marbled statues and painted ceilings of the Senate building.

They felt the release of walking freely in the corridors of power, after hiding in the shadows for most of their lives. Isaiah had expected more venom from the waiting crowds outside, or more opposition from the Senate security staff, but things had moved smoothly. They had been told to expect visitors from the Peoples of Earth and they didn't seem too worried by the notoriety of just who had turned up.

The press had been full of stories of Isaiah and Kaleb's past lives – their humble upbringings, the influences which had led them here. They had suffered through numerous 'tell all' tales in which people they hadn't seen or spoken to in a decade or more would offer what they seemed to believe was genuine insight into their ways.

It didn't make a blind bit of difference to their agenda. The more inane stories out there the better, in Isaiah's eyes. Not once did he read a single correct take on just how and why he had ended up as the leader of the most powerful cell of the PoE, or the influences which had led him to commit the acts which he took credit for. He liked that level of mystery.

The moment they entered the Senate chamber was one to savour for both men. They could feel every eye on them, every voice hushed. They could feel the heat and the hatred which was flowing their way.

Senator Royce stood slowly at the bench; the look on his face absolutely priceless.

The PoE had dealt with Royce through intermediaries and fed him exactly what he wanted to hear. He was an important tool in allowing them access to the government and sowing the seeds of disruption which they could not have managed through aggression alone. They knew he would blanch at the thought of getting into bed with the very face of terrorism though, so Isaiah and Kaleb had held back, keeping a low profile.

Royce had had his suspicions as the time drew near but now, as the big day arrived, he was beginning to see what he had got himself into. He had been told to prepare for the PoE leadership's arrival to help him plan for the war at large – and here he was, taking in the sight of Isaiah Redman and his most trusted companion in Kaleb Moynes.

"No no no! You two can't come in here!" Royce bellowed.

Isaiah laughed.

"You invited us here, Senator," he replied.

"No! I most certainly did not invite you two anywhere near our planet. Who let you in here?" Royce continued, rage stressing ever syllable.

"We have the documents you sent through. We are the PoE leadership you are expecting," Isaiah said with a smile to the room, as the chatter and whispers grew in the seats at the back.

"We did not make a deal with terrorists, Edward," Ramsey Pierce spoke up.

"Then I am afraid Mr Royce here hasn't told you the full story," Isaiah followed up. "We are, as I am sure you are all aware, the face and future of the Peoples of Earth movement."

He couldn't have timed his words any better. As Isaiah finished his introductory speech the doors once again flew open and the chamber was filled with the sound of marching boots.

"In case any of you were getting ideas," Kaleb spoke, looking at the gathered officials and state guards scattered around the outskirts of the room, "Please be aware we came in force."

A small battalion of Earth-born soldiers strode confidently into the chamber and took up position in formation in front of the grand double-door entrance.

"You can't just waltz in here with a troop of... mercenaries... and begin calling the shots. This is

Mars!" Royce screamed, his fury entirely unrestrained.

"I'm afraid you allowed this to happen, Senator Royce," Isaiah spoke slowly. "You made a deal. You signed the documents to allow my men into your capital. You stood down the Martian Guard." He smiled a sickening smile and looked Royce directly in the eye.

"You signed over the Senate to the Peoples of Earth."

***

Outside of the Senate building, an organised form of chaos was taking shape. PoE forces moved in numbers to secure positions around the building itself, while Southern officers made little or no fight in the process.

PoE guards stood at the doors of the Senate of Mars and the entire square was surrounded. The Southern Army retreated its position without any fuss – they had orders from their Senate leadership not to engage the Earthlings directly and had no reason to doubt those.

Before news broke that the PoE had effectively moved itself in to the Senate building, the Generals and Councillors outside of the building believed that all was well with the uneasy union they had forged.

Sebastian Raylor received a shaken phone call from Marien Lyndell in the late afternoon. She had witnessed the entire episode from the bench of the

Senate itself and, full of anger, she apologised to Raylor for the actions she and Pierce had taken.

Raylor allowed her to talk, trying hard to push down the feeling of betrayal – not just of their friendship, but of the people who they stood for and the belief in the freedoms for which they all fought.

He held his tongue and wiped tears from his eyes as he heard how the PoE had infiltrated the very seat of government he held dear. Lyndell told of soldiers walking the halls, faces covered and weapons drawn. There was fighting in the square outside, she said. She could hear screams and gun fire, but they were not allowed to leave the building.

Both sides had lost a civil war that neither had wanted in the first place. The Peoples of Earth organisation had made their play for Mars.

Raylor didn't give anything away to his fellow Senator. He spoke softly and sadly and agreed what a terrible state of affairs they had found themselves in. He questioned what might happen next and remained silent when Lyndell spoke of the former army of Mars, and where it might be.

He knew exactly where the army, and its loyalties, lay. He knew they would not answer the call of the Senate, even in these dramatically changing times. He asked about Royce – wondering if he would try to contact Harley Tyler and pull on his heart strings, knowing his fierce loyalty to his planet and his job.

Lyndell spoke quietly. She explained that Royce had kicked up a fuss with Redman and was forcibly removed from the Senate chambers. Nobody had seen him since, and so they feared the worst.

Raylor was cold to the news. Edward Royce had made his own bed and might now be laying very uncomfortably in it. He took no pleasure from the thought but felt a curious lack of concern for his colleague.

The call ended abruptly as Lyndell tried to speak of the numbers of PoE men occupying the chamber itself. Raylor listened intently but soon heard a gruff voice questioning Lyndell, followed by the sound of a dead line.

***

As the sun set, Raylor sat uneasily in the hastily thrown together communications trailer, at the back of a large convoy. Bellson was by his side, as Chairman Tyler gave his final orders.

The Armed Forces of Mars were assembled in no time at all. Tyler had kept them alert and close to the city. Bellson continued to call them 'The People's Army of Mars', but it stuck in Raylor's throat. Too close to the Peoples of Earth branding he was sick of hearing.

Tyler laid out the last of his plan to his Generals, then asked for confirmation that they all had taken in everything they required from him. Once he had received four affirmatives, he wiped the old-school white board clean – erasing his carefully drawn city plan, the Senate building and the strategic lines of advancement he had meticulously explained to his men.

The first missiles rocked the night air. Alarms and chaos.

Chairman Tyler had done his research. He knew every nook and cranny of the city he was sworn to protect and had several well placed contacts who provided him with vital information. He was very confident that he knew just where his foes would be.

The first waves of missiles were launched from the outskirts of the city – targeting the lookout points and strategic hole-ups of the Earth forces. As smoke and fire began to rise in the Martian night sky, Tyler's men moved with precision into the city.

They came from the west and south, knowing that the residential areas to the east and industrial zones of the north were not of much threat. The Martian forces took their foes by surprise in that first hour and made inroads quickly, dispensing any Earthling force with ease, and leaving small garrisons in defence of the newly cleared zones.

They came upon stronger resistance as they approached the two-mile stretch of motorway and transport hubs which connected the outskirts to the city centre. The PoE men had heard the gunfire and, to their credit, mobilised their defences quickly. Tyler looked on as he watched his men storm a hastily built roadblock and admired the way Earth forces had organised themselves – he had thought of them as a rag-tag bunch; self-trained and sloppy. The evidence in front of him suggested otherwise.

The night drew long and the incessant sound of gunfire never ceased.

Tyler lost good men, one after the other. Finally, they made a breakthrough as a PoE grenade detonated in error too close to their defences. The Martian team took full advantage, swarming the area before it could be defended sufficiently.

Once a chink in the defences was found it was only a matter of time – the Martians forced their way in and Tyler upped the alert level to crimson. He liked to have his troops looking for the disabling shot, nullifying the threat of their enemy whenever possible. It kept them on their toes, always thinking.

However, some situations called for a more deadly course of action. Working at crimson level meant that they would look for the kill shot without question. His men did not falter.

Tyler himself approached from the south, expecting more resistance from any lingering Southern forces along the way. He was pleasantly surprised to find none.

After close to three hours of constant pressing, his men found open streets and space to breath. They heard from the western front that they too had found their way through the pack and were within sight of the Senate square.

He relayed the orders to hold position and not to approach the heavily-defended Senate building until his force had joined them. He was wary of the PoE and didn't want any surprises. A full force, attacking from multiple angles, would give the best hope of a swift resolution.

Firstly though, he had his men head for the capital internment facility – what was once a basic prison –

which had been transformed into a slightly more-than-basic holding pen for political prisoners or your average up-standing citizens who had fallen foul of the law. Intelligence suggested that any Senate members who had anything to say about the recent changes to the hierarchy would be holed up there. Tyler felt uneasy leaving the place in the hands of the PoE – especially once news spread that the Senate building itself was under siege.

***

The internment centre was as heavily guarded as any armed forces training camp Tyler had ever seen. Gun turrets had been set at the gated wall side of the courtyard, while armed watchmen patrolled the surrounding area. Inside the courtyard stood a battalion of Earth militia – armed to the teeth with their old-style weaponry.

The 'traditional' weaponry never ceased to amaze Tyler's squadron and he made a point of hushing their chatter about it as they lay in wait – he didn't mind the banter and he actively encouraged this military-nerdiness in them at all other times, but in the middle of an operation as serious as this he knew when to bring the tone down to the appropriate level. His men listened.

He hated the thought that he would most certainly lose some of those very men in the ensuing battle. At the same time, he knew from his visual assessment of the enemy in front of him, as well as the condition of his own squad, that they had nothing to fear here.

The place was within their grasp, the plan was a sound one and the risk was worth the reward.

It took less than twenty minutes for his team to storm the walls. The gun turrets fell first, followed by the less-heavily armed patrolmen. The battalion stationed inside the walls were unmoved, awaiting their orders, when the last outer defence fell. Once that order came the battalion engaged with a ferocity and dangerousness that belied their numbers.

Tyler once again found himself impressed with their organisation, and their resolve. They were soon outnumbered but held firm. They moved in formation and made smart decisions, displaying great knowledge and skill in defensive manoeuvres. Still, he did not worry. His men were trained to handle these situations, day in and day out. What's more, they were hardened veterans of siege warfare. As impressive as the enemy ranks were, Tyler could see from their faces that many were young and eager, but inexperienced and liable to make mistakes.

The Martian forces moved with precision. No shot taken without gain, no movement wasted. The courtyard was cleared after a short, intense battle. Debris was still falling around them when they approached the building itself. The inside was less heavily staffed than expected and they quickly rounded up the remaining PoE members.

Tyler and his team advanced further, releasing several high-ranking government officials and Senate spokespeople along the way. In the last cell – a dingy, lightless block tagged on to the end of the row – sat Edward Royce. The fallen Senator sat despondently on the floor beside a cold metal cot. Tyler considered just how different he looked to the dapper, over-confident man he had once locked horns with at a Southern Army committee meeting, nearly a decade ago.

"Chairman Tyler. You've come for me?" Royce uttered almost inaudibly. He rose to his feet awkwardly, revealing his bloody and bruised face in the dim light. Tyler looked him up and down, taking in the ripped trousers and missing shoes. The man had been through an ordeal at the hands of his supposed allies.

"Bring him. Throw him in with the rest," Tyler spoke coldly as he turned and headed back up the long corridor.

"The rest? The rest of what?" Royce shouted after him, his voice almost cracking. One of Tyler's men reached out for his arm, pulling him forcefully towards the door.

"With the rest of the insurgents, I imagine," the officer told him.

"Insurgents?" Royce squealed, panic setting in. "I'm no insurgent! I am not a terrorist! Chairman!"

Royce scrambled to the floor, trying to break the grip of the army officer. He failed and squirmed for a moment on his knees, his arm still tightly held - like a small child trying to escape his parent's grip.

Tyler stopped his stroll along the hall and looked back at the Senator. He felt true pity for the man.

"I'm afraid, Mr Royce, that you have thrown your hat in with a bad bunch. You have allowed terrorists into our land, you have allowed an insurgent foreign force into our capital and you have invited mass murderers into our Senate house."

"I didn't intend for any of that. I just wanted to protect Mars," he spluttered in response.

"Then I am afraid you have singularly and spectacularly failed, Senator," Tyler spoke with authority.

"Now if you will excuse me, Mr Royce – I have to clean up after you."

The Chairman of the Armed Forces of Mars turned on his heels and left the disgraced Senator in the capable hands of his military guard.

***

Within an hour of leaving the internment facility, Harley Tyler was standing at the southern entrance to Liberty Square – the Senate building itself dominating his view. He spent a good while discussing plans with his most senior Generals and sending messages to his men positioned to the west of the square. The two teams had the final plan laid out to them within the hour and the preparations for the assault began.

Tyler led a team himself, taking out sentries at the south entrance to the Senate house. They passed the long stretch of square to get without incident, which made everyone nervous. How could they not see the assault coming? Why wouldn't they defend themselves?

The answer came as Tyler knocked on that southern entrance. The whistle was heard first of all, then the trail of smoke. The sound of the missile came milliseconds after, but by that point the dread inside Tyler had already taken hold. He looked back and watched as the missile tore a hole in the intricate brick floor of the square.

He watched as his own men were sent flying through the air, only to land in broken piles of rubble and bone. Their screams were drowned out by the shattering of stone and the explosions of the following missiles.

Pulling himself around, he barked orders. They had to move faster to find cover, and the best way to do so was to get into the Senate building. The missiles appeared to be coming from a window far above the door he currently stood in, as he beckoned his men towards it.

They piled inside, as many men as could fit. Bruised and bloodied, the injured trailed in behind.

An ambush awaited.

Scores of PoE men lined the dark corridors of the government building and gunfire rang out as soon as the liberators were all safely inside.

Trapped.

Tyler hit the floor hard and hoped his team would do the same. Smoke filled the air and he knew that the shooters were firing blindly into the abyss. He crawled into a recess in the wall and pulled a short range grenade from his belt.

He tossed it down the corridor towards the sounds of gunfire and waited for the blast. Hot smoke poured forward and screams again filled the air. The gunfire ceased for a moment.

He saw one of his generals find a moment to breathe and reach for his grenades in much the same way. He inched forward along the hall, using every small blast as a moments respite to claw his way closer to their goal.

The next hour was a blur. Tyler cleared his mind and remembered every moment of training he had ever learned. He took out men hand-to-hand, and wrestled rifles from the hands of hooded enemies. His men followed, rising to their feet now, the smoke clearing. Firing back.

Slowly the resistance grew smaller. Those who remained were already retreating into the bowels of the building.

Tyler's men reached the grand reception hall of the Senate and picked off the last few stragglers of PoE fighters who had taken positions on the ornate staircase which wrapped around either side of the room. His western team had secured the second hallway entrance and held firm there.

Tyler stepped up to the double-oak doors of the Senate Chamber and pushed them open with a heave.

CHAPTER TWENTY-TWO

A short burst of gunfire ripped through the air, and was followed by a shorter, more controlled spray from one of Tyler's men. The Earth soldier who had fired before thinking was dead before his next thought caught up with him. The air in the Senate Chamber felt heavy with fear, and Tyler could feel the nervous energy in the room.

He knew he had command of the situation, but the anxiousness pervaded and he knew that every member of the PoE group in the room was armed with a deadly weapon. He hoped they could see the writing on the wall.

Isaiah Redman sat at the bench looking down on the action as it played out. He shared a glance his partner, Kaleb Moynes, who skulked behind a portable monitoring system in the corner.

"My man tells me that our reinforcements will be here in a moment, Chairman." Redman spoke. "I'm afraid you will be outnumbered."

"I'm not here to discuss numbers or tactics. I'm not here for any kind of debate. Just the safe and peaceful removal of your forces from my Senate," Tyler responded.

"Your Senate?" Redman spat. "You claim the Senate for yourself? Haven't they demonised Mr Royce for doing just that very thing already?"

"It's my Senate, as it is for every other citizen of Mars. Step down from the bench and let's do this the peaceful way," Tyler spoke, remaining calm.

"Peaceful like the way your men just murdered one of my trusted guards when you barged into this private Senate function? That's peace in your twisted logic?"

"If your men shoot first, we will be obliged to take them out. There's no need for anyone to pull any triggers in this room now. Let's get this over with."

Tyler felt his heart pounding and the adrenaline flowing. He had been in countless situations such as this. Nine times out of ten it went the way it should – nobody missed a beat, nobody did the silly thing and nobody got hurt. But he felt the nervousness in the air. He knew the motivations of the Earth men. He got that tense feeling in his gut and he knew his instincts were never wrong.

The PoE moved first – a guard, tucked away to the left of the main entrance, stepped forward, taking one of Tyler's men by surprise. He didn't blindside him with a punch, or the butt of his gun, as they might have expected, but instead pulled out a small short-range device and fired a bullet directly into the temple of Tyler's man.

Chaos erupted in the chambers. The lone shooter was taken out immediately by the Martian team – however the soldier taking the kill shot was instantly besieged by two PoE goons, jumping onto him and yelling and screaming for their fallen comrade.

He muscled himself free enough to take a shot at one of his assailants, sending him to the floor. He grappled with the second attacker, arms twisting and bending impossibly. He managed to wedge him against the thick wooden beams which ran through the room and reached behind his own back to find something to restrain his foe with.

A gunshot fired from across the chamber. The bullet fired directly through the PoE man and struck the Martian solider in the neck. Both bodies fell to the ground, blood staining the hallowed floors of the Senate chamber.

The fight lasted all of five minutes. The PoE forces holed up in the chamber were not enough to withstand the assault, and they knew it. They sacrificed themselves where necessary, just to take out one or two of the infidels they had came to destroy.

Redman and Moynes now stood together at the Senate high table, watching their men go down for the cause.

Tyler's men fought bravely and, as ever, they continued to do so despite the loss of colleagues and friends by their sides. They did not take vengeance, or strike out on their own. They were a unit and they worked together to get the job done.

Every surviving member of the PoE faction was rounded up; hands tied behind their back and lined up in front of the Senate bench. Tyler himself marched up to the high table and wordlessly offered handcuffs to Redman.

Moynes jumped before Redman could offer any comment of his own. He lashed out at the Chairman, striking his face hard with his handheld device and then reached into his pocket for his knife. Tyler reacted quickly and stopped the man's hand as the blade swung towards his stomach. He twisted it hard.

"Kaleb!" Isaiah shouted, rooted to the spot.

The blade flew to the ground and Kaleb Moynes flung himself after it. Tyler's boot was immediately on him. He kicked hard, breaking ribs in the process. Kaleb squealed in agony, but grasped for his weapon still.

Tyler was calmness itself.

He pulled out his short-range pistol and checked the clip. He aimed it slowly at the flailing terrorist.

Isaiah reached for something below the bench, finally shaken from his stupor. Tyler's men had eyes on him and reacted as soon as they saw movement – in the blink of an eye three target sights were set on Isaiah Redman as he began to raise a semi-automatic weapon to his shoulder.

"No!" came a booming shout from the doorway, drawing everyone's attention. Time stood still for a moment, as all eyes switched to the double-door entrance to the chamber.

Sebastian Raylor stood in the doorway with a small force at his heels.

"Don't shoot either of them. Don't give them the satisfaction," he spoke authoritatively.

Tyler reacted first, turning his weapon around and delivering a blow to Moynes designed to knock him unconscious. Redman had stopped in his tracks, the weapon held now above his head as he glared at his would-be assassins. He looked for all the world like a man who was more than willing to let others die for his cause but didn't intend to share the same fate.

"Lower your weapons," Raylor shouted at the Martian men, before fixing his eyes on Redman. "You too. Put it down."

Redman barely moved a muscle, while all of the Martian men looked to Tyler for reassurance. He nodded, and they lowered their sights reluctantly. Redman held firm, arms above his head.

"This is your moment to finally make a good call, Isaiah," Raylor spoke to him directly. "You have made a hell of a bed for yourself. Come and lie down."

Redman wavered as he began to lower the weapon, pausing with it held at chest height, raising alarm in the Martian ranks again. One soldier raised his weapon, aiming it at Redman.

"Put it down!" Raylor shouted, looking at the Martian soldier.

"Hold on, Raylor, those are my men and in case you hadn't noticed there is an armed terrorist in the room," Tyler said.

"Chairman Tyler, I understand, and hope you'll forgive me for stepping on your toes. These are highly charged moments and I want to make sure we come out on the right side of them," Raylor replied.

"We all want the same thing, I'm sure. But I'm not sure allowing an armed man to wave his gun around an enclosed space full of his enemies is a good way to get us out of this."

"Drop your weapon or we will fire. You leave us no choice," Raylor spoke with resignation in his voice. "I came here to help you. I came here to ensure things don't turn out worse than they need to. We've all lost too many good men tonight."

Redman still looked stunned - man fighting for a lost cause, with none of the fight left inside. He looked at his fallen partner, Kaleb, motionless on the Senate floor with Chairman Tyler standing over him. Isaiah looked into the Chairman's eyes and knew the day was done.

Tyler took his cue, stepping forward with his hands out, and accepted the weapon from the leader of the Peoples of Earth.

Redman fell to his knees, a pitiful sight.

"Pick him up," Raylor said, matter-of-factly. "Bring him down here. Bring the others with him."

As he spoke, the small group who had accompanied him to the chamber emerged through the doorway. They were Martian patrolmen, alongside James Bellson. Marien Lyndell and Ramsey Pierce followed.

Raylor made his way to the bench and motioned for his fellow Senators to join him. Just as they reached the bench to take their seats, the last patrolman marched into the room with Senator Edward Royce in tow. He stopped in the middle of the room and took in the harsh stares of his fellow Martians.

The patrolman forced him to kneel, just as Redman and Moynes were sat next to him – the latter coming around from his enforced slumber.

"Ladies and gentlemen of the Martian public. Servicemen and Chairmen alike. I ask you to bear witness here tonight. These men will be trialled, fairly by the letter of the law."

"Seb," Bellson spoke out, "what do you mean trialled? They should be executed as traitors! All three of them."

He looked into Royce's eyes as he spoke and the hatred could be felt throughout the room. A rumble of agreement followed as the forces and Workers' Council reps flowed in, along with curious members of the public who had been gathered in the streets.

"Slaughtering these men makes us no better than they are. We do it right. We follow the rule of law. We offer a fair trial and judgement. This Senate will do the job it was voted to carry out or there truly is no justifiable reason to hold this Senate any longer."

***

The charges against each man were laid out clearly before the court. In matters of the state, high treason being one of the few acceptable reasons, the Senate itself may act as a court in its own right. Sebastian Raylor led the proceedings, and heard any witness accounts from those in the room, briefly.

He needed no accounts to be told to him. He needed not to ask Royce or his accomplices for their own side of the story. He had witnessed enough himself. He knew where their guilt lay. He waited patiently for all who wished to speak to say their piece. None changed his mind, nor even attempted to do so.

The Martian television crews arrived five minutes into the trial. He nodded when asked if they may cut to a live feed. He imagined every child at home, sick with fear for the world they were being brought up in, eyes glued to the screen. He wished that this would deliver some hope.

The final speaker stepped down. Raylor stood at the bench.

"You stand, all three, on charges of terror. You stand charged with insurrection. You stand charged with murder. Senator Royce – you have no blood on your hands directly. Murder doesn't fit when it comes to you. You don't have the guts for murder. You don't have the spine for it."

He watched Royce squirm, seeing the muscles of his jaw twitch where he wished he could spit some clever comeback, but thought better of it.

"You betrayed these people. You betrayed the wishes of the people of Mars, and in doing so you put the lives of every Martian throughout the colonies at risk. You allowed corruption and greed to reign and to rot at the heart of our democracy. You allowed it to rot the heart out of the Galactic Union."

"But I," Royce began to stammer awkwardly.

"Hold your tongue, Mr Senator," Raylor snapped loudly.

Royce broke down. Tears streaming down his face and onto his ragged suit.

"We have agreed on a sentence. You will all face a life sentence – a true life sentence – here on Mars. You will never know the freedom you tried to remove, ever again. Nor will you have the luxury of an execution, as is tradition for traitors. You will all live out a life behind bars - but it will be a life lived under a free and just Martian society, where you will witness everything you worked against come to fruition."

James Bellson led the cheers. The Workers' Council members joined in, followed by the public. Raylor caught the television crew applauding behind their cameras and microphones. His people were with him.

The three men were led away in restraints, with Martian voices ringing in their ears.

***

The cheering eventually died down to applause, then settled into chatter. The chambers were awash with hope and ideas. Senators Pierce and Lyndell looked shell-shocked as, just as they finally settled back into their seats, Raylor began talking to them of action – of getting Mars back on its feet, immediately.

"We have to make some big decisions tonight. We can't rest on our laurels till morning and allow more insurgent attacks throughout the night. We can't wait for retribution to come from the Peoples of Earth," he spoke urgently.

"I can't think straight, Seb," Pierce drawled. "I'm not sure what you want from me?"

"What do I want? These people expect us to take control now that we have slain the dragon. Wake up, Ramsey."

"He's in no state to take control of anything, Sebastian. Look at his eyes. He looks how I feel. Broken and beaten," Lyndell spoke angrily. "How could I know what is best for the people of Mars after all this?"

"For crying out loud," Raylor shouted, exasperated. "You were elected by these very people to handle situations just like this. You want someone to hold your hand? Someone to do it for you?"

Raylor threw his hands in the air and spun away from his fellow Senators. He looked across the chamber to see the expectant faces of their own citizens.

Chairman Tyler stepped out into the floor.

"Ladies and gentlemen, if I may?" he spoke loudly and clearly, bringing a hush around the large chamber.

"I cannot help but think of those who are suffering the after effects of a war we should never have fought, and those who will, this very minute, be attempting to escape justice for crimes committed throughout its course."

"I look to the Senate for orders, but all I see are two psychologically beaten prisoners of war. Two people who have been swayed and influenced to their breaking point, who can't now tell left from right - whether through indecision or trauma."

Grumblings began to be heard in the back – the public noticing maybe for the first time that the remaining Senate members looked less like the strong leaders they had elected and more like school children on a long and bumpy bus trip.

"I'll pull them around," Raylor spoke, with no confidence in his words.

"There's no time, Senator Raylor," Tyler responded for all to hear. "I propose we look to the Constitution. In times of great need there is a clause in the Senate by-laws. Article 505-B."

"He's right," Pierce agreed, barely able to make eye contact with anyone in the room.

Bellson caught on next, almost jumping on the spot as he looked to Raylor.

"Article 505-B. The Octavius Amendment," Bellson laughed.

Raylor was taken aback for a moment. He was aware of Chairman Tyler talking of tradition and of law. He heard his grave warnings of a mandate to relieve the planet from its crisis, and specifically to free it from the grip of the Galactic Union. His head was swimming, and his eyes only snapped back to reality when he noticed Tyler was now by his side; a deathly silence fallen on the room.

"Mr Raylor. With the blessing of your fellow Senators and myself, Harley Tyler, Chairman of the Armed Forces of Mars, we ask that you lead us at this time. Bring us back to normality."

Raylor stared into his face for what seemed like the longest time.

"Seb? Don't let us down. We need someone with strength and integrity and a vision of where we need to be, what we should all be aspiring to and how we go about getting it. You are that someone."

Tyler stuck out his right hand, and Seb Raylor took a deep breath before shaking it firmly.

"I accept," he stated quietly at first. "I accept," he repeated for the whole chamber to hear, at Tyler's urging.

The gathered crowd cheered loudly, and Bellson approached the bench smiling from ear to ear.

"What's your first step going to be, Fearless Leader?" he asked his new de-facto President.

Raylor looked around the room. Mars' decisions were now his decisions to make, just like that. He wondered how the hell he had got himself into this mess. He wondered what to do next.

He looked across the room and spotted the television crew still recording every moment.

"Are we still live?" he asked.

***

"To the group known as the 'People's of Earth', I speak to you as a warning. Do not come here. You are no longer welcome. Every citizen of the wider-galaxy is welcome on Mars, but on the condition that they live by the laws of the Free Martian People. If you cannot do this you will be punished in a just and fair manner. Hate cannot win and will not be allowed to thrive."

Raylor spoke directly to camera. The chamber was almost clear now, with only essential personnel remaining. The TV crew had set-up closer to the bench and Raylor had quickly written some notes for his speech. They amounted to nothing more than a list of names, but he had found the words to accompany them once the live feed had kicked in.

Only one name remained.

"Finally," he spoke then drew a deep breath. "Bernard Kiebler. President Kiebler and the Galactic Union.

"I announce officially, and unequivocally, as the leader of the Martian people that as of today all trade agreements are cancelled. All transport and shipping agreements are cancelled.

"If anyone is making their way here from Jupiter or on official GU business - turn your ship around. All ties are severed. We no longer recognise the rule of the Galactic Union.

"Mars stands alone."

CHAPTER TWENTY-THREE

K iebler snarled at his Chief Advisor, Donald Orsay. He had been listening to the man speak for ten minutes now and was no further forward in his understanding of the situation.

"Don, you have to get to the point sometime soon or I'm literally going to get out of my seat and tear your fucking head from your stupid square shoulders," he barked.

"I believe Donald was just getting to the relevant issues, if I'm not mistaken?" Scion stepped in diplomatically.

"Yes sir... Err... sirs." Orsay stammered. He had coped through many briefings in the past as Kiebler's advisor on the campaign trail, and again in vital meetings since he became President. However, this was the worst of the bunch. An update on the GU's abject failure to get a stranglehold on Mars and Jupiter's complete impotence in the situation so far. It made it worse that this was in front of the entire cabinet, and tensions were clearly running high.

"The bullet points, basically speaking, are that Mars holds the most advanced communication arrays and vast outpost equipment in the entire solar system. It is an essential piece of the galactic framework."

"Do we have any way of replicating this equipment ourselves?" Marlborough asked.

"Potentially, but at an astronomical cost," Orsay replied.

"Money is no object, Don. She's asking if it can be done," Kiebler butted in.

"I believe that part could be achieved, yes. It would take time and cause some serious issues in the meantime, but in theory yes it could work."

"Where does the theory fall down, Donald?" Scion asked, picking up on the look on Orsay's face as he spoke.

"The real issue isn't the infrastructure. Time and money can build anything. Our problem lies in the workforce. Jupiter doesn't have the skilled workers we'd need to create any of this from scratch. All of the best scientific minds are non-contactable on the outer rim habitation projects of Neptune and Uranus. The best manual labourers are all Martian. The logistics are impossible."

He finished talking and waited for the backlash. Kiebler just stood, mouth poised to explode into another tirade which didn't come. After a moment's pause he exhaled deeply and slumped back into his chair.

"Have terms been offered yet by the Martians?" Marlborough asked.

"Nothing at all," Scion answered, "except for the communication which drew us all here."

"Promising to shut down the galaxy at a day's notice. And they call us the threat to the future of mankind?" Kiebler spoke with a laugh.

"Turning off anything non-essential to Mars, they said. Playing us for fools," Marlborough added.

"The practicalities are the least of our worries," Scion spoke. "The fact is the people now see Mars in open revolt. We have seen this type of thing throughout history – word spreads, the notions of freedom and making your own fate take hold. Soon you have rebellions on your hands all over the world - or the solar system in this case."

"You think my people will revolt against us because the fucking Martians did? You're going soft on me, Dax," Kiebler said.

"I'm not suggesting they want to. I'm just pointing out that perception is key. They ate it up when we told them Mars was in league with the extremists. Now that has been unequivocally disproven."

"Partially, maybe. One of their Senators was tried for treason, remember?" Marlborough interrupted.

"The point is, they have also purged the PoE from their ranks and thrown a blanket ban on all Earth citizens. They have emerged from under the lies, or half-truths, and are stronger for it," Scion concluded.

"So we have to act very soon to change this perception. Make sure the people don't think for themselves," Marlborough said.

"I don't care what the people think. I'm done with this." Kiebler tossed his diary, pen and half the contents of his desk to the floor, almost nonchalantly.

"They voted for me, they have to live with it now. Next."

The group shared concerned looks for a moment, while Kiebler eyed each of them, wondering which one would be brave enough to stick their head above the parapet.

"It may not be just the perception to our own citizens which matters," Marlborough boldly spoke up. "The perception of Jupiter within the GU is changed. Mars was a powerful ally and the GU has lost that. Throw that in with the links between our cabinet and the PoE and we suddenly look like the aggressors, or at least the supporters of a corrupt government."

"Then my question is what the hell do I pay you for, Valerie?" Kiebler spoke, anger dripping from his words.

"I send you to the GU Handpick you for the role of a lifetime. You think you could have got that job without me? You think people suddenly thought 'Oh, look at Valerie, turns out she isn't washed up after all'?"

Marlborough was taken aback for a moment, unable to formulate the words to defend her position. She listened to the rant, trying not to look like every word was a crushing blow.

"You went to the GU and you have provided me with *nothing*. Now you tell me that not only are they *not* in our pocket, they are actively turning their heads to the Martian pricks who have ruined everything else we have going for us?

He spat the words with such venom the others in the room stood back awaiting the breakdown they were sure Marlborough was due to have.

"You useless, dried up, haggard old wretch. We look weak, Valerie. We look weak and you are doing nothing about it."

Marlborough leaned forward in her seat and took a sip from her glass of water. She gathered her thoughts for a moment before looking directly into Bernard Kiebler's eyes.

"You want to know why we look weak, Bernie?"

"Enlighten me, Valerie."

"We look weak because we are weak. Standing around here, crying about it. You are the leader of the most powerful planet in the known universe. Fucking use it."

Kiebler, completely taken aback, rolled back in his seat and stared Valerie Marlborough up and down.

"Remember your own words, Bernard. 'Change isn't going to come easily' you said. 'Some blood will have to be spilled'. Wasn't that it?" she moved closer as she spoke, emphasising every word.

A sickening smile began to grow on Bernard Kiebler's lips, then crawled slowly across his face. Marlborough was at his desk now, almost face to face with her President.

"Causalities are an inevitability of war," Kiebler spoke.

"Indeed they are," Marlborough replied.

***

Kiebler meant every word of his recorded speech that day. He couldn't remember a time when he could genuinely say that before – that he truly, honestly believed the words he was speaking to camera.

The energy of the day had fired him up, and his thoughts kept returning to one thing – that this was why he had wanted to be President. The thrill of the chase, the excitement of calling people out and taking bold actions. Some of it was sneaky, smart and thought out to the nth degree. Some of it was base and guttural and meant life or death for those involved.

This was why he wanted to govern. He wondered if he had just wanted to play war games all of his life, and decided he probably didn't want to know the answer to that or to follow the trail of psychological trauma which might lead him to it.

The morning started early with an emergency session of the High Court. He chaired the meeting himself, with Valerie Marlborough attending in her capacity as Galactic Union Chair. The various representatives of each major political group were invited along, as well as prominent – meaning voting – members of the GU. Apologies were made for those who wished to attend but were off-planet – the

Martian cull of communication arrays had already begun through the night, leaving many members unable to patch into the meeting.

It had taken the best part of two hours to fully convey the Mars situation, and its implications on the fragility of the GU to the gathered attendees. Once all was said and done, and Kiebler had had his say, a vote was called.

"That vote, taken this morning and verified by myself as President of Jupiter, alongside Ms Marlborough of the Galactic Union, was unanimous."

He spoke with pride and used all of his acting experience to carry his voice and emphasise the words perfectly. He was speaking live to as much of the solar system as could still receive the television signal. He was assured by his top men that this was a very high percentage of the human population. His words would be heard.

He considered it for a moment, and basked in it. He knew that everyone watching would see the enormity of this day. He knew that he could sell it as such. He smiled as he considered the fact that this particular speech would be replayed for generations to come – the true highlight of his Presidency.

"We recognise the actions of the Martian leadership as an act of war. We have voted to aggressively, and relentlessly, defend both ourselves and the interests of the entire solar system against this threat.

"A task force will be deployed to Mars to deal with the insurgent forces threatening our way of life here beyond the Belt.

"The GU and the Jupitoan government would like nothing more than to work with the Martian people to find suitable solutions to all of their issues. However, it seems many of these 'issues' are based in rumour and lies. We cannot accommodate this and we will not negotiate away our democracy.

"The rhetoric from Mars' new leadership threatens to undo many years of hard work to bring the Galactic Union together, and their actions in the early hours of this morning are a betrayal of everything they once stood for.

"They paint a pretty public relations picture for the media, but in reality they are traitors to the cause of humanity and will be dealt with in the swiftest way possible."

His heart pounded in his chest. He hoped that he wasn't looking too flushed on screen – the rush of blood and adrenaline was intoxicating and he could feel the giddiness overtaking him.

He lowered his head and bit his lip hard, fighting the urge to smile.

"Sebastian Raylor now holds us to ransom by threatening to turn off vital navigational apparatus. He has already begun the process of removing communication systems which are leaving many in the dark this evening. Many more will follow.

"They plan to renege on deals that were set-up – quite favourably, it must be said – to reward the

Martian government for providing these services to ourselves and our neighbours beyond the Belt."

He enjoyed hammering home the 'them and us' narrative - beyond the Belt good, the interior Planets bad. It helped to keep Mars in the same category as Earth, as well as painting it as a backwater world, left behind by technology and kicking and screaming against the winds of change.

"Jupiter will not be held hostage," he said with determination dripping from his professionally-honed voice. "The Galactic Union will not be held in contempt or be made the public patsy in a Martian workers' revolt."

He paused again for effect. His job was done here and he knew that he had turned in the performance which was required of him to sell this war. He just wanted to add some weight to his final statement, so that it was fully understood.

"The first wave of Jupitoan forces will cross the Belt at midday today. Mr Raylor – the ball is in your court now."

***

Marlborough knocked and waited. The door was slightly ajar. She peered in, inching the door open further and further until she heard heavy breathing coming from somewhere out of sight. She took a bold step into the apartment.

The exasperated breathing grew more focused as she closed the door behind her, leaving the room in total darkness. The noise of the door clicking into place signalled her arrival.

Kiebler stepped out from a doorway to her left, where light dimly filtered out into the hall.

"Valerie!" he spoke, excitedly. He held up a bottle of wine, with a corkscrew embedded into its top. "I can't get this damn thing open. It's an Earth vintage apparently." He shrugged and shot her a smile.

"It seemed appropriate," he laughed, turning to flick a switch on the wall which raised the mood lighting.

She returned his smile and allowed a small giggle, then watched as he returned to through the door he had appeared from. She took the opportunity to take off her coat and take in the apartment. As a temporary residence it wasn't exactly what she had expected.

"The apartment is lovely, Mr President. They're keeping you in comfort while you stay here, I see."

"Oh, it'll do for me," he replied from the other room. A loud 'pop' followed, and he appeared again, grin as wide as an ocean and an open bottle of wine in hand.

"Please – it's Bernic," he said. He reached for two large wine glasses from a nearby table and made his way over to the living room area, where Valerie was still perusing the decor.

"Here we go, Valerie," he said, pouring them both a hefty glass.

She glanced up at the large and elaborate clock mounted on the wall above a plush silver sofa.

"They should be arriving any minute," she said with a tremble of excitement in her voice.

"Fingers crossed. I've got Hasting on stand-by out there, ready to call in as soon as the full force joins him."

He handed her one of the glasses and took up his own.

"Cheers," he almost whispered while holding eye contact.

"To taking matters into your own hands," she replied as she clinked her glass against his.

Kiebler motioned for her to take a seat, then cosied up beside her on the grand sofa.

"You must feel very proud with all of this coming together so quickly," she said.

"It's funny, I feel happy that we are finally doing good work, but at the same time I feel a huge amount of frustration at the situation."

"You're frustrated that it has come to this?"

"No, not that," he replied. "I'm frustrated that I was ready to wipe out these 'Peoples of Earth' factions weeks ago. I sent Hasting out to the Belt for that very reason. Then before he can even get his feet under the table the Martians and the Earthlings implode."

He took a deep glug of his wine. Marlborough sipped at hers.

"I listened to him. I listened to Scion. I held back and let them tear each other apart, expecting to pick up the broken pieces at the end. Instead, this is what I get – Sebastian Raylor and his merry men."

"You shouldn't worry yourself with that, Bernie," Marlborough comforted him. She placed a hand on his knee.

"Even if you had taken out the Peoples of Earth before their problems with Mars began, the Martians would have had to be dealt with eventually. They have been mis-governed for too long. The people are rabid for a revolution."

"Maybe so. It just burns me up to think about it, we should have taken them all out months ago."

Kiebler looked at the woman by his side and considered the hand resting on his knee. As she sipped at her wine she caught his eye and the hand slid up to his thigh, the grip growing ever tighter.

"You know, Valerie, I was really impressed with you stepping up on this one. You got your hands dirty and made me see the light."

"I simply reminded you of your own outstanding advice. You would have arrived at the same thought yourself eventually, I'm sure."

"Don't play down your role in this, Valerie. The way you spoke to us all. It was vicious. And that plan! Aligning the Union and our government's goals with a simple vote – do you know how delicious that is?"

"I'm not sure what you mean?" she replied.

"Collusion, Valerie. The very thing the Martians and the protestors were accusing us of. Working together, too closely, corrupting the Galactic Union. We've solved it by doing exactly what they suspected in the first place."

He laughed a loud, hearty laugh and finished his wine with a gulp. Marlborough followed suit.

The comms display, integrated into the table in the middle of the room, buzzed into life at that moment and Kiebler reached out to answer it.

"We have General Hasting for you, sir," a voice came through the hidden speaker.

"Go ahead," Kiebler replied.

Hasting's voice came through loud and clear, using the military channels which were built and administered by Jupiter. Kiebler took some pleasure from the fact that the Martians wouldn't be able to shut this one down and that it would contribute to their downfall. The sweetest part, to him at least, was that it was all built from Martian designed plans.

"The last squadron has arrived, Mr President. All are battle ready. Awaiting orders."

Kiebler looked at Valerie Marlborough and she felt the utter glee in his smile and in his words in that moment.

"Launch the attack, General," he spoke in the most commanding voice he could muster through his grinning teeth.

His gaze remained on Marlborough and she met it with a smile of her own. He leaned towards her, as Hasting uttered some meaningless confirmations over the speaker.

He half expected her to back away but found her leaning into the kiss he offered, giving as good as she got. His hands pulled her closer, grabbing at her shoulders. He writhed her jacket from her as hastily as he could and she soon felt the warmth of his hands on the small of her back.

She felt his strength, pulling at her, urging her closer. He kissed her and she felt herself let go of any hesitation she had. Calm, level-headed, business-woman Valerie wouldn't approve, she knew. Relations with the boss were never her thing. She saw it as beneath her.

This was different. Her boss. Her President.

She felt every second as if it were an hour. In reality it was raw, lustful and over in just a few fleeting moments.

Marlborough lay back on the strange sofa in Kiebler's apartment and let out a sigh. Shirt still intact, skirt torn from her and flung to the far side of the room.

She had dreamed of this many times before and hoped that this time she wasn't about to wake up.

CHAPTER TWENTY-FOUR

T he impact rattled the walls of the old corridor and Raylor had to reach out to steady himself with his fingertips. The bombing hadn't ceased for eighteen hours now and the extent of the damage was becoming clear.

Many buildings on his way to the Workers' Council offices had been levelled completely. Piles of rubble stood, smouldering from untended fires, where once were tower blocks. Offices and government buildings had taken the brunt of the early assault and now the very walls of the Workers' Council offices shook with any nearby activity.

Raylor wondered how long the old building could stand. He wondered why they hadn't been attacked directly already. He guessed that Kiebler's forces expected the majority of Mars' decision makers to be huddled in the Senate building, with Raylor himself among them.

He entered the comms room and made a beeline for James Bellson, who was hunkered over a display in the corner of the room with Eliza Bergman.

"That one felt close?" Raylor offered.

"Couple of miles away, by the looks of it. Already retreating," Bellson looked up at his friend. "I can't figure out why they waste their time on those solo runs then back off so urgently," he muttered.

"They're trying to scare us," Raylor replied.

"It's working."

Bellson gave a wan smile and Raylor raised his eyebrows, while taking off his scarf and coat.

"The Chairman is here for you," Eliza informed him. "He's in your office. He didn't want to see this news coverage."

Chairman Tyler despised the media coverage of anything military-related. His wish was for a complete embargo on news outlets covering live war stories – it was dangerous for the reporters to get involved, and even more so for them to reveal movements and designs that his forces would prefer to keep secret.

Raylor headed for his office and swung open the door. Bellson followed him in.

"Mr Chairman," he said, shaking Tyler's hand. "Have you come with an update?"

"I have, sir. Argyre and Hellas have fallen in the south; Memnonia in the east is asking to give the go ahead on evacuation. Casius has been under siege through the night – an armed force was set down under cover of darkness and has the government on its knees. It's only a matter of time."

"Any good news?" Bellson asked.

"Only some slightly-less-bad news. Arabia isn't responding to radio calls. They've been silent since early morning, which could be procedural."

"It's unlikely they'd go lights out without warning?"

"It's unusual. They could have shut down comms to aid them in combat, but we wouldn't expect to lose contact for this long. I've got a team heading out there now but I wouldn't hold out much hope – if they are under siege we have absolutely no force available to facilitate a rescue."

"You still have enough men to guard the Senate?" Raylor asked, worried.

"I have posted every man I have now. Everyone within the capital is positioned in or around the Senate building."

"How's it looking inside?" Bellson queried.

"Every refugee from the destroyed buildings is being crammed in there. Children are being made comfortable, while those up to the task are being put to work helping with defences. It's packed, it's loud, it's hot."

"And it's all gone if they attack. There's little hope we can hold firm for long," Bellson spoke.

"There's still not been a direct attack on the Senate, though? Any ideas as to why, Mr Chairman?" Raylor asked.

"None as yet. They made strafing runs throughout the night but no sign of a bomb dropped.

My men are hardened soldiers, sir. They can withstand a ground assault longer than anyone you could pit them against – but they're only human."

"And when the bombs start to fall..." Bellson added, dejected.

Raylor considered it all for a moment. He couldn't get his head around much of the tactics of the Jupitoan armed forces and he wondered how much Kiebler had to do with that. Was he a military genius? Was he playing with them? Were his orders so incoherent that he was just stumbling to victory through sheer power of numbers?

"I've got to believe that there is some decency left. Something must have stayed Kiebler's hand so far, otherwise the Senate would be a mountain of rubble by now, with all of us under it."

"Seb," Bellson spoke, softer now. "I know what's at stake here. Trust me, I do. But this is suicide – we've made our stand now. How much further can we go?"

"What are you saying? We should give up?" Raylor relied, incredulous.

"It's not giving up," Bellson thought it through as he spoke, "it's cutting our losses. Maybe others will see now, across the system. They'll recognise what we tried to achieve and the lengths to which Kiebler has stretched to just to block us. Maybe we've changed their thinking by showing what we are willing to give up."

Raylor considered the point for a moment. He had never seen Bellson afraid of anything, and had rarely heard his voice quiver as it did now. It wasn't an endearing side to his friend, and he deeply wished to have his confident and ballsy partner back by his side.

"Are we still willing to give it up, James?"

Bellson had no answer. The question hung in the air, tangible, as Chairman Tyler joined Raylor in staring at the man in front of them. Bellson looked at his feet.

"Mr Raylor is our interim Leader, Bellson. You answer his direct questions." Tyler stepped up.

Bellson raised his head and Raylor saw the answer painted all over his face. He couldn't accept it.

"I don't want to die for this. I don't want anyone to die for this. If surrender is what it takes, and our punishment the only consequence, then so be it."

Raylor tried to suppress the rage which coursed through his body. He clenched his fists and bit down on his tongue. He wasn't sure if he was angry at his friend for giving up hope, or at the fact that there was so little hope to give up on.

He looked to Chairman Tyler, whose stare was still fixed on Bellson.

"Would you give us a moment alone, James?" Raylor asked.

Bellson stood wordlessly and left the office, closing the door behind him. He glanced back through the small window at his friend, knowing he was letting him down but feeling with all of his heart that he was right.

"I can't advise a way to win this fight, sir. We don't have the numbers or the air power to fight back adequately. Defending ourselves is the only plan," Tyler spoke calmly.

"You aren't suggesting that we surrender, too?" Raylor replied, incredulously.

"Absolutely not. We just can't fight them at their own game. My men will defend the city and its people to the last. You and the cabinet must be kept safe and that can't happen here."

"I can't leave the city, it'd create chaos."

"The only win Kiebler is looking for is your head on a pole. Don't give it to him so easily. This place will be in far more chaos without you."

Raylor mulled it over and quickly realised there was little he could do in terms of defending the city. His presence was drawing unnecessary attention from strafing parties, probably looking for his whereabouts. He was glad for the Chairman's level-headedness.

"I trust you with my city, Chairman. Our city. Acidalium must not fall with a whimper, you hear me?"

"Loud and clear, Mr Leader," Tyler responded. His demeanour changed, and Raylor sensed maybe a spark in his eye that he hadn't shown a moment ago.

"I have something I need to disclose, for your ears only," Tyler said.

"Please," Raylor spoke, motioning for him to go on.

"Remember the old days of the 'Glorious Martian War Machine'? All that hyperbole?" he asked.

"I've seen the footage. My dad used to tell me all about it. The great Martian warriors – the best that ever lived in all of the known universe, so they said."

"Yet they only ever seemed to fight amongst themselves," Tyler remarked glibly.

"What of it? You suggest another civil war right now and I'll strip you of your rank before sunrise," Raylor tried to joke. The Chairman leaned forward in his seat.

"There's a storage hanger – several, in fact – on the east coast. A military secret. Mars' great military past is still kept there, gathering dust."

"By 'military past' you mean...?"

"I mean great warships. The likes and size of which you've never seen. They're unwieldy, bulky, clumsy machines. But they pack a serious punch."

"We have a fleet? A secret fleet of warships?" Raylor couldn't quite believe the words he was hearing. Mars had left its war-like reputation in the long distant past.

"They're not much to speak of. I don't want to get your hopes up too much. They are an easy target in a fight and the sophistication of the Jupitoan fleets can easily blow us out of the sky. But for the time they stay flying – man, they're a sight."

"You think we can launch an assault with them?"

"We aren't going to launch them into the atmosphere and invade Jupiter or anything like that. They aren't even enough to repel the Jupitoan force that is here already. But if we use them at the right time they could provide an incredibly ballsy distraction."

"Thank you for this, Chairman. Every little helps. Hold on to that particular card until the time is right – it may not be enough to win us the war, but we might use it to strike a telling blow."

"Just upholding our Martian traditions. For our fathers and our father's fathers."

The two men shared a smile in the moment, and knew that they were on the same page in their mindset – two men fighting a war which was lost before it began but fighting on regardless.

"What's our next move, Leader?" Tyler asked.

Raylor pondered another moment, hoping he was making the right choice, and deep down knowing it was the *only* choice.

"We'll retreat to the safe zone in the northern sector – the industrial bunkers at Boreum should be under cover and still have comms in working order. At the very worst we'll draw some attention away from you here for a little while."

Bellson knocked at the door and walked straight in.

"Sorry to impose but it's looking more dire every minute out there. Do we have a plan?"

"Boreum," Raylor replied.

"So we hide in a cave until the end finds us?" Bellson asked.

"We hunker down and plan out our options. We'll be safer there – the industrial zones are notoriously impossible to navigate with electrical equipment on board and nobody in their right mind would bomb them."

"Kiebler isn't in his right mind! Hasn't he proven that already?"

"He has resisted wiping out a building full of evacuees, women and children. Bombing the industrial zone would be planet-wide genocide," Raylor replied.

Bellson flung his arms up the air. Raylor recognised it as the pent up anger and deep frustration that lay in his heart but also as the immature act of a young man with too many ideas, so much passion and not the will to see it through.

"I'll arrange transport," Tyler spoke, standing up from his seat at Raylor's desk.

"Take care of my people, Chairman," Raylor said, reaching out to shake his hand.

"I'm just watching over them, sir. Only you can take care of us now."

CHAPTER TWENTY-FIVE

"You're were sent here from the Saturn deployment?" Hasting asked, as he approached a man in his late thirties. His stubble and wiry black hair gave him a dark complexion, which was in direct conflict with the beaming white smile he flashed back at the General.

"I'm Lieutenant Tarab Arthur, at your service, General," he replied.

"You seem to have done a lot of damage on the way in – did you run into trouble?"

"Oh, nothing we couldn't handle," the young lieutenant laughed. He had flown his squadron in at sunrise with a direct order to report to Hasting and assist in the final steps to victory on Mars. They hadn't made contact with a single enemy vessel or ground force on their arrival, however Arthur had wanted to make his presence known.

"I've got reports of burning buildings outside of town. Several witnesses claiming some heavy-duty firepower was deployed," Hasting told him, stony-faced.

"I didn't want to waste any time. The Martians need to understand the danger they are in."

"Understand the danger? Lieutenant, if any of us truly understood the dangers we face in this whole endeavour we'd all be crawling back through the Belt and crying for our mothers. It's not your place to teach the Martian people anything."

Hasting had heard rumours of Arthur back on Jupiter. The men in his unit had heard stories of the life the Saturn deployments led – it was a cushy gig if you could get it. The leisure planet wasn't exactly a hotbed of military action – not in the past two decades at least.

Stories were floated of servicemen and women being caught out with holidaymakers and coming home from twelve-month stints with beer bellies and all-over-body tans. Hasting suspected that Lieutenants such as Arthur did little to bring that sort of behaviour to an end. Looking at his new right hand man's current condition he suspected he may actually be the subject of one or more of those tales.

"I want a report filed citing your reasoning and listing every type of weaponry used. Have it to me before we break this morning," Hasting demanded, then continued his walk through the command hub they had set up in the Martian capital.

Lieutenant Arthur took in the stares of those around him for a brief second, then followed hot on the General's heels.

"General, I don't appreciate the way you just spoke to me in front of my men," he called after his superior officer. "Believe it or not I am a fully competent leader of my force, and I will back any action taken by them in combat," he spoke confidently.

Hasting stopped in his stride and turned to allow Arthur to catch up. He eyed him from head to toe once again. He wouldn't have believed he was a day over twenty-years old if he hadn't read his history and profile in preparation for his arrival.

"Back them or not, you have just dropped a gang of outsiders into a warzone they know nothing about and flown in the face of established tactics. That's not to mention the possible victims of the attacks."

"Outsiders? With due respect, my men are as experienced and understanding of their roles as yours are. Different doesn't mean bad, General," Arthur stood his ground.

"I'm fully aware of each of their backgrounds, Lieutenant, as well as yours,"

"Then you'll have a good idea of what I think of your current tactics then?"

Hasting had read of the Lieutenant's limited field experience and could see the man was no less cavalier in his attitude than his record suggested.

"I suspected you might advocate a more aggressive approach."

"You're making strafing runs over known military targets. You're allowing political and populist figures live their lives despite the fact that we know exactly where they are and can track their every movement!"

"I'm using the tactics which will win us a war with the least amount of casualties. I am here to represent my planet's interests by keeping Mars on its knees. We are the bully here, not the executioner."

"If I may speak frankly, sir, I think you're being too soft," Arthur offered, with his eyes fixed on those of the General.

"President Kiebler wants to make an example of this whole operation. He's embarrassed by the way Mars has defied him. The Martians should be made to suffer. The galaxy should be made to see the consequences of crossing Bernard Kiebler and the Galactic Union."

"Did our President relay these thoughts to you privately?" Hasting asked with a degree of exasperation in his voice.

"No, sir," Arthur returned, "I spoke privately with Daxler Scion before leaving Jupiter. He assured me that was the case."

Hasting couldn't get a read on his new colleague but suspected he was being truthful. He had heard the rumour that Scion had some family hidden away somewhere – and the various rumours about just how legitimate parts of that family were. One of those rumours suggested he had promoted some family blood, under the radar.

It wouldn't come as a surprise to find out he had been doing so, right under the nose of Kiebler and his Generals. Hasting knew that this young Lieutenant's career so far had not suggested he should be here today, so he had to wonder. He pushed any judgement from his head and relied on cold, hard truths.

"Lieutenant – out here you answer to one man only, and that's me. In turn, I don't answer to private conversations you may have held with anyone in the known galaxy."

He fixed his serious stare onto the younger man.

"Do you understand me, Lieutenant?"

Arthur stared right back at him. Hasting gave him some credit for not backing down.

"Understood, General," came his forced response. "I just hope our President issues the order to blow the Senate off the face of the planet soon."

"That is not your business," Hasting snapped back. "We are military leaders. We're not in the business of murdering the innocent. The Senate building is packed with Mars' weak and elderly. Women and children. People who are not a threat to us, and whose own leaders know they are fighting a losing battle."

"The Senate building is a symbol of Mars' free government and as long as it stands it will be seen as a testament to Martian bravery in the face of adversity. The sooner it goes, the sooner this government, and many others out there, will fall at our feet."

Hasting pondered the words of his new protégé carefully. He considered just how dark a heart he must possess to think so coldly about the loss of life and liberty, even in an enemy.

"I am not willing to murder innocent people for political gain," he finally spoke. "President Kiebler may wish for it, but he has not passed such an order and I would be unwilling to fight for any leader who did so."

Hasting's stare lingered on Tarab Arthur's face for a moment longer. Both men knew they would never agree on the principle. Only one of them recognised just how monumental a problem that may turn out to be.

**

The lumbering old transport ship heaved its way through the thick industrial fog which masqueraded as air in Boreum. The vast structures of the region pumped out steam and smoke in abundance, whilst creating the atmosphere which all Martians thrived on. Breathing was difficult out in the open and no animals of any kind seemed to dwell in the north because of it.

Raylor looked out at the conical shapes of monumental funnels as they flew over their heads – grey and cold and unforgiving they appeared. He remembered visiting as a child with his school class and everyone staring in awe at the giant machinery. He had stood alone at the back of the group, looking on in fear at the noisy, imposing designs.

He had enjoyed learning of Mars' great past and wondered if that combination of history and fear was what had eventually pulled him towards serving the people of Mars. He felt a want within himself to be part of the great machine and to contribute to the future in some meaningful way. He had never quite grasped what that way might look like.

A reckless war. A folly the likes of which no Martian had ever attempted. That was his legacy now, he thought. Maybe the history books would see him as a man who tried to do his best for the people, even if the victory they deserved was impossible to achieve.

He thought it more likely that the next generation of children visiting this place would be here to see the site of his biggest failure – the leader who ran away and lost the entire system in the process.

"It's quite a sight, isn't it?" Marien Lyndell asked, stepping up to gaze out of the window by Raylor's side.

"It's terrifying, but soothing?" Raylor offered with a smile.

Lyndell laughed and shifted her gaze to the man rather than the view outside.

"Seb, you can't beat yourself up about coming here. This place exists exactly for our purposes now."

"I know," Raylor agreed, "I just can't help thinking I'm the captain who abandoned his ship."

The Boreum bunkers were designed in secret in Mars' long-forgotten past, to allow the government to escape the people. In times of stress, or sometimes civil war, the leadership could retreat safely and still have all of the operational abilities they required to lead and plan effectively.

The pair walked across the hanger-like hold of the vessel and joined the other leadership members at a small table. Ramsey Pierce offered a smile, Eliza Bergman a glance.

James Bellson sat in stony silence.

"What's our first order of business once we get settled?" Ramsey asked.

"We brainstorm our position – where would we like to be, realistically, and where do we think we can negotiate with Kiebler," Raylor replied.

"How can we possibly negotiate?" Bellson argued. "We have absolutely no position. We have nothing to offer except our own surrender. How do any of you envisage us getting out of this?"

His points were valid. He delivered them with barely concealed anger.

"We will talk it through. Decide amongst ourselves what we are willing to risk, what we are willing to give up. What we are willing to make a stand against."

Raylor stared at Bellson as he responded, and Bellson shifted his gaze quickly. Raylor didn't understand how he could have lost the respect and patience of his right-hand man so quickly but knew frustration and fear were playing their parts in equal measure.

"We have to be strong," he continued. "From here we can reach out to the other leaders, across the solar system. Rally some support. The universe won't stand idly by as Kiebler makes a mockery of the Galactic Union and attempts to crush the freedom of the Martian people."

"You think that will work, Seb?" Lyndell asked. "I know a handful of those leaders and I know where their interests lie."

"Money. Power. Respect. Specifically the money and power they earn from giving Bernard Kiebler their respect. You think they'll turn their backs on Jupiter's dollars, for our sake?" Bellson chimed in.

"I think it's the responsibility of all of humankind to hold each of us to the same level of respect and accountability. I have faith in people," Raylor stated.

"Then I'm afraid you are going to be severely disappointed," Bellson answered back.

"Kiebler is smart," Pierce spoke up to break the silence between the two. "He won't want to lose face in the eyes of the other leaders – no matter how badly they want to cosy up to him. His ego is a loose cannon firing against us, but it can work in our favour too."

"Exactly. Add to that the fact that these other planets must see the power play Kiebler has made for the GU and understand it as an attack on everyone's democratic freedom." Lyndell stood with Raylor, while Bellson did not stir from his seat.

"Thank you, Senators," Raylor spoke. "I have to believe all of those points ring true. With the buy-in of the other leaders we may just have enough of a voice to force Kiebler on to the defensive – politically if not militarily."

Raylor looked around the table at the glum and darkened faces gathered there.

"To do that I will need all of you to buy-in too."

Pierce and Lyndell nodded their approval.

"James?"

Bellson let the question hang in the air for a moment. In that moment even he didn't know which way his answer might fall. Finally, he looked up from the table and into Raylor's eyes.

"I trust you to lead. I will follow."

***

The landing gear screeched open and Bellson departed last of all. The smell of sulphur and mechanical oil was thick in the air, and he pulled his scarf around his head to double up as a breathing mask.

The group wandered into a huge, barren hanger. The walls were gun-metal grey and icicles hung from the rafters far up above. Raylor and the senators moved further into the open space, heading for a small office-like area near the centre.

"I'm going to find a comms room," Bellson shouted after them. Raylor gave a cursory wave while the others checked out their new toys. Bellson caught the flicker of a monitor out of the corner of his eye and the capital news theme tune sprung into life, echoing through the hanger and following him down the darkened corridor ahead.

He fumbled for a light switch and was rewarded with a stuttering florescent orange glow. He tentatively looked in each door as he wandered and finally spotted a bed. He heaved open the heavy iron door and dumped his travelling bags onto the floor, then looked around. He couldn't imagine spending many nights in this freezing hell.

He opened a zipper on his bag and rummaged for a smaller bag within. He opened it up and took out a small decoder box, a portable transmitter and a signal boosting aerial pack. He headed out.

At the end of the corridor he found stairs to the next level and on the next level he found a notice showing the layout of the building. He studied it for a moment and noted the way to the roof.

Ten minutes later he was stood in the freezing, heavy air, looking out above the barren wastelands to the south and the heaving industrial zone in the north. He quickly pieced together his communicator and switched it on.

It buzzed and whirred for a few moments while the portable antenna methodically spun half a degree clockwise and pinged for a signal. With a beep, louder than he cared for, it finally connected.

Bellson fiddled with the controls and made his call. The comms box spat out a hazy image as the video conference connected.

"Mr Bellson, such an honour," Daxler Scion spoke, his voice crackling through the static.

"Scion. I don't have much time. You know I wouldn't call you on this line without good reason," Bellson spoke, nervously.

"Indeed. Where are you, boy?"

Bellson hesitated for a moment.

"We're in the north. An old civil war hideout, as far as I'm aware."

He hoped he had kept his answer vague enough for the time being, but not so vague to inspire any distrust.

"Raylor is running away then? I wondered if the man was a leader or a coward – Mr Kiebler will be pleased with the outcome."

"No, he's not running. At least he's telling his people as much. He believes he can rally the Galactic Union – or at least those leaders who make up the majority of it – to see Mars' side in all of this. He thinks they'll take pity and put pressure on Kiebler."

"And you believe the pressure will break Bernard Kiebler? That he will relent?" Scion asked, with a hint of laughter behind his voice.

"I have my doubts," Bellson admitted.

"You can't truly believe this nonsense, James. You must surely see that Raylor is a madman. His efforts will be fruitless."

"I have voiced my doubts with him. He assures us his plan is solid, that he isn't giving up and that he sees some good will in Kiebler which will see him bow to the pressure."

"Fools. All of you," Scion spat, angrily. "Let me make things clear for you, James. Bernard Kiebler has no compassion for the Martian cause – and has no care for the other 'leaders' of the solar system. He has been riled, he has been hassled, he has been inconvenienced. He seen his new bride murdered on his wedding day and he has had to stand by and watch as Jupiter's neighbours have systematically raped and pillaged his beloved planet for too long."

Bellson shook in fear at the words as Scion delivered them with the kind of precision and vitriol that he had never witnessed before.

"If our galactic neighbours don't like what he has in store for Mars then make no mistake – they will be next. He has made this clear. He will take no prisoners. So, speaking of any good will Raylor has foreseen is optimistic at very best. I suspect he has gleaned this from the survival of the Martian Senate building, yes?"

Bellson uttered an inaudibly weak 'yes' while nodding his head.

"Then I am delighted to inform you that just this very morning, Mr Kiebler was made aware of the building's survival and that of those who dwell within it. He has ordered its complete and utter destruction. They will all be dead by sundown."

Bellson heaved a breath into his lungs, as tears came to his eyes. His chest pounded and his body shook, as he at least tried to maintain some semblance of participation in the conversation.

"Please," he managed to speak at last. "Please, spare them. I beg you to change his mind. I throw myself at your mercy – do not let the innocent ones be the victims of Raylor's mistakes."

"I cannot change the President's mind. The order is set. He is a hard man to convince."

"I'll do anything. I can be of great benefit to your cause – offer him my allegiance in return."

"I cannot go to him with such a paltry suggestion, boy. What have you got to offer the most powerful man in the Universe?"

"We have nothing."

"Give me something to barter."

"I have nothing"

"You have Raylor."

Scion's words fell like a hammer. Bellson felt the weight of them as they reverberated around him.

"Give me your location and I can save your precious Senate," Scion stuck the knife in harder.

Bellson closed his eyes.

CHAPTER TWENTY-SIX

G eneral Hasting sensed the excitement in the air and couldn't shake the feeling of dread it gave him.

He worked his way through the gathered troops on the muddy campsite they had settled into, on the outskirts of Acidalium. Mars' capital city looked battered and bruised in the background, as the soldiers jostled and laughed with one another on the field.

At the front of the site he found the enormous communications tent, where rain bounced off the roof and soaked the two armed patrolmen who stood guard. Inside, two technicians were busy setting up a large screen.

All of the lieutenants and captains were sat around the make-shift table, sharing a laugh with a particularly bawdy and enthusiastic Lieutenant

Arthur. They all straightened up and quietened down at the sight of the General entering the tent – all except Arthur.

"General, come and join us. We're sharing our favourite Martian war stories," the young Lieutenant smiled.

"I want you all stood to attention, immediately," Hasting barked. "That thing ready to go?" he asked, turning to the tech team.

"Yes, sir," came the response and the screen fizzed into action.

"Make the call."

Hasting took his position in front of the screen as the loud beeping indicated a connection was being sought. Within a moment the black screen was filled with the image of Bernard Kiebler's office, Daxler Scion appeared, standing alongside the seated President.

"Hasting! How goes the front lines?" Kiebler announced, cheerily.

"We're doing well, sir. The South is under Jupitoan control now. Several cities along the east coast have all been evacuated by the Martians, meaning there is very little resistance. The siege at Casius was broken at dawn today and the capital will follow soon enough. We understand the leadership have fled, leaving only the army in control here."

"Excellent work, General. You do your people proud." Kiebler's beaming smile flashed again, and Hasting's creeping dread crept further still.

"Dax has some intel to share, so I'll step aside."

Daxler Scion eased out of his seat and stood at the forefront of the screen.

"Gentlemen, and General Hasting. My sources within the Martian leadership have confirmed your suspicions. They have fled the city like the cowards we knew them to be."

"Do we have an update on their position?" Hasting asked.

"They have holed up in the Boreum region, hiding amidst the industrial smog. They call it a 'safe zone', so I'm reliably informed."

"Needless to say, General," Kiebler interrupted, "their safe zone must not be allowed to remain that way."

"Yes, Mr President. We will move our forces to the northern sector this evening and apply pressure on Raylor to surrender."

"We must not forget about the capital," Scion spoke, almost a whisper.

"I'll post a team here to continue the strafing runs and to maintain control. The capital is nothing but a symbol and a name now – it's Raylor and his men that we need."

"Hold your horses, Hasting," Kiebler jumped out of his seat and stood by Scion's side.

"I admire your approach but I don't want the capital to become an afterthought. It is a symbol, as you say. What news do you have of the Senate building?"

Hasting bristled at the mention of the Senate – he knew Kiebler's ways too well now and suspected he wasn't the type to leave any stone unturned.

"We have it locked down securely, sir. Patrols ensure nobody can enter or leave now. Their supplies won't hold more than a few days at best. They're going nowhere."

"How are we to know that the Martians haven't squirreled away enough supplies to last for months, General?" Scion asked.

"Never mind that – how are we to know they haven't squirreled away an entire battalion in that place?" Kiebler almost shouted.

"I am comfortable in predicting they have not, Mr President. The Senate is a refuge now. A symbol in name only. It will fall in a matter of days."

Kiebler remained silent a moment, Hasting watched as the cogs turned. He hoped the President was considering his place in history, or connecting with whichever faith he held within himself. He hoped against hope that the next words out of his mouth were not the inevitable.

He knew that such hope was madness.

"It is too big a risk," Kiebler finally spoke. "I want it burned to the ground, General."

Hasting felt the anger rise as he recognised his utter impotence in the moment. He was a military man to his core, and would follow orders blindly and willingly. However, these orders were unconscionable to him – and he hoped to any sane man.

"Mr President, I must ask you to reconsider that order," he spoke, taking a breath. "I live to serve my people, and my planet, but you ask me to take the lives of innocent men, women and children for no strategic gain. This is not a game we are playing; this is real life, with real consequences. We don't need to punish these people to win our war."

"General Hasting, it is not your place to question the orders of your President," Scion hissed.

"I simply ask for some reconsideration. To show some compassion."

"Compassion? For the Martians?" Kiebler exploded. "Compassion for their cause? For their betrayal? For climbing into bed with terrorist cells and murdering those dear to me?"

Kiebler seethed, almost frothing at the mouth. Hasting saw the bloodlust in his eyes and knew that all hope of reason was lost. The President was out for revenge and saw nothing less than mass genocide as a victory.

"General, mark my words and do not dare to question me again – I want the Senate in rubble before you leave the capital. I want the men, women and children dead. I want flames and ash to stand as the new symbol of Mars. Then the universe at large will see that Jupiter is not to be messed with. No, we are not playing a game, General."

The link shut down abruptly, with the last image being that of Kiebler throwing an object in a blur from his desk directly at the screen.

Hasting turned silently to his gathered leaders. He collected his thoughts as the men in front of him slowly began to chatter and bicker.

"Gentlemen, listen to me," he spoke with authority.

"We are men who live to be used as weapons to enforce the peace and the laws of our land. We have not asked for this war, but we fight it for our honour as it is what we have pledged to do."

A cheer was quickly met with a clamour and some jeering from the assembled men.

"We have no obligation to carry out orders which we deem to be illegal. What we have been asked to carry out is a senseless attack on innocent people. I urge you to turn down your weapons."

Several voices rose up at once – agreeing and arguing, applauding and complaining.

"What are we to do instead? We will be traitors!" one voice rose above the din.

"We can leave for the north tonight – gain the surrender of the Martian leadership and end this war before it goes any further. Let the Galactic Union tidy up the mess Kiebler has made."

Hasting hoped he could persuade those of the men who respected him already. He had no idea what the consequences might be for those who followed him – disobeying a direct order from your commander-in-chief was the ultimate sin in this line of work.

***

While the discussion raged, and Hasting fought off questions and attacks left, right and centre, Lieutenant Arthur made himself invisible at the back of the room. He picked his moment carefully and disappeared out of the back exit of the tent when all eyes were on Hasting.

He held his military-issue cap over his head to protect himself from the downpour and made his way to his own tent. He quickly found everything he needed – his flight bag, helmet and his handheld communicator which he attached to his belt.

He rushed off to the neighbouring tent and ducked his head inside. Two of his flight team were playing cards on a small fold-up table. He motioned for them to remain quiet, then signalled to his flight gear. They got the message.

He moved on to the next tent and roused two more of his men. Within minutes the five of them were all heading towards their aircraft, ready to fly.

It took a few minutes to plug in all of their equipment and run standard flight checks. Arthur looked around and noticed that several of the men he had left in the leadership tent were now filtering out and waking their own men for a debrief.

He assumed some form of plan had been agreed – perhaps all of the leaders had turned on their President, just as Hasting was suggesting.

He despised the idea of Hasting convincing any of the men that his way was best – who was he to judge on what was illegal and what was fair in combat? The President had issued his commands - it was the military's responsibility to carry them out to the letter, without question.

He fired up his ship's engine and began the takeoff procedure. He saw several faces within the camp look up at the sound. They were greeted with the sight of five battle-damaged craft taking to the skies.

He knew that some of those men would be loyal to Hasting and might even convince themselves that in the shadow of an illegal order from the President their chain of command dictates that Hasting become their de-facto commander.

Inevitably, that meant some would want to take to the sky to halt the actions of Arthur and his men. He knew any such actions would be futile; he had given himself and his team enough of a head start to successfully evade any resistance.

They flew in formation, with Arthur taking command and ordering strafing runs on the city streets underneath as they swooped for the main square and their primary target.

The Senate building loomed up ahead and Arthur eased back on his thrust.

"The kill shot is mine, gents," he spoke into his on-board radio.

The smell of smoke and debris was already strong in the air and he savoured it as he listened to confirmations of successful targets from his men. The streets of Acidalium were burning.

Tarab Arthur smiled.

His targeting computer gave a satisfying 'beep' as the image of the Senate building became crystal clear in his viewfinder. He flicked a switch to the right of his main dashboard and a warning alarm sounded twice.

A split second after the second alarm buzzed, the button at the tip of his launch control stick glowed green.

He reached for it and squeezed the button gently down. He saw the trails of air in his missiles' wake before he heard the squealing noise which accompanied them.

He watched as they streaked into the night, lighting up the air around them. He followed them with his eyes as they tore through the cold sky and quickly reached their destination.

The great domed roof of the Senate shattered on impact. A gaping hole opened instantly, only to be filled in milliseconds by a great ball of flame. The explosions echoed around the square and Arthur heard them over the raw power of his own engine.

He flew overheard and peered down into the destruction he had rained on the Martians. He saw walls crumbling and deep red flames lapping at the night air.

"That's a direct hit," he spoke cheerily into his radio. "Finish 'em off, boys."

He swooped past the square and circled back around, catching the sight of his four devotees blasting away at the last remains of the Senate building.

He smiled viciously. There would be nothing left standing after tonight. The rubble would be two stories high. There could be no survivors.

His President would be pleased.

***

Crowds had gathered as Lieutenant Arthur's men came in to land. He peered out of his windscreen and spotted the desolate figure of General Hasting, making his way through the crowd towards the landing bays.

Arthur flicked on his comms device and hailed Jupitoan Command.

"I need to speak directly with Daxler Scion," he spoke hurriedly.

The intercom buzzed as Command checked his credentials, then Scion's voice came through loud and clear.

"What news do you bring me, Lieutenant?"

"The Senate is destroyed. Mars is fallen. I have a direct request for President Kiebler, sir?"

"Certainly," Scion slithered back.

In a moment the blustering voice of Kiebler could be heard barking orders in the background. Arthur could see Hasting approaching now, wearing a look of weariness and fury rolled into one. He heard Scion relay his news to the President. Kiebler's booming voice grew clearer, overjoyed.

"Great news, Lieutenant, who do I have to thank for this victory?" Kiebler spoke.

"Sir, I led the attack charge myself. I believe I was carrying out your direct orders, unless I am mistaken?"

"No, my boy, you did exactly as commanded. Where is General Hasting?"

"I suspected General Hasting of potentially launching an insurrection, sir. He, and many of his officers, appeared to refuse your order. It seems they aren't happy that I have now carried it out to the letter."

Hasting had arrived at the landing bay, and was signalling for Arthur to disembark. Several of his men were also arriving and motioning to Arthur's men that they should remove themselves from their cockpits immediately.

"A General who disobeys his President is no longer a General, sir," Daxler said. "He is known by one name only."

"Traitor," Kiebler spoke, and followed it with a violent laugh.

"May I have your permission to arrest the traitor, and all who oppose me in doing so, Mr President?"

"Consider that a direct order," Kiebler replied. "I want him locked away while you lead the attack on Raylor's hideout – then I want him brought to me to pay the price for his crimes. Do you understand me?"

"Yes sir, I do," Arthur responded.

"See that it is done and I'll have a new General on your return, Lieutenant Arthur."

Kiebler cut the link with a final buzz and Arthur allowed himself a smile.

He released his cockpit door and stood in his seat to address the assembled crowd. He looked around and saw many more loyal and long-serving men than those that Hasting had in his pocket.

"My fellow Jupitoans. This man has defied orders from his President and betrayed each and every one of us. I have it on President Kiebler's personal authority that he is to be arrested and taken home to stand trial for treason and insubordination. Any who stand in my way in doing so will face the same charges."

He turned to the men who were still trying to hustle his flight team out of their ships.

"That includes you. Let my men remove themselves from their ships and assist me. Stand down or be taken down."

Cries of shock and anger came through the gathered crowd, but were accompanied by some cheers. The patriots were out there, Arthur knew.

Hasting stood up to him face to face as he finally stepped down onto solid ground. The deposed General did not utter a word, merely stared coldly into the eyes of his foe.

Arthur called for a guardsman to approach as reality sunk in for the gathered masses – they were all military men and knew the consequences of what Hasting had done today, whether they agreed with his actions or not.

Arthur took a pair of restraints from the guardsman and forced Hasting's hands into them.

"How does it feel to lose, General? I can't say I've experienced it for myself," he almost whispered as he leaned in close to lock the restraints tightly.

"You've come down on the wrong side of history, Tarab. Make no mistake, when this night is talked of in future generations, you will be the villain of the piece."

Arthur laughed hard at that. He laughed in his former-commanding officer's face, brazenly and raucously.

"Wilson, you poor deluded soul," he spoke. "You must realise – I don't give a shit about the history books. I'm here for now, for me. I only hope you live long enough to see me rise."

Arthur turned to his own men, taking stock of the situation around him.

"Someone take this disgusting, treasonous fool out of my sight. Put him on the battalion cruiser in the brig," he said loudly to anyone who would listen.

"We move to the north. The Martian leaders are holed up in Boreum. Our President has ordered their complete annihilation. Have your ships ready and the cruiser prepped for take-off within the hour. We end this war today."

His words were embraced by the many and reluctantly accepted by the few. Hasting's friends and followers were limited in the face of such insurmountable odds, and any hopes they had of restoring sanity and lawfully refusing any further orders from President Kiebler were gone.

The Jupitoan invasion force prepared quietly for battle, united in their goal to claim a victory for all Jupitoans and to return home before sunset.

CHAPTER TWENTY-SEVEN

ake sure you remain in contact with Harley Tyler and his men. They'll do whatever it takes to protect you."

With those words, and loud thump, the link disconnected. The image of the Senate hallways turned to black in Raylor's viewscreen.

He tried his best not to think the worst. He was calling from the most remote location imaginable, using tech older than he was. On top of that, he knew the Senate was subject to routine strafing runs from the Jupitoan forces. He imagined none of those factors could help with communication channels.

He hoped he was right.

He tried to retrieve the call but after a minute or two of listening to the dial tone buzz in his ears he gave up on it.

He imagined the worst.

He switched off the antiquated communication equipment and stepped outside of the small office. Marien Lyndell was at a desk in the room next door, Raylor slumped against the door frame on his way in.

"The link died."

"There's a million factors that-" Lyndell began to reassure him.

"I know, I know. I just can't shake the feeling. Something has to give, Marien. And we haven't heard a word back from any of the other leaders yet."

Raylor's hope that the other planetary leaders, those closest to the GU especially, would rally to Mars' wake-up call had proven to be fruitless. He knew that the poor state of the communication technology they had at their disposal could only be blamed up to a certain extent. Surely something had made it through eventually?

Receiving no responses meant only one thing to Raylor – Kiebler had utilised his powers of intimidation to ensure that nobody would be brave enough to stand by Mars' side; not even to add a dissenting voice to the conversation.

Mars was alone and Raylor was left to steer his people through the dark. Kiebler would be emboldened by the way things had turned in his favour at every point. Raylor suspected the unthinkable.

The Senate had been a symbol of Mars' resilience under attack.

It had to have been destroyed.

"It's the only course of action he can take now," Raylor explained to Lyndell. "He has us on the run, with no support from the entire solar system. He has destroyed the Senate and everyone in it to force us out of hiding."

Lyndell shook her head, trying to find comforting words to relieve his fears. She struggled to find anything positive to say as her mind raced to those she knew and loved, her friends and colleagues in the Senate. All innocent and all of them dead, if Raylor's take proved to be correct.

"We can go back, return to the capital and at least join the last stand," she eventually spoke.

"Maybe. We could send a scout somehow, to find out if our fears are correct."

Raylor wondered what good it would do. Should a scout find the Senate alive and well they will have risked someone's life for nothing. If the Senate was gone then there would be nothing they could do about it.

"More importantly, we need a new plan. If help isn't coming, and we are the only people who will stand against Kiebler, we had better make sure we make the most of what little time we will have left."

As Raylor spoke the words he saw the dread in Marien Lyndell's eyes – she knew as well as he did that any last stand by the few men they had left here would be merely a futile gesture.

Kiebler had launched his assault upon Mars – the legendary, mythical planet of war – and he had wiped them out with barely a whimper.

The outer doors slammed shut and snapped Raylor's thoughts back into the moment. He ventured out into the main hanger to see what the commotion was. At the far end of the room an officer was gesticulating wildly as people gathered around him.

Raylor strained to listen but couldn't hear the conversation. All he could hear was the faint sound of engines – aircraft engines, growing louder by the second.

The walkways above his head suddenly clanged with the heavy footsteps of someone running in his direction. He stepped out and looked above to see James Bellson, heaving as he tried to catch his breath.

"They're here," he said.

An explosion rang out and screams followed within the hanger. Chaos erupted around him.

"Here? How can they have found us so easily?" Raylor shouted, running towards the command centre in the middle of the hanger area.

As he arrived, several officers were cycling through the security channels on the video screen. The sights they showed were terrifying.

Jupitoan aircraft swooped low over neighbouring buildings, unleashing bombs and heavy fire. A large carrier ship and several smaller troop transports circled, looking for landing space.

"Are they insane!?" Ramsey Pierce screamed, staring at the carnage.

"They're firing on the terraforming cylinders," Bellson muttered, disbelievingly.

Raylor could barely speak.

"Kiebler doesn't care anymore," he said. "He's risking the life of every Martian." He looked to Marien Lyndell, and knew that she understood him; if Kiebler could attack here and risk life on the entire planet, then their fears about the Senate were proven to be correct.

"We have to leave immediately. Take what you need but do not hesitate – they are here to wipe us out. Let's live to fight another day."

With that, Raylor picked up a small comms unit and ran for the rear exit of the hanger, closely followed by every member of the team he had brought to Boreum with him.

The solid steel doors opened slowly and revealed the full extent of the damage outside as they did so.

The sky was bright with gunfire, while smoke billowed from dozens of different sites. Fires raged already and the sound of engines made it hard to hear. A pilot led the way towards their transport but their path was soon blocked by one of the large Jupitoan troop carriers as it came in to land.

There was little Raylor and his men could do They shielded their eyes from the dust and debris which was kicked up by the approaching ship and tried to edge as safely as they could towards their only hope of escape.

Then that hope was extinguished in the blink of an eye.

Tarab Arthur's squadron tore through the landing site in a blaze of fire, shooting at everything in sight.

The Martian aircraft were destroyed in a series of spectacular fireballs. The white hot shrapnel sprayed the surrounding area, catching several of Raylor's men, who screamed in agony and fell helplessly in the dirt.

Raylor stood in the eye of this hurricane and watched everything burn. There was no escape.

***

Lieutenant Tarab Arthur climbed from his cockpit amongst the debris of the Martian landing site. His troops had already lined up the prisoners, with the famous ring-leader Sebastian Raylor at the forefront.

"You must be out of your mind, recklessly blasting holes in the structures here," Raylor fumed.

"Mr Raylor. It's an honour to meet you," Arthur spoke calmly. "I'm soon-to-be General Arthur and I am here to arrest you on the orders of President Bernard Kiebler."

"Kiebler has no jurisdiction here – call it what it is!" Marien Lyndell interjected,

Arthur laughed.

"Jurisdiction or not, we are at war, Madam Senator. You are all prisoners of war. You may surrender at will but just to make you aware, Mr Raylor – you will not stop us from bombarding your little secret base. We won't allow your example to stand for any future cowards who would like to run from Jupiter's path."

"That's great," Raylor spoke, calmer this time. "Reckless and blind. That's Kiebler's way. Are you aware that some of the equipment you are damaging is the very same that Kiebler begged us to turn back on?"

"We'll rebuild it," Arthur shrugged.

"What about the atmosphere? The terraforming equipment is fragile and absolutely cannot be messed with. The magnetic field generator behind you alone could bring the entire planet to its knees. You're playing war games with the lives of millions of people."

"There is no game. We wage war on our enemies. It is too late to regret your actions now."

Arthur spoke with a swagger that riled Raylor. He knew the type from his days as a young fighter pilot – head stuck in his cockpit, thinking only of missiles and fireballs and the glamorous stuff.

"Fine. Wage your war. A little mass genocide will perfectly round off Kiebler's political career."

Arthur stepped forward and pressed his forehead against Raylor's. He had angered him with those words and Raylor hoped it might buy some leeway, if only for a few moments.

"Senator, you push your luck. I have a duty to honour my President and while he asked for prisoners he never quite specified who it should be."

Arthur pulled a pistol from his flight jacket holster and held it against Raylor's chin, forcefully pushing upwards. Raylor held firm, using all of his restraint to keep his own hands behind his back.

"If I'm the first to go, so be it," Raylor spat.

"I like that," Arthur smirked. "So be it." Even as he began the motion to pull the trigger, he felt the air shift around him. James Bellson pounced, leaping to his right and tackling Tarab Arthur to the floor. Arthur's men reacted quickly, pulling guns of their own, but holding off from firing for fear of shooting their own man.

Bellson wrestled the gun out of Arthur's grip for a moment and pointed it towards his foe but Arthur was physically bigger and stronger – he flipped Bellson onto his back and rolled with him, ending up sitting atop his opponent.

"Martian slime. I'll happily massacre you all and tell Kiebler you died in the fire."

He held one hand around Bellson's throat while the other worked to pull the gun back under his own control.

"Stop! Stop! I'm the man on the inside! I'm Scion's source! Kiebler wants me alive!" Bellson blurted, terrified.

Arthur stopped in the moment, holding the prone Workers' Council man still on the ground.

"You? You're the traitor?"

Arthur laughed. Bellson paid no attention. His eyes were fixed on Raylor.

Raylor felt the crushing heartbreak of the words as they had spilled from Bellson's mouth. He knew that his friend was put out and that he had his problems with their plan – or with his leadership in general. But he also thought he was committed to seeing this through for Mars, whatever the outcome. He would never have believed that James Bellson could betray his friends, his government and his people.

James Bellson was the closest thing to a patriot that Raylor could ever imagine.

"I'm sorry, Seb," was all the Council man could muster as Arthur stepped off and offered a hand to pull him from the floor.

"Sorry? That's... it?" Raylor stammered. "That's it?" he repeated. It was all he could think to say.

"Sonofabitch!" Ramsey Pierce shouted, earning himself the butt of one of the Jupitoan's rifles to his face.

"You gave us up?" Lyndell asked.

"I had no choice. We should have surrendered back in the capital, Seb. You must see that now. We ran out of options."

Bellson spoke through tears, his words seemingly genuine and his pain clear for all to see. Raylor simply stared at him, showing none of the emotion which broiled under the surface.

"How, James? How can you sell out your own people like that?" he finally spoke. "Was it for fear? You sold out your friends? Do you see the colossal mistake you've made?"

"I didn't sell out anyone. I betrayed my state, I admit, but I did it for its own good. Mars has already lost. There's no way out of the situation we have managed get ourselves into – that you led us into, Seb. There is no way to win, not even to reach a settlement, unless someone makes it happen."

"So you made it happen, at the expense of us all?" Raylor asked.

"At the expense of the old state. It can move on now. Evolve. Mars lives to fight another day."

Bellson gave a weak smile, hoping his friend would see it his way this time.

"You don't get it, James. The state cannot be held more important than the men and women who defend it. Not more important than the ideals they hold. You have betrayed us all and put not nearly enough faith into the cause we all stood for."

Bellson stood motionless, as tear ran down his cheeks.

"I have saved the lives of innocent people – please understand that. The very people you are talking about. Did you forget about them, Seb?"

"Which people?" Raylor asked, his face contorted now in confusion.

"Our people in the Senate building. I made sure they were part of the deal. They won't have to suffer for us now."

"James, did you make... Did they promise...?" Lyndell began to ask but was interrupted by the mocking, hysterical laughter of Tarab Arthur, followed by that of all of his men.

"You made a deal with Jupiter to bring an end to this war. I'm sorry to tell you that Jupiter does not grant the wishes of infidels."

He roared with laughter again. Bellson's eyes fell from Raylor to Arthur and back again. The moment felt like an eternity in Bellson's mind.

"They slaughtered them," Raylor spoke, almost a whisper. "They murdered our people, James."

Bellson lurched forward and for a moment Raylor thought he was about heave or faint. He hadn't noticed that Bellson still held Arthur's gun. As he fell forwards he sprung the gun out once again, pointing it towards the Jupitoan soldier.

"No!" cried Raylor, as Bellson let off a volley of shots.

The blasts narrowly missed Arthur, with one just barely grazing his shoulder and causing a nasty slashing burn. Bellson had fired on the turn and he was no soldier or marksman. In truth, he had never fired a gun in his life.

Raylor's heart sank as he watched the blasts sail past their intended target and blow a sizeable hole in the outer walls of the magnetic field generator. Deafening alarms sounded immediately. Gushing steam poured from the opening.

The generator had stood for centuries, placed there by Mars' terraformers in the very beginning. The magnetic field was vital to maintain Mars' breathable atmosphere. Now it was bleeding chemicals into the open air. Raylor had read countless reports and 'What If...?' scenarios based on the failure of the field. He knew that they had only a matter of minutes before the atmosphere of Mars would begin to bleed into space.

The chaos caused by the blaring alarm helped Raylor to focus, and distracted the Jupitoans just enough to gain some ground. He gave a nod to Pierce and Lyndell and made a dive for the nearest guard. His fellow Senators joined him, grabbing the guard's arms as Raylor pulled his weapon from his hands.

Within seconds the soldiers were refocused, but Raylor and his team were already advancing towards the open bay doors of the troop carrier the Jupitoans had arrived on.

Bellson saw them make their move. He saw the soldiers raise their weapons, saw Arthur pulling himself together out of the corner of his eye, heading in his direction.

"Seb! Run!" he screamed, gaining everyone's attention for the briefest of moments.

He used his moment wisely – unleashing a barrage of fire at the nearby spacecraft of Lieutenant Arthur, which quickly found the fuel hold and sent it up in a ball of flames.

The distraction proved crucial, as Raylor and his team ducked their heads in light of the explosion and found their way onto a vacant enemy craft.

Raylor himself stood at the bay door and pulled the lever to lock it closed. Before he did so, he took one final look at his beloved Mars.

The last sight he saw was of his friend James Bellson, smiling back at him. He smiled all the while, as Arthur finally reached him and disarmed him of his weapon.

Raylor witnessed the fatal shot as hell began to rain down upon them all.

***

Raylor slumped into a chair and relived the last few moments over and over. He was aware of shouted conversation and heated words being shared amongst his people. His ears still rang from the alarms and his head buzzed from everything that had occurred. He couldn't piece together anything in the correct order.

His friend had betrayed him.

His friend had sacrificed his life to save them.

His friend had killed them all.

He snapped back to reality at that thought. Mars was a ticking time bomb now, and he had a responsibility to his people.

"Somebody get me a comms device – anything I can use to patch into the Mars defence network."

Several people jostled around the small crew room looking for suitable equipment.

"Are we sure there are no enemy fighters left on board?" he asked.

"Yes sir," came the response from a Martian guard. "We've checked everywhere. We locked the pilots away in the brig, along with those who were already held there."

Raylor nodded his appreciation.

"Who's flying this thing?"

"We have it under control," the guard said as he hurried away.

Raylor turned his attention back to the task at hand. The displays around the ship were beginning to light up as the Martians hacked the systems and took control. One viewing screen fizzed into life and Raylor saw atmospheric readings quickly calculating and adjusting.

Mars' artificial atmosphere was leaking out at a fatal rate. The most optimistic calculations showed eight hours til complete loss of breathable conditions – the end of life on Mars.

Raylor hoped that figure would get better, but knew in his heart that once the perfect balance of conditions was lost it would create a snowball effect. All oxygen would be sucked out into the vacuum of space at an ever quickening rate.

Mars would be a ball of rock before the day was done.

He shook off the mortifying dread that filled his stomach. The planet may die today, but lives could be saved if he acted fast.

The makeshift crew had set up a small comms device in front of him. He watched as they quickly punched in the defence network codes. The speaker crackled then was filled with noise.

"This is Mars central command. State your clearance codes."

"Zero, delta, alpha, delta, zero. Senator Sebastian Raylor."

The line fell silent for a moment.

"Patching you in, Senator," came the voice.

Raylor shifted in his seat impatiently.

"This is Chairman Harley Tyler. Is it you, Raylor?"

"It's me, Chairman," Raylor replied with a smile. "How are you holding up?"

"I'm relived you're alive, sir. We are holding in here, but the capital is no longer under our command."

"That's OK, Chairman. That loss is on me, not you. There are bigger issues to be dealt with and time is against us."

"The capital is smoke and ash, sir. I'm not sure what else there is to be done."

"Listen to me, Tyler. The capital is no longer an issue. I need you to listen carefully. The atmosphere is bleeding into space. The entire planet will be gone soon. We have to act now."

"Sir, I... What can be done? All of the tech people, the scientists, engineers... They're all gone."

"Don't worry about that. We need to focus on saving those who are left."

"They massacred them, Seb," Tyler said, his voice dropping low. His sadness hit Raylor hard.

"I know. We'll be next if we don't make our move, Harley. Listen to me – is the communications tower still intact?"

Harley took a moment to gather himself, his thoughts drifting to the Senate building and how he wished he could have done more to protect it. The attack had come in the middle of the night, out of the blue. The fighters scrambled as fast as humanly possible, but it was too late.

"I believe it is, sir," he finally responded.

"I need you take it, Tyler. We don't have long. Can you do it?"

"We don't have much of a force left, sir."

"Unleash the aircraft you told me about. Give it everything you have left. This is it, Chairman. Nothing gets left behind."

Raylor waited for confirmation from his military leader. He sensed the turmoil in his Chairman and understood the feeling of loss he must be going through.

"I'll see you on the other side of this thing," Chairman Tyler offered, and the line went cold.

***

The communications tower stood as a beacon of industrialisation in the centre of Acidalium. At four-hundred and eighty metres, it was the largest man-made structure outside of the industrial zones in Boreum, in the far north.

Tyler's men approached with caution. He knew that Jupitoan forces had held the tower for days now and that gaining entrance wouldn't be an easy task.

However, the news of the atmospheric drop was reaching the streets now and as they approached he witnessed troops moving out of the building. Truck loads of Jupitoans were leaving the capital.

"Finally some good news," he said out loud, passing his night vision sights to one of his men.

He despatched a team to the south entrance and positioned himself directly across the main street from the front door. He waited for the signal that his men were in place, then took out his short-wave radio.

"Launch."

With a simple word, Chairman Tyler unleashed hell.

The screech of engines overhead was almost instant, as four cruiser-class, short-range fighters buzzed across the sky. They were followed by two hefty looking machines, whose sound reverberated off every building and window.

The short-range fighters began to blast at Jupitoan outposts which Tyler had scouted meticulously over the past few days. They held small pockets of troops, each meticulously placed to aid in any offensive.

Tyler put them on the defensive immediately, ensuring the fighters sprayed them with gunfire constantly.

The bigger ships dropped heavy bombs on airstrips and landing bays. He wanted every Jupitoan grounded, every ship waiting for clearance to take off to be destroyed. If Martians were to die with their planet, then he would make sure their Jupitoan invaders would suffer the same fate.

As the war machines passed overhead, Tyler led his men into the street and fired the first shot at the communications tower. Windows shattered and wooden frames splintered as his team followed his lead in showering the building with bullets.

Jupitoan troops began to spill onto the streets to engage. Tyler trusted the men he had left – some of his very best were still standing by his side. He heard the echo of gunfire coming from the alleyways behind the building. He knew that his men were right on time in joining the attack and splitting the Jupitoan defensive force into two.

Soon the strewn bodies of unprepared Jupitoan men lay in the streets, as Tyler's squad picked their way through them and walked into the lobby of the building. He gave signals to his explosives experts and they set off to the large lower floor rooms.

Tyler himself prized open the elevator doors and dropped a grenade into the shaft. He and his men ducked around the corner and began to climb the stairs as the sound of the blast shook the building behind them.

Dust fell from the ceilings and the stairs themselves shook.

Two more blasts followed – and Tyler knew it was his explosives team, ensuring the ground floor was inescapable, while he had cut off access to the lower levels.

The only way was up.

He placed a small detonator on each floor along the way and kept climbing. Every few floors there would be a flurry of gunfire or the odd slip or grunt from some hidden enemy guard. Tyler's men were a tightly knit group, well honed through the years to expect and intercept any such challenge.

They quickly dealt with any soldiers they met along the way, as they continued to climb higher and higher.

Tyler had studied the plans of the building and knew where he was heading. Midway up the tower there was a service level and from it he could gain access to a second stairwell. Once they arrived at it he split his group again, leaving one group on the original stairs while leading another up the new path. He sent a solitary trooper to scope out the service floor and handed him a munitions belt full of grenades.

"See an elevator shaft – light it up," were his only words of wisdom.

The second staircase led Tyler outside. It zigzagged across the sleek metal surface and he forged ahead into the whistling wind. Rain began to pound down from the sky.

In the distance he could see strange colours mixing into the horizon and knew it was the effect of the atmosphere filtering off into the black of space. It was mid-afternoon but the sky grew dark. He wondered how long it might be before the stars became visible in the sky above. Then he wondered if they'd live long enough to witness them.

Small Jupitoan fighters were now buzzing around the sky too and every now and then he caught a glimpse of one of the small Martian crafts darting past and firing at them.

As they finally approached the top floor of the tower he felt the wind direction change and the sound of heavy engines filled the sky. He looked up to see an ancient Martian freighter landing on the roof of the building and knew that his men had the better of the Jupitoans out there.

He counted to three and burst through the fire exit door on to the top floor. Three men followed, guns aiming into the darkened room. He saw movement and acted quickly.

"Smoke!"

One of his team immediately launched two smoke canisters over to the far side of the room. It billowed up quickly, reducing enemy vision to zero, and allowed Tyler to move in closer. He slid his night vision goggles back on and picked off two men by the main entrance.

Screams and fire followed.

He estimated twelve to fifteen enemy fighters were hidden within the large room. His men methodically picked them off one by one.

The second stairway was cleared by the men who had continued up it, and now all of Tyler's men stood in command.

"Somebody find a light switch," one of the men shouted.

Tyler looked at the array of technology at his disposal. Desks lined the room from the walkway where he stood, to the very front where an enormous screen towered over it all. Each desk held its own gadgets. He flicked some switches on the panel in front of him until the mini-screen lit up and green lights flashed in the panel.

"Comms do your work," he said, and stepped away from the desk.

Two communications men swooped in and began typing, flipping switches, spouting jargon to each other. Tyler only followed so much and waited for the nod from the experts.

When the nod came, he stepped forward again and pressed down the radio receiver.

"Are we live? The full network?" he asked.

"Yes sir. The emergency channel is engaged – every TV, radio, digital station on the planet is part of the override. She's all yours."

"That's quick work," he smiled. "Patch in Senator Raylor."

***

Raylor had been waiting by the receiver for longer than he cared to think now. He had heard from Tyler when they left the military base but all had gone quiet since.

The light blinked green.

He sat up.

"We have Chairman Tyler for you, sir," his comms officer spoke triumphantly.

Raylor pumped his fist in celebration – at least his head of armed forces was still alive.

"Chairman! It's good to hear you made it."

"That's a positive, Senator. We have taken command of the communications tower here in Acidalium and read you loud and clear."

A cheer rang out amongst Raylor's men and he heard it reciprocated by Tyler's soldiers.

"The emergency channel is ready to go?"

"At your word, sir."

Raylor took a deep breath.

"Let me address our people, Chairman."

"Yes, sir."

Tyler gave the order and Raylor's comms device flashed red then green. He saw the monitors on his own ship cut off from the transmission of Jupitoan news they were watching, and bring up an image of the Martian military insignia.

"People of Mars. This is Senator Sebastian Raylor calling on all known channels," he paused for breath, the gravity of the situation weighing heavily on his chest. "I'm afraid the war is lost. It's impossible to ask that you not panic at this time, but I do it anyway. Please be aware that the atmosphere generators have been compromised and the news you are hearing is not false – Mars has a matter of hours now until it returns to its natural state."

He breathed heavily, and held it in. He found it impossible to find the words that were vital to the survival of the Martian race, but he persevered.

"We must evacuate calmly and carefully but immediately. I repeat – you must evacuate Mars immediately. All military and civilian transports are to be commandeered. Leave nobody behind. Help your fellow man and allow us all to retreat to safety. Follow evacuation plans and set a course for Saturn or Neptune – I will ensure the safe havens are notified and are awaiting us with all of the help they can muster."

His heart pounded through his chest. He knew that this was his defining moment in life. He led the Martians into a fight they could not win and now he was leading them across the galaxy, leaving their home behind.

"I want to apologise for everything that has happened. We did what felt right, we did what was good and we believe in everything we made a stand for. We stand tall for it even now, as we lose our home, as we know that have not lost our Martian spirit – it will go on with us and live to fight another day."

Tears streamed from Raylor's eyes as he held a hand over his mouth to smother a sob from deep down.

"Good luck, my fellow Martians. Stay strong, stay safe and stay together."

***

Harley Tyler listened to Raylor's speech with his men around him. He felt his heart strings tug and felt nothing but honour to serve a man of Raylor's belief and courage.

All the while, he heard the sound of engines drawing closer.

He flicked the switch to bring the giant screen online and cycled through the security channels until he found the camera mounted on the roof.

The Martian freighter still sat there, awaiting their escape, but now a Jupitoan warship hovered above.

In the blink of an eye the Martian vessel was gone – a ball of flame enveloping the ship, the camera and anything else in its path.

The engine noise grew louder still as the Jupitoan craft drew in to land.

Tyler reached into his pocket for a small device – no more than a button with a simple unlocking index.

He looked at the faces of his men and they looked back at him in total understanding.

He keyed into the index and the green button lit up brightly in his hand.

"You have served me well over the years. You gave me your all, I could not have asked for a moment more from any one of you. This is goodbye, men."

He saluted his team as they had done to him on thousands of occasions. They returned the gesture.

He looked to the button.

The sound of engines grew louder, louder, louder.

Finally, they died out.

Tyler pushed the button.

Every explosive device throughout the building, which Tyler had carefully placed on each floor, inside and out, exploded in the same instant.

Every floor gave way, every window shattered, everything stopped.

The tower fell in a matter of minutes, taking Jupitoans and Martians alike.

CHAPTER TWENTY-EIGHT

K iebler's office was a celebration.

Daxler Scion stood uncomfortably in front of the President's desk and waited for the clamour to calm down. The gathered flunkies and hangers-on whooped and hollered, while Valerie Marlborough applauded and smiled.

Kiebler was ecstatic.

"You're sure, Dax? The capital – done?"

"Yes, Mr President."

"And Raylor's running again!" Kiebler screamed in delight. He hadn't felt this good in a while and he turned directly to the drinks cabinet. "Jupiter will dine on champagne again, while Mars eats the dirt it was built on!"

Another cheer from the followers halted Daxler's announcement.

"Sir, if I may," he offered above the din.

Kiebler motioned for the room to quieten down and he listened intently while popping open his best champagne.

"Lieutenant Arthur reports that severe damage was done to the infrastructure of the environment generators in the assault. The Martians sabotaged their own planet when they saw the end was nigh, sir."

Scion lied to Kiebler, just as Arthur had lied to him. He had seen through the young Lieutenants charade at once, but hadn't said a word. He knew Kiebler wouldn't suspect a thing; such was his hatred and mistrust of the Martians.

"Sabotaged?" he asked.

"Indeed."

"As in..?"

"Mars will return to the barren wasteland it once was. Land and structures alike, all reclaimed by the natural order of things. The atmosphere is bleeding as we speak."

Kiebler let out another howl of delight, and drank directly from the bottle.

"Get me Tarab Arthur on the comms, right now," he barked to an aide, who quickly got to work.

"Dax, this is incredible news. We won! Imagine the looks on their faces as their plans fell apart. They've lost it all."

Even Scion managed a smile at that.

"What's more, Mr President, imagine the faces of the other leaders out there in the solar system. Think of the powerful message this sends. Jupiter will not be challenged."

The thought gave both Kiebler and Scion a chilling feeling deep down to their bones, which they both savoured. Ultimate power over all comers; the ideal outcome from a terrible mess.

Valerie Marlborough remained silent throughout. Her thoughts flashed to the people now racing, screaming, torn from their homes. She thought of the huge displacement of the Martians if Mars truly was destroyed. She worried about the plight of these people first of all and her political mind couldn't help but wonder if they had won a war to alleviate immigration across the stars and simultaneously created the biggest surge of immigrants the solar system would ever see.

"Lieutenant Arthur here, sir," came a voice, as the holographic comms unit sprayed out its image into the centre of the room.

"Tarab! You gorgeous boy! You have really outdone yourself – and General Hasting – on this one!"

"Thank you, sir. We were only following your orders."

"Looks like you got a little banged up there, son?" Kiebler said, pointing at his Lieutenant's shoulder where he held a bloodied bandage over the exposed skin.

"It's just a graze. Nothing could keep me out of this fight, Mr President."

"Glad to hear it! Now listen – there's some vital equipment out there on Mars. I want you off planet before she dies but make sure you get what we need. Have the ops guys sent you lists?"

"Yes, sir. My men are loading the transports now. We'll be tight for space, but we can just about make it home."

"No, no, no. Don't bring it here. Dax will send you precise co-ordinates. I want that stuff in the Belt, there are folks waiting for it to arrive."

"The Belt, sir?" Arthur asked, puzzled.

"You heard me right, kid."

"Forgive me but - is the Belt manned, sir?"

Kiebler gave an instinctual, wicked laugh, which gave way to a giddy cackle as he tried to respond.

"We have much to chat about when you arrive home... General Arthur."

Kiebler saluted his newly promoted officer and saw the look of pride in the young man's face, then called for the signal to be cut.

The faces in the room all looked in awe at their leader, wondering what his words were hinting at. He let them wallow in it for a moment, feeling the joy of being the centre of attention, just the way he liked it.

"Ladies and gentlemen, let me tell you what I have been working on while you've all been off winning me a war."

***

Raylor's ship cruised safely behind the pack, following a fleet of Martians on their way out of the system. Mars was a distant dot in the rear-view now and all on board took great efforts to push away any feelings of sadness for the time being.

There was no avoiding the crushing despair hanging in the air however, nor the feeling of absolute hopelessness which Raylor held inside.

He checked the comm channels for the hundredth time to find no word from Tyler and, surprisingly, no gloating updates from Kiebler as yet. He figured it wouldn't be long until the President stepped onto his soapbox to tell the world about his great victory, and the many lives he tossed aside in the winning of it.

He concluded that Chairman Tyler was gone. He knew there was very little chance that he would get out of the communication tower alive.. The evacuation had gone as well as could be hoped and Raylor comforted himself with the knowledge that Harley most likely gave his life to allow his fellow Martians the chance to live.

A bright flash in the forward view caught his eye. Then another.

He leaned forward to peer out of the window as the pilots adjusted their flight path, shielding their eyes.

"What is that?" he asked.

"It appears to be cannon fire, sir," came the reply.

An alarm buzzed overhead and the pilot reached up to silence it.

"What's happening here? Cannon fire from our ships?"

"It appears something is firing on us, Mr Raylor. From inside the asteroid belt."

Raylor stood from his seat and moved closer, hoping the extra few inches would give him more clarity on the field many miles ahead. The asteroid belt loomed in the distance, another flash of light occurred just in front of it.

The on-board radio crackled into life but no words could heard, only screams.

Another flash and this time the radio lit up with chatter from the fleet. All of a sudden every Martian ship was talking, all at once. He could only make out every other word but pieced together the information tentatively.

The Belt was moving. The asteroids were closing in. Something was firing on the fleet.

"Sir?" the pilot looked to Raylor for direction.

"Full ahead, now!" he shouted, annoyed at the hesitation. "We won't be leaving our people in there, no matter what it is."

The ship lurched forward as the pilot applied some forward velocity. Soon the fleet ahead became clearer and the damage already caused became obvious. Smoke poured from several of the vessels, while two sat immobile in the sky.

"Open all comm channels, let me speak," Raylor demanded.

The pilot flicked his switches and the radio mic opened loudly.

"Attention whoever it may concern. You are firing on an unarmed and non-hostile refuge fleet. Cease fire immediately."

No verbal response was given, however another flash from the Belt saw more damage to one of the fleet. Raylor was furious now, grabbing the radio mic with both hands. Before he could speak again the audio channel whirred and cut out to complete silence, then was replaced by a solitary voice.

"You have reached Jupitoan airspace. The Belt is closed. Return home or be eliminated."

The voice was Kiebler's.

It was clearly a recording, triumphant and gloating in true Kiebler style. Raylor's mind was spinning – he had heard the rhetoric around 'Blocking the Belt' during the election campaigns on Jupiter, but everyone agreed that it was just laughable nonsense from the joke candidate.

So what was this? Kiebler was no joke and now the entire solar system was paying the price for Jupiter's willingness to laugh along with him.

Ahead of the fleet the asteroid belt was very visibly moving. Each rock was inter-linked and it moved as one, forming a barrier and closing ranks around the fleet. Jupitoan spacecraft now flooded out, as if from nowhere, flanking the Martians.

Some of the fleet had nowhere to turn now as they were shepherded forward towards the belt – any manoeuvre came with the risk of flying into one of their own vessels, while turning around would mean engaging directly with the Jupitoan ships.

The Belt closed to a solid wall as they arrived. With no time to change course several of the Martian ships crashed directly into the rock.

Raylor watched in horror. Everything in his life had lurched from bad to worse, all day long, and now when he thought it was over it had become worse than ever before.

He seized the mic again and flipped the switch to open a Martian channel.

"Steer clear of the rock. Do not attempt to navigate the Belt. It looks impenetrable. We'll have to take our chances with the fighters. Avert your course and hit your thrusters as soon as you are clear."

The ships began to take heed and several turned off to the left, attempting to drive directly through their Jupitoan chaperones.

The enemy fighters fired on them. Not many Martians got through. Those who did were followed swiftly.

"Get up behind them, we're one of the only ships with weapons," Raylor ordered.

The pilots swung into gear, swooping the craft down and below their own fleet, then ducking out to the left. They came up behind a Jupitoan fighter and blew him out of the sky.

"Yahoo!" the pilot hollered, while Raylor was busy racking his brains for a strategy.

"Keep at them, protect as many as you can. Tell the other military ships to do the same. The civilian ships must get out alive; they're all we have left to protect."

He stormed out of the cockpit and through the living quarters. He didn't understand how such a monumental construction could have occurred without anyone's knowledge.

He marched to the brig and stood before the huge gun-metal grey cells.

"My fleet are taking devastating losses out there. The asteroid belt is a wall of... something now. Somebody give me answers or so help me God..."

He spoke with an edge to his voice that could only come from a man on the brink of sanity. His spirit was broken, his hope gone, and his pride battered. He needed answers.

"Speak to me now. One of you knows about this. These things don't happen by magic. They don't happen overnight. If I have to have you torn apart limb by limb, don't think that I won't."

One of the ship's original pilots stepped forward and spat on the floor in front of Raylor. His fury took hold - he leaped for the cell door, reaching through the bars and grabbing the pilot by the jacket cuff. He pulled him close, as if trying to remove him from the cell through the metal bars themselves.

"Tell. Me. About. The. Belt." He growled through gritted teeth.

"He can't tell you anything," a voice spoke from the corner of the cell.

Raylor loosened his grip slightly to peer into the darkness.

"He can't tell you anything because he knows nothing."

The brig was kept in semi-darkness at all times. Raylor wished now that he had dragged a squadron of men with torches along with him.

"Somebody knows something. I want it now," Raylor spoke into the dark.

"None of these men know a thing. Don't waste your anger on them. Kiebler kept it all a secret – his big surprise for the mid-term elections, or for some unlucky victim who crossed his path before then. I'm afraid you are just that today. I am truly very sorry for that."

The stranger spoke calmly and clearly. He wasn't a grunt or a pilot.

"How do you know this?" Raylor asked, dropping the pilot without a second glance.

"Because President Kiebler only shared such plans with his inner-circle. I have seen it for myself."

General Wilson Hasting stepped out of the shadows to look the Senator in the eye.

"I'd be willing to tell you all about it, Mr Raylor."

"All I need to know right now is how to get through it."

"There is no way through it. It is a complete and utter block on all things. Nobody can break through it. Nobody can fly to Jupiter without Bernard Kiebler's express say so."

"You're lying. It can't be unbreakable."

"I know of no way in or out, unless you're on their side."

"That's a monumental piece of work," Raylor almost whispered.

"It is an affront to all of mankind, Senator," Hasting said. "Tell your people to turn around. The only way out is to run."

Raylor looked at the General intently. He recognised him as the leader of the army which had led the invasion of Mars. He recognised him as a Kiebler pawn. He did not know why he should trust a word that fell from the man's mouth.

He wondered how he found himself to be a prisoner. The General held himself well and had always struck Raylor as a decent man when he'd heard reports of him in the past. He felt an urge to trust and saw no other way to proceed. His people's lives were hanging in the balance.

He pulled out a comms unit and reported to his pilot.

"Retreat. Order the entire fleet to retreat. By any means necessary." He paused. "Set a course for Earth."

He stared Hasting up and down.

"I'll send for you when this is through. If your intel proves incorrect you better hope we get blown out of the sky before I see your face again."

Raylor left the brig alone, leaving Wilson Hasting alone and exposed in a cell full of his peers.

CHAPTER TWENTY-NINE

"Valerie, drink up," Kiebler admonished his Secretary of Communications, while brandishing an especially old looking bottle of brandy.

Marlborough forced a smile and sipped from her champagne glass.

"I'm breaking out the good stuff, Val, you need to catch up and savour it with me," he spoke, without once glancing at his companion. The staff had cleared out thirty minutes earlier, and Kiebler had asked her to stay behind to finish off the champagne. She had reluctantly agreed, although she already felt light-headed from the alcohol. Her head spun from the revelations of the night too, and the latest had sent it into overdrive.

The commanders at the Belt had called through to inform their President that his newest doom-laden scheme was a success – the Martians were dying or running scared. Kiebler had lapped it up, and made directly for the expensive brandy.

Marlborough felt ill at ease. The Belt had seemed such a fantastical idea that it charmed everyone during the campaign. The finances and logistics of it all were unthinkable and she had cast it from her mind after the election – there was no way they could build it, no chance anyone would fund it and no need to be able to do the things Kiebler wanted it to perform.

"Val. Are you OK? You've gone quiet on me."

She looked up at her President, standing over her with two elaborate tumblers full of brandy and no ice.

"I'm fine, Mr President. I think it's just been a long night."

"What's on your mind?" Kiebler asked, sensing her anxiety.

"I'm still in shock that the Belt – your Belt – is fully operational. I don't know how you did it, Bernard."

Kiebler smiled and slinked his body onto the sofa beside her.

"Well Valerie, I reached out to several old friends, colleagues, businessmen. I used my contacts and I used the power of this office to convince a few people to loosen the old purse strings - and to tighten their lips about it."

"But it's a colossal undertaking – the size of the thing!"

"You flatter me, Valerie," Kiebler replied with a repugnant smile.

"As a banker I would hate to ask what terms you got on the financing."

"You're not a banker any more. You're my secretary."

"Secretary of Communications, sir," she corrected him, "and head of the Galactic Union, I might add."

"It all amounts to the same thing, Val. You're here to support me and I'm here to give the people what they voted for. I get the feeling you aren't too keen on the way I kept this all from you?"

"My issue isn't with you keeping it a secret from me, or from anyone. If anything I'm impressed with how well you pulled it off."

Kiebler ran his hand along her leg.

"You know me. I am a man of vast talents."

"I know that, sir," she spoke awkwardly, sitting up a little; just enough to force her President's hand to fall from her exposed leg. She pulled down her skirt to cover up as subtly as she could manage, but she knew that he had noticed.

"My problem lies in the power the Belt grants us – or you. I wonder if it's a step too far."

"Too far?" Kiebler nearly choked. "I promised the people a revolutionary means of reducing the numbers of immigrants, vagrants and leeches that were clogging up our streets. I have delivered that in stunning fashion."

"But under the circumstances don't you feel... just a little murky?"

The silence was insufferable. She couldn't tell if the swirl of emotions which briefly flashed across Kiebler's face were good or bad, although she suspected she could guess. He gulped down his drink and stood from the sofa.

"I don't mean to offend, Mr President," she said, trying to allay his anger. "I only mean to say that it's unfortunate we have created the strongest deterrent against immigration and provided a guarantee of Jupiter's future as the largest and most influential planet in the known galaxy tonight – on the night when an entire planet is about to die. It's entire population will be in need of a new home."

"Valerie, I think you have had too much to drink."

"Sir..." she tried to speak.

"No! You are done giving your views on this. Have you forgotten the values we spoke of? The reasons we do this? The Martians wanted a fight and we gave it to them – the loss is theirs and theirs alone to deal with."

Kiebler was fury personified now, his brandy glass a million shards of tiny crystal-like pieces on the floor after it shattered against the wall.

"Suddenly you care for them? All of those who plotted against us? Attacked us, in league with the bastards who killed my wife? You want me to sympathise now, after all they have done?"

"I only want to make sure we are doing the right thing. I'm not sure if we've strayed too far from what is right, and into what is right only for us."

She flinched as Kiebler turned angrily, so sure was she that he was about to strike her. He didn't, to her relief, but his posture and gesturing were enough to make her quiver. She had spoken truth to power before, but even then she knew she was feeding him what he wanted to hear deep down.

He didn't have time for the truth. He didn't have a heart for compassion.

"We have won a war tonight, Valerie. We have destroyed the very people who stood up to us and rejected Jupitoan values. We have shown the galaxy that we cannot be bullied and we cannot be held hostage. Nothing stands in our way from here on out."

Marlborough eased out of the sofa seat where she was firmly planted. She rose to her feet and stood side by side with the fuming President.

"Sir, I'm afraid we can't agree."

Kiebler laughed.

"There is no 'we', Ms Marlborough. You work for me and you will do as I ask."

"As leader of the Galactic Union I cannot do that, sir. I must look to use that position to right some of the wrongs we have caused tonight. I want Jupiter to soar, but I can't let it be on the back of atrocities which could have been avoided."

"You spiteful bitch. You can't bear to see the way I'm making history here. Are you jealous that you can't rightfully be President yourself? You'll do anything to try to upstage me, to scrawl your name onto my page in the history books."

"No, sir. I am simply seeing things straight for the first time in a long time," she replied, dredging up every last bit of courage to remain looking her President dead in the eye.

"Well Valerie, let me help you see straighter still. The Galactic Union? It's mine. It's been mine since day one of my Presidency. Everyone on that council is fully bought and paid for – including you. You don't want to play ball? So be it."

He strutted over to his desk and pressed the intercom.

"Get me Dax, immediately."

"You paid off the GU from day one?" she asked, confused.

"You have no idea of the things I can do from here. Trust me on that, if nothing more."

The intercom buzzed.

"Mr President – is there a problem?" Daxler Scion's voice came through.

"Dax. Prepare a notion to be forced through immediately. Wake everyone for the vote. I want the Galactic Union officially under my control by sunrise. Ms Marlborough is relieved of her duties as of this moment."

"As you wish, sir," Daxler replied, sounding as surprised as Marlborough looked.

"Oh, and write me a speech to pass this news on to the people. It's about time the victorious Bernard Kiebler spoke to his public."

He slammed his hand down on the intercom button and Dax was gone.

Marlborough stood rooted to the spot. Kiebler approached her again.

"See, Valerie. The man you fell for just happens to be the most powerful man that ever lived in this little system of ours."

He ran a hand through her hair softly.

"You know my mother always told me to reach for the stars, and now they're all in the palm of my hand."

"Would she be proud of you now, Bernard?" Marlborough asked.

"Who gives a fuck," Kiebler spat, grabbing her chin and forcing a kiss onto her lips. She pulled away as hard as she could and he let go with a laugh.

"You'll call me Mr President from now on, should you get the chance. Pack your things. I'll make my speech sometime tomorrow. If you're still on the grounds at that point I'll have you arrested and standing trial for treason before the night is done."

He turned his back and returned to his bottle waiting for him on his desk.

Marlborough hesitated for just one moment as anger and disappointment flooded her senses. She wanted to take revenge in an instant. She looked at the glass, which was still gripped tightly in her left hand.

She considered the relief it would bring. The sheer joy of being free of Bernard Kiebler.

She considered the consequences. The utter despair at the years she'd lose, assuming she even made it out of the building alive.

She considered the man she had admired and worked with so closely. The man she'd encouraged to be his absolute worst self. Somehow he'd managed to go further than she could have imagined.

She considered the love she still felt for the man inside. The thought made her feel ill.

She ran.

She ran from the office and down the grand staircase, passing her own office and within it her belongings. She left the building on foot and never looked back.

Valerie Marlborough wanted to live to fight another day, and in that moment simply hoped that another day would come.

CHAPTER THIRTY

R aylor dreamed of violent storms and winds which tore down buildings. Everything around him was engulfed in flames and yet he tried to run from them anyway. Worse still, the more he tried to flee, the more people followed.

He pleaded with them to stop, to turn back, to go their own way, but they stood silently while he spoke and fell into line behind him again as soon as he set off.

He awoke to the bleeping of an alarm and wearily opened the porthole shutter.

Outside of the craft the blackness of space had been illuminated by one shining light. Two thirds of the planet Earth glowed brilliant green and blue, while the remaining section dropped off into magnificent shadow. Raylor felt something powerful when his eyes eventually managed to focus on it and his passion for the task ahead was renewed.

He looked around the blackness that surrounded them and could see the moon sloping gently into view in the distance. He hadn't seen the planet of his ancestors this closely before but had watched every rose-tinted, 'those were the days' type of TV show he could find when he was young. He had a deep appreciation for the birthplace of humanity.

He joined the cockpit crew again as they approached orbit. Earth had very little technology and only one manned space station, to act as a gatepost to any visitors. Raylor surmised that they didn't get many visitors to begin with.

The pilot had a hard job explaining their business to the crew of the space station until Raylor whispered a few words into his ear. They explained they were leading a large envoy and would like to stop to negotiate a rest break for their crews. Raylor asked if his lead ship could land and he could meet with an official to discuss terms. They didn't take long to approve his request.

The message was sent to the remains of the fleet that they were to settle into orbit and await orders. Raylor's crew readied themselves and plunged down into the atmosphere.

They could never have prepared themselves for what awaited.

As they broke through the clouds, the bright sunshine began to bounce off a bright green and wondrous blue landscape below. The crew crowded around windows and into the cockpit to glance out at the sights.

The oceans stretched for miles around, while dense forests filled the distance. Tiny islands passed underneath and birds were disturbed as the craft drifted closer to ground level.

They approached a verdant green island with a towering mountainous region which stretched north to south. The pilot swooped low to give everyone a better view; the crew whooped and cheered as monkeys scurried from the treetops and deer sprinted for cover at the foot of the hills.

Raylor had never witnessed such sights before. Mars was a beautiful place but he had heard all his life of the artificial nature of all things beyond Earth, and how rich and colourful the birthplace of humanity was.

The rumours of Earth's vividness were not exaggerated, he saw now, and he knew that his crew had held the same doubts before seeing it with their own eyes. He stared in awe at the planet below him and at the joy it had awoken in his crew.

The task at hand was made no lighter by the happiness. He soon snapped back to reality and exited the cockpit, leaving the other crew members in their reverence at the views they had discovered.

The ship approached the landing pad of the Earth leadership camp and Raylor knew he had one chance to convince them of the Martian's plight. He headed directly to the brig and pulled out a key card when he arrived at the cells.

"Wilson Hasting," he spoke softly.

Hasting stepped forward almost immediately. Raylor nodded his recognition and entered the key card, opening the door. He stepped aside and gestured for Hasting to join him.

Hasting was bemused by the situation but reluctantly stepped forward. Several of the other prisoners moved towards the open door but Raylor quickly swing it shut, leaving Hasting looking helplessly back at his fellow Jupitoans.

"Come with me," was all Raylor offered.

***

The landing pad was wider than it had any need to be. Raylor thought it looked like an old transport hub which had been allowed to fall into disrepair over a couple of decades. The Earthlings had little need for space travel and their fuel sources for inner-atmosphere flight had dried up centuries ago. He knew that the leadership rarely accepted off-world visitors, so he supposed the quality of their spaceports was fairly low on their list of priorities.

The craft carrying the Martians touched down on the blue-grey stone slab and the pilot released the lock, allowing Raylor a chance to peer out.

A long, low building, with a shabby dried-out blue paint job and dusty old windows, lay parallel with the landing area. No faces could be seen in the windows and no welcome party appeared out of the door.

Raylor wondered about this but his thoughts immediately turned elsewhere. He stepped down the ramp and into the warm sunshine. He looked around and let it soak in.

He breathed in his first taste of the pure natural air of planet Earth.

He couldn't have imagined such a thing would have such a strong impact on his emotions and yet he found his eyes welling up. The air itself tasted different here – the freshness and the sense of life was undeniable. He realised now the impossible job the generators back on Mars had been attempting to achieve – no machine could ever replicate this authentically.

He snapped himself back into the moment and headed back onto the ship. After a few minutes he re-emerged with the entire crew following behind. Ramsey Pierce and Marien Lyndell walked directly by his side. He ensured that Wilson Hasting was escorted by two armed guards at the very rear of the group. They approached the old building and Raylor looked around with a shrug – there was still no hint of anyone inside. He knocked on the door.

He knocked and then he knocked again – harder each time. He turned to his fellow Senators with a resigned look in his eye, then tried the handle on the door; it swung open with ease.

Inside was dull and dusty. Raylor recognised the old equipment as ancient versions of their modern comms and some early spaceflight paraphernalia. He wondered when the last flight had left from this port and concluded that it couldn't have been within his lifetime.

They pushed ahead into the dark building, down a long and narrow staircase, lit only by two old-style halogen light bulbs. At the bottom of the staircase lay a wider corridor, with light flowing in from the opposite end. The group trudged onwards and as their eyes adjusted to the light they saw two men up ahead, guarding a wide arch way which opened out into bright sunlight.

"State your name and business," shouted one of the guards.

They were dressed in long flowing robes, with an almost floral pattern unlike anything Raylor had ever seen. They held long spears in hand, with sharpened tips and no sign of any form of mechanical weapon at all.

"I'm Sebastian Raylor, Senator of Mars. We have been given leave to rest and speak to your leadership."

"You cannot enter The Circle with so many," spoke the second guard. "Chose your party carefully and approach."

Raylor looked around at his group, wondering how many was acceptable. He decided to pick the easiest options and gave his fellow Senator's the nod. He also picked out the pilot from the ship, thinking his account of the struggles they went through to get here may come in handy. He passed up Eliza Bergman, Bellson's assistant, and saw the disappointment on her face as he did so. He knew she had a wise mind on her young shoulders, but this wasn't the time for her. He resolved to speak to her later about his choice and walked directly to the back of the group.

"You're with me, General," he said to Hasting.

The two armed guards by his side escorted him to the front of the group and they accepted the supportive nods and well wishes from those left behind. Raylor led them to the archway.

The Earthling guards stepped forward and crossed their spears in their path.

"No weapons, no technology. The Circle is a sacred place to us and we will have it respected."

"You need to understand that this man is a prisoner. We must be wary of him," Raylor said, motioning to Hasting.

"Then we advise that you do not bring him with you."

Raylor turned to his party. He felt strongly that Hasting needed to be a part of the conversation which was in front of him. He sighed and reached a hand out on to his own guard's shoulder.

"Stay with the group. I'd rather have you two armed and ready out here, than guarding a prisoner while the rest of the group sits unprotected. Give him to me."

They stood aside and allowed Hasting to step forward. The former General took this in without a word, but looked hard at Raylor. He knew the pressure on the man and had no intention of making things any more difficult for him.

"I'm trusting you to be of some use in there. I'm counting on the rumours and reports I hear of your valour and honour. Don't let me down," Raylor said. Hasting simply nodded his acknowledgement.

The Earthling guards did a final pat down check of the three Senators and the Jupitoan and concluded that they were safe to enter The Circle.

Stepping through the arch was a step into the unknown. As Raylor's eyes adjusted to the harsh light of day he realised just how monumentally unknown this place was to them all.

The Circle was at least two hundred metres in diameter and surrounded by stone seating which tapered upwards, giving it the look of an ancient amphitheatre. Everything was carved from chalky-grey stone and the floor looked to be solid concrete except where patches of fertile grass and flowers had been planted.

All around the area stood large stone pillars – carved with intricate designs and each telling a story. Raylor couldn't keep his eyes on any single one of them long enough to take it all in

In the middle of the circle stood a flat, rectangular platform and behind that a larger platform with a pristine white tent rising above it. The first platform was host to a number of people, all of whom looked anxious at the sight of the visitors.

More people milled about the circle floor. They were dressed, much as the guards had been, in floral printed robes and loose fitting clothes. Several people had marked out small areas of their own where they displayed paintings and small works of art that they had produced. People wandered, laughing and idly chatting as they perused the various items on offer.

Lyndell and Pierce admired the artwork and let out some barely audible gasps of wonder as they stepped further forward. The colours astounded them and the brightness was reflected in the smiles and attitudes that the locals flashed back at them.

Raylor focused his attention forwards. He could not allow the alienness of it all to distract him from his goal. He was as blown away by the sights as any of the others, but his eyes had been drawn to the bigger of the two platforms in the centre of the circle. Hasting's eyes had been drawn to the same spot.

Under the tent was an ornate wooden table and behind it sat three dour looking figures. It was clear from their position, and the fact that the Earthlings did not interact with them, that they were people of power and reverence. Raylor noted that while his eyes were locked to them, all three sets of eyes returned his gaze.

The group stepped up onto the lower platform and approached the tent.

"Make way for the visitors. Grant them an audience with the Jisan," a nattily dressed man on the edge of the platform bellowed loudly, then rang a tiny handheld bell.

The people moved quickly as they gathered up belongings and jumped down to the circle floor. A crowd gathered as Raylor and his team edged closer still to the Earthling leaders.

"We come to you in a time of desperate need, your lordships," Raylor spoke loudly.

"Please refer to us as Jisan," the central of the seated figures replied. She was dressed in a lily-white outfit which was something between a dress and a robe. She wore a headpiece woven with flowers and lace, which sat in a bewitching cone atop her head.

"I'm sorry, I meant no offence. We don't know this word?" Raylor responded.

"It means to respect, or at least to show it. But we are not offended," the Jisan to the left spoke now. "I am Nanadev Jisan, one of the chosen to lead in Earthly matters in this peaceful time."

Raylor nodded, and his crew followed suit.

"My sister on the end here is Sahakar Jisan, and you have already addressed our honoured partner Ramdas Jisan." Both of the ladies nodded their welcome. "Please, tell us where you come from, and of your desperate need."

"I am Sebastian Raylor, Senator and elected leader of Mars. We come to you on behalf of all Martians. I'm sorry to report that Mars is no more. Its atmosphere is lost, and the vast majority of its people along with it."

A gasping, shocked expression murmured through the gathered crowd.

"By 'lost' you mean what, exactly?" Ramdas Jisan asked.

"I mean destroyed by forces working for a man named Bernard Kiebler – President of Jupiter."

"We know of Mr Kiebler," Sahakar Jisan replied.

"Then you will know that he has schemed and plotted against Mars and now he has finally taken his war too far," Marien Lyndell blurted out.

"We know nothing of Mr Kiebler's actions, nor of any war."

"We could spend weeks standing here telling you of every twist and turn which has befallen us in the past few weeks alone, but we would waste valuable time and I'm sure you have little interest in the actions of the universe at large," Raylor spoke, trying to take charge of the situation.

"You are correct, sir," Nanadev Jisan replied.

"Then let me tell you the basics and pray that you will see our plight. We have been at war with Jupiter for some time. Mr Kiebler has committed atrocities beyond those considered acceptable in such circumstances. His men have destroyed our cities, and murdered innocents. At his orders they have dismantled the very structures which helped to build Mars and which kept its atmosphere breathable for all of these years."

"Then you are refugees of a fallen civilisation?"

"We are the last surviving members of a wronged people," Raylor retorted.

"Mr Raylor, your anger will not win you any hearts here. For what do you seek our aid?"

"We need your hospitality and your kindness. We need food and shelter. We need to prepare for the next onslaught of Kiebler's fury."

"I'm afraid we cannot offer you asylum if you mean to fight, Mr Raylor. Nor can we harbour your stay here if such an act might draw the wrath of Jupiter."

"We can't just sit back and-" Raylor began to speak, before Nanadev Jisan held up her hand.

"We are a peaceful people," she said softly. "Understand that we have no machines of war. We will not be drawn into a conflict and we will not invite the wrath of another power upon us. I'm sorry but we cannot help."

"No machines of war? Your people burned down buildings, blew apart entire blocks in our cities. You have explosives and means of space travel outside of our knowledge," Ramsey Pierce spoke angrily.

"You refer to the Peoples of Earth organisation, sir," Ramdas Jisan replied. "Do not refer to them as our people. You know not of what you speak."

"What Mr Pierce is trying to say is that there are means to help us, available here on Earth," Raylor tried.

"Senator, I would expect better of a leader of people. I have told you we have no armed forces and no technology to wage a war. We have nothing to fight with and no reason to do so. If you came here only to urge us to war then you have made a grave error and I will kindly ask you to leave us."

Ramdas Jisan spoke for the group - the others remained silent now. The gathered crowd was deadly quiet too.

Raylor stood exposed and empty. He could not think of words which would ease the situation, nor any reason why the Earthlings should allow him to stay. He cursed the fact that they had rolled in and blurted out every thought, not playing the cards they had been dealt correctly.

Equally, he didn't know what Earth could realistically offer them. His fleet had no other options - they had to find refuge on Earth or else they were cornered in an increasingly bleak quadrant of the solar system. There was nowhere left to run.

"We apologise for any misconception, Jisan," Wilson Hasting stepped forward and spoke. "We do not confuse you with the terrorist cells who have waged an unholy war on our communities and recognise that they are as much a menace to your people as they are to our own."

The Jisan nodded their acceptance of his words.

"My friends speak out of frustration. We have travelled a long way and they have watched many of their friends and family die on that journey. There is truly nowhere left to turn."

"We wish to offer our assistance but vengeance and bloodshed are not ours to take. We cannot help in this way," Sahakar Jisan said.

"Then offer them homes and protection from the unforgiving wind and rain. Let them rebuild their community and their lives on your world. As a boy I witnessed the fractious nature of war on Saturn and as a man I have watched it destroy lives throughout the system. I have seen the desperation in the eyes of those who have been beaten and have recognised in those times that they are only human, just like me. Like all of us.

"I've stood by Kiebler's side when he has launched these attacks. He has no remorse for anything he does. It takes very little for him to decide on the most grievous of actions. I understand that Earth does not want a war and cannot fight one by any means. But believe me; war is coming to us all sooner or later. Bernard Kiebler will see to that.

"For now I ask that you embrace these people as refugees. Give them your compassion and it will be repaid. Give them your hearts and they will embrace you wholly. The Martians are a people without a place to call home. Give them that, at the very least."

The Jisan considered this bloodied and broken looking man with wonder.

"Who is this man who speaks so passionately for the Martian people, Mr Raylor?" Nanadev Jisan asked.

"This is Wilson Hasting. He is a captive soldier of our enemy. A Jupitoan General."

"His words speak to all of us," Sahakar Jisan said.

"Far too many have died to bring us all here. Far too many Martians have fallen today. Please listen to his words," Raylor pleaded.

The Jisan looked at each other for a long moment, and whispered unhurriedly to each other.

"Mr Hasting," Ramdas Jisan spoke, after a few anxious moments. "You ask for us to provide a home to the homeless. You wisely point out that we are all of the human race, no matter our birthplace or stature in life. To this I would say that Earth is the home to human life, and in that case you are all, indeed, home."

The words took a split second to sink in. Hasting was the first to break into a smile. Raylor looked at him for what seemed to be an eternity. The silence was broken by the loud 'Whoop' from Ramsey Pierce, which was quickly echoed by Senator Lyndell as she pulled him in for a celebratory hug.

The gathered crowd cheered along too, accepting the Jisan verdict without question. Raylor saw smiles and tears in the faces of those gathered and it made his heart swell. He reached out his hand to Hasting, who shook it willingly.

"Thank you, Jisan," Raylor said, turning back to face the Earthling leaders. "We have no words to truly express our appreciation."

"Your words of thanks are not needed, Senator. Only the promise that you will not look to bring destruction to Earth out of your wish for vengeance and that you will stand by our side should our fate be war, as General Hasting predicts."

"You have my word, Jisan," Raylor replied.

"Then call your fleet, Senator Raylor. Tell your people to come home."

CHAPTER THIRTY-ONE

A low afternoon sun hung in the air as Kiebler walked across the pristine lawns of the Presidential grounds. He slipped on some sunglasses he'd had tucked in his jacket pocket and felt the relief. The previous night's hangover was well earned, but ill timed. He waved to a small group of well-wishers who had gathered on the street, peering into the gardens through the thick black steel fencing. The girls squealed and the older gentleman – maybe the father, he couldn't focus his eyes on them clearly – gave a wave back then clapped his hands.

Kiebler wondered at the mentality of these people. They showed up to catch a glimpse of their President, and they stood in awe at everything he did. Even a simple wave of his hand warranted a round of applause.

He had never been one of those types of people. He had grown up not knowing the first thing about politics and wouldn't have cared if the President had turned up on his own street and joined in a ball game. Of course, he'd always had his competitive streak so he imagined he'd have taken any chance to wipe out the newcomer should such an opportunity have arisen.

He couldn't imagine admiring someone so much to want to take a bus downtown and stand on the street in the frosty winter air, just for the chance to lay eyes on your hero. He wondered if all of his supporters had some kind of mental disorder. Could he have won an election based purely on the vote of the mentally handicapped?

He knew that wasn't really the case. He had seen this type of behaviour in his previous life as an actor. Fans turned up on set in their droves like moths to the light. Sometimes they would camp out at the studio gates for the chance to spot him heading from his trailer to the soundstage three times a day. He could never understand that hunger to be near the flame even when they knew they couldn't touch it.

He arrived at the covered podium at last and watched as Daxler ranted at a producer. Sam Heighway stood nearby and averted his gaze, hoping the producer would take all of the flack. Dax finished up and noticed the presence of the President.

"We'll need this thing turned around, Dax," Kiebler said, pointing to the sun bearing down on them. "I can't address the nation in these," he said and removed the sunglasses.

"Of course, Mr President. I have told our friends here to make the change already.

As they spoke the producer grabbed two crew members and had them lift the entire tent structure up on the spot and turn it ninety degrees, then repeated the trick with the podium itself.

"I trust you had a fine celebratory night with Ms Marlborough, sir?" Scion asked.

"If you're referring to my bleary eyes and worn out complexion, Dax, I swear I'll send you to Mars."

He smiled at his Chief of Staff and patted him on the shoulder.

"We had some words last night. I dare say she is feeling worse than I am right now. I trust you have arranged everything I asked?"

"Yes sir. You got the copy of your speech?" Daxler replied.

Kiebler had received the speech early – the messenger had awoken him from a deep sleep. It came attached to an invite to make his speech sometime before noon, which he'd dismissed with a polite "Fuck off," and gone back to sleep.

He'd awoken in the afternoon to find a revised speech and a new slot time for his television appearance. He'd spent the last hour revising the speech mentally, adding finishing touches here and huge swathes of dialogue there.

Daxler Scion could write a good speech, he acknowledged that. However, he was too much of a politician to always hit the right note. Sometimes Kiebler wanted to be forceful and to the point. He'd learned not to let Daxler in on his rewrites until he performed them. There was less of a debate to be had by that point.

"Wonderful speech as always, Dax," he smiled.

Scion seemed to wallow in comments such as that. Kiebler saw him almost shiver at the appreciation and knew that in a very faintly different reality Daxler Scion would be wrapped up in an overcoat, standing at the gates hoping to catch a glimpse of the President of Jupiter.

"Dax. Speak to the watch command as soon as I'm on the air. I want them to ensure Valerie Marlborough is off the premises and her access rights are removed immediately. If she's anywhere to be found within these grounds, bring her directly to me."

He savoured the look in Scion's eyes. He could see ever so clearly the vicious streak that he loved about his number two and knew that was the very thing that elevated him above the super-fans and losers at the gate; Daxler Scion wasn't afraid to shed a little blood and get his hands dirty when the time was right.

"We're ready for you, Mr President," Heighway said and motioned towards the podium. A small crew was gathered to set up and hold mics and other equipment, while Heighway was present just to ensure things ran smoothly. Kiebler was grateful for the lack of fuss.

"How long have we got?" he asked.

"We are live in one minute, sir," Heighway confirmed.

Kiebler had always loved the limelight. He revelled in this one.

"You're about to witness the defining moment in my career, Sammy boy. And quite possibly in Jupiter's entire history come to think of it. Turn on those lights."

He stepped up to the podium and looked straight down the lens of the camera. He had his speech folded in his pocket but he didn't bother to remove it. He'd read it three times before leaving his room and wanted some room to manoeuvre. He watched Heighway for the countdown.

"Five, four," he spoke before silently mouthing the rest of the countdown, accompanied by highly unnecessary hand signals.

"Good day, my fellow Jupitoans. Today is a momentous day in our history and I would like to take a few moments of your time to recognise that fact."

Kiebler smiled and tried to look as relaxed as possible, knowing every eye on the planet, perhaps the entire civilised solar system, was on him.

"Early this morning I received reports that Mars' leadership had fled from their bunkers after sabotaging vital atmospheric equipment in the north of the Boreum region. I'm sure by now you have all seen the news updates and are aware of the consequences of these actions. It is regrettable that the Martian forces saw fit to abandon all that they have fought for, and the hard work which all of our forefathers played some part in many years ago.

"The destruction of Mars has brought great sadness to my heart. I extend my sincere condolences to all of those who are affected. Unfortunately, those who are responsible for these cowardly acts have escaped the net and are yet to face the consequences of their actions. Mark my words; they will be made to face those consequences.

"I'd like to congratulate our armed forces, our great heroes who continue to fight the good fight for all of our well being and come home with yet another Jupitoan victory under their belts. I'm sure you will join me in honouring them on their return.

"As a result of the actions of those few Martians, and some dissident voices here within even our own government, I have held crisis talks with the Galactic Union leadership overnight. It was clear that our solar system requires a strong hand to guide it through the coming months and I have offered that hand.

"As of this morning, the Galactic Union has been folded into the Jupitoan government itself. All of its entities and enterprises are now under governmental control, its obligations and assets are the property of Jupiter and the organisation itself will cease to be.

"Let me take a moment to thank Valerie Marlborough for her hard work in getting us to this point. She has been instrumental in forming the Galactic Union and Jupiter into one well-oiled machine in preparation for a day such as this. She deserves all of the credit."

He couldn't help but smile at that and had to look down to his podium to help suppress a laugh. He held his breath a moment then looked back to the camera.

"Jupiter will now govern all of those planets previously held under the stewardship of the GU The galaxy at large needs to be kept safe from the insurgent forces who threaten the freedom of us all. Jupiter will be proud to take on that honour."

He felt the giddy feeling of victory rise up within him and wondered if any man had ever felt so powerful in the history of all of humankind. He had studied the great ancient histories of Earth, with its Roman Emperors and overpowering dynasties and he had devoured books on the great ruling overlords of Saturn back in the early days of its colonisation.

None of them had felt power on this scale. None could boast control over whole planets, never mind the entire star system.

He felt like a God. A self-made God, risen from nothing, with only his own wit and charm to build a legacy on.

"I have a message to those who wish to take us on now, at our boldest moment. I have a message for anyone who wishes to challenge the military might of Jupiter. And I have a message to my people – you, the voters – who backed my ideas to block the Belt wholeheartedly and allowed me to ride this great tidal wave.

"I have had the greatest minds of our time working on this project, and their efforts were tested with absolute success last night. The Belt has been blocked and Jupiter now controls the space at our borders."

He allowed a few seconds for people to let that information sink in. He wished he had a crowd to truly take in their appreciation. Somehow the shocked look of Sam Heighway and the gleeful smirk of Daxler Scion weren't quite enough of a reaction for the colossal achievement he felt he had made.

"It will stop those who have nothing from coming to Jupiter to take what is ours. We have earned the right to live in peace and to enjoy the fruits of our labours. Let the bottom-feeders at the wrong end of the system work for themselves - they will get only what they deserve."

He paused again, trying to adopt a more solemn tone. Here he was, an actor, back where he belonged in front of the camera. He knew how to manipulate it to perfection.

"That unfortunately now includes all surviving Martians. Your Senators have betrayed you and you have fallen foul of the great Jupitoan Belt as a result. Let me make this clear – you survive because I allow it. You were not pursued to Earth because I said so. You live because of Bernard Kiebler.

"Now that Mars no longer exists, and the Earth leadership has agreed to take you in as refugees, I am granting you all citizenship of Earth. That will be ratified by my government this evening, as Earth remains within the remit of the Galactic Union legislature as agreed in the van Hession Agreement.

"It's ironic isn't it? You have fought a brave and foolish war for your freedom – only to find yourselves even more firmly under Jupitoan control than you could have possibly imagined."

He allowed himself an open laugh, failing to see the benefit of hiding his true feelings on the matter. He hoped the Earthlings would allow Raylor a television just for tonight. He hoped that his Martian counterpart saw just how juicy and darkly depressing the irony was.

"Incidentally, I should add to our old friends - gone but not forgotten – those who threw down their weapons and refused the direct orders of their President. You are hereby cast out as traitors and cowards, with warrants on your heads. There is no escaping the law."

He thought of the time he had spent in conversation with Wilson Hasting and felt sick to his stomach. He had tried to make an impression, hoping to mould this starry-eyed, naive, liberal General into a legend the kids of Jupiter could look up to and be terrified of all at the same time. His betrayal had hurt the most, and yet had been the easiest thing to predict of all that had gone on.

"Finally, a message to our enemies. The Martians. The rebels. The terrorists. And to all of the other planets across our glorious solar system.

"There will be no more referendums, no more workers' unions. You will fall in line or... Well, you've seen what happens if you don't."

With a smile and a wink, Bernard Kiebler signed off to begin his reign as the most powerful man in the known galaxy.

And he really liked the sound of that.

EPILOGUE

The sun was setting when Raylor emerged from the Martian ship where his crew had retired for some much needed rest while the remains of the fleet touched down and were shown around.

The afternoon had been a blur as their Earthling hosts gave the guided tour of the site they lived within and explained some of the history of the place. Raylor found it fascinating but had resigned himself to taking a repeat trip when his senses weren't quite so dulled, his brains not quite so fried.

What he had taken in was that the site was an old military base – and he sensed that 'old' on Earth meant 'seriously old' – and its current inhabitants were just one sect of many, scattered across the globe with similar set-ups. They had everything they needed and lived a simple existence within a small valley, never wandering too far from it and never worrying about the problems of their neighbours out amongst the stars.

He admired that way of life to a degree. It sounded peaceful. He knew after a while he'd find it boring. Then he'd find himself in trouble and looking for a way to leave. As it was, at Mars' most desperate hour, it was the perfect place to be.

They had watched Kiebler's address from the cockpit of the ship when they returned after their tour. Some of the crew flew into a rage, others could do nothing but laugh at the outrageousness of it all. Raylor stood at the back of the group and let it all sink in quietly.

Towards the end of it he'd flashed his eyes onto Wilson Hasting, who had similarly hung back. He saw the man's eyes spark with anger and yet he could see that he was also full of sorrow for what he had lost. His sense of duty was so powerful that he felt bereaved of his home, despite the fact that it had betrayed him.

Raylor had taken to his bunk and tried to shut his eyes. He heard the crew dissipate soon after and the restless sounds of them all trying to catch some sleep before their promised supper. Their first Earth-made meal. He hoped it tasted just like home. If it didn't he knew they'd just have to get used to it.

The thoughts of Mars rattled through his brain. He swung from agony at the loss of their planet, to the pain of all of the lives lost along the way. He couldn't stop the feeling of guilt creeping into his heart. Every thought came with it attached, prodding at him and letting him know that it was all his fault.

He could have averted war. He could have led the fight elsewhere. He could have waved a white flag. He could have been Bellson. Every time he pushed the thought down it would spring back up on him in some unexpected way. He opened his eyes and decided sleep wasn't going to come.

Outside, he wandered the area beyond the site for a while, as the deep orange light of the falling sun painted long shadows around him. He found himself pushing through undergrowth, and across fields.

In the near distance he could hear the sound of water, and he pushed ahead to find it. The field held horse paddocks and he watched as the animals considered him curiously then went back to their business.

At the edge of the field lay a small dusty track, with little bushes at ankle length which nipped at his legs. He followed the path for a moment as it rose, then opened out into the most majestic view he had ever seen.

A smooth outcrop lay at his feet, flat enough to take a seat and enjoy the vista it presented – a view of the ocean, as far as the eye could see. The sun's fading rays bounced off it, and waves rolled gently in. It took his breath away for several minutes, and it wasn't until he shook himself back into the present that he noticed the silhouetted figure sat on the edge of the rock up ahead.

"They have – *had* – oceans on Mars," he said. "Nothing quite as grand as this. They were all artificial. The real ones weren't self-sufficient enough so we had to give them a head-start."

Wilson Hasting turned to see his uninvited visitor. He gave him a nod, and moved his coat which he had laid down by his side. Raylor took a seat.

"They have them on Saturn too. All man-made, like the rest of the solar system beyond what you see in front of you. They're beautiful in their own way, but nothing compares to these surroundings. Cliffs and fields and the rocks below – they never think to recreate that stuff."

"I wouldn't have thought of it either," Raylor offered back. "Until I stumbled upon this one just now, I doubt I'd have ever thought about how beautiful a cliff top could be."

He laughed and Hasting slowly joined in. They fell silent for a few moments, just admiring their new home and the wonders it had presented to them in just one day.

"I guess they can replace anything nowadays. Replicate anything in existence. It'll be a matter of time before some brain at the far end of the system decides to build some Mars themed leisure planet. They'll pull the original design docs and make some adjustments to keep the kids amused."

"They can't replicate it all. They can't recreate the feeling of a planet that was built by years of labour, by honest hard-working people. They can't recreate the freedom we have all lost," Hasting replied. He reached into his coat and pulled out a small hip flask.

He took a swig and offered it to Raylor, who gladly accepted.

"To all of those who lost their lives for Raylor's folly," he spoke, raising the flask in the air.

"I'd bet those people would follow you into war again, given the chance."

"I don't know about that. I damn sure know I wouldn't ask them to."

The sun had dipped lower still and the two sat in shadow, watching the dying light. Hasting looked up at the last sliver of the sun's sphere on the horizon.

"I have to hope that on some planet out there at the tail end of the solar system someone is sitting, just as we are, looking up at that sun. They're looking at it and wondering about us. Wondering how many of you Martians yet live. Wondering how they can help to make things right."

Raylor was touched by the Jupitoan's words, but couldn't see past the bleakness that clouded his every thought. The weight of his people's woes was on his shoulders. He had gambled with it and lost.

"I hope you're right. But I think we have witnessed the end to a united galaxy. Kiebler has tightened his grip, just like we said he would. Like it or not, those planets beyond the belt are under his control now."

"They won't all accept it. They can't. As my granny used to tell me; 'We're all born under the same sun'. They've seen what he's capable of doing to his fellow man, no matter which rock they call home. You'll see. They'll have to stand up to it sooner or later," Hasting said.

"Then we've not seen the last of civil war amongst humanity," Raylor lamented. "That which divides us will only make us stronger."

Hasting took a long draw from the flask, gazing off onto the darkening horizon.

"I remember my dad talking about the day they packed up and left Saturn when I was just a baby. He'd fought out the long, cold war against the Uzstazi and when it was over they were granted leave to return home to Jupiter. They talked about that day with so much pride. The fact that they lived through it. They fought the good fight, and they survived.

"They begged me not to sign up when I was sixteen, but I wanted to feel what they had felt that day. I wanted to pay back my planet for the life it afforded me. I see them, now and then, and they worry and they fret, but they're glad I'm following in their footsteps and they're proud of their boy.

"I hoped they would never see another war. I hoped they could live out their days in peace out there. But now it's coming. Now I feel for all who live under this maniac."

Raylor took in Hasting's tale and somehow it made him feel better about his plight. The more he thought about it, the more he believed that war was inevitable and Mars was just the first to step out onto the battlefields.

It was coming for everyone now and no decision he could have made would have avoided that. Kiebler was at fault for it all. He was looking for a fight and now that he had won one he would only be empowered to do it again.

"Freedom was never easy to come by, Hasting," he spoke quietly. "Never in all of human history was it easy to win or was it given freely. No matter where you were born, your roots come back to here. To Earth. A planet whose history was built by those who fought oppression, those who threw down false gods. Those who stood up to the powers that be and said 'No!' to them all."

He thought for a moment, choosing his words carefully.

"Maybe we can't win. Maybe hope is lost. But we fight on anyway, because that's what our founding fathers – the fathers of humanity itself – taught us to do."

"Live until you can't fight anymore. Fight until you can't live anymore," Hasting added with a smile.

"Will you say 'No' with us, General Hasting?" Raylor smiled back.

THE END

ABOUT THE AUTHOR

Andrew R. Davidson is an author with very little back catalogue and a mountain of ideas. Born and raised in the North East of England, he has dabbled in short story and screenplay work for over a decade before committing to this, his first feature novel.

His second attempt is currently under way, while a collection of short stories and other works – entitled *Coming / Soon* – is, indeed, coming soon.

ACKNOWLEDGEMENTS

This book would never have gotten off the ground if not for a rambling conversation on after a particularly boring day at the day job – so thanks to Adam for helping to provide that initial spark.

Thanks to Dylan for the constant flow of encouragement – I hope you still think I'm a good writer after reading this...

Huge thank you to all of my family – Mam, Dad and Iain as well as Darren, Claire and Jack – who have been there throughout it all and maybe don't know just how much they have helped in a million little ways (not limited to dealing with late nights, mood swings, self-doubt and three house moves along the way).

Literally couldn't have done it without all of you, and a special shout out for Malcolm & Sue for your help and your time and for some vital proof-reading and editing skills!

Finally, a world of thanks to Sharon & Philip – for giving me a home and giving me heart. This is all for you and because of you, and I thank you.

AUTHOR'S NOTES

Let me start by thanking you sincerely for taking the time to read my words – I'm honoured that you have made it to the end!

That Which Divides started out as a curious "What If...?" scenario in which I'd conjure up a world where celebrities could be elected as Presidents and exiting decades-old institutions for the good of the people were preposterous creations. I suppose I should thank the real world for not only making my inventions true, but for making the reality so much more bizarre and terrifying than the fictional.

I can't stress just how thrilling it is to have this work out in the world, with the promise of so much more to come. Please visit my website (see link below) for news on upcoming releases and events, and take a moment to sign up to my mailing list – I'll be sending previews of *Coming / Soon* into inboxes everywhere from early 2020.

Thanks for reading,

Andrew

https://andrewdavidson1981.wixsite.com/iwritethings

Printed in Great Britain
by Amazon